LATE
BLOOMERS

LATE BLOOMERS

A NOVEL

Deepa Varadarajan

RANDOM HOUSE

NEW YORK

A Random House Trade Paperback Original

Published in the United States by Random House, an imprint and division of Penguin Random House LLC, New York.

RANDOM HOUSE and the HOUSE colophon are registered trademarks of Penguin Random House LLC.

Library of Congress Cataloging-in-Publication Data
Names: Varadarajan, Deepa, author.
Title: Late bloomers: a novel / Deepa Varadarajan.
Description: First edition. | New York: Random House, [2023] |
Identifiers: LCCN 2022017703 (print) | LCCN 2022017704 (ebook) |
ISBN 9780593498026 (trade paperback; acid-free paper) |
ISBN 9780593498033 (ebook)
Subjects: LCGFT: Domestic fiction. | Novels.
Classification: LCC PS3622.A724 L38 2023 (print) |
LCC PS3622.A724 (ebook) | DDC 813/.6—dc23/eng/20220411
LC record available at https://lccn.loc.gov/2022017703
LC ebook record available at https://lccn.loc.gov/2022017704

Printed in the United States of America on acid-free paper

randomhousebooks.com

2 4 6 8 9 7 5 3 1

First Edition

Book design by Caroline Cunningham

For Nishan and Sania

Every arrangement in life carried with it the sadness, the sentimental shadow, of its not being something else, but only itself. . . .

—Lorrie Moore, BIRDS OF AMERICA

Maybe we can start all over.

And give love another life.

—Beyoncé

PART ONE

I

SURESH

All these internet women lie, I tell you. All of them. Funny that the anonymity draws everyone in. But it's also what keeps you from trusting a word.

Sometimes the lies are about the fundamentals: previous marriages, whether they have kids, what line of work they're in. Oh, and age. Age is a big one. The last date I went on was with a woman whose profile said forty-one. Impossible! There wasn't a chance that Ms. Mittal (formerly Mrs. Mittal) was a day under fifty.

My son, Nikesh, laughed at me when I told him about that one. "But, Dad," he said, "*you* are fifty-*nine.*" Well that may be, but I didn't go around grossly exaggerating for sport. I was more reasonable about it all. On my profile, I described myself as "Suresh Raman, a healthy and active, five-foot-ten, fifty-five-year-old divorced man of Indian origin."

All right, so fifty-five was four years ago, the height was a rough estimate, and "active" was only an accurate description if it included toenail-clipping while watching CNN in my carpeted den. But these were reasonable deviations from the truth. RDTs, I called them. So long as you kept it reasonable, where was the harm, really?

It was early evening now. I parked my SUV in front of a small, white brick house. I had to quash my misgivings—for the next few hours, at least. I reminded myself: This was a first date, a new woman, a clean slate.

I sniffed under my arms. Good, still powdery fresh. I'd left my house in Clayborn, Texas, two hours ago, but I blasted the AC the entire drive to Austin. Whatever my doubts about lying internet women, I'd never want a date to see unsightly wet patches blooming across my shirt.

I checked my reflection in the rearview mirror. Even at this hour, the late-August sun beamed harsh and unforgiving. My eyebrows looked like two furry worms wriggling around a pockmarked forehead. I licked my forefinger and tried pasting down the errant hairs. But it was useless. Hairs kept popping up in every direction. Oh well. Perhaps the restaurant would be dim and Mallika wouldn't notice the unruly duo dancing above my eyelids.

Mallika. We'd been emailing each other for two weeks. Now, this one did not seem like a liar. I couldn't be sure, of course, as I'd yet to see her in the flesh. At the moment, she was still three parts fantasy to one part reality—a concoction of my hazy, lonely brain. Though given the mendacious tendencies of these internet women, it was hard to maintain any fantasy for long.

Mind you, this wasn't just abstract cynicism talking. It came from months of experience. And in my months of experience, I'd learned that even when these internet women weren't lying about important things, like age, then they were lying about ridiculous things—things I wouldn't have even cared about had they told me the truth. But when I discovered they'd lied about it, I had to assume it meant something.

Last month, for example, I went out with this divorced real

estate agent from Baton Rouge named Usha. She lied about all kinds of trivialities. *Favorite Food: Italian.*

Trusting this preference in her profile, I suggested going to the Olive Garden on our first date. It had been a tiring six-hour drive from Clayborn to Baton Rouge, but I wanted to show her that I was sensitive to this detail about her—that I cared enough to remember. Upon hearing my suggestion, she shrugged and explained that Italian wasn't really her favorite. She wanted a steak. Feeling rebuked, I asked her why she didn't just say "steak" on her profile. She replied that she was afraid of scaring the divorced and widowed Hindu vegetarian men from answering.

Now, I wasn't an unsympathetic man. Or a vegetarian. And while I questioned the sanity of anyone who enjoyed masticating thick slabs of beef, I understood that a forty-two-year-old divorcée with two teenage kids needed to expand her pool of possibilities in any way she could. Only that wasn't all.

Over the course of that evening, which began and ended at Matthew's Steakhouse, I discovered that in the dozen emails and phone conversations leading up to our fateful meeting, she'd lied about her car (a Honda not a Volvo), her glasses prescription for nearsightedness (minus four, not minus two), her tennis elbow (she didn't even own a racket), and her subscription to *National Geographic* (ha!). None of those things in isolation would have caused me to do more than raise a puzzled eyebrow. But read together, the insignificance of those lies added up to one significant thing: She was a liar.

There had been countless such evenings. During the long (and sometimes multistate) drives back home, when disappointment sat in the back of my throat like undigested food, I'd say to myself: "Enough, old man, enough of this silly business." But at such moments, I too was a liar. For within minutes of pulling into my garage, I'd head straight for the buzzing glow of my computer. I'd check for new responses, answer the promising ones, and update my profile—the three-step ritual that had become second nature to me, like the windshield-to-rearview-mirror-to-speedometer visual reflex of driving.

Nikesh called me "hooked." I'd describe my dating mishaps to him, and he'd say, "If they're so bad, then stop; or just stay local, at least."

Local? What was the point of trying to meet an Indian woman in Clayborn? They were all friends with my ex-wife, Lata, who'd left me, and would therefore be biased against me. And a non-Indian woman? That was too foreign to contemplate. But I didn't say any of this to my son. Instead, I'd meekly reply, "You're right—this is the last one. No more." But he wouldn't believe me. He'd chuckle and chide, "You're hooked, Dad."

He was right. I had yet to go on a good date, but I wasn't ready to stop.

Out of the corner of my eye, I could see a curtain flutter in the front window of Mallika's house, a ripple of black hair against the glass. Was Mallika peeking out? Was she wondering why I hadn't gotten out of the car yet, hadn't crossed the dried expanse of lawn to her front door?

I thumbed my brows one last time. I ran my palms over my grayed—but mostly full—head of hair. I unbuckled my seatbelt, leaned forward and then fell back again, my back hitting the leather with a loud smack. Why couldn't I sit here for just a little while longer? Just a few more moments to savor the Mallika of my hopeful imaginings and delay the inevitable disappointment.

For a second, I considered pulling out my phone and dialing Nikesh. I could ask him to tell me a joke and lighten my spirits. But then, maybe I shouldn't bother him at this hour. Six o'clock in Texas meant it was seven for Nikesh in New York. He would likely be busy—either at work late, or giving Alok a bath, or coaxing him into bed.

It startled me sometimes to think that Nikesh, my youngest, was no longer so young—no longer that spindle-legged teenager with an unruly mop of hair, but a thirty-year-old man with an eleven-month-old son of his own, working long hours at a prestigious Manhattan law firm. My grandson, Alok, was by all accounts a sweet-tempered boy like his father. Thankfully, he'd inherited none of the Nordic sternness of his mother, Denise, a woman that neither I nor Lata had even met before Nikesh married her—correction, before he eloped with her, telling us about it only after the fact. No doubt Lata was still licking her wounds from the shock of their elopement. For my part, though, I was relieved not to publicly perform the role of delighted father of the groom. At least Nikesh had spared me the indignity of reciting some fraudulent speech about the joys of marriage in a Hilton ballroom, while our friends (Lata's friends, mostly) squirmed and Lata glowered behind me.

In truth, I couldn't find much fault with Nikesh. Oh sure, he might tease me now and then for being hooked on internet dating. But at least he was indulgent and kind to his aging, addled, romantic-idealist father.

My eldest, Priya, on the other hand, hurled harsher words my way: *post–midlife crisis; act your age; ridiculous; embarrassment.*

I tried not to take it too personally. It had been almost a year since Lata moved out, but the wound was still raw for my daughter, a thirty-five-year-old history professor in Austin. Oh sure, give her macro-level changes—civil wars, fallen empires, mass famine, and pestilence—those were her bread and butter, she couldn't get enough. But throw some micro-level change her way, and she turned on you.

Though in all fairness, I couldn't entirely blame Priya for being skeptical. If someone had asked me a year ago, I would have said the very concept of internet dating was ridiculous. Just a fast-food model of human connection. If nothing else, it was a sport left to the young. I couldn't say for sure when my scorn started to subside. But if I had to place a date on it, I'd say it was about a month after the divorce papers were finalized—maybe the thirtieth evening in a row that I found myself glued to the evening news, a Crate & Barrel plate (chipped in the corner, so Lata left it behind when she moved to her own apartment) balanced on my lap, dragging a butter knife across the unyielding skin of a microwavable bean-and-cheese burrito. (It was a bitter month for my digestive system; even now, my gastroenterologist refers to it as "that unfortunate burrito period.")

That particular night, after loading the dishwasher with the handful of kitchen items Lata left behind—the aforementioned chipped plate, a mug that came free with a purchase of gas at the neighborhood Exxon station, a fork, an oversized spoon useful for scooping out generous amounts of salsa and sour cream— I readied myself for bed. I climbed onto the mattress, pulled the comforter to my chin and switched on the bedroom television, hoping to catch the Leno monologue before falling asleep. But just as the comedian began his routine, the oddest thing happened: I started to weep.

It was the first time I'd cried like that since Lata left me. But for some reason, at that particular moment, it struck me how much I missed her. Even during the worst phases of our thirty-six years of married life, when silences were thicker than the cement foundation underlying the two-story house we'd designed together, when our hands had long forgotten what the touch of a bare stomach or the soft inside of a thigh felt like, we could still take solace in one consistent form of togetherness. Late at night, every night, before nodding off on opposite sides of a king-sized bed, we'd watch the Leno monologue together. (Leno by default, because Lata could never stand Letterman's self-congratulatory laughter while delivering a joke.) And for those precious few minutes, we could be consoled by the intermingling sounds of our laughter. By the feeling that we weren't completely alone, together. It might not seem like a romantic or even an interesting marital ritual. But it was ours. Now, it too was gone.

The following day, I found myself typing three unlikely

words into Google: "Indian internet dating." What I discovered
was a cornucopia of sites promising romantic fulfillment:
Shaadi.com; DesiDating.com; IndianSingles.com. The sites
seemed endless. Was there one for every flavor of desolation?
Lonely-Middle-Aged-Ukrainian.com? Aching-for-Contact-
Papua-New-Guinean.com?

In the end, though, some combination of loneliness and curiosity got the better of me. And late one night, unable to sleep, I
logged on to a site. Within days, I'd read dozens of profiles, com-
pleted one of my very own, and made a discovery I hardly dared
hope for: women wanted me. And not just one or two, but scores
of them. Shalinis. Malinis. Sri Devis. Purvis. Forty- and fifty-
somethings from all over the country responding to my ad.
Good-looking too, some of them, in their pictures (though, of
course, this was all before I became aware of the lying phenomenon). My initial reaction was to assume something was wrong
with them. What else would propel them to go to such
lengths—to meet me of all people? Not that I was a particularly
insecure man. I knew I was okay—maybe not a prize bull but
not a smelly boar either. But their responses—so obsequious, so
eager to make contact. *You sound like a fascinating man. Your profile really caught my attention. Your answers were so funny, so clever.*

A few weeks of covetous attention and, as my children would
say, it started going to my head. I began seeing myself less and
less as a portly, indecisive man, who rarely knew the right things
to say, who bungled his first marriage, who loved his children
but felt his absentmindedness often bordered on neglect.

Instead, I'd entered a new world—one that enabled me to
have what, left alone with dust and memories in a four-bedroom
house, I secretly desired most: an escape from myself.

"Mallika?"

A petite woman, seemingly younger than the forty-three she

claimed to be, answered the door. She had honey-colored skin, kohl-rimmed eyes, and a slender, curvaceous figure encased in a form-fitting orange dress with embroidery on the bodice.

"Suresh?" Her voice was soft, with the lilting undercurrent of an accent.

For the next few seconds, we stared confusedly at each other. Her confusion was easily explained. It was likely due to the fact that I'd become a stuttering fool, incapable of forming a single declarative sentence: *Mallika? Yes, uh . . . I'm Suresh?* Who could blame her for looking so uncertain in front of a strange man who seemed painfully unaware of his own name. But the excuse for my befuddled state was even easier to explain: She was stunning.

In all my months as an internet dater, I'd grown accustomed to a certain disillusioning phenomenon: the face-to-face letdown. Weeks of buildup over phone and email culminating in disappointment at first sight. But standing on Mallika's doorstep, I felt none of that customary dissatisfaction, that feeling of air seeping out of my stomach like a needle-pricked balloon. I watched the dusky sunlight bounce against her silky hair, and a dizzying fume of elation wafted over me, almost as sweet as her rose-scented perfume.

"Shall we have Thai food for dinner?" I asked as soon as the fuzziness left my head.

"My favorite—you remembered. There's a place called Bangkok Garden close by."

Relief flooded through me. So far, so good: no sign of mendacity.

Holding the passenger door open for her, I noticed the smoothness of her right leg, the glistening sheen of her peach toenails, the peek of cleavage as she climbed into the car. I shut the door and walked briskly to the other side. Gulping discreetly, I scolded myself for behaving like a skin-starved schoolboy and started the car.

Soon enough, we were nestled in a corner booth at Bangkok Garden. A young waitress placed two sweating bottles of Singha and several steaming plates between us. I sipped my beer with relief, hoping it would loosen my tongue and counteract the near-paralyzing effect of her beauty. Perhaps sensing my nervousness, Mallika began to talk. She spoke exuberantly and at length: about her fondness for snow, her inexplicable fear of rabbits, her embarrassing habits like watching Ron Popeil infomercials late into the night and listening to country music stations while mopping her kitchen floor. She described her job, working as an administrative assistant for an elderly ophthalmologist who was going blind himself. She asked me about my job, and feeling more relaxed now, I told her how I'd worked as a systems analyst at Central Texas State University for almost thirty years, before taking an early retirement last year.

"You must have liked it—to have stayed there for so long?" She spooned pad thai onto my plate first and then onto her own—a gesture of generosity that touched me.

I chewed a forkful of noodles and considered her question, deciding to answer it honestly. "Well, it was a good job. Reliable, paid decently, and I rarely had to work weekends. But I can't say I liked it. It was inertia that kept me there, really. And a lack of imagination about what else to do. And, of course, I had a wife and two children to provide for. My wife, Lata—I mean, *ex*-wife—didn't work. She works now—part-time at a library or some such thing. But she didn't work back then, so I was the sole breadwinner."

Mallika nodded, forking a broccoli floret. "I can't say that I much like working for an octogenarian ophthalmologist either. But it does pay the bills, which is important, now that I'm . . . you know, on my own."

I spooned two mounds of rice and green curry onto my plate, and then silently scolded myself for not offering some to Mallika first. Maybe she didn't notice. "So how long have you and your husband been divorced?" I asked, trying to distract her from my selfish food-serving practices.

"No, we didn't . . . I mean, I'm not divorced. I'm a . . . a widow."

I paused, spoon hovering in midair. Widowed? This young? In our emails, this had not come up. I'd assumed she was divorced, like me. Mallika's cheeks flushed, and I struggled to mask my surprise.

"I-I'm s-sorry," I stammered. "How did your husband, I mean, your ex-husband—wait, are they still called husbands, if they die? Forgive me—that was insensitive. I don't know the proper terminology. But how did he . . . die?" I whispered the word "die," and then felt ridiculous for whispering.

Mallika picked at her Singha label. "Well, he died a few years ago. His name was Ajay. I'm sorry, but do you mind if we talk about something else?" She stared at her shiny nails scratching bits of paper off the glass. When she finally looked up, her expression was hard to decipher. I saw pain in her eyes, but was there something else in there too? Guilt or shame, maybe? Her face flushed again and she looked away.

I shook my head, trying to free it from irrational thoughts. I was being ridiculous. She didn't want to talk about her dead husband on a first date. It made perfect sense. There was nothing fishy about it. Those other internet women were just making me paranoid.

"No, of course we don't have to talk about it. I'm sorry." I busied myself by scooping rice onto my plate.

"Don't be. It's just that tonight has been really nice. Let's not spoil it with unhappy history. There will be time for that later." She smiled at me during the last sentence, and I tried not to gawk at her face—those radiant pink cheeks, those curling lashes, the delicate curvature of her cheekbones.

Later. There would be a later.

My stomach began to churn. For years, I suffered from too much acidity in my stomach. I lived with a near-constant, low-level discomfort in my gut, easily exacerbated by spicy pickles, public speaking, employment evaluations, fights with Lata, and too much Taco Bell. But this—this was an entirely different topsy-turvy feeling in my abdomen.

Was it hope? Hope that there was actually someone out there in the world capable of making me feel joy, maybe even love? That such a person existed? Or was this feeling in my gut anxiety? Anxiety that, even if the chance of finding such happiness was possible, even if it was right in front of my face, I'd manage to bungle it somehow.

My wife—*ex*-wife—always said I suffocated her with my pessimism, sucked the joy out of her like a Hoover. In her characteristic myopia, she never stopped to consider that maybe she brought out the negativity in me, that my so-called pessimism was more acute in her judgmental presence. But bygones. Divorce was good for nothing if not the copious amounts of alone time. A perfect opportunity for self-reflection and reexamination. And it was possible, just possible, that I could be, at times, a tad disagreeable. A bit of a complains-first-thinks-later sort of person. All right, so I could be a real donkey. But that was all going to change. Mallika would only see the reformed me. The jovial me. The new and improved, happy-go-lucky Suresh Raman.

We made lighthearted conversation for the rest of dinner. A mint lemonade for me, a tea for her. A shared plate of sticky rice with mango. At the end of the night, I walked her to her front door and let my hand linger on her shoulder. She pecked me on the cheek and thanked me "for a wonderful evening." She closed the door with a sweet little wave.

All right, so maybe the date ended more chastely than I might have wished. But wasn't this a commendable thing too? My Mallika was a virtuous woman. A lovely, modest, old-fashioned kind of woman. The kind of woman a man could marry—would be lucky to marry. The kind of woman that some man already

had the great luck to marry and the greater misfortune to lose—
through death. Likely a car accident. Or a heart attack. Or cancer.

At any rate, he was gone, and I was here, standing on Mallika's doorstep, inhaling the lingering scent of her perfume.

Blissfully, thrillingly alive.

2

LATA

When Professor Greenberg, a History of Jazz professor at the university, handed me the slim plastic CD case across the checkout-and-return desk, I started to place it in a pile of disks for scanning and shelving. But then he stopped me.

"No, wait," he said, "it's not from the library. It's for you, Lata. I burned that CD for you."

"Burned it? For me?" I placed the CD case on the oak counter between us, and stared at it, confused.

"Remember our conversation the other day when you mentioned that you had never listened to jazz and didn't own any jazz CDs? Well, I made you a compilation of some of my favorite vocalists singing standards I thought you'd like—just to ease you into the genre. There's also a card—well, a folded sheet of paper—inside the case listing each song and artist."

He spoke very fast, and when he stopped, I had no idea how to respond.

Since beginning my position as a library assistant five months ago, a position I'd seen advertised on the bulletin board of my favorite bookstore, I'd come to learn that libraries had their regulars (much like bars, I'm told). And Professor Greenberg was definitely a regular. Nearly every other day, I'd start my shift expecting to see his tall, trim frame in a listening carrel, earphones peeking through his gray curls, his head bobbing as he scribbled notes.

And it was true that a few days ago, I had said something to him in passing about not owning any jazz music. But we weren't friends or anything. To my mind, we weren't even casual acquaintances. Until today, our interactions had consisted of little more than the "hello, thank you, you're welcome" formalities of checkout and return. I didn't think he knew my name, so what could he mean by giving me this CD?

I'd been staring at his gift for several seconds without saying a word. My silence was clearly making him uncomfortable. Although he was at least sixty, he had a boyish face, and a matching inability to mask distress. A few students stood behind him in the checkout-and-return line, and they watched us with a mixture of curiosity and impatience. Both wanting and fearing further explanation from him about what prompted this gesture, I quickly thanked him for "burning me it . . . I mean, making me the CD," and turned to help the spiky-haired boy next in line.

"So, Lata, what's the deal with you and jazz-professor man?" Deanna, another library assistant, appeared next to me with a teasing smirk.

I pretended like I didn't hear her. I tried to seem very busy piling the returned books into a neat stack. I closed my eyes for a moment and focused on the texture of book covers between my fingers, the not-unpleasant smell of yellowing, mildewed pages.

But Deanna was not a person you could easily ignore. She was a graduate student who specialized in something called ethnomusicology. From what Jared, the head librarian and our boss, had told me, Deanna was a kind of genius. Barely twenty, she was one of the youngest PhD students at the university. To look at her, though, you'd never guess that this hundred-pound girl—who had rings through her eyebrows and a tattoo of a giant lotus on the back of her neck and often wore long sweaters that she (purposely!) shredded with scissors—spent her hours applying for research grants and coauthoring papers with gray-haired professors. But sometimes I wondered if Deanna's accelerated schooling had stunted her social development. She seemed to have a hard time getting along with others. With the library patrons, for example, it was not uncommon to see Deanna yelling at some unsuspecting student for returning a biography with pencil-marked pages or for using a cellphone inside the library. This tiny feather of a girl liked to fight.

But for some reason, Deanna had taken a liking to me. She listened patiently—though with an amused expression on her face—when I read from a hepatitis pamphlet I'd picked up from the doctor's office about the dangers of tattoo needles, or when I suggested she eat something other than popcorn and Reese's peanut butter cups for lunch. I'd even started packing extra food for her along with my own lunch, and come noon, when we'd break in the back room, I'd shake my head at her Ziploc bag of popcorn and cajole her into trying some idli and sambar. When I started this, she was hesitant, but lately, she'd been eating them with relish; she'd let the idlis soak in the sambar like a well-practiced South Indian and then scoop up the spongelike pieces with her purple-polished fingers. Watching her eat so hungrily, I'd wonder: Who was her mother, and how could she let her daughter waste away like this? Priya might be a grown woman, but even so, I still made occasional trips to her apartment to stock her freezer with Tupperware containers of homemade sambar and idlis, rasam and tamarind rice. I knew that during busy work months, Priya, like Deanna, would probably live on cereal rather than take the time to cook proper meals.

As a way of distracting Deanna now, I mentioned the lunch I'd brought. "Guess what, Deanna? It's idli day today."

"Nice try, but I'm not letting you off the hook so easily. Spill it, Lata. What's the deal with you two?"

"Deal? We have no kind of a deal." Self-consciously, I touched my left ring finger. I felt the raw skin where my wedding ring used to be. "I've barely spoken three words to him before today."

"Well, those three words must have made some impression, because he likes you."

"Who likes who? Sorry, my dentist appointment ran late." Jared snuck up behind us, smelling of sweat and spearmint gum. "So, ladies, who are we gossiping about?"

"Nobody," I said quickly—too quickly.

"Uh-huh. Who's your not-so-secret admirer?" Jared plopped into a swivel chair with a grunt and twirled around to face us.

"It's nothing, really. Professor Greenberg made me a CD compilation. That's all. It's nothing . . . just a kind gesture." I focused my eyes on the book I was stacking—*The Structure of Atonal Music*—and pretended to read the back cover.

Jared fluttered his eyelashes and said in an artificially high voice: "'I have always depended on the kindness of strangers. I don't tell the truth. I tell what ought to be the truth.'"

The corners of Deanna's mouth twitched. I could see that she was trying hard to keep a critical comment to herself.

Jared was officially our boss, even though he didn't act very bosslike. He had graduated from college over two decades ago, and though he worked full-time managing the music library, he spoke often about his aspirations to be a theater actor. Deanna suspected that his frequent dentist and doctors' appointments were all a fraud and that he was really sneaking away to auditions in Houston and Austin and Dallas.

"Jared's smoking crack if he thinks that a balding fatty in his forties has a serious theater career waiting for him," she'd say. "People have the most idiotic dreams for themselves."

She had a sharp tongue, that Deanna. But in this case, her words seemed true. As I looked at Jared now, his body slumped in the sagging chair, his teeth just as yellow and coffee-stained as they were this morning when he left for his "dentist appointment," I struggled to imagine him reaching any professional heights beyond his current library position. And yet, off he went, week after week, speeding out of the library door with the same urgent look on his face . . . and despite his best efforts, week after week, month after month, his life remained exactly the same. Completely unchanged. What made him keep trying? Blindness? Stupidity?

This irrational dreaming, this clinging to the belief that it was never too late or that anything was possible—I'd never been able to decide whether it was an admirable quality in white Americans or a ridiculous one.

Though really, who was I to criticize Jared for his dreams, irrational or otherwise? Here I was, barely a year into a new life—a woman who had chosen to get divorced at fifty-six, who had started a new job after never having had one before, who had decided to move out of her old house and live alone in an apartment three miles away. Maybe my friends were all thinking these same things about me—that thirty-five years in this country had confused and corrupted me, had turned me into some kind of irrational-dreaming Lata. My younger sister, Parvati, who still lived in Chennai and had watched over our parents until they died, certainly thought so.

"Hey." Deanna tapped my shoulder. "Did you check inside the CD cover? Maybe Greenberg wrote his phone number in it."

"Sorry, what am I looking for?" I opened the CD cover gently, as if it was made of breakable glass instead of cheap plastic.

Deanna grabbed the case from my hands and tugged the paper in the front—the printed list that Professor Greenberg had mentioned. She unfolded it, scanned it, and shook her head.

"No phone number. But that doesn't mean he's not interested. He doesn't strike me as that suave of a guy anyway. He'll be back."

Deanna refolded the paper, tucked it into the plastic cover, and handed the case to me. "The question is, Lata, what will you do when he does come back?"

"Yeah, Lata—are you interested in our cherubic Coltrane aficionado or what?" Jared asked.

"Cherubic what?" My head was swimming. I wanted to get away from them before they could ask me any more questions.

"You two are too much. It's just a small, meaningless gift. It's been a long day. I'm going home." I stuffed the CD in my purse and hurried to the door before they could say another word.

It was usually the post–evening news hours that deflated me.

After returning to my apartment from work, I'd heat up a light dinner, maybe two chapatis with curried eggplant or potato sagu, and eat it while watching NBC News. After that, I'd flip the channel to watch the first part of Jim Lehrer on PBS. But, come seven, I'd be at a loss for what to do. I might read a magazine. Or half-heartedly knit. Or call one of the kids. Maybe if I was lucky, Nikesh would sit Alok, my little *laddu*, in front of a computer and Skype with me for a few precious minutes. But when all that was done, I'd hear the silence in my apartment grow loud as a blender.

When I first moved into this apartment, I savored these silent post–evening news hours. I would make myself tea, sit on the loveseat with a blanket over my lap, and watch movies. One channel in particular played an endless stream of romantic comedies—*Pretty Woman, When Harry Met Sally, Sleepless in Seattle.* When no movies were on that station, I'd watch old Bollywood movies. Not the newer ones with the half-naked girls and the heroes with muscles as large as bodybuilders', but the

older ones from my youth—the seventies movies with Jaya Bha-
duri and Sharmila Tagore and Hema Malini, those wide-eyed,
long-haired beauties who could make Amitabh or Dharmendra
melt with the simplest gestures. Actresses that didn't have to rely
on the overly sexy, twisty-jerky dance numbers of today to make
men melt.

In those first few weeks alone in my apartment, the evening
hours flew by as I drank my tea and watched my movies in peace,
free from Suresh's angry grumblings: *Why are you wasting your
time watching this? Why can't we watch something useful, like the
Discovery Channel? Such a silly, unrealistic plot—why would that
rich man marry a common prostitute?* Strange, though: For all his
complaining, he would always hang around until every movie's
end.

This apartment was set up for me by my friend Mala and her
husband, Dr. Chandrasekhar. It was their condo. They'd owned
it for years, usually renting it out to graduate students or visiting
lecturers. Mala had initially questioned my decision to leave the
house to Suresh. "He should leave the house, not you," she
scolded. "After all that effort you put into designing it, decorating it. It's where your children grew up. It's near your friends—
Maneesha and Deva and I all live close by, and we can keep an
eye on you."

I didn't know how to tell her that that was precisely why I
wanted to move. I didn't want to stay alone in a four-bedroom
house where my kids grew up but no longer lived. I didn't want
to walk out my front door to check the mail, only to find Mala's
husband sneakily inspecting my car tires or roof shingles at his
wife's urging, just to make sure that everything was still ship-
shape now that Suresh was no longer around. And living close
to my friends would have made it harder to say no when they
invited me to a Diwali party or a Pongal celebration or a Saturday potluck. The last thing I wanted was to bring my signature
lemon rice to one of those parties and face the quickly disguised

looks of concern and pity, the false expressions of good cheer. No indeed. Far better to live farther away. Not wanting to drive to and from their parties late at night—that was an excuse my friends were more likely to accept.

When Mala couldn't persuade me to stay in my house, she offered to rent me their condo at a reduced rate. I didn't need the reduced rate. Since Suresh kept the house, he had to buy out my share. If I had wanted to, I could have easily bought my own condo, or even a small house, for that matter. But I didn't feel like making the effort to search for a new place, and Mala wouldn't hear of letting me pay the same rate as a stranger. So it seemed an easy and practical decision to move into the Chandershakers' condo. At least for the time being.

The space was pleasant enough—two small bedrooms, a large kitchen with a gas stove, clean carpet, fresh beige paint, and a balcony overlooking a swimming pool that I never used because I couldn't swim. And after I got the job at the music library, the apartment provided the added bonus of being a quick drive to work.

But after the first few weeks of enjoying my solitude in the apartment, I'd come to dread these evening hours, when every cricket chirp and dog bark sounded like an accusation, a scolding: How has your life ended up like this? Why are you fifty-seven and living alone in someone else's small apartment?

But today, I was too distracted to even dread the evening silence. All I could think about was that CD at the bottom of my purse, just waiting for me.

I was standing barefoot in the dining room, wearing a cotton nightgown, staring dumbly at the purse on my dining table. The purse was a fiftieth birthday gift from Priya—an oversized Coach tote. Usually, the sight of the bag's smooth, taupe leather comforted me. Not today, though. I was too busy trying to imagine what I could possibly say to Professor Greenberg (what was his first name, even? Leonard?) the next time he came into the library. Was it enough to say I liked the CD, or did I have to be more specific, identifying particular songs?

I slapped my palm to my forehead. I was being ridiculous, a fool, an *asadu*. What was the big deal? The man made me a CD. I could play it on my CD player as I drifted off to sleep. After all, wasn't jazz supposed to be relaxing? Like the music they played in elevators. Like that Kenny G fellow—soft saxophones and flutelike sounds?

I stuck my arm into my purse and pulled out the CD. A bit of lotion streaked the right corner. A tube of Lubriderm must have leaked in my purse. I wiped it away, opened the case, and unfolded the printed page. I wasn't wearing my reading glasses, so I squinted to read it. At the bottom, I could make out the words: *For: Lata Raman. From: Leonard Greenberg.*

It was simply stating the obvious—that the gift was from him to me. But seeing our names written together like that, in such close proximity, I sat down on a chair.

He had taken the time to make me this gift. He chose these songs because he thought I might like them. He typed this page of song titles, this inscription. All for me. No one had made me a gift in such a long time. Not since the kids were in elementary school, bringing home ill-constructed crafts made of popsicle sticks and dried lima beans for Mother's Day.

No man had ever made me a gift before. Suresh wasn't the gift-giving type—neither store-bought nor homemade. My father—my kindhearted schoolteacher father—used to whittle me wooden animal figures when I was a little girl. He died of a stroke twenty-two years ago. My mother held on for two decades more, dying of pneumonia just eighteen months ago. It was not lost on me—the fact that I had stayed married until both of my parents died. I had always been a dutiful daughter. I was, until their end.

For: Lata Raman. From: Leonard Greenberg.

My heartbeat quickened. Was Deanna right? Was this more

than a friendly gesture? Did Leonard want to date me? It was all too much to think about right now. I was just learning how to live alone. I didn't need this.

I folded the paper back into the CD case and shoved it into my purse.

I pushed it as far away from my body as I could manage.

3

PRIYA

"Voilà!" With a flourish, I opened the lid to reveal a gloopy orange mound.

Ashish sniffed suspiciously. "What is it?"

"Macaroni and cheese." I scooped out a hefty portion and dumped it on a plate, wincing a little at the plopping sound.

The recipe said it would turn out creamy. That it would slide off the spoon. Not plop. Well, whatever. Wasn't it the taste that really mattered anyway?

I sat next to him at a small maple dining table I'd rescued many years ago from Goodwill.

"You first." I propped my elbows on the familiar wavy wood grain, cupped my palms around my cheeks and watched closely as he chewed and swallowed.

"Well, what do you think?" I widened my eyes and tried to jokingly mimic the solicitous gaze of a housewife who'd spent the day toiling over a stove for her husband.

We were, after all, playing house on a Friday evening. We were sipping Vinho Verde and trying to ignore the ticking of time. It was seven now. If we finished dinner soon, we'd have just enough time for sex and a shower, so Ashish could get home by nine. That was when he turned into a pumpkin. That was when his wife, Chalini, returned from her monthly book club meeting. I didn't ask Ashish what book they were reading.

"Ashish, say something already. How's the mac 'n' cheese?"

He nodded thoughtfully and held up a finger to quiet me. He forked another bite and grinned mischievously. "I think you did not miss your calling by becoming a historian."

I laughed—a bit louder and longer than necessary. I was trying to mask my disappointment. For a moment, I allowed myself to wonder if Chalini could cook—if she whipped up aromatic biryanis and dhals for Ashish on a daily basis. Ashish had never mentioned her cooking.

My phone beeped on the table. I peeked at the screen, relieved for the momentary distraction. A missed call from my father—from earlier this afternoon. I must not have heard it during my completely wasted culinary labors. At the thought of my father, I rolled my eyes—a reflex these days.

"Uh-oh. Who is it?" Ashish asked, buttering a sourdough roll that I had no role in creating. It was bakery-bought and therefore edible. He tore into the roll and chewed with satisfaction. The macaroni lay untouched on his plate, congealed and fluorescent.

"It's my dad. I'll call him back later—when I've got more wine in me." I sipped, letting the bubbly tartness wash over my tongue. "He's probably just calling me en route to one of his dates. He drives all over the country to meet these weird Indian women he finds online. It's so embarrassing."

I spat the words out, harsher than I'd intended. My inability to make an edible macaroni for Ashish was bothering me more than I cared to admit. I'd chosen macaroni because it was supposed to be easy. Unfuckupable. Ashish reached for another roll, and I resisted the urge to take the butter away, to punish him in that small way.

"What's the big deal?" he said. "Your dad's like what, sixtyish? So he's got a few good decades left, and he's trying to find someone to spend it with. I don't see why it should bother you so much. It's not like he's still married to your mom."

"You're right. He is not. Married."

I glared at him, and he held his hands up in surrender.

I turned the wine bottle upside down. Two sad drops dribbled into my glass. "Perfect," I muttered, letting the bottle clang against the table.

The orange mound on Ashish's plate glistened up at me—mockingly. Ignoring his look of surprise, I grabbed his plate and scraped the macaroni back into the red casserole pot. The pot was brand new, a Le Creuset knockoff I'd bought at T.J. Maxx a few days ago, just so I could make this shitty dinner. Now I couldn't stand the sight of it. In three quick strides, I carried the pot across the room and hurled it into the trash bin.

There. Dinner was done.

It didn't feel particularly good, being a hypocrite.

After all, for months now, I'd been giving my dad grief. Grief about the divorce, about his cross-country dating sprees, about the younger women he pursued like he was some kind of Don Juan–cum–Amitabh Bachchan.

And to be fair, these women weren't even all *that* young. From what Nikesh told me, the old man had the decency to stay a good ten years away from my general age group. That was sort of commendable these days. Reality television had, after all, set the bar so low. Regardless, I'd lectured him and belittled him and felt ashamed of him. I'd acted like some Mother Superior when in fact I was the contemptible one, having an affair with a married man.

The married man in question was Ashish Trivedi, an economics professor at Travis College, where I taught as well. It was a small college, dwarfed both in size and stature by its more illustrious neighbor, the University of Texas. Ashish and I first met about a year and a half ago, at a chamber music recital on campus. The cellist, Camille Kim, had invited me. Camille was a student in a small seminar class I taught. Usually, when students invited me to their campus events—plays, water polo matches, protest rallies—I'd feign interest and politely decline. But Camille was one of my favorite students—a shy girl who raised her hand infrequently, but always made insightful comments. I encouraged her to speak more in class, because I had a feeling she censored herself unnecessarily. (Why was this always the case with students who had the best things to say?) So I decided to make an exception for Camille—and go to her recital.

As Camille and the other musicians warmed up their instruments, I snuck into an empty row toward the back of the recital hall. Halfway into a Bartók piece, a tall Indian man slipped into the same row as me, one seat over. He looked to be in his late thirties, had cropped hair with slightly graying tips, and dressed more Oxford than central Texas—tweed jacket, dark jeans, loafers. It suited him, though, lent him an impressive, learned air, like if you asked him to, he could probably describe the political situation in Lesotho, or somewhere random, right off the top of his head. I half expected to hear an English accent when he said, "Excuse me, is this your program copy?" It was, in fact, a faintly Midwestern accent. I told him it was my copy, but he was free to keep it.

He smiled at me then, a high-wattage smile that was incommensurate with the smallness of my gesture. I did notice, however, that his teeth were nice and extremely white. I also noticed his eyes, which was unusual for me. I never noticed eyes unless they were creepy or untrustworthy. Like Vladimir Putin's, for example: They were beady little windows to his clearly nefarious nature. But Ashish's eyes were nothing like that. They were beautiful: large, richly lashed, inky black orbs. And they insisted upon eye contact, penetrating eye contact—something that unnerved me at first, but then grew on me, assured me that I was the sole recipient of his attention. They made me feel seen.

During intermission, we chatted. He said he loved classical music and often stopped by the recital hall on his way home in hopes of catching a performance. I said I was only there at a student's behest, that I preferred Motown and soul, and probably drove my neighbors crazy by playing Aretha Franklin and Etta James at odd hours of the night and belting along in my too-high voice.

"What I wouldn't give for a sexy alto voice, instead of this annoying bird squeak," I added.

"You're too hard on yourself, I bet. Your speaking voice is sexy enough." He seemed startled by the intimacy of his own comment.

"Oh, well, thanks. Maybe it's the concert hall acoustics or something. I guess I should get a similar setup for my bathroom."

I mumbled the last bit, and immediately berated myself for its stupidity. The fact was, adulthood had turned me into a totally inept flirter—or at best, an unintentional one. That a flirtatious exchange was even happening would hit me about two and a half seconds after the fact, at which point, in trying to decide whether I wanted to continue to purposely flirt, I'd simply miss or mangle the moment. My flirting abilities had been on a steady decline since a short-lived peak around the age of twenty-six, a sort of standout period for me, when I'd finally been able to view myself less meanly, to see what other people probably saw when they looked at me—a woman who, if not uncommonly pretty, was just on the cusp of it.

The concert resumed then, and Ashish smiled and turned his attention to the stage. Just before the lights dimmed, I spotted his wedding band. During the rest of the concert, I felt a bit heavier. This scenario had become all too familiar. I'd have a nice chat with a good-looking man, feel that momentary surge of excitement, and then, inevitably, I'd see that shiny gold buzzkill. When the concert ended, I used the excuse of needing to congratulate Camille to walk speedily away. But there was a throng of admirers to wade through, and in the end, I gave up and left through the side door. As luck (or unluck) would have it, I reached the parking lot just as Ashish was pulling out of his space—a space that, sure enough, was near mine.

He rolled down his window as I came near. "Hey, there you are. You left so fast that I forgot to ask if you wanted to meet me for lunch tomorrow."

I tried to gauge the spirit of his invitation. He appeared relaxed, with no sign of nervousness or guilt. Was it possible that he just wanted a new colleague-friend? Why not, I'd thought— I could use a new colleague-friend. The professors in my department were mostly wizened old white men—all nice enough, but not exactly prime friendship material. So I'd accepted his invitation, and we arranged to meet at a Mexican place the next day.

Maybe that's how all big transgressions start—with a tiny acquiescence. (Do heroin addicts feel this way too?) You say yes to something seemingly innocuous, like lunch at a taco dive, a quick beer after work, a midday coffee run to the Starbucks across the street. And before you know it, you're in a three-day-a-week, fourteen-going-on-fifteen-month arrangement with a married man. A married Indian man, no less—a fact that makes it worse somehow, makes you feel both guiltier and more invested in the relationship.

He comes to your house every Monday afternoon (before his evening class, after your morning one), midmornings on Wednesdays (before your afternoon office hours), and an extra, variable day of the week, when he can slip away from Chalini, a woman you know little about except that she's a pharmaceutical sales representative who'd stopped having sex with her husband about two years ago, around the time she found out she was infertile.

Chalini. A woman you wouldn't recognize if you bumped into her in the produce section of H-E-B—which you very well might, since his house, which you drove by once out of curiosity, is not too far from yours—but whose life you now have a distinct hand in fucking up.

I lacked many things. But I wasn't without a conscience. Really.

"Ashish, have you told anyone about me?"

We were lying on my bed, spent. The trash can macaroni was forgotten now—though the faint smell of burnt onions and browned butter lingered in the air. The covers lay crumpled on the floor, and the fluttery sounds of Debussy or Chopin or some Frenchish sort played softly in the background. Ashish's music collection had been seeping into mine. But I didn't mind. His classical music was growing on me. Above the delicate piano trills, I could hear the sudden thumping of my cat, Ann Richards, against the bedroom door. She was a sprightly stray, who like her namesake (the unquestionable high point of Texas gubernatorial politics), sported blinding white hair and a feisty attitude. Her door-thumping was an act of protest—she hated being ignored.

I ran my hand through a tuft of hair on Ashish's stomach, watching the coarse coils straighten between my fingers and then curl again as I let go. He cupped his hand over mine, to stop my tugging. "Just my therapist. That doesn't count, does it?"

I propped my head up. "Since when do you see a therapist? I didn't think Indian men your age were into that kind of thing."

"My age? I'm only a few years older than you. And what do you mean—Indian men aren't 'into that kind of thing.' What kind of thing?"

"You know . . . mental health."

Ashish laughed. "Haha. Thanks a lot. Look, darling, don't pigeonhole us, okay?" He said this last bit in a thick, put-upon Indian accent. "It's no big deal. I started seeing a therapist in graduate school because Columbia's medical insurance covered it, and I've gone to one off and on ever since. Therapy's great—you should definitely try it."

"Well," I said. "Nearly a decade of off-and-on therapy, and here you are, shuttling between your wife and mistress—ugh, I hate that word—special friend, gal pal, whatever. Clearly, therapy's done you a world of good."

He shrugged. "Look, these things happen. They're not ideal situations, but they happen."

His nonchalance disturbed me. I wouldn't call Ashish a callous person per se, but he was one of those people who thought feeling guilty was a waste of time. He seemed to throw out misgivings like yesterday's trash. I hid my discomfort with sarcasm. "Well, if that's the kind of earth-shattering revelation you're paying the big bucks for, you should really consider getting a new therapist."

"Jeez, tough crowd." He moved down the bed and started biting the soft part of my waist.

I yelped and threw my hands up. "Okay, I give. You're the picture of mental health. So, what do you tell this therapist about me?"

"I can't tell you that. That's the point of therapy. Unlike you, she's a neutral third party." He started kissing my stomach.

"Your therapist is a she? Who are you—Tony Soprano?" I laughed.

"You're enjoying this too much." He looked a little hurt.

I adopted a sober look. I'd been trying to keep it light, but in truth, I was desperate to know what he told this therapist about me, and what she told him about being with me. Maybe she was telling him to leave his wife. Did therapists do that kind of thing?

"Okay, I'll be serious now," I said. "Really, what do you tell her about me? I won't be offended, I promise."

He hesitated. "I told her that you still haven't quit smoking, which is disgusting, that you have an irrational aversion to cilantro and naked feet, and that whenever I'm playing with one of your breasts, you want the other one to be left alone, as if you can't take any pleasure without an equal measure of deprivation."

"What? You told her all that? Okay, okay, I'm not getting mad or anything. So—what else do you tell this therapist?"

He was silent for a moment. "Well, last week I told her that I was in love with you."

He stared at me, trying to gauge my reaction.

"Oh." I shifted my gaze away and focused on a crack in the ceiling. "What did your therapist say when you told her that?"

"That I should tell you."

"Oh."

"Oh? Is that all you have to say?"

"Are you still married?"

"Come on, Priya. You know it's complicated."

My chest felt heavy. I squinted, so that the ceiling crack became a blur. If I just kept staring at it, I could stop myself from crying. "Well, then, I guess I don't have anything to say."

4

SURESH

After dropping Mallika off, I noticed the gas gauge nearing empty.

I pulled into the first station I could find. I removed the fuel nozzle from its cradle and started to hum. To a passerby, I must have made a foolish picture, standing in the middle of the Exxon with a goofy grin on my face, clutching a gas pump and humming. But I didn't care. The date had surpassed all my expectations. I wasn't a bungler after all.

Wanting to capitalize on this rare feeling of triumph, I considered visiting Priya. I'd called her this afternoon, but she never answered. Why didn't she answer?

Her condo wasn't far from here—maybe ten minutes away. But then, I knew she'd be suspicious if I landed on her doorstep uninvited at nine o'clock on a Friday night. I'd have to deal with her questions—her relentless, uncharitable questions: "Why are you in Austin? Don't tell me it was for one of your ridiculous internet dates? Is she at least older than me? I mean, do you fancy yourself some kind of Indian Michael Douglas or something, because let me tell you, that old man looks ridiculous with Catherine Zeta-Jones, simply ridiculous."

How inside out things had become. Once upon a time, my children followed me from room to room, chanting "da-da-da-da" and clutching my pant legs with a love so primal and suffocating that I'd pretend to have a number two, just so I could escape to the quiet of the bathroom.

Why didn't I appreciate that unquestioning devotion more when I had it? And when exactly did the tables start to turn? How did I become the needy one, the one so desperate for my children's approval, fighting for their time, fearful of losing their attentions and affections?

I clicked the nozzle back into its cradle. I grabbed a squeegee from a pail of curiously gray water and scrubbed the windshield. With no other task available to me, I dialed Priya's number. Her phone rang once, twice, three times.

"Hello." Her voice sounded scratchy and low—as if I'd woken her from sleep.

"Hello, Priya! It's your dad!" I was practically shouting into the phone. When nervous, I spoke a good ten decibels louder than necessary.

"I know it's you, Dad. Your name comes up automatically. Are you okay?"

"Oh, I'm doing fine. Just fine. And you? How is . . . work?"

"Good, I guess. Busy."

"Good. Busy is good. Very good to be keeping busy. Good."

Silence.

"So, Dad, is your stomach still giving you problems?"

Ah yes, the digestion-related questions. She was clever, my daughter. Make no mistake: This line of inquiry, while appearing innocent, was really quite devious. It allowed her to play the part of a concerned child without having to really ask, hear, or know anything about my life. She could plant herself in the trouble-free zone of superficial conversation, digestive inquiry serving as the functional equivalent of discussing the weather. Maybe even more than that, she derived a certain satisfaction from casting me in the light of an ailing old man. She'd ask about my stomach, my heart, my cholesterol, my blood pressure, my joints, and by asking me all the health-related questions she had once reserved for obligatory phone calls to her grandparents in India, she could snuff out all images of her serial-dating, virile, vital father. She could suck all the life out of me. But I didn't say this to her, of course.

"I'm fine. Stomach is fine."

"Well, that's good. I'm glad to hear you're taking care of your health. It's so important *at your age*. So, um, look, I should probably go. It's getting late, and I need to finish some work stuff."

"If you need to go, then of course it's—"

"Thanks for calling, and take care, okay?"

"Priya . . . Priya?" She'd hung up already.

A car honked behind me, a gray Nissan waiting for a turn at the pump. I waved apologetically, got back into my car, and pulled into a parking space in front of the gas station convenience store. All the while, Priya's parting words pulsed in my head: *Take care. Take care?* As if I were her colleague. Or a customer. Or the postman.

If I only had an inkling of it before, the cost of my romantic renaissance was becoming clear to me now: patricide. A slow and agonizing patricide, a symbolic killing of father by daughter with each uncomfortable conversation, accusatory glance, and exasperated sigh!

Or was I just making too much of it? Maybe children never liked thinking of their parents as sexual beings, as people who needed to be touched and admired to feel alive. I rarely thought of my own parents this way. My parents had slept in separate beds until my father passed away. And yet, I couldn't help but sense that Priya's sentiments transcended this general unease—

went beyond instinctive squeamishness. She felt betrayed. And for that, I wondered if I was partly to blame.

Lata and I were never really open with the kids about sex and dating. There were never explicit prohibitions or rules on the subject—as was the case with many of our Indian friends and their children. But it wasn't a topic of open discussion. I never walked into Nikesh's room after he spent what seemed like an abnormally long amount of time in the bathroom to have any kind of "special talk." As far as I knew, Lata prepared Priya for her transition to womanhood by going on a shopping expedition to the feminine hygiene section of Wal-Mart. Beyond that, any description of birds, bees, unwanted pregnancies, boy parts, girl parts, and fluid by-products was left to bloom in the unspoken background. Lata and I never even discussed how we should address the topic with our children. I wasn't sure, in retrospect, how to account for this gaping hole, except that if it ever occurred to us, by the time the realization pushed beyond the barricade of our unease, it was too late. Our children were in their late teens, and by then, it was safe to assume any gaps in their knowledge had been filled in by television, movies, and detailed accounts from their American friends, who by that point were no doubt accumulating firsthand information. (In our parental blindness, we would, of course, never assume the firsthand knowledge of our own children.)

My son, as it turned out, did figure it out on his own. I found a condom in the glove compartment of his car two days after he went to the junior prom with the Jacobs girl—"that Jacobs girl," Lata called her. I didn't say anything to Lata about it. I knew she would overreact. I didn't tell Nikesh either. He was terribly territorial about his car (now I know why), and it would have been too difficult to convince him that I wasn't snooping, just updating his proof of insurance card. In a way, I was relieved. At least he was being safe. I was even a little proud and envious of his sexual exploits, his freedom, which to me at seventeen would have been unthinkable.

And now, ironically, I relied on his experience, which he gained without our knowledge or explicit approval. I sought his advice when it came to making awkward first-date chatter or deciphering the ambiguous signals that women sent. Oh, we didn't engage in any kind of locker-room talk—that would be far too uncomfortable, for both of us. And though he seemed to view my search for companionship more as a joke than as a serious endeavor, he was still the closest thing I had to a friend.

But with Priya, everything was so difficult. She didn't exactly blame me for the divorce—though she never understood why two late-fifty-somethings needed to put the official stamp of failure on a three-decade partnership. She had to know that I didn't misbehave in any terrible way during the marriage. And insofar as there were fights, long silences, doors slammed, wasn't Lata as much to blame as me? It was, after all, Lata's decision to leave in the end. I would have stayed. Surely, Priya saw that.

No, it was just my performance as a divorced man that appalled her. I called it the Jimmy Carter predicament in reverse— the way he was maligned during his presidency and adored after. I was adored, well, at least liked well enough by my daughter during my marriage. And reviled after. A father's fall from grace. The inevitable descent from the parental pedestal. I distracted myself with high-sounding phrases. The truth was: I missed my daughter.

Here's the terrible secret of being a parent: You always have a favorite. Not in the sense of who you love more, or whose happiness you want more, or who you'd save if you could save only one of them. (Note to all parents: Never watch *Sophie's Choice* with your children, no matter how old they are: fifteen, nineteen, twenty-five. Inevitably, they'll ask the dreaded question.) I loved both my kids deeply, would sacrifice life and limb for them without a second thought. I just mean a "favorite" in the sense that you understand them. They make sense to you, as much as any creature outside of your own head can make sense to you. In some way, they are a version of yourself—similarly wired, correspondingly flawed, and deeply resentful of your own shortcomings because you embody what they fear they will become. You know this child—it's the one you fight with the most, worry about the most, the one who you secretly pin your innermost hopes on, because you see in them the opportunity for your own redemption. Priya was this to me. *Is* this to me.

And I worried for her. My children differed in their fundamental makeup. Nikesh would never be alone. He was the one that people immediately liked. He got this quality from Lata. Any social life I'd had in this town was because of her—I knew that. Which might explain why no one ever sent *me* condolence biryanis in neat Tupperware containers or invited *me* to a Diwali dinner after the divorce.

But Priya: She was a difficult combination—sensitive and not easily reached. She was thirty-five, unmarried, and lived alone in a scantily furnished condo. As far as I knew, she wasn't seeing anyone and had never been in a relationship serious enough to tell her mother or myself about. On the outside, she seemed confident enough, but on the inside, she was a soft-shelled crab like her father—easily bruised. She always needed encouragement. And at crucial moments, Lata and I failed her. By our very example we failed her. And I worried that, like me, she would one day find herself growing old, all alone.

The glass door of the convenience store opened and a young couple walked out. The man carried a six-pack of beer, and the woman dangled a large bag of chips from her fingers. They were holding hands and laughing.

I felt an ache in my chest, imagining my daughter alone. I flipped the ignition and began making my way to Priya's.

"Dad?" Priya answered the door in a purple robe and slippers. "What are you doing here? Has something happened?"

She looked at me with such uncensored concern that for a split second, I considered inventing an ailment for myself. Something empathy-inducing but treatable, like gout.

"No, no. Everything is fine. I just haven't visited you in a while, and . . . this seemed as good a time as any. Does there have to be a reason for a father to visit his only daughter?" I adopted a stance of nonchalance, shrugging my shoulders and holding my palms up.

"But you just called me. Why didn't you say that you were on your way over?"

"I thought it would be more fun this way. Surprise!" I did not mention that she had essentially hung up on me.

"Okay, well, thanks for the surprise, I guess. Come on in." She opened the door wider, and I stepped inside.

I hugged her awkwardly, clasping an arm around her shoulders and pulling her sideways into my chest. "Are you sure you're okay?" she repeated, scanning my face for signs of disease.

"Yes, I'm fine. What about you? You're looking thin. Are you eating properly?"

Priya had always been trim. In high school, she had played volleyball, a sport with ungainly squatting movements that I could never get excited about, though I was relieved she'd found her way to sports instead of fat. But now, her cheekbones stuck out more than usual, her robe hung off her shoulders, and skin puffed around her eyes. At her age, she needed to take better care. She was an attractive girl, at least when she tried to be. I knew it was superficial, but I was always proud of her good looks. Priya had intelligent black eyes, clear skin, and thick long hair—when she put on some makeup and dressed with care, she looked as telegenic as a TV news anchorwoman.

"You know, Priya, I hope you're not trying to diet. I mean, I've seen these supermarket magazines, and the girls on the covers look like famine survivors. Fashionable or not, it looks very bad."

"Daaad," she moaned. "You've barely walked in the door and already you're lecturing me. If I've lost weight, it's not on purpose, okay? I've just been stressed lately. I've been working a lot."

She nudged me out of the doorway. I removed my shoes in the entryway and followed her into the living room, then sat down next to a pile of unfolded laundry on the couch and inhaled the clean scent of detergent.

"Sorry about the mess. If I knew you were coming, I'd have cleaned up."

Stacks of books teetered on top of a long brick fireplace mantel, and still more books were crammed into tall wooden bookshelves. But aside from one large *Texans for Obama* poster, the walls of her living room were bare. As far as I could see, my daughter had very little interest in decorating. Such a difference from her mother. Lata couldn't stand empty walls, was forever crowding them with paintings of flowers and mountain landscapes and fruit. When Priya was a girl, I'd applauded her disinterest in dolls and lace and various aesthetic pursuits. Her preference for books over frilly nonsense was a point of pride for me. But now, I wondered if this lack of competence in the domestic arts had somehow contributed to her unmarried state.

I scanned the room for any evidence of a boyfriend. Not that I had any idea what to look for. Maybe a boyfriend would leave behind some reading material, something that Priya would never buy for herself, like *The Wall Street Journal* (if he was a business type), or *Sports Illustrated* (if he was a sporty type), or *GQ* (if he was a stylish type). I looked hopefully at the coffee table. No magazines. Just an empty wineglass and an ashtray with crumpled cigarette butts. My heart sank.

Priya grabbed the ashtray and clanked it on the mantel. "It's for guests," she mumbled.

"Oh sure, 'for guests.' You think I can't tell those cigarettes were freshly smoked. You are steadily killing yourself." Smoking was now another worry to add to the Priya column, somewhere between "unmarried," "father hater," and "too thin." I knew she'd experimented with smoking in college, as many kids do. On more than one occasion, I'd caught a whiff of her nicotine-tinged breath. But I assumed she'd grow out of it. She was too smart to be a smoker. The girl had a PhD for goodness' sake.

"Dad, please don't start." She sighed dramatically. "We all have our vices. Speaking of which, are you really in Austin just to visit me? It's past nine already. I take it that I'm the lucky beneficiary of your latest dating disaster."

The condescension in her voice sucked the air out of me. "Don't speak to me like that. Whatever you may think, I'm your father."

For a moment, she looked ready to fire back. Then at the last second, she seemed to think better of it. She stared at her toes and shrugged. "Well, I'm sorry, but you show up here out of the blue, and all you've done is criticize me."

I sighed. This wasn't how it was supposed to be. Hardly ten minutes since my arrival, and already we were fighting. I'd envisioned a very different scenario at the gas station. Maybe some magical moment of understanding, her teary-eyed apologies over steaming mugs of hot chocolate.

"Okay, it's forgotten. Let's start over. Do you have any hot chocolate?"

She furrowed her brows. "No, I'm not ten years old. But I have coffee. Or tea."

"No, I can't drink caffeine in the evening. I won't be able to sleep." I tried another tack. "So, tell me about your work."

Best I knew, Priya was working on a book. Though honestly, I'd never understood her choice of specialty: European medieval history. As far as I could tell, she studied the antics of long-dead white people who didn't even speak proper English. If she was studying the antics of long-dead people, couldn't they have been Indian, at least? But over the years, I'd learned to keep that particular opinion to myself.

She raised her eyebrows skeptically. "Dad, I know you're not really interested in my work." She picked a fleck of red polish off her thumbnail.

We sat silently for a few moments. Then I burst. "I know we haven't talked about this in a while, but are you seeing anyone?"

Priya stopped picking at her nail polish and looked warily at me. "Why do you ask?"

"Why do I ask? I'm worried about you. It's time you settled down in life. You only have a few childbearing years left. Work isn't everything, you know." I knew she didn't want to hear this, but the words spilled out before I could stop them or think of better phrasing.

Her eyes narrowed. "I hardly need you to remind me of how many childbearing years I have left. And I don't need a lecture on finding marital bliss from you, of all people. I'm surprised you even have time to worry about this, what with all your weirdo internet women. Why don't I just put an ad up on one of your Indian dating sites?"

I knew she was being sarcastic, but I chose to ignore it. "I think that's an excellent idea. There's no shame in it, really. People your age do this all the time, left and right."

"Yes, Dad. I am aware that people my age use this amazing thing called the in-ter-nets for this purpose." She rolled her eyes—an infuriating habit that she'd picked up as an adolescent and never grew out of. "But it's not my cup of tea, okay? I revile social media. I refuse to join Facebook. I'm a medieval historian who likes dwelling on our technologically deficient past. And besides, the thought of sharing any kind of dating venue with you—virtual or otherwise—grosses me out." She paused, allowing the words to sink in and pierce me.

"Anyway," she said, "for your information, I am seeing someone. I have been for a while now." She walked toward the mantel and positioned herself near the ashtray. She pulled a cigarette out of her robe pocket and lit it.

I was too distracted by her admission to scold her for smoking. "You have? Does your mother know?" She didn't answer. "Well, can I meet this mystery boyfriend figure?"

Her eyes shone with anger. She crushed her barely smoked cigarette into the ashtray, causing a dismaying sizzle. "Sure. But just so you know, he might bring his wife."

For a moment, we stared at each other—unblinking. What did she mean by "his wife"? Was she joking? I looked at the edges of her mouth for the beginnings of a smile. But no—she just wiped her eyes and glared at me, sad and defiant. I was stunned, aghast. For once, the ability to form words had left me. And then, without a word of explanation, my daughter walked out of the room.

5

LATA

"So I have news," Mala said, handing me a steaming cup of tea.

I blew into the cup, and ginger-scented heat warmed my face. "What is it?"

It was Sunday afternoon, and we were in her large, light-filled dining room. A plate of Girl Scout cookies sat on the glass-topped table between us.

"Meena is pregnant!" Her cheeks flushed with excitement as she reached for a Do-si-do.

I felt a pinprick of jealousy and tried to squash it. Mala's daughter Meena was a sweet girl married to a neurologist. They already had one child—a three-year-old boy. They lived half a mile away, and Mala saw them every week. I was happy for my friend. I was. But at this moment, it was hard for me not to think of Priya, deep into her thirties and not even close to mother-hood. Or Nikesh and my grandson, living fifteen hundred miles away, visiting only once or twice a year. I knew that comparing your own children to those of your friends was a foolish and corrosive habit. It changed nothing and made you feel disloyal to your own blood. But sometimes, you just couldn't help it.

I clapped my hands together and pasted a big smile on my face. "Mala, what wonderful news! You must be thrilled."

Mala beamed. "I'm so excited. I think it's a girl this time. Meena doesn't want to find out yet, but I can already tell by the way she's carrying and all her morning sickness. A granddaughter to go with my grandson—a perfect set!"

As Mala chattered excitedly, I glanced down at my purse, resting against the leg of the dining chair. The CD was still there, burning a secret hole in the buttery leather. I still hadn't listened to it. I hadn't even opened it again since the other night. But last night I had the strangest dream about Professor Greenberg. He and I were sitting in an airport lounge. Intercontinental, Hobby, DFW? I couldn't tell. That part didn't matter. He had a soft pretzel in his hand. Every few seconds, he'd tear off a piece for me to eat. Each time he handed me a piece, I laughed. He wiped a grain of salt from my lip, and I woke up, sweaty and warm.

"What is it, Lata?" Mala must have seen something in my face. "Is everything okay?"

For a moment, I thought of telling Mala about it—about Professor Greenberg, the CD, my dream. But this was not the kind of relationship we had, even though I considered her to be one of my dearest friends. Maybe it was my fault that we didn't have that kind of confessional closeness. After all, for so many years of our friendship, I had hidden a part of myself from her, unwilling to admit to Mala or anyone else the thing that I had known for a long time. The thing I'd known since my kids were young: that I was deeply unhappy in my marriage. Instead, I had let Mala and all my friends believe I was not so different from them. A woman who, like them, had married young to the man her parents had chosen, followed him to America, supported his career, faithfully taken care of his home and children. And if I had complained to them about my husband along the way, it was in the same joking and recognizable way as the other women had, about petty annoyances and minor grievances. Just little cracks in the surface of a marriage. Nothing hinting at a rotting foundation underneath. In a way, I had been lying to Mala for most of our friendship. Or at the very least, concealing an important truth about myself.

But Mala wasn't stupid. She must have suspected. After all, she'd borne witness to Suresh's ill temper, his moodiness descending on a dinner party like a rain-filled cloud. In fact, one of Suresh's many outbursts had happened here, years ago, in this very dining room.

Even now, the memory of it embarrassed me. We and a few other Indian families were having dinner at the Chandrasekhars' house. The men were talking about the Iran-Contra hearings. It was all anyone was talking about in those days. From the kitchen, we women could hear them, yelling about Oliver North and that uglier, bald one—that Poindexter fellow. After a while, I could make out Suresh's voice, louder than the others, mocking President Reagan: "Ha, that liar, acting like he didn't know. Wearing his Mister Rogers sweater like he's some kind of innocent grandfather. He's no innocent, I tell you!"

Well, if there was one thing everyone knew about Dr. Chandrasekhar at the time, it was that he loved Ronald Reagan. He had a framed picture of him in his office. But Dr. Chandrasekhar was a calm man, and polite about hearing his hero maligned at his own dinner table. He simply said, "We shouldn't presume anything."

The other men, who might have agreed with Suresh, took this as a cue to restrict their mocking. But not Suresh. He wouldn't stop. On and on he went about what a crook Reagan was, as the other men remained silent or tried to change the subject. Furious, Suresh turned on his friend: "You're a simple-minded man who wouldn't know a corrupt leader if he landed in your lap. Just keep your stupid delusions. That's just like you doctors, isn't it?

Charging astronomical fees, cheating insurance companies, and completely ignoring reality!"

Where that doctor business came from, I had no idea. Everyone at the table looked confused and embarrassed. We left immediately, both red-faced for opposite reasons. Dr. Chandrasekhar was willing to forgive and forget: "It was just a heated political argument. Such things shouldn't come between friends." But Suresh wouldn't let it go. No doubt he felt embarrassed and was too stubborn to admit it. So instead of apologizing, he came up with crazy justifications for his rude behavior: "These doctors, they're so smug. So ostentatious. You know, I always suspected there was something not quite right in the head with that Chandrasekhar."

It was no use arguing with Suresh, telling him that he was being the "not quite right in the head" one. He would just respond with some nonsensical comment about doctors.

And Suresh's behavior with the Chandrasekhars was no isolated incident either. Other friendships had crumbled over the years because of some angry outburst. Honestly, the man's mouth was a ticking time bomb. And do you think he spent a single second wondering how it affected me? Of course not. One weekend after another, I'd implore him to attend some dinner party, some weekend gathering, and he would say some version of the same thing: "No, all that man talks about is college basketball. And his wife is worse. She's a loud-mouthed know-nothing, and her cooking tastes like my foot. You go if you want. You know the way—you don't need me to come with you."

But I did need him to come. Not because I couldn't find my way there. Not because I couldn't carry a four-quart pot of sambar from the car to the party or pick up a bouquet of tulips at the grocery store or make pleasant conversation on my own. But because it was embarrassing. It was embarrassing to have to constantly explain and make excuses for his absence. It was embarrassing not to be able to invite others to our house and make the invitation ratio an equal one-to-one, for fear that Suresh would be in one of his sour moods. Because socializing was a team sport. You made friends as a married couple, you got invited to parties as a married couple, you attended parties as a married couple, you said "goodbye" and "thank you" and "this gulab jamun is excellent" and "next time, you must come over to our place" as a married couple. It was like pairs ice-skating. Maybe you could do the double-jump-axel-thing by yourself, but you'd never get up as high or land as far as you could if your partner was throwing you. Alone, it just wasn't the same. Each time, standing on a friend's doorstep in jewels and a freshly pressed silk sari, idlis in hand and an apology ready on my lips, I felt like a spectacle.

Mala was staring at me, her eyes wide and concerned. "Lata?"

Yet somehow, despite Suresh's antics over the years, Mala had stayed my friend. I felt a rush of gratitude toward her. I took a sip of ginger tea and shook my head. "No, Mala, nothing is wrong. Just a bit of a headache. I think it's because I forgot to eat lunch. Nothing that a few cookies can't fix. And this tea too. It's delicious." I took another sip and reached for a coconut-flecked Samoa. .

"You are looking so pretty and slim, Lata. Unfortunately, Raj and I are going the opposite direction." Mala puffed out her cheeks like a poori on the stove.

Mala had been fretting about her weight for decades. She shrugged and bit into a Do-si-do. A fleck of peanut butter dotted her lower lip. She had a weakness for sweets. And for accumulating exercise equipment that she never used. A stationary bike. A NordicTrack. A treadmill. I wondered over the years what she did with them. By now, she'd have enough dust-covered equipment to fill a home gym.

"You know, Raj and I are thinking of taking golf lessons."

I nodded, indulging her. So in a few weeks, she'd be adding a set of golf clubs to that list of unused equipment.

"What is it that we're thinking of doing?" Dr. Chandrasekhar walked into the dining room, his cheerful, boisterous voice filling the room. Even on a Sunday, he was dressed as if heading off for work—in a short-sleeve polo shirt and pressed tan pants. Mala was dressed nicely too—in wide-leg black pants, a flowing red silk top, and a gold jewelry set with small rubies. I smoothed the wrinkles in my navy capri pants and dusted a cookie crumb off my cream blouse. I knew better than to wear jeans to Mala's house.

"Golf lessons," Mala said, batting his hand away from the Do-si-dos. "Those have peanut butter, Raju." Raju was her pet name for him. "You hate peanut butter. You'll like this one better." She lifted a Samoa up to his face.

"What would I do without you?" he said, taking the coconut treat from her hand.

"Starve, probably." She giggled. "Though a little starving would do us both good." She patted his large belly, jutting out over his belt buckle.

"But I need energy for all this golfing we're going to be doing." He did a silly imitation of a golf swing and Mala laughed.

They were always like this—happy together. Even now, after all these years, Mala became lighter, giddier when her husband was around. And Raj too, he always appreciated her. There was an easiness to them, the way they talked, the pleasure they took in doing things together, in trying new things—like this golfing business. They probably wouldn't stick to it for more than a week. But then they'd laugh about it and find something new to do together.

Did Suresh and I ever have this?

I couldn't remember a time when his coming into a room made me breathe easier, when his presence lightened me. For years, in fact, it had been the opposite. At so many moments, I had imagined leaving him, starting over. But I couldn't bring myself to do it. There were too many reasons not to. Disrupting my kids' lives. Devastating my parents. Some people would think I stayed for financial reasons, that I was economically dependent on Suresh. But that wasn't really it. After the kids left for college, I had taken computer courses at the local community college to improve my skills. I had always been a good student, diligent and hardworking. I knew I could find a job if I put my mind to it. And I had—one that I liked.

No, for all those years, I had stayed because I didn't quite believe I was entitled to leave. Women of my mother's generation (of every generation, really) had survived far worse in their marriages—abusers, alcoholics, men who stood silent while their wives were berated by cruel mothers-in-law. Suresh wasn't that. He had never raised a finger toward me. He didn't drink. He wasn't the cheating type. He didn't gamble. You couldn't really call him a bad man. So what right did I have to leave? Who did I think I was to take such drastic action, to cause pain to my children, to my elderly parents, to bring gossip on my family when Suresh wasn't any of those things?

But the man could never be calm! Always moody, always angry about something. Maybe he was suffering from depression or some psychological ailment all those years, and we just didn't know it. After all, we didn't grow up in a generation where people knew about psychiatrists and therapists and antianxiety pills that could numb a man into calmness. In those days, if you were a pain to be around, no one went looking for a chemical reason behind it. You were just a bloody pain who caused pain to everyone around you.

But here's what I did know: I'd spent thirty-six years like a woman treading on a field of landmines. Not long into our marriage, I found myself weighing every word out of my mouth, every gesture, wondering and worrying what kind of reaction it would trigger from Suresh. Everything became an advanced math calculation: Is it worth mentioning this or that, asking Suresh to do this or that, knowing that he will overreact? I started treading so carefully that I felt myself disappearing. For the last few decades, I hardly recognized myself.

So what if Suresh wasn't a bad man? Why was being married to a non-bad man, who made most moments of your life harder to manage, who turned you into a stranger to yourself, better than not being married at all?

And then, one day you wake up, your kids are grown and moved away, and you realize that you've spent a lifetime with a man you don't like all that much. And as much as you've told yourself over the years that it could have been worse, that he isn't a bad man, that he doesn't drink, doesn't cheat, doesn't gamble, that he was a decent-enough father to your children, that you should consider yourself lucky, that you aren't entitled to ask for more, that you are too old to start again, that other people will talk, that your children will suffer, that you are being selfish in wanting anything else or anything more—none of these things can mask or make up for the biggest, most obvious fact of all: that you don't really like the man you are married to.

And if that was your only choice, you'd rather be alone.

"That's enough cookies for you, mister." Mala waved her husband away. "This is a ladies-only tea."

"Okay, okay, I can take a hint. Nice to see you, Lata." He waved goodbye, and then grabbed another Samoa before Mala could pluck it away. He winked at us and fled.

"You sneaky man!" Mala widened her eyes at her husband's disappearing back, a small smile playing on her lips. "He's hopeless." Mala turned to me, shaking her head.

I smiled weakly at her. I bit into a cookie. I could barely taste it. A dry, crumbly paste on my tongue. I hadn't left my marriage with the expectation of finding anyone new. I was content to live the rest of my years alone, calm. I'd escaped a field of landmines for a quiet, empty field. That itself felt like a victory. I had two children I loved, who loved me in return. I had a grandchild I adored. I had so many things to be grateful for. But at moments like this, watching Mala with her husband, a husband who clearly delighted her and delighted in her, my life seemed like a failure. Like I had missed out on something precious that the world had to offer. Something I was afraid to admit I even wanted.

I dug my hand into my purse. The sharp plastic point of the CD cover pricked my finger, sending a jolt through me.

I wanted to listen to it. I wanted to listen to it right now.

"Mala." I lifted a hand to my forehead. "My headache is getting a little worse. I'm sorry to cut our teatime short, but I think I should go home and lie down."

"Oh no." She touched my arm. "You can rest here if you want. I have Advil. Are you sure you can drive?"

"I'll be fine getting home. I just want to be in my own bed. Thank you for the tea. And congratulations on the baby. You are . . . a very lucky woman." I pecked my worried-looking friend on the cheek, grabbed my purse, and left her house as quickly as I could manage.

In the car, I leaned back against the hot leather seat and inhaled slowly. I turned the key in the ignition. I pulled out the CD, set it on my lap, and exhaled. Just as I was about to open it, I heard a beeping from my purse. It was the voicemail alert on my phone.

My heartbeat quickened. Was my dream last night some kind of sign, a premonition? Was it possible that Professor Greenberg was calling me to ask if I liked the CD? Could professors at the university access the phone number I had listed on my employment form? Oh God. I grabbed the phone.

Suresh. The voicemail was from Suresh. Not Professor Greenberg. Of course it wasn't from him. The man didn't even have my phone number. Dreams were not signs. Dreams were meaningless.

I felt stupid. And relieved. And disappointed. And then worried. Because a call from Suresh was unusual. The last time he had called, it was because a jury duty summons for me had been mistakenly sent to the house. Was it another jury duty summons? Was something wrong with the kids? Quickly, I checked the message.

"Lata? Lata? Why aren't you picking up?" Suresh's impatient voice blared through. "I have something urgent to discuss with you. I won't go into the details on a voicemail message, but I think you should know that our daughter has turned into an unrecognizable stranger. Call me back!"

I hung up, confused. Why was Suresh raving about Priya being a "stranger"? I listened to the message again. It made no sense.

He didn't say she was sick or injured. Just "unrecognizable"? Was it possible she had cut her hair unrecognizably short, and now he was worried that she looked too boyish to marry? Oh God, she wouldn't chop off her hair like that, would she? Or maybe he thought Priya was a stranger because she didn't call him enough?

I groaned and rested my head against the steering wheel. This was typical, overreacting Suresh. Creating a giant fuss about nothing. Well, I didn't want to talk to him. I would just call Priya myself when I got home. I could skip the unnecessary middleman altogether. I shoved the phone far down into my purse.

I opened the CD case and slipped the disk into the player. Music flooded the car—a trumpet, a piano, a woman's sparkling voice. My body relaxed. I pressed the gas pedal and headed home.

6

PRIYA

"*Kannamma*," my mom's anxious voice greeted me on the phone, "is something wrong with you? Your father left me a very odd message about you."

I was in my office, hunched over a large wooden desk. Noon sun glared through half-opened blinds. I'd already been here for hours, grading—the bane of professors everywhere.

Summer term ended last week, and all that stood between me and three weeks of vacation before the start of fall semester was a stack of ungraded essays. I'd barely made a dent in the stack, but upon hearing my mother's worried tone, I dropped my red pen on the desk.

"Dad called you? What did he say?" I bit my lip and braced myself.

My mom clucked, her signature sound of disapproval. "He said you were an 'unrecognizable stranger.' What does that mean? Did you cut off your hair? Did you get one of those boy cuts or whatever they're called?"

"What? No. Why would you ask that?"

"Oh, thank goodness. Because you know women do not look

good in those boy cuts. Except for that Halle Berry. Just her. But no one else, okay?"

"Mom, enough with the hair. I didn't cut it off. I don't plan on cutting it off."

"Okay, so if it's not that, what is it? Have you not been calling him? Is this why he feels like you are being a stranger to him?"

I relaxed my grip on the phone and sank into my chair, relieved.

He hadn't told her. Not yet, anyway. Or rather, his attempt to share the news through veiled euphemism (*stranger?*) had been conveniently misinterpreted. With a tiny smile, I reached for a mug of coffee. I'd reheated it in the staff microwave a half hour ago. I took a sip and grimaced. Predictably, it was cold.

"Because you know, Priya, you and Nikesh are all he has these days, and you should call him more. He's probably lonely in that house all by himself."

I felt a surge of affection for my mother. Little did she know how misdirected her concern was, how my father was working feverishly to replace her with a younger version.

"Oh, I'm sure he finds ways to keep busy," I said.

"What's that?"

"Nothing. I just mean . . . he's taken up gardening, as a hobby or something. It seems to keep him busy."

"Really? Your dad gardens now? Well, I guess that's a good thing. You should tell him that the bushes need regular pruning. And the eggplant growing in the back garden, it needs to be—"

I cut her off before she could bombard me with instructions for every plant in the yard. "Mom, why don't you tell him? I'm never going to remember these instructions."

"Oh, well, it's his garden now. He can do whatever he wants with it. So, is there anything . . . else?" At the end of her question, Mom inhaled a quick but noticeable breath.

Anything . . . else. This was how my mother ended all our

phone conversations. The expectant pause, the tremulous hope before the word "else." This was the point in the conversation where I imagined my mother bracing herself, desperate for some kind of announcement. That is, the nuptial kind—the kind that would finally relieve her of the fear that I'd die childless and alone. While my father's lack of subtlety took the form of antagonistic questioning in my living room, my mother's took the equally exasperating, though less confrontational, form of the pregnant pause.

What they both failed to realize, however, was how hypocritical their disappointment was. I mean, what did they expect? Ever since I was old enough to understand the concept of boyfriends and dating and sex, I'd understood something else too: It was a taboo topic in our house. My parents were so viscerally, palpably, heartbreakingly uncomfortable with all of it, with what they'd unwittingly unleashed by immigrating here and having children in this country of seemingly ubiquitous teenage pregnancy and date rape, that I knew better than to bring boys home or ask for my parents' romantic advice or share my heartbreaks over someone not liking me enough. Like gays in the military, I'd operated under a strict "don't ask, don't tell" policy for well over a decade. Until one day, I turned thirty, and everything changed. As if some light switch went on, and my parents became obsessed—obsessed!—with my lack of a husband. All of a sudden, they were paralyzed with disappointment that I hadn't spent those "don't ask, don't tell" years maneuvering my way toward a partner like their friends' daughters had—a destination arrived at, mind you, through dating and kissing and having sex and doing all those things my parents had demonized for so long. As if it was entirely my fault that I hadn't succeeded at the very thing they'd spent years weirding me out about. I wanted to scream, "Well, what the hell did you people expect?"

But instead, I stuffed the indignation down my throat and

swallowed. "Nope," I said. "That's it—nothing *else*, Mom. What about you—everything okay? The library, the condo, you know, life in general?"

"Me?" She paused for a second. "Oh, I'm . . . fine."

"That's not very convincing."

"I saw Mala Aunty. Her daughter—you know, Meena—is pregnant."

"Again? Didn't she just have a baby, like yesterday?" Inwardly, I groaned. Meena-fucking-Chandrasekhar. The girl was about as interesting as masking tape, but she'd married a doctor before she'd turned thirty and was cranking out babies. So in the eyes of my mother and her friends, she was perfect.

"Not yesterday! Meena's son is already three. Mala gets to see him all the time." Her voice quavered. "I'm sorry. I think I just miss you kids."

And just like that, my anger turned to shame. My mother was alone. She was growing old in a crappy condo. She spent her days working in a library with obnoxious, college-aged freaks.

Honestly, what kind of daughter was I? If I was even a half-way decent one, I would have found a way to be married already, with two kids, a big house in the suburbs, and a comfortable guest room where my mom could spend the rest of her days—ideally, providing me with free childcare and a steady stream of sambar. At this moment, I couldn't help but feel like life had gone terribly off track somewhere, for the both of us.

"I miss you too, Mom. Maybe I'll come down for a visit one of these days. And I think Nikesh was planning a trip soon too." I hoped the invocation of my equally absent brother would lessen my feelings of guilt. It did—a little.

"Nikesh?" Her voice brightened.

Funny how the mere sound of his name could perk her up, cheer her in a way that even a ten-minute-long conversation with me could not. But I guess that was okay too. After all, I'd spent years coming to terms with this inequity. Nikesh was her only son and her youngest. Her baby boy. Her baby boy who'd gone to Harvard Law School and who'd recently given her a gorgeous grandson. Anyway, at a certain point in life, resenting the more emphatic love of a mother—an Indian mother, no less—for her son started to feel like resenting the orbit of the moon. It was just a fact of the universe, and sooner or later, you grew to accept it. Maybe if you were lucky, you'd get the consolation prize of a father's favoritism. But even then, a daughter shouldn't fool herself. Even with a stellar sort of father, that's an unequal trade. A father's love is just a different kind of animal— less concrete, less consuming, less concerned with the details.

"Yes, Mom, *Nik-esh*. Remember him? Your son. High-powered attorney on Wall Street. He's got that blond wife you hate and that perfect dumpling of a child you adore. That guy."

"Priya, why do always have to be so sarcastic? You're just like your father. You know, sometimes I feel sorry for your future husband." Mom liked to invoke my pitiable, fictional future husband whenever I exasperated her.

"And of course I don't *hate* his wife. I don't hate . . . Denise." Mom struggled to pronounce her name. No matter how hard my mother tried, in her accented English, Denise's name always came out sounding more like "Dennis."

"Denise is . . . fine. She's very smart and . . . organized." Through the phone, I could detect the superhuman effort it took for my mother to name any virtue of the woman who'd eloped with—who'd stolen—her darling boy. That Theory-suited, Pilates-toned thief in the night.

"Right," I said. "You and Denise are best buddies. You're Oprah and Gayle, okay. And that's good news, because the last time I talked to Nikesh, he said he wanted to bring the baby and Denise down for Alok's first birthday. I think he wants to have some kind of party for Alok here. Though I don't know why they'd have it in Clayborn instead of New York. I mean, where's it going to be—McDonald's? I can't imagine Denise going for that. I'm sure she'd rather die than inhale the vapors of stale canola oil and mass-produced beef."

Okay, so my sister-in-law was not my favorite person in the world either. Though mine was not the primal, Oedipal (reverse Oedipal?) dislike my mother tried so unsuccessfully to mask. And I wasn't hurt or offended by Nikesh and Denise having eloped without inviting any of us, as my mother seemed to be. Honestly, it was one less dateless wedding for me to suffer through. No, my misgivings were of a more quotidian nature. For example: Denise was the kind of woman who'd wear four-inch Louboutins and pearls to the airport. I mean, how could you genuinely like a woman like that? A woman who needed to present such a well-curated version of herself to the hot mess of humanity at LaGuardia?

Though, to be honest, Denise wasn't even the worst woman Nikesh had ever brought around. At least she had a brain in her head. She was a junior partner in commercial litigation (whatever that meant) and had a $1,000-billable-hour-$500,000-a-year kind of brain, from what Nikesh told us. Somehow, she'd marched those pinchy, impractical shoes straight up the ladder of a testosterone-dominated profession. You had to give her kudos for that. That was more than I could say for some of the dopes Nikesh had forced on us before.

Like that Janine character he'd dated at Brown. Junior year, he'd brought her home for Thanksgiving. Unlike me, Nikesh had no compunction about parading his college significant others in front of my parents—though in Janine's case, he really should have. She was a waif-like redhead with a vacant face and a whispery voice. For an entire weekend, Janine referred to Nikesh as "my sweet," stroked his neck like it was cat fur, and hardly ate a bite of her masala dosa. I disliked her instantly. So did my parents. Fortunately, the following summer, Janine discovered meth while visiting her grandparents in South Dakota, and she dropped out of school and all our lives. According to Nikesh,

Janine was clean these days, a born-again Christian happily married to a furniture designer in North Carolina. So really, the demise of their relationship had worked out well for everybody.

Yeah, given his history, Nikesh could have done far worse than Denise. Alas, maybe my biggest problem with Denise was that she wasn't Elena. Elena was the woman my brother really should have married. Elena was Nikesh's law school girlfriend, a Mexican-American girl with explosive, curly black hair, dimpled cheeks, and gestures so emphatic, you worried she'd knock herself out by accident. Elena ate two helpings of everything and accidentally snorted ginger tea out of her nose when Nikesh did his weird impression of a Russian oligarch ordering a sandwich. It took me less than an hour to love Elena. I think even my parents had liked her, though they were too stubborn to admit it. At that time, they weren't quite ready to admit defeat—i.e., the non-Indian daughter-in-law. Though in all fairness to my parents, that was then, years before they'd called defeat on their own marriage. Years before last November's election of Barack Obama, which warmed our collective souls, reaffirmed our faith in humanity, and ushered in a "post-racial" American dreamscape. If Nikesh had shown up with Elena now, who knows—they'd probably feel different about it all. One would hope, right? Hope and change.

Well, it didn't matter now because Elena was gone. Nikesh never told us why they broke up, never explained why we were forever deprived of her adorable snort-laugh and the potential bevy of dimpled, Spanish-speaking baby Ramans. I tried asking him a few times in my customary artful fashion: "Let's get queso at Taco Cabana. So, um, whatever happened with Elena? Where'd she go?" But he'd just get this tragic look on his face until eventually I let it go. *¡Oh, Elena, qué lástima!*

"Priya? Priya, are you still there?" my mother shouted, forcing me out of my ruminations. "Alok's birthday is in a few weeks—Labor Day weekend. Did Nikesh say whether they're staying with me or your father? Or maybe Denise prefers to stay in a hotel? Do you think I should make a reservation at the Hilton for them?"

"Mom, you're not their secretary. If they want a hotel, they can make their own reservation. Or they can get some underling at their fancy-pants law firm to do it for them."

"Well, I'll call him and find out. We have to figure out where to have this party. Unless Nikesh insists on having it at the house . . . your father's house."

She was silent again. Maybe she was racking her brain for party venues that didn't require coordinating with my father. Or maybe her musings about Nikesh's family life had led, once again, to mental hand-wringing about my own nonexistent one. It was time to beat a hasty retreat out of this conversation.

"Good idea, Mom. Call Nikesh. I have to go anyway. There's a student at my door," I lied.

After hanging up, I stood and massaged a crick in my neck. Still standing, I began rereading the essay I'd started before Mom's call interrupted me. Four pages in, and I still didn't have a clue what Kenny Stark was going on about. The awkward syntax and compulsive misspelling didn't help. What was the matter with undergraduates these days? Was it really so hard to use spell-check and proofread before turning a paper in? The essay I'd assigned was on the impact of bubonic *plague* in thirteenth-century England, and Kenny Stark kept referring to it as bubonic *plaque*. Like it was some dental problem. I sighed. At this rate, I'd never finish.

I stretched. Arms raised, I scanned the room for any diversion that wasn't Kenny Stark's incoherent essay. I peeked through the window blinds at the courtyard. Trees stood unmoving in the airless heat, and the grass, usually abuzz with students, lay eerily empty. The entire campus sat silent, except for the whirring of several industrial-sized air-conditioning units.

When I had interviewed for the job at Travis College six

years ago, I was struck by its quaintness: the manicured court-yards, the clusters of shady pecan trees, the orange-roofed stucco buildings in Spanish-colonial style. At a time when history departments relied on adjuncts to teach, I knew I was lucky to get the job. Though it was becoming less clear if I'd be keeping it. Given the recession and drops in enrollment, looming budget cuts had every department cutting corners—starting with caps on conference reimbursements, and ending, somewhere down the road, with terminated contracts. Not even the tenured folks were safe. When push came to shove, we were all dispensable.

I bent over to touch my toes and paused halfway, eye to eye with the blinking cursor on the Google search bar. That little jerky cursor was beckoning me to go off task. Luring me with the promise of myriad sites more interesting than Kenny Stark's essay. And somewhere in that online abyss lurked my father's dating profile.

I'd looked for it once—about a month ago, when I was working late at my office. What a creepy thing to embark on, the search for your father's dating profile. If only Freud had lived to see the internet age in all its perversity. But I'd wanted to know—what did Dad say about himself that made these women reach out to him? What was this romantic persona that he'd created for himself? About twenty minutes into my search, I'd chickened out. I wasn't really ready to know after all.

According to Nikesh, Dad wanted to try it "our way" this time—the dating and courtship and falling desperately in love bit. And instead of telling Dad how ridiculous that sounded, Nikesh just encouraged him. In fact, my stupid brother seemed so charmed by it all.

"Why do you have to be so hard on Dad?" he'd say to me. "The guy had an arranged marriage that didn't work out, and now he's trying to find love our way. It's kind of brave, really. Can't you be cool about it?"

The question was galling on so many levels. First, there was the whole hypocrisy thing again. I mean, how was it that I had to spend a decade hiding my dating life from Dad because it made him uncomfortable, and now, all of a sudden, I was expected to cheer him on and dole out advice over brunch like we were Carrie and Samantha on *Sex and the City*?

And then, there was the sheer futility of the project. I mean, did Dad really think this was going to end well for him? Even if you had youth and looks on your side (which, let's face it, Dad did not), the whole dating and courtship and falling desperately in love bit was rife with complications. It was a shitshow most of the time, full of pain, embarrassment, and rejection. I knew this. I knew it from experience.

So really, what chance of success did Dad have here—this nearing sixty, divorced Indian man with a failed thirty-six-year marriage in his back pocket, this garrulous systems analyst who'd poisoned his first marriage with perpetual moodiness?

Nikesh could just go ahead and be Mr. Cool Guy all he wanted. But me—no way. I wasn't going to play along and pretend like this was a great idea.

7

NIKESH

"My mother wants to know our plans for the birthday trip. Are we staying with her, my dad, or at a hotel?"

I stepped into the steamy bathroom and watched Denise pry a toy frog from Alok's hands. Ignoring Alok's red-faced howling, she began rubbing a soapy washcloth methodically over his fingers, palms, arms, underarms, and neck.

I winced, grabbed two squares of toilet paper and stuffed them in my ears. "What should I tell her?" I shouted.

"They're *your* parents. Why are you asking me? Can't you just figure it out?" She sounded irritated, her standard tone with me these days.

Damp strands stuck to her cheeks and forehead, her face pink and sweaty from steam and frustration. It surprised me—the sight of her so disheveled. Not that it should. We had a baby, after all, and life with a baby meant spit-stained shirts and permanent undereye circles. Disheveled went with the territory. It just contrasted so sharply with the woman I spent all day with at work. At work, Denise wasn't the exasperated mother of an eleven-month-old, who wore yogurt-splattered jeans and snapped at me with near constancy. Instead, Denise-at-work was the firm's star junior partner, and my boss to boot, who got paid three times my salary, wore crisp, tailored suits, and spoke with a practiced calm honed from years of meeting the frantic demands of Wall Street clients and overcaffeinated senior partners. Denise-at-work was a recognizable version of the woman I'd met two years ago. Denise-at-home . . . was another story.

I bent over the tub and fished the frog out of the soapy water. "Buddy, look, the frog is dancing. The frog is jumping on your BELLY. . . . It's on your NOSE. . . . It's on your HEAD!"

For an instant, Alok stopped bellowing, distracted by the squishy bath frog tickling his body parts. Denise's shoulders relaxed against my own. But then, Alok spotted the wet washcloth in Denise's hands, and his screams began again—even louder this time, which I hadn't thought possible.

How could such a small creature, barely twenty pounds, produce such decibels of sound? It was a question I asked myself often, in different iterations: How could such a small creature, with his tiny anus, produce so much shit? How could such a small creature, with his olive-sized stomach, regurgitate so much foamy spit-up? How could such a small creature upend every aspect of my life?

"Nikesh, can you stop goofing around and help me out here?" Denise grabbed the baby's towel—orange, with a hood in the shape of a tiger—and hurled it at me. She stomped out of the bathroom, the white soles of her feet thudding against the blue tiles.

Sighing, I turned to Alok. "Come on now, little man."

I lifted his quivering, dripping body out of the tub and wrapped him in the towel. I rubbed his hair with the tiger-shaped hood and started singing: "*The wheels on the bus go round and round, round and round, round and round.*"

Slowly, Alok's screams dulled into soft whimpers. I cradled my son to my chest and carried him down the narrow hallway:

past the study, the second bathroom, the guest room, and finally, into his room, which was right across the hall from ours.

It was the promise of three-plus bedrooms—and a small yard in back—that had led us here in the first place, out of Manhattan and into Brooklyn. Soon after we learned Denise was pregnant, she called a broker, and for a seemingly endless number of weekends, we found ourselves crisscrossing Brooklyn's pricier neighborhoods, leafy enclaves full of charming brownstones, farm-to-table eateries, and artisan coffee shops that had been luring pregnant couples out of Manhattan for well over a decade. Admittedly, our approach to Brooklyn real estate was not particularly original. Taking our cue from friends at the firm, we'd first looked at Brooklyn Heights and Park Slope. Quickly realizing that those neighborhoods were pricier than the Manhattan ones we were leaving behind, we eventually settled on a condo in Boerum Hill. It was bright and modern, with newly laid wood floors, spacious rooms, and large corner windows framing a quiet, tree-lined street. Through the window in Alok's room, I could see leaves dancing in the late evening breeze, the sky tinting purple.

My stomach gurgled. I'd skipped lunch, and it was well past seven now. Faint sounds floated from the kitchen—the fridge door opening and closing, microwave buttons pinging. Denise was probably making a quick dinner for herself—warming up a frozen tikka masala from Trader Joe's or maybe that leftover Thai takeout I'd planned on eating. I knew better than to expect Denise to warm up a dinner for me too. Probably, by the time I was done dressing Alok, doing the two obligatory readings of *The Very Hungry Caterpillar,* and coaxing him to sleep, Denise's dinner dishes would be dripping from the rack. She'd be settled into the study's Aeron chair, huddled over her laptop, tapping away until the wee hours of the morning.

That was how it was these days. Her in one room. Me in the other. I couldn't remember the last time we'd actually eaten dinner together. Or had sex. Or had a conversation that didn't end in a fight.

I laid Alok in the crib and blew strawberries on his soft belly. I breathed his clean soapy scent—a smell that could make me forget anything, for a few moments at least. Alok giggled, batting at my face. I nuzzled his tender chest, his dimpled thighs. Alok laughed louder—a giddy warbling sound—baring all six of his teeth and clapping with delight. I breathed him in again and again, feeling every muscle in my body loosen and relax.

It was everything, these moments. I tried to memorize them, to imprint the feeling onto my brain. If only you could bottle it up and fan it under your nose like smelling salts when you needed to fortify yourself; a bottle you could reach for at 3:00 A.M. when you were grinding your teeth and doubting your life choices; when the image of a different woman than the one sleeping beside you made you hard and jolted you awake; when the baby across the hall felt less like your salvation and more like your jailer, dictating your time, keeping you trapped in a job and a relationship that didn't feel quite right sometimes, made you feel like you were maybe living the wrong life—someone else's and not yours.

God has a plan for each of us.

It was the kind of thing Elena used to say. Religious gobble-dygook that I'd always chalked up to her Catholic upbringing. But here they were now, those words, flashing through my head like ticker tape, keeping me from falling asleep. I tugged the sheet up against my chest and shifted on the bed. The room was pitch black—not a trace of dawn through the curtains.

I turned over onto my stomach and inched my face closer to Denise's sleeping one. Even unconscious, she wore an expression of urgent competence: eyebrows raised, lips pursed. I'd read somewhere that during sleep, the mind organized information from the day, helping the sleeper remember it—memory consolidation, it was called. I pictured a maze of neurons behind Denise's sleeping face (though, in my mind, neurons resembled sperm because I had no idea what actual neurons looked like). I imagined that those sperm-shaped neurons in Denise's head were doing their magic right now, consolidating legal theories, sorting out the missteps and omissions of her client, Stephen P. Garner, the CEO of a once notable hedge fund that federal investigators had charged with defrauding investors.

Garner was a longtime client of the firm—and a longtime golfing buddy of one of the firm's founding partners. And in a funny way, wasn't Garner responsible for my present sleeplessness too? After all, if Garner hadn't falsified financial statements, pilfering millions for himself and his Argentine mistress, would Denise Collins—a thirty-nine-year-old divorcée, only daughter of a Minneapolis hardware store owner and a real estate agent (both killed years ago in a car accident), a first-in-her-class graduate of NYU Law, the firm's youngest female partner, a demanding boss maligned by male junior associates for being a ball-breaker—have wandered into my office all those many months ago looking for help?

On that particular day, like most days, I'd been at the office late. But I wasn't reviewing documents, as per usual. Instead, I was slumped over my desk, gaping at my email. It was a position I'd been frozen in for two hours, rereading the same message: *Hey Nik, I have some news. I'm engaged. Hope all is good with you. Elena.*

Engaged? I didn't even know she was seeing anybody.

Congratulations. Glad to hear you're doing well. Nikesh.

That was the response I'd managed to come up with in the span of two hours. But to be fair, I'd gone through several iterations.

(1) *What the fuck? Engaged? Seriously?*

(2) *Is he a religious nut-bat like you?*

(3) *I'm happy for you, El. He's a lucky guy, whoever he is. He's a guy, right?*

(4) *You're telling me this over email? You couldn't pick up the phone and call me, the guy you lost your virginity to, the guy who told you he'd love you forever, the guy who wanted to marry you first?*

(5) *I don't know what to say. I guess I should say congrats, right? But what I really want to say is, why didn't you love me enough to marry me? Why does it still hurt?*

In the end, I decided to go with something more formulaic. For the sake of dignity and self-respect and what have you.

"Ahem." Bleary-eyed, I'd looked up to see Denise at my desk. She was dressed in an expensive-looking cream pantsuit, her blond hair pulled back, her expression a mixture of annoyance and curiosity.

"Nikesh Raman, right? Second-year litigation associate? Are you busy right now, because I need some help, and you seem to be the only one around. Where is everybody? One of the biggest indictments of the year is coming down any day now, and there isn't a warm body to be found."

"It's the Thursday evening before Fourth of July weekend. If I were a betting man, I'd say two-thirds of the firm is halfway to the Hamptons by now. Stuck in soul-crushing traffic, if there's any justice in the world."

"Touché." A smile played on the edges of her lips. She sat down, crossed her long, slender legs, and laid a manila folder on her lap. "So why are you still around, then?"

"Me? Excellent question." I laughed, almost mockingly. Ordinarily, I'd never be so brazen with a partner. In my two years as a junior associate at Tiller, Craft & Levine, I'd learned to cultivate the right mixture of ass-kissing-deference and confidence. But after Elena's news, I wasn't up for the usual charade.

"Well, I'm trying to figure out how to tell an ex-girlfriend who told me that she's getting married over email that (a) I care, (b) I don't care, (c) she's a shitty person for telling me over email, (d) I'm over her, and (e) I'm not over her. The project's taking longer than I thought."

"Well, what've you got so far?"

I turned the laptop toward Denise. Her eyes ran quickly over the sentence. "May I make a few changes?"

I was too surprised by the question to do anything but nod.

She stood up and leaned over the desk. Even in my dismal state, I noticed her shapely breasts. Close up, her face was smooth and unlined. She went a bit heavy on the eye makeup, but no one could deny that she was attractive. Really attractive. A perfectly manicured, Scandinavian kind of hot. The very opposite of Elena. Elena was a kind of pretty you didn't notice right away; it sort of crept up on you. Like the mess of black curls that ran down her back. Hair that, when you first looked at her, vaguely resembled an unwieldy bush, until one day, the beauty of those licorice curls made you stop breathing for a second.

Denise was tapping a key, and I looked to see what she'd done. She'd erased my message.

"Hey, what do you think you're doing?" She might be my boss, but that was private correspondence she was messing with.

"Look, Nikesh, it's best to leave this message unanswered. If she cares that you don't care, then she'll write again. If she doesn't care whether you care or not, then why should you? Either way, playing stupid games over email will just make you feel like crap. Trust me: There's nothing like a messy divorce to teach you that a one-sided struggle for a relationship is futile. So, are you ready to do some work now?" Her eyes sparkled with challenge.

I was ready, as it turned out. And over the next few months, I discovered a few other things too: that Denise, the legendary ball-buster, was witty and reliable; she never complained about work or went off the deep end or suffered fools; she was blissfully vigorous in bed. Our courtship was brief, though. About four months in, Denise told me she was pregnant. She was almost forty, and I was twenty-eight. She'd been married once and divorced once. She'd worked with a single-minded vision for years and become partner at one of Manhattan's most prestigious law firms. She told me she was having the baby, that she'd do it with or without me, but she hoped it was with me.

And what about me?

I'd never been married. Or divorced. I wasn't even thirty. All I knew was that I'd been in love once before, that it had blown up in my face, and standing in front of me was a woman I admired and liked and was maybe even growing to love—even if it wasn't the blinding-knock-you-on-your-ass kind of love I'd known before—telling me she was going to have my baby and she'd do it with or without me but hoped it was with me.

So what did I say to her? I said we'd do this together, of course. Because what other answer was there, really?

I'd slept through Alok's morning cries. Again.

That was the thing about insomnia. Once you finally managed to fall asleep, you'd sleep through anything—garbage trucks, car alarms, your baby's morning cries. It was the third day in a row I'd overslept, leaving Denise to handle Alok's pre-nanny morning rituals alone. She was going to be pissed.

I found them in the breakfast nook, next to the kitchen. Denise was crouched in front of the high chair, spooning yogurt into Alok's mouth. She was still in her pajamas, a thin streak of pink goo on her forehead. An oversized mug of coffee sat untouched on the counter.

Spotting me, Alok cried "da-da" and waved his arms, knocking the spoon in Denise's hand and spurting strawberry yogurt toward her face.

"Hey, sorry. You should have woken me up. It's my turn to do breakfast, isn't it?"

Denise wiped her forehead with the back of her hand. "Nikesh, I'm not your mother. I'm not going to shake you awake in the morning."

"I said I'm sorry. Did I complain when I stayed up with him two nights in a row last week?" Why did she have to make a federal case out of everything? "I'll take over now. You go get ready for work." I grabbed the mug on the counter and sipped. The coffee was lukewarm and bitter, but it would do.

Denise waved her hand dismissively. "Forget it. I'm almost done." She spooned more yogurt into Alok's mouth, and cooed: "Good job, buddy. Just one more bite."

Alok smiled and clapped, basking in the praise. He seemed to be in a cooperative mood, which lessened my guilt about sleeping late.

"I'll wake up with him tomorrow. I promise." I pulled a loaf of bread out of the fridge. "Hey, will you tell the nanny the dates we'll be out of town in Clayborn?"

Denise was silent. She walked to the sink, washed out the empty yogurt bowl, shook it free of wet drops, and placed it in the dish rack. "I've decided not to go." She turned toward me, her jaw clenched.

"What? The whole point is to go there for Alok's birthday. You're seriously going to miss his first birthday?" I stared at her, incredulous, the bread loaf swinging limply in my hand.

"No, because neither of us are going—not me or Alok."

"Why? Is this your way of punishing me for sleeping late?"

Denise rolled her eyes. "Don't be ridiculous. This has nothing to do with that. I'm not punishing you for anything. But I can't do this lying thing anymore. Every time we see your parents, I have to act like we're married because you told them that we are.

I have to lie. And I don't like it. I especially don't like having to lie in front of Alok."

"You see them once a year—maybe twice, at most. What's the big deal? You don't have to lie. You just don't have to correct them when they refer to you as my wife. And it's not like Alok knows what's going on anyway." As if on cue, Alok began drooling and saying "bye-bye."

Denise grabbed a dishcloth and dried her hands. "I don't understand why after all this time, you still haven't told them the truth." She threw the dishcloth on the counter and looked accusingly at me.

"I meant to tell them. You know that. But the timing was never right. They've been going through a lot this past year, and I didn't want to add to the stress. I thought you understood that." Alok began slapping his hands on his high chair tray, a sign that he wanted out. I broke away from Denise's critical gaze and hushed him. "Alok, I'll be right there to get you out."

"I didn't push it the last time we saw them because their divorce was still fresh," Denise said. "It would have been hard for them to deal with news of their grandson being illegitimate or whatever, on top of everything else. I was raised by devout Methodists. I get that it can be hard for parents to accept these things. But it's been a year now. You need to man up and tell them. So that's the deal. Unless you tell them, we're not going."

"Da-da-da-da!" Alok had reached the end of his tolerance for this conversation. And so had Denise, it seemed.

She grabbed the dangling bread loaf from my hand and pushed me toward our son. "And you can get Alok ready for the nanny. I'm already late."

8

SURESH

The date was going poorly.

For the last hour, I'd been sitting on a plastic-covered couch in Aparna Sharma's living room. We were watching a movie I couldn't quite follow. It was called *Love Actually* or *Love Appropriately* or some such thing. As far as I could tell, it was about an improbably young-looking British prime minister and some unrelated characters whose purpose was unclear to me.

Aparna Sharma—who liked being called "Pinky"—was a recent internet acquaintance. After my date with Mallika, I'd been so full of hope that I discontinued my nightly perusal of profiles, my diligent responses to inquiring internet women. Mallika and I had even made plans to meet in Clayborn for our second date. I'd sent her my address and a link to Google Maps with the exact directions from her house to mine. But when the day of our date arrived, she called to cancel, sounding vague: "I'm sorry, Suresh. Something has come up with work. I'll have to reschedule."

That was five days ago. And since then, not a peep from her. She'd stopped responding to all my phone calls. After phone calls one and two went unreturned, I'd given her the benefit of the doubt. Maybe she was busy at work. Though honestly, how busy could that octogenarian ophthalmologist be keeping her? After phone calls three and four, I'd become anxious. Had she decided I was too old for her? Did she want a man with more hair? After phone calls five and six, I'd become despondent. I just had to face the fact she didn't like me.

And with that bitter realization, I'd forced myself to email this woman—this Aparna Sharma. This Pinky.

Why had I chosen her, of all people? I struggled to remember my reasoning now. Her name had struck me, I suppose. It had a nice, rhyming ring to it: *Apar-na Shar-ma.* And she was not too far, only a few miles out of town. So little gas money would be wasted. To be perfectly honest, after all my fruitless efforts with Mallika, I had assumed a date with Aparna would be easy to coordinate. And that part, at least, had turned out to be correct. After just one email exchange, two phone calls, and a fifteen-minute drive from my house, I found myself sitting here on a late afternoon, in the apartment Aparna shared with her daughter and granddaughter, watching this silly movie.

But while it was true that setting up this date and driving to it had taken little effort, the date itself was proving to be a different story entirely.

"Aparna, is this movie about a British prime minister? Because this fellow looks too young. And who are these other people?"

"Pinky. I keep telling you—call me Pinky."

"Okay. Pinky."

For God's sake, why did she insist on that? A grown woman called Pinky? I could never understand these North Indians and their pet names. All this Bintu, Pintu, Binky, Pinky, Cookie nonsense. What kind of self-respecting individual embraced such a nickname after the age of seven?

And to add insult to injury, this Aparna didn't even look like a Pinky. To me, "Pinky" suggested someone with rosy cheeks (what else justified the "pink" in "Pinky"?), supple lips, bright clothes, and a ready smile. But this Pinky was nothing like that—and, of course, nothing like her comely picture. This Pinky was a rather severe-looking woman with sharp cheekbones and a hooked nose—like a hawk's face. She was dressed in drab colors: navy blouse, gray pants. And as for a ready smile—ha! This woman hadn't smiled once since my arrival—not once during the movie, and even more damning, not once in response to any of my ice-breaking jokes.

All right, so maybe she just didn't understand my jokes. Even I could admit that they were better in their original Tamil. Something got lost in the translation to English, so I couldn't put all the blame on Pinky's bony shoulders. In fact, it had become a real frustration of mine on dates: I found it harder to be funny in English. Now, don't get me wrong: I have an enviable command of the English language. Truly enviable, thanks in no small part to English-medium Catholic schools and years spent memorizing English grammar rules to avoid the wrath of nuns. And after more than a half century of daily usage, I can honestly say that English is a perfectly adequate medium of expression in many respects. I can be angry in English. Joyous in English. Frustrated in English. But funny? Not so much. Funny requires one's mother tongue.

I took a deep breath and tried again. "So, Pinky, is there a reason you wanted to watch this movie? Are you interested in British politics?" I looked at her doubtfully. Her coffee table had no newspapers or general interest magazines. No *New York Times* or *Time* magazine. Just a few of those supermarket tabloids with scantily clad actresses on the cover. I sighed. Hopefully they were purchased by Pinky's daughter and not Pinky herself.

"This movie is not about British politics. It's a romance movie." She looked at me like I was slow in the head. "My daughter, Somya, rented it from Netflix."

This Somya-daughter character was another mystery. Apparently, she worked evenings as a motel receptionist, lived at home with her mother, and had a two-year-old daughter, Divya. I wouldn't be meeting either of them, as they were at the mall for the afternoon. But this Somya didn't seem to have a husband to speak of. Pinky hadn't said a word about him—no story of death, divorce, nothing. There were no pictures of him in the house as far as I could tell, even though there were many pictures of Somya and Divya and a plump, bearded man that I assumed was Somya's father. But in all those pictures, not a single glimpse of the baby's father. It was as if he didn't exist.

My eyes fell on a framed picture of Divya on the fireplace mantel. She was plump and smiling—the antithesis of her grandmother—wearing a pink dress with white stockings, propped against the solid blue background of a Sears photography studio. It was not unlike the pictures of Priya that we once displayed on our own mantel.

I shuddered at the thought of Priya in a situation like Somya's—raising a child without a husband in the picture. Though who knew what Priya was doing with this married man of hers. Did he already have kids of his own? Was he going to get divorced and marry Priya, forcing her to play stepmother to his children instead of having her own?

For God's sake, what was the matter with all these Indian girls today? Why couldn't they find decent men, get married, have children—all in that precise order—and give their aging parents some peace of mind before they died?

All I knew was that it had been a week since I'd heard from Priya. Ever since leaving her place in Austin, I'd been waiting—for a phone call, for an explanation, for an apology, something, anything. But nothing—not a peep.

On the television screen, a girl undressed and jumped into a lake. Then a man undressed and jumped into a lake. The characters' nonsensical antics reminded me of those silly romance movies Lata was so fond of. Were women simply incapable of watching something useful, like CNN or the Discovery Channel?

Lata too had failed to call me back. Did she know about Priya and the married man? How could she have let this happen? For God's sake, why had every single woman in my life chosen the exact same moment to become completely unreliable? It was too much for any man to bear, really.

Pinky held the remote listlessly in her hand, her finger hovering above the volume button, as if she couldn't decide whether to raise or lower it. She caught me staring at it and asked, "Is the movie loud enough for you?"

"The volume is fine. I'm having trouble following, though. I just don't understand why the prime minister of England has jumped into a lake."

She gave me a quizzical look. "That is not the prime minister." She shrugged and turned back to the screen.

This movie was giving me a headache. I considered asking Pinky to turn the stupid thing off, but at least with her focus on the movie, I could furtively study her face.

It was a sad face. Defeated, even. Etched in the lines around her mouth, the wrinkles in her forehead. As if she'd suffered some real tragedy—bigger than divorce, perhaps. I glanced once again at the mantel. Next to the framed picture of Divya was a picture of Pinky's ex-husband—or late husband, was it? Above his bushy beard, his expression was rigid, unsmiling. Maybe this husband had abandoned Pinky after Somya had her illegitimate baby. Or maybe this husband was a drunkard who gambled away their life savings, leaving Pinky with nothing but this shabby two-bedroom apartment and its paint-peeling walls, worn carpet, and cheap, plastic-covered couch.

Poor Pinky. Poor Pinky with the hawk face. I didn't know the reasons why, but this apartment echoed with sadness. Suddenly, I felt a pressing need to run away, to escape this place before it could infect me with its melancholy.

As if she could read my thoughts, Pinky grabbed my hand. "It's very hard, no?" Water filled her eyes.

Her question surprised me, as did the sudden weight of her hand on mine. My fingers stiffened. "What is hard?"

"This living alone. This being alone."

I sighed and patted her hand. "Pinky, you're not alone. You have Divya and Somya." I swept my free hand in the general direction of the pictures.

"Yes, but I . . . I miss my husband. He died four years ago. Heart attack. One day he is here. Next day, he is gone. Just like that." She sniffled and pulled a crumpled Kleenex from her pants pocket.

"I'm sorry." I felt guilty for my earlier imaginings. The bushy-bearded man in the picture had been a kind husband after all. Just an unhealthy eater, probably. Too much buttery naan and paneer.

"At least he died quickly. Not prolonged, like cancer," she added, nodding in the direction of his picture. "A heart attack is better than that, don't you think? How would you want to die?" She looked expectantly at me.

Honestly, what kind of date conversation was this? Here I was, making all this effort. I had offered her jokes, and when that didn't work, I tried to start a conversation about this senseless movie. And to all of that, barely a word in response. And now, all she wanted to do was yammer away about death.

I rubbed my temple. "I don't know how I want to die. Sleep, I suppose." I consoled myself with the thought of how little gas I'd expend driving home. Not even a tenth of a tank. Maybe not even a twentieth of a tank.

"Yes, yes, sleep, of course, everyone would choose sleep," Pinky said, sounding exasperated. "But, if that's not an option, would you want it to be slow or sudden?"

"Sudden" seemed like the obvious answer. After all, who wanted a prolonged, months-long battle with liver cancer or something? But then, sudden death had its disadvantages too. For one thing, you couldn't say goodbye or set things right with anyone. What if tonight, for example, on the short drive home, some teenage drunk driver slammed into my car, shattering my bones and killing me instantly? Sure, it would be a sudden death, but then, the last moments of my life would have been spent with this sad woman on a plastic-covered couch. My final memories on Earth. At least with a prolonged disease, my last lucid moments could be orchestrated better. I could spend them with my children. I could hold Alok on my lap and breathe his baby smell a hundred more times before drawing my last breath. On balance, the sudden death option seemed exceptionally grim. But not wanting to prolong this discussion a second longer than necessary, I gave Pinky the simpler answer. I gave her the answer she wanted, the answer she probably consoled herself with when she thought of all those last moments her husband's sudden heart attack robbed her of.

"Sudden. Definitely sudden."

Pinky nodded, satisfied. She squeezed my hand once more and released it, the warmth of her abruptly gone. The fluorescent light of the TV flickered over her face, giving her skin a bluish hue.

She was right. It was so hard, this being alone. In a few months, I'd turn sixty. Far from young. Not even middle-aged. Death wasn't some glimmer in the distance, assured but out of reach like the moon. It was close now—a porchlight right outside my house, casting its somber glow on my daily steps.

I leaned back against Pinky's plastic-covered couch—

suddenly exhausted. I reached for her hand. She was still holding the remote control. I covered her hand with mine, feeling her warm knuckles against my palm, and closed my eyes.

We were not so different, really. Two aging, lonely people on a plastic-covered couch, waiting for death to take us away, sudden and unexpected.

9

LATA

"Now come back to child's pose. Just relax into it. Breeeathe. Clear your mind."

At the front of the mirrored room, Olive, the evening instructor at YogaLife studio, demonstrated the pose.

The backs of my legs were sweaty. My exercise pants were sticking to my thighs. I tried not to think about the patches of wetness making crescent moons under my buttocks. I breathed in the rubbery smell of the pink yoga mat that Deanna had brought for me, and tried to clear my mind, just as Olive instructed us. I tried not to think about the achiness in my left knee, a knee that hadn't felt quite right for over a decade, ever since I'd tripped on a flight of stairs, carrying a box of books into Nikesh's college dorm.

I closed my eyes. I tried to remember the sound of Ella Fitzgerald's voice—giddy and bright. *A-tisket, a-tasket, a brown and yellow basket.* There, that was better.

I had listened to the CD so many times now. Dozens of times. In the morning, while I made my tea and toast. In the evening, when I loaded the dishwasher. At night, as I brushed my teeth and got ready for bed. I loved it.

"Kiss your sit bones to your heels," Olive's low, melodious voice instructed us. "Extend your arms farther and exhale."

I did not know what sit bones were. Sith bones? Sitz bones? Or how to kiss them to my heels. But I knew how to exhale. I let out a deep, long breath and stretched my fingers to the edge of the mat. I felt relieved that we were on the ground now, rather than standing.

This child's pose was easier than some of the other poses we'd gone through. The crescent lunge. The dancer's pose. I'd nearly fallen on my face during that one. I'd caught myself at the last second, landing on my forearms with a thud. Olive had stopped her own pose to ask if I was okay. It was humiliating. But other than my punctured ego, I was fine. Brought low by the dancer's pose. And to think, I had spent a decade of my youth learning Bharatanatyam, molding my body into every shape my exacting dance teacher had demanded of me. But now, here I was, struggling to follow the instructions of Olive, a forty-something woman with a soothing voice, a perfectly flat stomach, and a gray-streaked braid dangling down her back.

It turned out that my mother was right all those years ago when she told me I didn't have the natural grace to be a dancer. I had believed her then. I had quit dancing, even though I loved it. As a girl and then as a young woman, I had believed much of what my mother told me. Too much. She was loud and certain about everything. I was quiet and doubting. I had believed her when she told me that with my too-dark complexion, I was lucky that a man like Suresh had agreed to marry me. A man headed to America. A man with so many prospects. I had wanted to delay marriage, to use my college degree, maybe even apply to graduate school. My mother said I would never get in on my merits, and that my father didn't have the kind of money to bribe a spot for me. I had believed her then too. Even my father, a reasonably progressive man for his day, could not support my rejecting a promising marriage proposal for the pursuit of a career.

And so I gave up before I really tried. I did what everyone told me to do. I followed a man across the globe. I supported his career—one that everyone rooted for, his parents, my parents, literally everyone. And the irony was, Suresh himself didn't seem to care all that much about it. He was a very smart man but lazy. I watched his growing apathy in his PhD program. I watched him slink away, blaming everyone but himself for failing to finish his dissertation—his advisors, the other students in his program, and of course me. He even blamed baby Priya and her inability to sleep soundly through the night—though it was not as if Suresh ever got up to tend to her. That was my job. And as I watched and listened to his ever-growing list of grievances, while a baby suckled on my sore nipples, a seed of resentment began to grow inside of me. How was it, I wondered, that my fate had been sealed to this man, who had everyone rooting for him to succeed, but who couldn't be motivated to try harder, who never did anything but complain? And then, along with resentment came regret. Even shame. Because I had let it happen. As a young woman, I had not trusted myself. I had lacked the kind of confidence that was required to challenge a mother, a father, an entire society's expectations. And yes, maybe it wasn't fair to blame myself for that. But I knew other women who had pushed forward. Old friends from college—not many, but a few, who'd marched fearlessly toward graduate programs and medical school, ignoring all the naysayers, swallowing their own doubts. Sometimes, in my darker moments, I wondered what would have happened if I had been more like those women. Where would I be?

Well, at least Priya would never have to feel this way.

"Exhale. And expel any negative thoughts out of your body."

Was Olive reading my mind? She was right of course. I

needed to free myself of negative thoughts. There was no point looking backward. That never did anyone any good. And besides, I was a working woman now. Whatever opportunities I failed to take in my youth, I had found my way to a job now. I'd even made a new friend there—one who convinced me to try this yoga class.

I turned my head and watched Deanna. Her eyes were closed, her body folded over on the turquoise mat beside me.

A few days ago, I had told Deanna that I wanted to find a new hobby to fill my evenings. She suggested I come with her to a yoga class. I was skeptical at first. I used to watch my grandfather practice yoga on the roof of our house. Unshaven and clad in a thin white lungi, he'd stretch and bend and meditate, oblivious both to me and the noisy vendors carting fruit and vegetables on the streets below. Trying not to disturb him, I would count the number of times the wind made his *poonal* string flip-flap in a thin diagonal across his chest as he did his exercises. I'd never considered trying it myself. At the time, I'd considered it to be the boring ritual of my grandfather—not at all appealing to a young girl obsessed with dance and cinema. But when Deanna brought up the subject, I'd been tempted to reject yoga for the opposite reason. It seemed all too glamorous now— a hobby of young celebrities and fad-chasing college girls, not divorced Indian women in their sixth decade of life.

But Deanna was insistent. "It's not what you think it is. You won't be the oldest woman there, I promise. Just give it a chance."

At that moment, I'd thought of Mala and Raj, buying matching polo shirts and visors, learning to swing golf clubs and putter in the green, or whatever it was called. They weren't worried about looking stupid. Why should I be nervous about trying new things? Wasn't that one of the benefits of living alone? There was no Suresh to mock me as I left the house in my newly bought, formfitting yoga pants, asking if I thought I was some kind of Spice Girl now. (Honestly, I had wanted to wear loose-fitting pants, but Deanna insisted that formfitting was better for yoga.)

Well, at least Deanna had been telling the truth when she said I wouldn't be the oldest woman in the class. I lifted my head off the mat and peeked at one woman, two rows in front of me. She looked over sixty, her hair cut in a gray bob. I'd been sneaking glances at her the entire class. She wore very loose clothes, and when she did the downward-facing dog pose, her shirt fell toward her neck, revealing her entire midsection, spotted and floppy like chapati dough. But she didn't seem to care. She did every pose perfectly, her face serene and glowing. Every time I looked at her, I felt equal parts inspired by her obliviousness and grateful that Deanna had warned me against wearing loose clothes.

"Now, let's move into warrior pose," Olive said. The women all around me began to rise.

Oh God, we were standing up again.

I took a deep breath and tried to mimic their movements. Right leg forward, knee slightly bent, left leg lunging back and unbent. Arms forming a straight line, aligned with the shoulders, fingers together but not held in fists. I looked at Deanna's face. Her expression was stern, resolute—like she was preparing for battle.

I tried to imitate it. I narrowed my eyes and focused on an egg-shaped water stain on the wall. I pretended like I could zap it with my gaze. I kind of liked this warrior pose. For a moment, I believed I was strong, powerful, weaponized. My knee was aching less. Drops of perspiration dotted my upper lip. I sniffed the faint vinegar smell of sweat in the room.

I had not been this close to so many sweating women in years. The last time was in the eighties, when Mala had bought a Jane Fonda workout video. She invited me and a few other women to her house three times a week to work out together. This was a few years after Nikesh was born. I still hadn't shed the baby weight, and I'd hoped an exercise group would motivate me. In actuality, we probably consumed more calories than we burned. Dressed in sweatpants and oversized T-shirts, we'd kick and twist along with Jane for about fifteen minutes, at which point someone would collapse on the couch, and Mala would take that as an excuse to suggest a snack and tea break. And after a half hour of gossiping and eating, it would be time to pick up the kids from school. Our exercise group lasted about a month, just enough time for each of us to gain a few more pounds.

In truth, I was never able to maintain any kind of exercise program when the kids were at home. It was not until the kids left for college that I discovered the one form of exercise I could actually stick to: morning walks. For the last twelve years, I'd wake up at six and take a brisk four-mile walk. I did it every day, unless it was raining. And I credited that simple act of walking with helping me maintain my weight. Who knew it could be so easy? As I stretched my warrior arms out farther, I eyed the slight jiggle of my upper arms. I felt the small bulging of my stomach over the waistband of my new yoga pants. Well, so what if I wasn't Jane Fonda–level fit? Or Olive-level fit. I was healthy. I was strong. It was good enough for me.

"Okay, now let's move into triangle pose." Olive tilted her body at the waist, letting her outstretched hand graze her foot.

I bent along with her, touching the sandpaper skin of my feet.

"Feel the stretch all along your leg, in the back of your thigh, your hamstring," Olive said.

I did. I felt it all. It felt wonderful. Maybe Deanna was right about yoga. There was something to this. Had Jane Fonda herself abandoned aerobic workouts for yoga? Maybe I'd start coming here with Deanna a few evenings a week. I could buy my own yoga mat. And another pair of yoga pants. And a few fitted shirts. Life was still full of surprises. You just had to be willing to look foolish and try something new.

"Pssst, Lata," Deanna whispered. "Don't look now, but your special friend is here." She jerked her head toward the back of the room.

At the waiting area, a few people were taking off their shoes and preparing for the next class. Professor Greenberg was there, stuffing his shoes into an open cubby. I spun my head back around and widened my eyes at Deanna. What was he doing here? This was a yoga class. Men didn't do yoga. My grandfather did, of course. But white American men? They didn't. Did they?

"Okay, now move back to downward-facing dog. Then drop your hips toward the floor and lift your chest into upward-facing dog," Olive said.

Why were there so many positions named after dogs? And when was this class going to end?

I didn't want to mimic a dog in front of Professor Greenberg. Maybe he didn't see me. Maybe he had no idea I was here. Maybe he was sitting in the waiting area, his head buried in a book about Charlie Parker or Miles Davis or Thelonious Monk. I'd been doing research in the library, learning some names.

The rest of class passed in excruciating slowness. Five minutes felt like fifty. I felt ridiculous doing a pose called happy baby, holding my feet in the air and rocking side to side like an infant, all the while knowing that he might be watching. I wanted to hide. I was so embarrassed. Why had I worn these unbreathable, formfitting pants? I was sweating through them. I wish I'd never said yes to this insufferable yoga class. Oh, that pushy Deanna! This was all her fault.

And then, finally, it was over. We lay like corpses, closed our eyes, and Olive told us we were done.

I wanted to bolt upright and run out the door, but that would only call more attention to myself. So I waited for all the women to gather their slippery mats and walk herdlike to the cubbies. I would duck my head and follow them, hoping he wouldn't see me.

I rolled my mat and started walking as close as I could behind Deanna.

"Lata, what are you doing? You almost tripped me," Deanna said.

"Oh, sorry. I'm just . . . my knees are a bit wobbly after the class."

"Well, don't fall now because your biggest fan is waving at you."

Oh God. He saw us. He was waving, a big smile on his face, a green yoga mat rolled under his armpit.

"Hey, Professor Greenberg. First the library, now here. You're not stalking us, are you?" Deanna wagged a finger in front of his face.

He laughed. "Nope. This is my regular yoga studio. I mean, it's the only yoga studio in town. I usually come in the afternoons, but I had a faculty meeting today, so here I am at the late show."

Students from our class were trying to exit while students for the next one were trying to enter, and the three of us had created a roadblock. We moved to the side, to let people pass.

"The late show? You sound like Lata. It's only eight-thirty." Deanna grabbed her flip-flops from a cubby and shoved them on her feet. Summer or no summer, I didn't understand how she could drive in those shoes.

I reached into the cubby beside hers and pulled out my sneakers.

"Hi, Lata." He waved again, just at me this time. He was dressed in navy exercise pants. They looked like pajamas. I was glad he wasn't wearing shorts. Men often looked ridiculous in shorts.

"Hi . . . Professor Greenberg."

"Len. It's Len."

"Len." I smoothed the sweaty strands of hair off my face and wondered if kohl had smudged below my eyelids. "So . . . you do yoga?"

"I do. I have for a few years now. What about you?"

"This is my first class."

"She's a yoga virgin." Deanna stuffed a stick of gum in her mouth. "Well, not anymore. We popped her yoga cherry." She began chewing, completely oblivious to my reddening face. Oh God, what was the matter with this girl?

"You guys want one?" She held the gum packet toward us.

Len shook his head. I took one and unwrapped it, mostly to distract myself from my own embarrassment. As I folded the minty stick into my mouth, I tried to think of something to say.

"So, I listened to your CD." The words flew out of my mouth before I could stop myself.

Len's face brightened. He shifted his yoga mat to his other armpit. "You did? What did you think?"

"It was . . . wonderful. I really like that Ella Fitzgerald. Her voice is so clear and bubbly, like a stream. And that Billie Holiday. She has a voice that is sad, but beautiful. A voice full of tragedy. And Sarah Vaughan, she . . ." I was babbling. Was I even pronouncing their names correctly? "I just . . . loved all of them. Thank you again for making me the CD."

"I'm so glad you liked it." He was staring at me in a way that made me nervous. His eyes were the color of walnuts.

"Okay class, let's get started," Olive called out. She had just finished our class, and now she was teaching another one, right away. Goodness, what stamina that woman had! Did yoga do that for her too?

"I think your class is starting." I pointed at Olive, whose feet were spread apart, her arms stretched to the ceiling.

He didn't seem to hear me. He set his yoga mat on the ground and ran a hand through his curly hair. "Lata, so . . . there's a jazz quartet playing in town next Saturday. They're visiting from

Houston, not very well known. But it will be pretty good, I think. I have an extra ticket. Would you like to go with me?"

Go to a concert with him? Just the two of us? I clutched the sneakers in my hands.

Deanna popped her gum. Loudly. We both turned and stared at her. Sticky white goo covered her lips. She mouthed "sorry" and shrugged.

"Now exhale." Olive's sonorous voice filled the room. "Close your eyes. Quiet all negative thoughts."

I exhaled.

I closed my eyes.

10

PRIYA

Travis's gym stood alone near the east end of campus. In the pre-dusk light, the stucco building looked saggy and tired.

Our college gym was most definitely not one of those gleaming sweat palaces that had bloomed across institutions of higher learning in this sports-obsessed state. It looked the part of a budget-strapped liberal arts college with no state-ranked athletics to speak of.

I stepped inside, inhaled the musty air, and surveyed the room of sad, arthritic-sounding machines. Needless to say, I didn't come here often. Once every few months maybe—when I'd had one too many takeout dinners. Or a day like today, when I'd take any distraction from grading.

I squeezed the rolled-up *New Yorker* in my fist and headed toward an unoccupied bike. It was bike by default, since the treadmills, ellipticals, and stair-steppers required bobbing around in a way that would make reading the magazine's small text impossible. Next to my chosen bike, a girl pumped away on an elliptical machine—her face red and glistening, her blond ponytail whirling behind her head, her eyes glued to an *US Weekly*. I looked longingly at her magazine. Why did I bring a *New Yorker* to the gym anyway? Was I really going to absorb an article detailing military failures in Afghanistan or dissecting the mortgage foreclosure crisis? After four hours of grading, a story about a starlet's eating disorder was probably all I could manage.

I set the cycle at the easiest setting and thought fondly of the trashy magazine stack next to my toilet. My secret shame. (Well, one of them, anyway.) The first time Ashish spent the night (his pharma-rep wife traveled often for work), he'd said nothing about them. The second time, he walked out of the bathroom holding an *OK!* magazine with an amused look. "Nice reading material you've got in there." On the cover, a barely clothed Kim Kardashian puckered her collagen'd lips and glowered.

Maybe a few years ago, in advance of a man staying over, I'd have hidden the tabloids and replaced them with *Economist*s or *New Yorker*s to project a certain image of myself. But I didn't see the point of hiding my trashy magazines from Ashish. After all, what was a stack of glossy tabloids hidden in the bathroom compared to a wife hidden at home? It was one of the few perks of dating a married man: There was less reason to present a sanitized version of yourself. Dating a liar paradoxically created incentives for honesty—well, about the trivial things anyway.

After twenty minutes (during which I'd failed to read a single highbrow word), I hoisted myself up from the bike. The blond girl next to me still pounded away. Sinewy calves, triceps, and biceps bloomed with every step, push, and pull of the elliptical. My twenty minutes on the bike seemed like a joke by comparison. At best, I'd burned off the calories in a piece of toast.

I sighed. I didn't want to go home. I didn't want to go back to my office. I didn't want to get on another cardio machine. I glanced again at the blond girl—her muscles poking out with each determined step, as if trying to escape from her skin. Alas, maybe I'd give the weight room a try.

The weight room was separated from the cardio room by a single door with a brass handle. The old-fashioned door betrayed the humble origins of the gym—the building once housed impoverished scholarship students. I looked around for an unoccupied machine that seemed minimally taxing. And then I spotted him.

Ashish. Laughing and adjusting the weight setting on a machine for a woman whose face I couldn't see. Gasping, I ducked behind a stack of weights before he spotted me.

Peeking around the weights, I could only see the woman's back. Her black hair was twisted into a high bun, like a dancer's. A peach-colored tank top showed off her shapely arms. As she pushed a bar up over her head, a diamond sparkled on her ring finger, lit up by the fluorescent lights overhead.

Chalini? He'd brought his wife to the campus gym?

She swatted playfully at him, though they were too far away for me to hear what he'd said to her. She pushed the bar up and down, up and down, while he talked and laughed and repositioned her shoulders when she strayed out of form. His hands rested lightly on her shoulders—her toned, glossy-with-perspiration shoulders. A lock of hair escaped her dancer's bun, and he tucked it behind her ear. A gesture so familiar to me, I couldn't breathe. I felt like the weights I was crouched behind had been hurled at my stomach.

So this was what he did when he wasn't with me? He went to the gym with his wife and told her jokes and guided her movements on weight machines and pushed her hair back when it fell out of place?

Of course he did. Why wouldn't he? She was his wife. After the gym, they probably went to Whole Foods together, where he handed her melons to smell and squeeze for ripeness, where they debated what kind of fish to buy for dinner. Or maybe they went to Starbucks, where they waited in line for lattes and he'd readjust her purse strap when it slid from her shoulder. They had rituals and jokes as a married couple. They lived their lives out in the open as a married couple.

For obvious reasons, Ashish and I spent most of our time together inside my condo. We didn't go to Whole Foods or try new restaurants together for fear that someone, some friend of theirs or mine, would spot us. Austin wasn't small like Clayborn, but it wasn't that big either. Once, for my birthday last March, he took me to a Mexican restaurant on the River Walk in San Antonio, about an hour's drive away. It was disastrous. Neither of us had been able to relax. We fought the whole drive home. I went to sleep alone and then to Whole Foods alone the next morning to buy myself a bagel.

I crouched lower to the ground, until my knees gave out and I sank to the floor. My fist curled tightly around the *New Yorker*. I felt the pages dampen from the sweat of my palm. I couldn't decide whether to scream or cry. I rested my head against the weights and shut my eyes.

I needed to end this relationship.

I'd almost gotten married. Years ago.

I'd met Darren Norton in a Medieval History class my last year of college. He was my professor's teaching assistant. If my father had ever met him (which he hadn't), he would have called him "Nordic-looking." Darren was tall, pale, and very blond. So blond that I didn't pay much attention to him at first. In general, I'm not attracted to blond men. They have a hazy, blurry-at-the-edges quality that I find off-putting—like looking through an out-of-focus camera lens. And besides, in this class, it was nearly impossible to pay attention to anyone but Professor Faisal, a stout, androgynous woman, who never failed to captivate us with tales of Rome-sacking Visigoths, ruthless popes, and strange-named characters like Clovis and Pepin the Short. Most people assumed that a class like Medieval History would be a bore. They were sorely mistaken. In Professor Faisal's capable hands, it was more like a biweekly story hour. Her class was the reason I'd become a medieval historian.

The first time I really noticed Darren was a few weeks after our midterm exam, an in-class essay on Charlemagne. I was sure I'd nailed it, but two weeks later it came back to me with a bright red "C" in what I would later discover was Darren's customary scrawl. Sitting across from him in the windowless cell that he called an office (how uncharitable I was then toward the depressed budgets of history departments), I told him he'd made a mistake.

"This section I wrote on Charlemagne's attempts to standardize money—I see you didn't make any comments next to it." I jabbed at my paper. "Maybe you missed it. Aren't all graduate students sleep-deprived?"

He stared at me, his expression amused. "Yes, very sleep-deprived." He was wearing a navy corduroy blazer that had a vintage air, though the sleeves were short on him. He was a tall man with long limbs. He grabbed a red pen, crossed out the "C" and replaced it with a large "A." "Okay, then. All fixed."

"That's it? You're not going to reread my essay?" Was he joking with me?

"Nope. You convinced me." He smiled. Wait—was this his way of flirting? He ran a hand through his blond hair. It seemed to have become a little less blond in the past five minutes. More light brown than blond, really.

Still, his haphazard regrading philosophy disturbed me. "Is this how you grade papers? You just stick your finger in the air, and whichever way the wind blows, that's the grade?"

"You wanted an 'A,' and you got an 'A.' Don't question it. Just pretend you're a freewheeling Viking or something."

"Why would I pretend to be that?" I asked, my voice filled with disdain. "Weren't they, like, raiders who were drunk on mead all the time? And mead is basically beer, right?"

He touched his chin. "Hmm. I thought it was more like sweet wine. You know what, I'm not really sure what mead is." He looked mildly ashamed about this, which made me dislike him a little less.

"I don't either. I pictured it like Guinness," I said. "But thicker, you know? More mealy. Less distilled or hygienic or something. Look, that's not really the point here."

"Really, because you seem awfully hung up on this mead thing," he said. "Are you thirsty? Do you want to get a Guinness? Or . . . any drink?"

"What?"

"A drink. A beverage. Preferably alcoholic. Have a drink with me?"

"Well, you're . . . um . . . old. Er. Older." Heat filled my face. I was twenty-one and he was twenty-eight. I smelled of unfettered promise and hope and youth, and he had that spacey look of overwork and dissatisfaction that I'd start to recognize a few years later. He seemed taken aback when I insinuated he was old. When you are twenty-eight, it is impossible that you might seem old to anyone. Sometimes, when I remember such things, my thirty-five-year-old self wants to smack my smug twenty-one-year-old self in the face.

You know, some people would have called Darren awkward. Nikesh had called him awkward. But awkwardness has its charms. Awkwardness is a seriously undervalued trait these days. I'd met some of Nikesh's New York law firm cronies. They were slick. Slick lawyers with their slick lawyer girlfriends, or slick lawyers with their slick trophy wives, or slick lawyer wives with their slick investment banker husbands, a cross-pollination of slickness that bred slicker and slicker offspring.

After a moment's hesitation, I shrugged, stuffed my rechristened A-paper in my backpack, and walked with Darren to an Irish pub near campus. We ordered pints of Guinness and started talking. And we didn't stop until 2:00 A.M., when the bartender kicked us out. After that first date, we were pretty much inseparable. About a year into our relationship, I became pregnant. I'd waited three days too long to refill my birth control prescription. I was barely twenty-two years old. I hadn't graduated from college yet and was knee-deep in graduate school applications. A baby was out of the question. Marriage was out of the question—for me, anyway. Darren suggested we talk about it, about marriage; he offered to propose, to do the right thing, or whatever cliché men use in those situations. But I told him I was too young. I couldn't imagine having a baby until I finished graduate school. Darren drove me to the clinic, tried to distract me from protesters holding signs of bloody fetuses, sat with me in the waiting room, and drove me home afterward. He sat on the bed next to me, rubbed my back, and whispered that one day, when the time was right, it would happen for us—a baby to be welcomed and cherished. *Cherished.* A word that sounded so strange, so old-fashioned. I hated that word, and I hated him for saying it, for reminding me that the baby I'd gotten rid of would never be cherished. I'd shifted away from him on the bed, felt the friction of a maxi pad between my legs, and cried.

Nothing was really the same after. I started graduate school and Darren finished his PhD. The long conversations and the sex had become sporadic at best. Darren accepted a teaching job at Case Western and suggested a bit too casually that I should stay behind to finish my program before joining him. And soon after that, he told me not to bother joining him at all. He'd met someone new, he said. A sociologist named Cara.

Two years ago, I'd bumped into Darren at a history conference. Apparently, he and Cara were married and had three children— a boy and twin girls. To his credit, he couldn't quite look me in the eye when he told me that. And he had the decency not to show me any pictures. Though he did tell me their names: Edward, Lisbeth, and June. Three children to be cherished.

Chalini had finally finished her set of repetitions. She stretched her smooth, lean arms over her head and bent them against her back, massaging her triceps. Ashish took the pin out of the weights and set it at a higher level. It was his turn now. As they switched positions, I could finally see her face. She was young—younger than I'd imagined. Thirty at most. Her skin was flawless, the color of peanut butter. Her eyes were anime-character wide. Her nose was a bit large, but she was undeniably pretty. Beautiful, even. Of course I should have known this. She was a pharma rep, after all. They were always good-looking, as per the evil genius of pharma companies. She threw her head back and laughed in response to something Ashish said, revealing a row of small, even white teeth.

I felt a snapping sound in my head, like the splitting of a branch. I wanted Ashish to see me. I wanted him to know I was here—that I could see him. As I approached them, Chalini's eyes widened with friendly curiosity. She smiled at me, clearly trying to place me, trying to figure out if she'd met me before. Ashish was on the machine, his back toward me. He pulled the bar up and down, grunting, sweaty and oblivious to me.

I tapped him on the shoulder. "Hey there."

He turned. Astonishment filled his face.

"Oh, h-hey," he stammered. "What are you . . . um . . . doing here?" Ashish wiped the sweat off his forehead with his wrist.

He stared at me and then at Chalini, as if unsure what to do next. Then he placed his arm around her shoulders—whether out of habit or deliberate choice, I couldn't know.

My heart fell. I had allowed this to happen. I had believed him when he said he loved me. I had let this man make a fool of me.

Hot tears burned the corners of my eyes. I dug my nails into my palm and ordered myself to stay calm. The idea of crying in front of him—of her—was simply unthinkable.

I smiled and shrugged, feigning nonchalance. "I'm exercising, of course. What else would I be doing at a gym?"

Chalini's eyes were losing their friendly glow. She stared at Ashish, her full lips thinning into a taut line. "Ash? Aren't you going to introduce me?"

"Yes, of course. Sorry. Chalini, um, this is Priya. She works in the history department. She's working on a paper with Doug, and he introduced us a few weeks ago. Priya, this is my wife, Chalini."

Chalini held out her hand, her eyes friendly once more. I stared at it, confused by Ashish's explanation. *Doug?* Who the fuck was Doug? And how did Ashish come up with that lie so fast? As if he'd been practicing for this very moment—when I'd run into him and his wife.

Regaining my composure, I took Chalini's hand and pumped it with as much fake exuberance as I could muster. "Yeah, that Doug. He's a real character."

Chalini's smile widened. Her shoulders relaxed.

She believed us. To her, I was just some weird historian who worked with her husband's friend Doug. I could see her mind working, taking me in, assessing my age, my faded gray shorts, my untoned legs, my awkward gestures. She had decided I wasn't worth worrying about.

"I know, right?" Chalini nodded. "The last time Doug came over, I told Ash to hide the whisky or else Doug would start some incoherent tirade about the Fed, then start an impromptu eighties dance party in the kitchen until four in the morning and fall asleep in our tub. Who knew an economist could party like that?"

Terrific—so she was witty too. The kind of woman I might even be friends with, were I not sleeping with her husband. I wondered if mistresses often thought that sort of thing upon meeting the wives. After all, the same man had chosen both of you—presumably, you had some shit in common.

I glared at Ashish. He was staring at his shoes, avoiding my eyes. It was unbearable.

"Sure, that sounds like Doug. Well, I'd better go. Lots of grading to do. Nice to meet you, Chalini." I waved and walked away as fast as my untoned legs could carry me.

Just after midnight, I finally finished them all.

I stuffed the last stack of graded essays—bloody with red ink—into my backpack. I tugged the zipper closed and felt a rush of satisfaction.

My phone beeped, and I pulled it out of my pocket. Another call from Ashish—his fourth since the afternoon, and none of them answered. This one, like the others, was followed by a text: *Hey, call me please. Priya, call me, okay? Please.* Also unanswered.

My momentary post-grading buzz dissolved into a cocktail of shame and fury. I walked into the bathroom, flipped the light switch on, and watched the perimeter of mirror bulbs illuminate my exhausted face.

I leaned in, inspecting the circles under my eyes. My age was starting to catch up with my skin. These days, every stress-filled, hungover, sleep-deprived, cigarette-infused moment seemed to stick in ways that no amount of catch-up sleep or vegetable juice or exercise could undo. I feared that one day, I'd wake up to find that the haggard, drunken, overworked face I'd gone to sleep with wasn't just some temporary aberration, but my actual face. My aging, sagging, late-thirties face.

Well, at least this old face had gotten the job done. I'd finished my grading. Despite the afternoon's humiliating spectacle, I hadn't shirked or sacrificed any professional duties. I could take heart in that, at least. And despite the late hour, I wasn't even going to scrimp on nighttime hygiene rituals. No skipping out on the cleanser, or toner, or moisturizer, or contact lens cleaning, or teeth-brushing. The flossing—well, that I'd skip. It would be my one reward for vigilance.

Satisfied with this tiny consolation, I reached for my tooth-brush. It sat in a four-holed toothbrush holder on the counter. About halfway to my lips, though, I realized I'd grabbed the wrong toothbrush. I was holding a blue toothbrush with a monkey-shaped handle. A kid's toothbrush in the shape of a Disney character or something. It was Ashish's toothbrush. Ashish had beautiful white teeth and compulsive tooth-brushing habits, so I'd bought him this toothbrush to keep at my house. The monkey-shaped handle was supposed to be a joke.

He'd looked confused when I first gave it to him. "I don't get it," he said. "Why a monkey?"

"Because you look like a monkey. Your ears stick out. Like a cute monkey's." I'd expected a laugh, but he looked irritated.

"You can't call an Indian man a monkey. That's an ethnic slur—not a term of endearment. Weren't you paying attention to the 'macaca' incident?"

"That's a preposterous comparison. I'm not some Republican senator. I'm the woman you're sleeping with. Take a joke." Now I was irritated. Ashish could be such a prig sometimes.

I pinched his arm. "And anyway, so what if I call you an ethnic slur. Isn't that one of the perks of dating your own people? You can hurl racial epithets at each other with impunity?"

He'd laughed then, wrapping his arms around my waist. In the bathroom mirror, we'd looked like one of those perfect, matchy-matchy, brother-sister-looking couples in a toothpaste commercial. Like if we embraced for a second or two more, the Crest logo would appear under our reflections.

"So that's the benefit of dating your own people?" Ashish said. "Too bad you weren't around to defend those anti-miscegenation laws back in the day. Those Southern politicians could have used your whole 'don't let the races mix, or it'll be the end of postcoital, racist nicknames' argument. It's a real winner."

"Very funny, monkey-face."

Alone now, I shoved the monkey-brush in the medicine cabinet and slammed the mirrored door shut.

I grabbed my own toothbrush and began moving it in fast, frothy circles. As I brushed, I stared at the now-empty, four-holed toothbrush holder on the counter.

When I was young, my family lived in a smallish house in Clayborn. It had only two bathrooms, and for some reason, my mother insisted on keeping one a pristine guest bathroom, so we all shared the master. There was a four-holed toothbrush holder in there too, and it was always full. Each morning, we'd all fight for mirror space as we brushed our teeth. The bathroom had terrible shellfish wallpaper and cracking linoleum. But I couldn't help remembering it now—how we'd shared it, how our four toothbrushes had sat together in that toothbrush holder, two adult-sized and two kids' toothbrushes, crusty with the remnants of paste, leaning into one another.

I spat the last bit of toothpaste out of my mouth, gargled violently, and thrust my brush back in the holder. I gripped the sides of the sink. I stared at my lone toothbrush and was struck by the thought that I'd never see the sight of four crusty toothbrushes jostling each other again. No kids' toothbrushes touching my own. Not even one toothbrush next to mine. Just one toothbrush in there until I died.

I started to sob. I crumpled to the floor and pressed my face against the purple bath mat. The fluffy fibers tickled my face until my crying slowed to a hiccupping whimper. I stayed there, face to rug, until I finally dragged myself to bed.

The next morning, I woke to puffy skin pushing against my eye. I lifted my head off the pillow and felt around the nightstand for my phone. I took a deep breath and dialed.

"Hi." My voice cracked. "Can I . . . come see you?"

11

SURESH

"Lata, I can only assume you no longer care what happens to your children. It's astonishing, really, because you've always been an attentive mother. It's probably the trait that I've most admired about you. Your devotion to your children—our children. I've heard from the kids that you have a job now—at a library or some such thing. But I find it shocking that you've become so obsessed with a career at this late, *late* stage of your life that you can't find five minutes to discuss the well-being of your daughter with the man you called a husband for thirty-six years."

I had more to say, but Lata's voicemail cut me off before I could finish.

I was in my car now, driving home. I'd left Pinky's before the movie ended—abruptly letting go of her hand and lying about an errand I had to do before dinnertime. She didn't ask me to stay. She seemed as relieved to see me go as I was to leave. I hoped never to see her again.

Despite the evening hour, I was running the AC full blast. I leaned my face toward the vent. As cold air caressed my forehead, my anger began to dissipate and a twinge of remorse took its place.

Perhaps my voice message was too harsh? Maybe I shouldn't have called Lata on the way home from a terrible date.

But why was Lata behaving this way—why couldn't she return my calls? Was it possible that Nikesh or Priya told her about my internet dating—and now she was angry with me? True, I never expressly told the kids not to tell her. But I just assumed they wouldn't. Maybe for a while, I'd even hoped that they wouldn't—in case Lata ever came to her senses and decided she had made a big mistake. It had seemed wise to leave that door open, just in case.

Well, so what if she knew now? That was still no excuse for her to ignore my calls. She should be above such pettiness—especially when the welfare of one of our children was at stake.

A few minutes later, I pulled into my garage, and a new worry entered my mind: Was Lata sick? No—unlikely. Lata's immune system was very strong. That was another thing I'd always admired about her. Even when the kids were young and brought home virulent germ cocktails from school, she didn't get sick. I, on the other hand, would succumb instantly. Like the kids, I'd stay in bed, feverish and miserable for days. But somehow, Lata would go on like always, picking up prescriptions at the pharmacy, fetching us cups of orange juice and Sprite, making soup for the kids and pepper rasam for me. Oh, that pepper rasam. It felt like an eternity had passed since I'd last tasted it. The spicy tamarind flavor on my tongue was always the one consolation of being sick.

I walked into the house, trying to imagine the smell of pepper rasam cooking on the stove. But I couldn't—smells were too hard to remember. I sniffed. Just the faint scent of 409 and a mild eggy odor lingering from my midday omelet.

How many months had passed since I'd inhaled the glorious smell of mustard seeds simmering in ghee? I turned on the gas burner. Small blue flames leapt into orange ones. Maybe I could try to make pepper rasam for my dinner tonight. Oh, who was I kidding? I wouldn't even know where to begin. And Lata didn't work from paper recipes, so there was nothing to even use for guidance.

In truth, the kitchen had seen paltry action since Lata left. I'd never mastered more than the basics of South Indian cooking. All right, less than the basics. I tried to make a sambar once, a few months ago. I spit it out after one sip and tried to make do with a bowl of rice, yogurt, and store-bought spicy pickles. The makeshift meal was wholly unsatisfying, and since then, I'd stuck to a repetitive regimen of omelets, canned soups, Domino's pizza, and frozen burritos.

But the underuse of the kitchen was a shame for reasons that went beyond my deadening taste buds. The kitchen was arguably the best part of the house. It was, as our architect had described it, "a cook's dream," with a Sub-Zero refrigerator, chef-quality gas stove, and a marble-topped island in the center. These indulgences, of course, had little to do with me. In fact, when Lata and I were designing the house, I'd protested the needless extravagance of the kitchen:

"Who cares if the stove is gas or electric? Electric is cheaper. And who needs a marble-topped island? We're not taking a vacation on it. It's not a destination in the South Pacific. It's a countertop. Formica will do the job just as well for a quarter of the price."

At my suggestions, Lata and our architect—some local man named James Trotter—traded disdainful looks. Lata reproached me: "You don't understand anything about kitchens. When was the last time you used one? Electric stoves don't work well for our kind of cooking. I need a gas stove, or nothing will taste right. And Formica! Formica is for struggling graduate students or young families who can barely afford their first home. We've saved for over a decade. We already live in a house with Formica countertops. The house we're building is the last house we'll ever live in. We'll probably die here, and I refuse to die on Formica."

Just as I was about to alert Lata to the statistical improbability of her falling over dead on a kitchen island—Formica or no Formica—the architect interjected, "You know, I hear what you're both saying. But I want to point out that in terms of resale value, modern, upscale kitchens are one of the key things prospective buyers look for. You'll be hard-pressed these days to find a three-thousand-square-foot house without a Sub-Zero in the kitchen and marble throughout. Now, look, I'm not pushing you in one direction or the other. It's just something to keep in mind."

He was a savvy fellow, that Trotter. His Texas accent was thick, nasal, and congenial. He smiled at us with all the sincerity of a car salesman and stood with his hands in his pockets, trying to fool me with his assumption of neutrality. When he thought I wasn't looking, I caught him giving Lata a nod of encouragement. Lata, realizing she had an ally in her vision, quickly made "resale value" her new mantra, not only for the kitchen but for a variety of expensive fixtures we didn't need: a Jacuzzi in the master bath, built-in mahogany shelves in the study, and perhaps most absurd of all given the broiling Texas climate—a fireplace.

But strangely, for all our bickering over the details of the house—over doorknobs and ceiling heights and carpet thickness—it was one of the happier times in our marriage. For the first time since the kids were small, we didn't run out of things to say to each other. The new house had given us an inexhaustible topic of conversation. Suddenly, we *wanted* to talk to each other, to trade ideas, to convince the other, to be convinced. During the four months we spent discussing the design of our new house, our excited voices filled the far more modest house we lived in at the time—the starter house we'd been living in ever since we moved to Clayborn. That affordable, young-married-couple house with peeling sunflower wallpaper that

Lata hated in the dining room and Formica countertops that Lata refused to die on and an oversized pecan tree in the back-yard that we'd both be sorry to leave. It was the house where Priya broke her front tooth on her fifth birthday, her face crash-ing into the corner of a wooden dining table as she bounced a red balloon; the house where we brought Nikesh home from the hospital, watched him take his first steps and grow tall enough to fend off the sneak attacks of his older sister. It was the house where Lata and I first glimpsed the potential boundlessness of our growing dislike; where, in the heat of an argument over whether we should spend the money for the whole family to fly to India for her father's funeral, Lata had said with a calm matter-of-factness that slowed my blood, "I should never have married you."

And then, it was—for at least a four-month period, when we were designing our imminent escape from it—the house where Lata and I grew the slightest bit back together, like mended bones. Perhaps we both sensed the potential for a fresh start in the new house. Perhaps we both hoped our problems could be solved by new rooms and new walls, new paint and new ceilings, new beams, new fixtures, new appliances. By newness. A new-ness that could make us new too.

I watched the flames dance on the burner for a few seconds more. The air above the stove warmed my face. I turned the burner off, letting the orange flame grow thin and blue, and a second later, fade into nothing.

Sitting cross-legged on the carpeted floor of the upstairs game room, I swirled the glass tumbler in my hand. Funny that I still thought of this room as the game room, even though no games remained here. Not a single board game or toy or any evidence of our children's boisterous childhood.

Instead of dinner, I had made myself a concoction of whisky, four cubes of ice, and three splashes of water. In truth, I wasn't much of a drinker. On occasion, I'd have a few beers with pizza or Thai food. A mango margarita now and again with Mexican food. But nothing stronger than that—not usually.

I dipped my finger into the liquid and stirred the cubes around, listening to the pleasant pinging sounds. I took a sip and cringed at the medicinal taste. How could this drink have such an inviting amber color but such an odious flavor? Even ice and water couldn't blunt the bitterness of this—this Johnnie Walker Black Label.

I'd found the Black Label bottle in the back of the kitchen pantry. It was hidden behind a large burlap sack of basmati that Lata purchased years before at an Indian grocery store. I would never have bought the whisky for myself. It was a gift from that Chandrasekhar, for my fortieth birthday.

Against my express wishes, Lata had thrown me a fortieth birthday party. I had told her I didn't want one. Who wanted to wear a silly hat and cut pineapple cake in front of sixty clapping guests like a seven-year-old? Wasn't that the consolation of growing older—that people could no longer force you to make a spectacle of yourself? But did she listen? Of course not. She had said, "What will people say if I don't throw you a fortieth birthday party? Mala threw her husband a surprise fortieth, Maneesha threw her husband a surprise fortieth. How will it look if I don't throw one for you?"

Why were women such slaves to their fellow busybody gossipmongers? Wasn't the important thing what I wanted for my birthday? In the end, of course, Lata did exactly as she wanted. She spent days soaking, grinding, and pickling items in preparation for the fifteen or so dishes she put on display. She steamed mountains of idlis. She ordered trays of gulab jamun. She enlisted the kids in decorating the house with streamers and a big banner in the dining room that said: HAPPY BIRTHDAY SURESH, FORTY YEARS YOUNG. She glared at me as I cut my cake, warning me with her eyes to play the part or risk her wrath. So I cut the bloody cake. I endured the slaps on the back. But I drew the line at a party hat. "If you make me wear this hat, Lata, I'll turn this cake knife around and stab myself in the chest with it. Is that what you want? Blood on the cake? What will all your friends say about that?" It was around that moment that Lata stopped talking to me at the party, a silence that lasted for three days.

At the end of the night, Chandrasekhar approached me in my study, where I'd escaped for a few minutes of quiet. He was late to the party, straight from rounds at the hospital. He discovered my hiding place and came toward me with a gold-wrapped box.

"Good man, you are over the hill now," he said, laughing heartily. He slapped me on the back and held out his offering. "Let me tell you what helps every man during a midlife crisis: Johnnie Walker Black Label." He winked at me, a large, exaggerated wink, like we were conspirators in a bank robbery.

I waved my hand in protest. "Raj, I don't really drink hard liquor. You should keep it. If you leave it with me, it'll go to waste. I'll just have to tend to my midlife crisis by buying a sports car and dyeing my hair blond." I tugged a clump of my hair for emphasis.

"Oh, ho, you are such a joker, Suresh. Really, take it. Try it, you will like it. This was the favorite scotch of Winston Churchill."

At that moment, something erupted inside of me. Between Lata's hostile silence, the endless hours of blathering party guests, and now this idiot anglophile who'd invaded my one moment of solace and refused to take back his useless gift and leave me be—it was too much. I grabbed the box out of his hands and said, "Raj, what the hell do I care what Churchill's favorite scotch was? The man was an unapologetic racist who called Gandhi a half-naked *fakir*! Why should I give a damn what he liked to drink? You want me to have it? Fine, I'll take it. I'll bury it in a closet and I'll never drink a sip of it. But thank you, Doctor. From the bottom of my middle-aged heart, thank you." Chandrasekhar left me alone after that.

Remembering this now, I held my glass up in a mock toast to clueless old Chandrasekhar. "Cheers, good man. To you, and to dear old Winston too."

A giggle escaped my lips. I took a few more sips. It was beginning to taste less like medicine and more like metal. What happened to whisky after sitting unopened for nineteen years? Could it spoil? Wasn't age good for alcohol—improved it or something? If only the same could be said for man.

I took two more sips. The length of my sternum warmed. So did the tips of my fingers. It felt soothing, this whisky coursing through my veins. I reached for the bottle and poured.

Why hadn't I done this drinking thing more often during the years? God knows all the times it would have been nice to blunt the sharpness of life, to blur its disappointments. Was it possible that with some things, we couldn't shake the lessons of our youth—the vices deemed too taboo by our own parents? Maybe they infiltrated our bloodstream as children and stayed with us long into adulthood. My parents, after all, were simple people. They lived all their lives in a small house they'd inherited from my father's parents. My father would never have wasted his factory manager income on alcohol. My father didn't even smoke, though his cousins and older brothers did. I remembered my uncles gathered on our front stoop, their sweat-stained undershirts stretched over rice-engorged bellies, sharing smokes and guffawing over the antics of their coworkers, the corruption of politicians, the profligate spending habits of their wives. And my father would stand with them, his slim frame propped against the railing—not saying all that much, and never with a drink or cigarette in hand, but smiling and nodding. He was too much a responsible family man, not prone to excesses of any kind. Well, except one: His only indulgence was a daily shoe polish from the boy on the corner. That was his lone extravagance, his one concession to vanity: perfectly polished shoes. That too I could re-member: the gleaming black leather of my father's shoes set against the sea of my uncles' overused Bata sandals—sandals that advertised the yellowing, calloused soles of their feet. As a boy, I'd hover around all those feet, marveling at their gnarled repugnance, tracing the tributaries of cracked skin with twigs until they shooed me away.

Such a responsible family man to the end, my father was. His last words to me were to take care of my mother. And what dis-mal luck that woman had. She had to live through the death of one daughter, my sister Laxmi, who died at twenty-three of leu-kemia, and then she'd lost her husband, my father, at the en-trance to middle age. And me? Me, she'd lost to a vast, distant continent that she didn't understand and hated to visit. During her life, she'd come to Clayborn a total of three times, and each time, her bags were packed and India-ready a full week before her scheduled departure. More than once, I asked her to come live with us: "It's my responsibility to take care of you. You can't live alone. What if you fall down the stairs and break your hip? Who will find you?"

"The vegetable man comes every morning," she said. "The woman who washes the dishes comes every night. The woman who cleans the floors comes every afternoon. The question is not, 'who *will* find me,' it's 'who *won't* find me.' Can you say the same in your country?"

I tried to persuade her. I knew it was my duty, as her only son, to take care of her—whether she wanted me to or not. But se-cretly, I was glad she refused. Because the truth was I didn't want her here. I didn't want her day-to-day updates about the eczema on her legs or the aching of her hips or the increasing difficulty of her bowel movements: the litany of physical troubles that started plaguing her soon after widowhood. Not even fifty when my father died, and she already sounded like an old woman. A tiresome old woman. Was it possible that she knew I felt this way? That she sensed my relief when she boarded the plane back to India? That she sensed my relief each time we reached the end of our weekly Sunday calls, right up until the day she died five years ago?

I tipped the glass back, letting the rest of the drink flow into my mouth.

If only I'd had more patience back then. If only I'd understood the humiliations of feeling your body begin to fail, and the added insult of having to bear it alone.

She had been right after all. If I fell down the stairs and broke my hip, who would find me in this country? Who would even know? I could be dead, rotting for days before the neighbors noticed, before anyone found me.

I was more alone now than I'd ever been in my entire life. More alone than I'd have been in India. She'd been right and I'd never believed her. This was a terrible place to grow old alone.

Forgive me, amma.

I wiped my eyes and poured myself another glass.

A buzzing on my left buttock woke me. Groggy and unfocused, I sat up with great effort. My throat felt dry, my head dizzy.

The bottle of Johnnie Walker was horizontal now—half its contents spilled and soaked into the fibers of the beige carpet, an amber blob that resembled the vestiges of excrement. A strong liquor smell filled the air. I must have knocked the bottle over in my sleep. I stood the bottle back up and capped it. I considered getting a water-soaked towel to clean it, but the mere effort of sitting up exhausted me. I lay back down. The buzzing on my buttock, which had stopped for a moment, resumed. With a great deal of focus, I turned on my side and answered the phone.

"Dad? What took you so long to answer?"

"Nikesh?" I hadn't been drunk since my college years, but if memory served correctly, this fuzzy, dizzy, blurry state was drunkenness. I attempted to disguise it with effusiveness. "My kind, brilliant son. How are you? How's my grandson, the light of my life, the apple of my eye?"

"Um, Alok's fine. We're all fine. Are you okay? You sound . . . different."

"No. Wait, I mean, yes. I'm okay. I'm excellent. I was just . . . ah, sleeping, you know."

"Sleeping already? It's barely nine. You're not sick or anything, are you?"

"My dear boy. You're such a good son, you know that? You call your father. You check on his health. You would find me if I fell down the stairs and broke my hip. You'd find a way to get me to the doctor. I know you would." The phone slipped from my ear, so I couldn't hear what Nikesh was saying. I pushed the phone back up. It slipped again because my elbow kept collapsing on the carpet. Folding and unfolding. Folding and unfolding, causing the cellphone to drop. I watched my elbow with fascination. It was like watching a tiny house of cards fall.

"Nikesh, do you remember building those card houses with me when you were small? Remember how we would stack the first row like teepees? And then we'd stand back, and wait to make sure they didn't topple? And then, we would take turns placing cards on the tops of the teepees, connecting them to one another? Remember that? And one time, we made a card house five stories high! Five stories! It was incredible! Remember?"

"Dad, why are you going on about broken hips and card houses? Tell me what's wrong." His voice quavered.

Oh, Nikesh. My softhearted boy.

"Dad, look. It's not healthy for you to be in that house by yourself all the time. You need to see people. What happened to that internet lady? You know, the one from Austin that you were so excited about? What's her name—Mallika?"

I started laughing. A strange, hollow laugh—even to my own ears. "Oh, I don't know. She is not interested, I think. She canceled our second date. Five, six times I've called her now. And no response. What can I do?"

"Well, that's okay. Get back on the horse. You've got to keep trying. And in the meantime, call some of your friends. What about . . . um . . . those uncles we used to hang out with?" He sounded dubious. And worried. I didn't like hearing the worry in his voice.

"Nikesh, *kanna,* don't worry. I sound strange because I've had too many drinks . . . with my friends. And you see, I am not used to it, this drinking."

"Oh—you're drunk!" His relief was obvious. At last, I'd said the right thing.

"It's all right, you had your heart broken by a girl. You're entitled to a few drinks. In fact, I've done this myself. Whew. I thought you were going crazy for a second." He laughed. I loved the sound of my son's laugh.

"Okay, Dad, here's some advice. The best thing to avoid a hangover is greasy food. Order yourself a pizza, drink lots of water, take two Advil, and sleep it off. I'll call you in the morning. Bye, Dad. I love you, okay?"

The phone slipped again. Not because of my folding elbow this time, but because my cheeks were wet with tears.

I was sitting by the front door, waiting for the pizza delivery man.

Nikesh was right. The effects of the water and Advil were starting to kick in. My head felt less heavy; my vision was clearer. All I needed now was that greasy mushroom and cheese pizza I'd ordered twenty minutes ago.

Though it was dark out, I could see the silhouettes of desert willows and crepe myrtles swaying in the late evening breeze. The scent of white jasmine, climbing in vines along the wooden fence, filled the air. When Lata lived here, I knew nothing about gardening. I never imagined I'd have the patience for plants. But gardening work had turned out to be easier than I thought. And to my surprise, it was even pleasurable—digging my fingers into soil, adding fertilizer, pulling weeds, and seeing the tangible results a few months later. At the sight and scents of my vigorous plants, I felt a rush of pride. I had done that. Instead of letting them die, I had nurtured them to life, made them bloom.

A car slowed down in front of my driveway. A green Honda Accord without a Domino's sign on top. Was that the pizza guy? Did pizza deliverers drive their own cars from time to time?

The car was turning onto my driveway. I could now see that the driver was a woman. A woman with long black hair. Was it Lata? For a second, my heart leapt. When Lata had lived here, she'd driven a navy Camry. But maybe along with her new job, she'd bought a new car—this Honda. My heart began beating faster.

Had my voicemail knocked some sense into her? Maybe she felt so bad about not returning my calls, she decided to make amends in person. I puffed out a breath into my hand, smelled it, and felt relieved that the whisky odor was gone. The car door opened. I stepped hurriedly off the front stoop and walked toward her. "Lata, is that you?" My voice rang out in the darkness.

The woman screamed. Moonlight illuminated her frightened face. "Suresh, you startled me. I didn't expect you to jump out like that."

It wasn't Lata. It was Mallika.

"I suppose it's strange for *me* to say I didn't expect *you*, right? I mean, here I am, showing up at your house unexpectedly." She smiled in a doubtful, embarrassed way.

I was speechless. Mallika was here—right in front of me, in my driveway.

I felt incapable of forming a sentence or even a lucid thought. I rubbed my eyes. Was this all just a delayed aftereffect of the Johnnie Walker—a hallucination of some sort?

"I know I haven't called you back in a while, but things have been kind of a mess for me. And I . . . well, I couldn't really explain what was going on over the phone."

As she spoke, my senses returned. She wasn't a liquor-induced hallucination. She was real. She was here. And she wasn't alone. The rear door opened, and a little boy stepped out.

"Mom, I'm hungry. You promised me McDonald's French fries." He tugged on her sleeve.

The boy, who looked seven or eight, pointed at me. "Who's that guy?"

PART TWO

PART TWO

12

LATA

I'd said yes.

Why in the world did I say yes? What was I thinking?

I wasn't thinking. I blamed all that yoga breathing. All that inhaling and exhaling and excess oxygen and then that Olive telling me to quiet my negative thoughts in her hypnotic voice. My brain had silenced itself, and I had stupidly said yes to the concert. And now I needed to find a way to say no. To tell him I'd made a mistake. To tell him I had other plans—even though I didn't, and he'd probably see through my flimsy excuse.

Or maybe I could call in sick to the library today. And tomorrow. And every day after that.

My bones felt cold. Maybe I really was getting sick. I put a palm to my forehead. I was fine. I shook my head and scolded myself. I was being foolish, an *asadu*.

In the kitchen, I tiptoed around, trying to make as little noise as possible—steaming milk for tea, toasting slices of bread, closing cupboard doors gently. I didn't want to wake Priya.

That was the other big surprise: Priya was here. How could I possibly go to a concert with Len when Priya was here? What would she think? It was out of the question. If Len came into the library today, I would just have to tell him that I couldn't go.

The truth was, I didn't even know why Priya had come or how long she was staying. She had been here for days already, and most of that time she'd spent sleeping. I'd return from my morning walk and she'd be sleeping. I'd come home to check on her at lunch and she'd be sleeping. I'd return from work at the end of the day and she'd be sleeping. The only time she wasn't sleeping was between the hours of midnight and 5:00 A.M., when the rest of the world—me included—was sleeping. Instead of sleeping then, she would watch television. Last night, around 1:00 A.M., the sound of television gunfire woke me.

"Priya, I think you are feeling depressed." I sat down on the couch next to her and removed a warm bottle of beer from her hands.

She squinted at me. Light from the screen reflected off her glasses. "Mom, why are you awake? It's late."

"I am awake because you are awake. I am awake because you sleep twenty hours a day. I am awake because you are watching a police detective show at one in the morning instead of sleeping like a normal person."

"It's not a police detective show. It's a show about prison guards."

"Priya, please tell me what's wrong. Why are you depressed?"

"I'm not depressed."

"Are you having some kind of trouble at the college?"

"No. It's fine."

"Did they fire you?"

"What? No! They didn't fire me."

"Did one of your articles get rejected?" My daughter was very smart and capable. But she did not handle rejection well. Even as a girl, anytime she got into an argument with a friend or received a "B" on a paper or lost a volleyball tournament, she'd hide and cry in her bedroom closet. I always knew where to find her.

"Work is fine. I'm just . . . tired, okay? I need a few days to decompress."

"Is it your dad? Did you guys have an argument? Is that why you're depressed?"

"Mom, I don't want to talk about it right now. I just need to get away from my normal life for a little while. Then I'll be okay. Go back to sleep. I'm going to sleep soon too. As soon as this show is over."

"What makes you depressed?" I asked Deanna. We were shelving sheet music in the Choral Works section.

"Lots of things, I guess. That's a weird question. What's with you?"

"I know it's a strange thing to ask. But my daughter—you know, Priya, I've told you about her—she's been staying with me these last few days. I don't know how long she's planning on staying. But all she does is sleep—morning, noon, and evening. And then she stays awake all night watching strange television shows about prison guards. I keep asking her what's wrong, but she won't tell me. She just says she's too tired to talk."

"Maybe she had a fight with her boyfriend or something,"

"No, I don't think it's that. She doesn't have a boyfriend. Or maybe she does. I don't even know." Why didn't I know this? Wasn't a mother supposed to know if her grown-up daughter had a boyfriend or didn't? Of course, I'd never had any such conversation with my own mother. I'd had an arranged marriage at the age of twenty. Why was it easier for me to have this kind of conversation with Deanna, whom I'd known for only a few months, than with my own daughter?

"So why don't you ask her if she had a fight with her boyfriend? If she has a boyfriend? If she had a boyfriend until they had a fight? You know, something in that general area."

"We don't really talk about that kind of thing."

"Why not?"

"I don't know. She doesn't bring it up. And I feel strange asking her. If she wants me to know she's dating somebody, she'll tell me. Do you talk to your mother about those things?"

"Not really. I mean, I might if she was around, but I barely see my mother. She's meditating in an ashram in some remote corner of Oregon. Her guru-person lives there. I don't even think she has a phone. I'm lucky if I talk to her once in six months."

"Once in six months! Why is she in an ashram? Is your mother Indian?" I looked doubtfully at Deanna's dyed-black, spiky hair.

"No." Deanna laughed. "She probably wishes she was, though. She's just a hippie."

"Oh." I pictured some long-haired woman wearing bell-bottoms, a flowered shirt, and dark sunglasses. No wonder Deanna's mother didn't care about her daughter's peculiar eating habits. She was probably off somewhere smoking marijuana and listening to strange music. "I'm so sorry."

She laughed again. "It's not like she has terminal cancer or something."

"No, I'm just sorry you don't get to see her more often. So where is your father?"

"Oh, he's there too."

"You're joking. Really?"

Deanna nodded, her expression serious. "You want to hear something crazy? Before he met my mom, my dad was a fourth-generation Southern Baptist. Now he's more likely to have a Bible up his ass than on his nightstand. You can imagine how much his parents like my mom." Deanna laughed once more, but it sounded insincere.

Poor girl, she was basically an orphan. And here I was asking her what things depressed her, forcing her to talk about her absentee family. Her arms looked so frail and thin reaching for the high shelves. I would have to feed her more. I made a mental note to bring her a large Tupperware of lemon rice.

Maybe Deanna was right about Priya. Maybe she was depressed because she had a fight with a boyfriend. Was it possible Suresh knew something about it? For days, I had avoided his calls, and then he stopped calling. I could only imagine how impossible he would be if I called him now, after all this time had passed, to ask about Priya: "Oh, so now you want to know what I have to say. So now Ms. Busy-Busy-Working-Lady finally has some time to pick up the phone and call her lowly ex-husband. Oh thank you, Queen Elizabeth, I'm so honored that you would deign to acknowledge a simple peasant like me."

I winced at the thought of calling him back. Though I knew I should. It might be worth bearing his theatrics to find out something useful about Priya.

Parenting never ended. Your kids turned twenty, then thirty, even forty, and they never stopped needing you. It was terrible and wonderful. Even if Priya didn't tell me what was wrong with her, at least she wanted to be around me when she was sad. I took some heart in that. I might not be the kind of mother who knew how to talk to my daughter about her boyfriend problems, but at least she still thought of my house—and me—as her refuge, her safe place. That was something. I had not thought of my own mother this way. Deanna did not think of her parents this way. I had been a good mother—a loving mother. Though, having your depressed, unmarried, adult daughter, show up midweek and drink beers on your couch at one in the morning was not exactly a marker of successful mothering. My mother was hard on me, but it had given me a kind of toughness, a resilience, that my own daughter did not seem to have.

I sighed. There was no winning as a mother. Whatever kind of mother you were, there were costs. If you were harsh, your kids resented you and avoided visiting you. If you were soft, they had trouble functioning in the world as adults. I suppose all you could do was act in the ways that came naturally to you and just hope for the best.

"Lata, look who just walked in the door." Deanna nudged me. "Your soon-to-be date." She winked at me.

Oh God. Len. He was dressed in khaki slacks, a striped button-down shirt, and sneakers. His curly gray hair poked out of the sides of a blue baseball cap with the words *Montreal Jazz Festival '88*. His glasses sat low on his nose. A computer bag hung off one shoulder. He walked toward the reference desk and looked expectantly behind the counter. At the moment, it was empty, since Jared was at an "appointment" and both Deanna and I were shelving at the other end of the room.

"I'm going to cancel," I said to Deanna. "I shouldn't have said yes. It was a mistake."

"What do you mean 'a mistake'? You don't like him?" Deanna asked.

"No, it's not that. He's a nice man."

"Okay, so you're not attracted to him. You think he's ugly?"

"What? No! He's not ugly! He has a kind face. A smiling face. I like his eyes."

"Okay, so you hate jazz or something? You don't want to go see this boring quartet? I mean, that I understand. But just go to dinner, then."

"No, it's not that. From the little I've listened to, I like jazz. I really like it."

"Then I don't see the problem here. It's just one date. What's the big deal?"

Of course she didn't think it was a big deal. She had probably been dating since she was in middle school. Isn't that what girls in this country did? I remembered when Priya came home one day in the sixth grade in tears because her friend Madeline had a boyfriend, and because of this Madeline had stopped sitting with Priya at lunch. I'd hugged my daughter, wiped away her tears, while panicking on the inside. A boyfriend in sixth grade? I couldn't understand it. Of course, I never expected Priya to have an arranged marriage like me. I did not want that for her. But dating at age twelve? I didn't want that for her either. Deanna too had probably had her first boyfriend at the age of twelve. Maybe even earlier. She had no idea what was going on inside of me. She didn't seem to understand that I'd never had a "date" in my entire life. So for me, it was a big deal. A very big deal.

I got married when I was twenty, in 1972, the year after I graduated from an all-girls college. Perhaps the closest experience I'd ever had to a date was when my classmate Lalitha's older brother Venkat used to follow me home. He never spoke to me; he just followed me after class, staying a foot or two behind. After a few weeks of Venkat's silent following, I finally confronted him, exclaiming, "Why are you following me?" My boldness had surprised me. I'd always assumed that if words were spoken between us, he would initiate them. He ran his hand sheepishly over his face, grazing the few sprouts of hair on his upper lip and chin, sprouts that hadn't quite attained the status of a full-fledged moustache and beard, but couldn't be dismissed as the mere fuzz of a boy either. He shrugged, and said he followed me because he liked my hair.

In those days, my hair attracted attention. It was much like Priya's hair now—thick, straight, and shiny. And back then, my hair fell to my hips. But even though I'd encountered reactions to my hair before, I hadn't known what to say in response to Venkat's compliment. So I said nothing and continued on my way. But the rest of the way home, I'd felt a prickling heat in my back. The next day, I'd waited impatiently for class to end. But when I began my trek home, there was no lumbering shadow behind me. Venkat wasn't there. He never returned to follow me home, and I was too embarrassed to ask Lalitha about her brother. But the point was this: Those silent walks home with Venkat were the only "dates" I'd ever had before I got married. And they weren't even dates at all.

As for my first date with Suresh, if it could even be called such a thing, it hadn't taken place until after our wedding. We barely spoke the few times we'd seen each other in the crowded living rooms of our parents' houses before our marriage. Our wedding night—could that be called a date? It had been embarrassing—terrifying, even—disrobing in front of a man I barely knew. But then, Suresh had been kind. He turned off the light and said, "It has been a long and tiring day. Let's just lie down and sleep." It had been such a relief, really. I started to cry, my shoulders shaking in the dark as I lay next to him, my new husband. But he didn't mock me. It was a rare moment of him doing and saying exactly the right thing. He cupped my shoulder with a single palm, and the weight of his hand was comforting without being pressuring. And somehow, at that moment, it gave me hope that one day, the dread feeling of being married might go away. The next day, he took me to a movie. A very famous film. Sharing a bag of spicy popcorn, we were tentative and overly courteous—careful not to bump our hands together in the bag, to let the other have the first pick at the darkest, most flavorful, chili-seasoned kernels. But as the movie went on, we became more comfortable—bumping greasy palms and knuckles in the bag, drinking from the same straw.

But even if it had been new for us, could such an outing between a husband and wife be called a date? When you both knew the outcome: that you'd go home to your life together, sleep together, wake up the next day, and the next, and the next, and the next.

Unless I found a way to cancel this date with Len, I'd be

picked up at my apartment by a man I barely knew, a man I'd exchanged perhaps ten sentences with. The irony, of course, was that I already knew him better than I'd known Suresh when I married him. For Len and I had actually conversed—just the two of us, uninterrupted by overbearing mothers and fathers and aunts and uncles and siblings. And Len had already given me a gift.

But here was the crucial difference. While my dates with Suresh had no real purpose other than to go about our life together, the purpose of this outing with Len was a mystery to me. What was the point of all this? How would this end? This kind of date was like taking an exam for a class I'd never attended. I didn't know where to start.

"Look, Deanna, it's a big deal to me, okay? And anyway, I can't go on a date when my depressed daughter is at my apartment."

"Don't be silly. Your daughter might not even stay the week. And who cares if she does? You're not doing anything wrong. You're going to a concert. Not an orgy. Get a grip, Lata." Deanna pushed me toward the reference desk.

Bossy, sharp-tongued girl. Well, she could just forget that Tupperware of lemon rice.

"Good morning, Professor Greenberg, can I help you?" I used the most formal speaking voice I could manage. Formality was the tactic I'd decided upon during the walk to the reference desk. It would put me in the right frame of mind. None of this "Len" business.

If he was confused by my formal manner, he didn't let it show. He adjusted the brim of his cap and smiled. "Got some books to return here." He handed me two books, and I busied myself with the scanner, while scanning my brain for the right words to say.

Maybe I could just blame Priya for having to cancel. I could tell him my daughter was visiting, that she was sick, that I had to take care of her, and that's why I couldn't go. No—that was too inauspicious. You should never lie about your child being sick. No matter how expedient.

"Actually, returning books is not really why I'm here. The truth is, I have something for you." He dug his hand into his computer bag and pulled out a CD case. "Since we're going to see the Douglass Quartet on Saturday, I thought maybe you'd like to hear them before we go. I should warn you, though, it's all instrumental. No vocal greats on this CD." He spoke excitedly, gesturing with his hands, waving the CD case.

I would tell him the truth. That I couldn't accept this CD, because I wouldn't be going with him to the concert on Saturday. Because I didn't know how to date. Because I was too old to learn how. Because I hated this nervous, sick feeling that had been bubbling in my stomach ever since he gave me that first CD, even though I loved that first CD and had listened to it so many times I was sure it was going to get a hole in it. Because . . . Because . . .

Priya! I dropped the scanner.

Priya was at the far end of the room, pushing through the entrance turnstile, dressed in jeans and a yellow sleeveless shirt. My eyes widened, disbelieving. What on earth was she doing here? A part of me was relieved that she was awake and wearing something other than pajamas at noon. But this was the worst moment for her to be here. What if she saw Len? What if she heard him talking about our date?

Len paused his spirited chattering, a concerned look on his face. "Lata, are you okay?"

"What? Yes, I . . . thanks for the CD." I grabbed the case from his outstretched hand and shoved it in my purse before Priya got any closer. "Maybe we can talk about the concert another day," I whispered, my voice barely audible.

"Okay, sure. I get it, you're working," Len whispered back, leaning in closer. "But why are we whispering all of a sudden?"

Oh God, he was leaning in so close that our heads were not even a foot apart. And there was Priya standing right behind him.

"Mom?" She sounded agitated. Though maybe I was mishearing the agitation part because I was agitated. My heart was beating so fast. I had to calm down. I wasn't robbing a bank. I wasn't doing anything wrong. To Priya's eyes, I was having an innocent conversation with a library patron.

"Priya, what a nice surprise. This is my daughter, Priya. This is Len—I mean, Professor Greenberg. He's just returning something to the library." I spoke quickly.

Len smiled and extended his hand to Priya. "Very nice to meet you."

"Hello." She shook it politely, and then stared at me, as if awaiting further explanation.

"Well, thanks for returning your items on time, Professor Greenberg." I returned to my overly formal librarian voice. I picked up the scanner, hoping it would make me look more official. I didn't know what else to do. The formality sounded ridiculous to my own ears. He was going to think I was a crazy woman.

If he was offended or confused, he didn't show it. "I'd better be heading off to my class. I hope you like the CD, Lata."

"What CD?" Priya asked as soon as Len left.

"Oh, just some jazz CD he wanted me to hear." It wasn't exactly a lie, even if I didn't mention that he'd made the CD specifically for me, that he'd made it in preparation for our Saturday date. A date I still hadn't canceled! Tomorrow—I'd do it tomorrow. If he came in.

"He seemed awfully concerned about you liking it. What's his deal?"

"He's a jazz history professor, so he wants everyone to like this kind of music." I waved my hands, as if it was all a big nothing. Priya frowned, looking unconvinced.

Luckily, Deanna was making her way toward us with an empty book cart in tow. "Oh good, Deanna's here. I've been wanting you to meet her."

"Deanna," I called. "This is my daughter, Priya—the one I've been telling you about. And, Priya, this is my colleague Deanna. She's one of the youngest PhD students in the whole university." I prayed that Deanna would, in this instance, have some measure of tact and sense, and refrain from saying anything about Len in front of Priya. She knew that I didn't want Priya to know. I squeezed the scanner in my hand. My knuckles were starting to turn white.

"Hey." Deanna nodded.

Priya eyed Deanna, her expression growing more amused at the sight of Deanna's shredded leggings, pierced eyebrow, and neck tattoo. "Nice tattoo. Hibiscus?" Priya said.

"No. Lotus."

While the two girls discussed the specifics of Deanna's body mutilation, I relaxed my grip on the scanner and sat down. Deanna would not say anything. If she was going to say something about Len to Priya, she would have said it already. She would have asked me right in front of Priya's face if I had canceled my date with him. I exhaled slowly.

Deanna was my friend. I could count on her—well, sometimes. As for Priya, I still had no idea what she was doing here.

"Priya," I interrupted. "You never told me why you were here. Is something wrong?"

"No. I wanted to see where you work. I thought I'd surprise you and take you to lunch."

"Oh, lunch," I said, relieved. She just wanted to have lunch with me. It was a sweet gesture. Why was I always doubting these girls? Priya, Deanna. I really ought to give them more credit.

"Lunch would be nice. Deanna, why don't you come with us?"

Our waiter hadn't returned since taking our lunch order. We'd been waiting twenty minutes for a simple order: three egg rolls, vegetable lo mein, and broccoli stir-fry.

The restaurant was filled with the sounds of the lunch crowd: forks hitting plates, groups in casual business attire talking, waiters listing lunch specials. A group of customers two tables away had been seated after us, but somehow they'd already received steaming plates of food. At the sight of their dishes, Priya burst.

"We should have gone someplace else." She tapped a chopstick on the table.

"You said you wanted Chinese. This is the closest place—and it's the best," Deanna said.

Deanna's voice was very calm, which struck me as strange. Usually, any inconvenience would send her into a fury. But Priya's impatience was having the reverse effect on Deanna. With someone else occupying her usual furious role, Deanna had apparently decided to play the opposite. This relaxed, imposter-Deanna reached leisurely for the teapot in the center of the table and poured herself a cup. Priya glared at her slow, contented movements.

"What's the point of being the best if people never actually get to taste their food?" Priya continued to tap her chopstick on the table. Deanna rolled her eyes and sipped her tea.

Maybe inviting Deanna to lunch was a bad idea. I had figured with her there, Priya would be less likely to ask questions about Len. And that at least was true. Priya seemed to have forgotten all about him, thank God.

But I'd also hoped that the two girls would hit it off, prompting Priya to talk more freely about what was bothering her, why she was still at my apartment, and when she was planning to go back to work. I had hoped it would be as it was when Priya was younger—when she and her giggling girlfriends forgot where they were and whose parents were around and let unintended details fly out of their mouths without even realizing. That's how I had learned that Priya, at age seventeen, had gone to a Madonna concert in Dallas the same weekend she told me she was at a debate tournament in Austin. She and her high school friends had spoken of their weekend adventure months later at our kitchen table, forgetting I was a few feet away, at the stove. I pulled crispy pakoras out of oil while silently screaming panicked questions: Where had they stayed? Had boys gone with them? Was alcohol involved? But I never said anything to Priya. To say something would have made her more watchful the next time. I just lingered silently in the background, letting the giggling girls drop pieces of information like colorful mosaic tiles that I could collect and arrange around the picture of Priya I already had. In my own way, I was trying to know her. Nikesh was easier in that way. He always told me more about his life than Priya did—not everything, of course, but more. At least, he used to, when he was younger. Then one day, he stopped. He got married without telling me, without inviting me—a fact that hurt me, shamed me, every time I remembered it.

I looked at Priya and then at Deanna, sitting on either side of me. No hint of a giggle from either of them, not even a smile. Both were no doubt cursing me for having forced them together. I wondered if Len had any daughters. Or sons. Had he been married before? I pictured him with a tall, blond-haired woman. A woman who, unlike me, walked around the front yard wearing shorts on hot days. I imagined this blond-woman-in-shorts kissing Len on the mouth as he entered the house.

"I think your chopstick is starting to splinter," Deanna said, placing a hand over Priya's tapping stick.

Priya glared at the slim white hand with chipped purple polish and heavy metal rings that prevented her from further tapping.

"If it was bothering you, all you had to do was ask me to stop," Priya said.

I sighed with resignation. Priya wasn't a giggling high school girl anymore. And Deanna wasn't even her friend.

It was stupid to think I'd learn anything this way.

13

NIKESH

"Knock, knock, sugar." Sheila's sizable frame filled the doorway. "Got something for you."

Sheila had been my secretary ever since I started at Tiller, but she'd been at the firm long before that—at least twenty years. She was in her late fifties and boasted a thick Long Island accent. Today, she wore bright green pants and a matching shirt. Thick earrings in the shape of isosceles triangles dangled from her ears. Chunky bracelets clinked as she trudged to my desk holding a large interoffice mail envelope.

By and large, Tiller was a cold, clinical place. One of Manhattan's oldest and most prestigious white-shoe firms, it prided itself on a stuffy inscrutability. If you stick your nose in the air and sniff hard enough, you can practically smell the backroom cigar smoke of halcyon days. I could never figure out how Sheila, with her garish outfits, thick accent, and irreverent laugh, had ever made it through Tiller's censorious hiring committee. But thank goodness she had.

"You're a sight for sore eyes, Sheila. A blinding sight in that outfit too." I took the envelope from her hand and shielded my eyes, teasingly.

Sheila did a theatrical half twirl. "Gotta liven this place up with color. All the gray and black suits make me feel like I work at a funeral home."

I laughed and tossed the envelope on top of a stack, intending to open it later. I had a million things to do before lunch. Two unfinished memos. A dozen unanswered emails. A call to a pro bono client challenging a denial of disability benefits.

"Maybe you should open that envelope first," Sheila said.

I stared at her, confused. It wasn't like her to make recommendations about my work priorities for the day.

"Denise came by and gave it to me. I asked her if she wanted to give it to you herself, but she said she had a meeting to run to." Sheila raised her eyebrows meaningfully. "Is everything okay?"

Despite Sheila's friendly way with me, I could never get a read on her feelings about Denise. She was perfectly cordial and professional with Denise, of course. You didn't survive as an administrative assistant at Tiller for two decades by divulging your true sentiments about the partners. Sheila was way too smart to voice her opinion about Denise—or anyone else, for that matter. But I suspected that she, like everyone else, had been caught off guard by our sudden relationship.

I shrugged and avoided her wide, concerned eyes. "The baby's been going through some tough toddler-transitioning recently, but we're managing."

"Oh, that little bundle!" Sheila, perceptive woman that she was, redirected the conversation to less bumpy territory. She reached toward the bookshelf and picked up a framed picture of Alok—one of him grinning on a park swing. He had four teeth when that picture was taken: two on the bottom, and two on the top, like vampire fangs. It was my favorite picture.

"I want you to bring him by again so I can squeeze those

sweet cheeks. Like his daddy, this one." She winked, put the picture back, and floated out of the room, closing the door behind her.

If only every person in my life could be deflected as easily as Sheila. I eyed the interoffice envelope with suspicion. Why didn't Denise just drop the damn thing off herself?

I groaned and opened the flap. It was hard to believe it now, but once upon a time, an interoffice mail envelope from Denise was something to look forward to—inside jokes, coded raunchy messages. What were the chances that this envelope contained a naughty haiku? The chances were zero. Less than zero. I pulled out a single slip of paper with Denise's neat, even handwriting: *Have you told them?*

Were the theatrics necessary? She couldn't have sent a fucking text instead? I crumpled the paper and threw it into the trash bin. It missed, landing on the dark gray carpet, just a foot from where Sheila had been standing a few seconds before. I groaned again, and let my forehead fall against the desk.

It wasn't as if I hadn't tried to tell my parents. Just a few days ago, I called Dad with every intention of telling him. But then, he'd sounded so strange, a little unhinged even. I was relieved at first to discover it was alcohol at work and not senility. But the relief was short-lived: Dad wasn't a drinker. Growing up, I'd seen him come home from work cross and dejected, but he never reached for so much as a beer to take the edge off. At most, he would reach for the remote. Or a bag of Doritos. But not alcohol. Dad said it was about that Mallika woman not calling him back—that led him to get drunk.

Maybe this whole post-divorce loneliness was getting the better of him. I felt a little guilty, maybe even a little responsible. Had I been too encouraging about this online dating stuff? Honestly, I never saw the harm in it. And contrary to Priya's frequent accusations, it wasn't because I was some selfish jerk who thought my parents' antics were some big joke designed to

amuse me. Not even close. Watching them divvy up photo al-
bums and bath towels, helping Mom seal boxes with packing
tape, carrying out one half of a married life into a rented
U-Haul—there hadn't been anything funny about that. Watching Dad putter about aimlessly in the yard as Mom moved her
stuff out, not offering any help, of course, but unwilling (or
unable) to leave the scene—there hadn't been anything funny
about that. About any of it. Sure, I didn't necessarily understand
why they would bother getting divorced at their age. But then
again, they never seemed to make each other very happy. My
entire childhood, I would wonder why my parents never kissed
each other or hugged each other or teased each other or lit up
around each other like some of my friends' parents did. I'd always chalked it up to cultural differences—some generational
Indian aversion to physical displays of affection. But deep down,
I knew it was more than that.

And then later on, when the divorce dust had settled a bit,
they even seemed to grow into their separate lives. Like when
Mom called during a midday break from the library, a tinge of
excitement in her voice as she described how campus security
had stopped a homeless man from leaving the library with four
books stuffed under his shirt. A liveliness I hadn't heard from
her in years. Or when Dad called me with tales of dates-gone-
south (the "steak-eating vegetarian," the "thinly disguised Com-
munist," all those women who "fooled him with an airbrushed
picture") from a strip mall in Dallas or Chattanooga or Baton
Rouge. This Dad-turned-Kerouac traversing the countryside in
search of love. It all made me think that divorce had been the
right decision for them after all.

Priya could kick and scream all she wanted, but that wouldn't
stop me from thinking there was something admirable about
what they were doing—this trying to start over thing. Something brave about the two of them trying to cobble together new
lives while other Indian people their age were settling into

creaky lawn chairs with chilled mango juice in hand, reconciling themselves to deadened marriages and eventless retirements. Because as far as I could tell, my parents had gotten a raw deal. They'd hit their twenties at precisely the wrong moment in India. A generation too early. Before the Infosyses and Intels and call centers dotted the landscape. Before an educated, enterprising person didn't have to travel ten thousand miles away, leaving everything they knew in search of opportunity. Before economic prosperity triggered the social and cultural evolution that would morph the concept of arranged marriage into a convenient kind of dating service provided by one's parents. Like Mom's cousin Padma, twenty years her junior. She'd met her husband, Ashok, through her parents, but imposed a cadre of conditions before agreeing to marry. They'd gone on lots of dates to figure out if they liked each other's smells and voices and tastes in movies. And they did. She was a manager at Dell; he was a VP at Cisco. As a couple, they emanated happy vibes.

But Mom and Dad didn't get the chance to do that. They'd seen each other twice maybe, across a crowded room filled with family members who were all banking on the match; so really, what kind of a choice did they have? What could they even base their decision on? If the boy didn't have a cleft lip or the girl's skin wasn't as dark as a car tire, did they have cause to object? Okay, so maybe it was unfair to generalize this way. There were certainly happy people of their ilk, after all. And maybe Mom and Dad didn't even see it in those stark terms—that they got screwed. But I did. And if they were finally trying to find a little happiness, to make up for some lost time, and in the process breaking, at last, the bonds of duty and obligation and the keeping up of appearances that had served them so sorrily up until this point, who was I to resent them for it? Why should Priya or anyone judge them for it? It sure as hell sounded like a good idea to me.

Or it did anyway.

Now I was starting to feel less sure. What if all this change was too much for Dad? What if it had all come too late in the game for him? He was getting on in years, almost sixty now. And his age was starting to show. The last time I visited Clayborn, he asked me to bring down a suitcase from the attic because his back was acting up. On the same trip, we had to refit his glasses with anti-glare lenses because he couldn't see while driving at night. Bit by bit, his faculties were declining. And where was Priya in all of this? Why wasn't she helping? What was the point of having a sibling that lived two hours from your parents if she couldn't be bothered to tend to them?

Teeth gritted, I dialed Priya's number. Two rings and straight to voicemail. Even her voicemail prompt conveyed irritation; it was the auditory equivalent of an eye roll. Sometimes, I found it hard to believe that we ever used to be close. And it certainly didn't help that the last time Priya visited us in Brooklyn, she'd been a bitch to Denise. There was no sugarcoating it. Priya pounced on any chance to make uncomfortable references to the age difference between Denise and me. She'd even asked about Elena in front of Denise. And she hadn't seemed all that interested in playing with Alok either—in getting to know her only nephew. Before Priya had arrived for that visit, I'd planned to confide in her about the whole fake-marriage business. But about four hours in, all I could think about was finding any excuse to drop her ass off at LaGuardia.

A beep signaled the end of Priya's voice message prompt. I hung up, disgusted.

Well, that still left Mom. She lived a few miles away from Dad. Geographically, she was in the best position to check on him. But what was I going to tell her? *Dad is really depressed because you left him and his internet dates aren't working out. Could you go check on him?*

Defeated, I tossed the phone on the desk and turned to face the window. From my perch on the fortieth floor, I could see the helicopters delivering important people to the roofs of downtown buildings. The East River glittered in the distance—Brooklyn just beyond.

How had it come to this? Dad had spent over three decades of his life caring (in his flawed way) for a wife and a daughter, neither of whom seemed to care all that much about what happened to him. He had me too, but I lived fifteen hundred miles away. What could I do for him? It was impossible not to feel for the guy. Had he really screwed up so badly? What would I do if, three decades from now, I discovered I'd pursued the wrong career, married the wrong woman, alienated my kid?

The scary thing was it wasn't that hard to imagine. Because the wrong life wasn't just one big fork in the road that you chose incorrectly. Well, unless you killed a person or something. For most people, though, it wasn't one bad decision or blunder. It was a series of choices, a bunch of opportunities to change course that you didn't take—that added up to the wrong life. That turned you into a sixty-year-old getting drunk alone in your empty house with too many regrets and no one around who cared to check on you. Dad was a cautionary tale. A road map of what not to do.

I stood and walked toward the photo of Alok at the park. I picked it up, brought it to my face, and kissed his forehead. After setting it down, I bent over and picked up the crumpled note from Denise. I uncrumpled it, folded it into a small square, and slipped it in my pocket.

All I needed was a little more time. I'd figure out a way to make everyone happy.

There were more dads than usual at the park today. Wedged in between the Tibetan and Caribbean nannies. Hipster dads, the bulk of them, decked out in their skinny jeans, checked shirts, and impressive facial hair—that calibrated combination of rumpled chic.

I pushed Alok on the baby swing and watched them. The bearded hipster dad crouching at the base of a slide, coaxing his tutu-clad daughter to let go of the plastic rails. The mustachioed hipster dad coaxing his attractive mixed-race toddler to drink the "wa-wa" from a sippy cup. The hipster dad with silver sideburns peeking out from his fedora pushing his twins in a double-wide City Mini stroller toward the two empty swings next to Alok's. He nodded at me in a noncommittal-dad-greeting style. I nodded back and pretended not to watch as he extracted his twins from their stroller harnesses and wedged them into the swings. Girls? Boys? One of each? It was hard to tell, as they were dressed in identical onesies patterned with bicycles. What was this guy doing here at four in the afternoon? What were all these dads doing here? Didn't any of them work for a living?

My explanation for being here at this hour was to avoid Denise. I knocked off work early in case she decided to follow her passive-aggressive note with a drop-in. Our nanny, Yvette, had been surprised to see me at three, but she didn't complain when I sent her out the door three hours early with the same two hundred dollars she got every day.

I hadn't been to the park with Alok in a while—not for over a week. Yvette brought him here nearly every weekday. I brought him on the weekends. And Denise almost never did, not because she had philosophical objections to parks, but because she had philosophical objections to making forced conversation with other moms. Though in fairness, park dads were probably an easier lot than competitive park moms. Dads did more looking at phones than talking. And even the chatty ones were usually just looking to commiserate about their lack of sleep.

"So how old's yours?" the silver-sideburned dad nodded at Alok.

"Almost a year. Yours?" I nodded in the direction of the twins in bicycle onesies.

"Eight months. Twin boys. They just started sleeping for a six-hour stretch."

"Nice. Twins must be tough on the sleep."

"Harder on my wife than me. She's the one who has to breast-feed them both. We had to get extra breast milk from a woman we found on a parenting blog."

"We did that too. It weirded me out at first, a stranger's breast milk. But they say it's better than formula."

"Definitely better than formula."

At these moments, I felt confident that the gulf between my father and me was wider than an ocean. The idea of my dad pushing a baby me on a swing while chatting to a stranger about Mom's breast milk challenges was completely unimaginable. It was absurd. That entire generation of Indian men—and the non-Indian ones too, probably—had left all the inconvenient details of parenting to their wives. In my profession, we had words for people who chose to ignore all the inconvenient de-tails. Malpractice. Negligence. We were a generation of boys raised by a generation of negligent fathers. And now we were fathers, trying hard not to be like our fathers.

I brought Alok's swing to a halt with both hands, tilted it back, kissed him on the forehead, and then pushed him even higher. Alok squealed with delight and clapped his hands.

"So what do you do?" I asked.

"You're looking at it."

"Full-time dad, huh?"

"Yup. What about you?"

"Corporate lawyer playing hooky for the afternoon."

He nodded. "My wife's a lawyer. She's a partner at Miller Wakeman. After the twins came, we decided one of us needed to be home, and she liked her job way more than I did, so it's me. Stay-at-home dad. I love it. So much better than being a financial analyst. Maybe one day I'll finally start that novel in my head." He chuckled and brought a hand to each of his son's swings, pushing them in tandem.

I nodded. "Sounds like a good life."

When Alok was born and Denise's twelve-week maternity leave was nearing its end, I'd flirted with the idea of quitting too. The thought of leaving my tiny boy with a total stranger for ten-plus hours a day seemed like lunacy. (That was before we met Yvette and could see how loving and patient she was with Alok—even more than I was, at times.) In those early weeks, during the wee hours of the morning while Denise caught up on sleep, I'd rock a crying Alok back and forth and feed him bottles of procured breast milk, mulling my options. I could quit, I'd tell myself. Denise made more than enough money to support us. She loved her work. I pretty much hated it. So why not? I could take care of Alok and figure out what to do next with my life. On one of those sleepless nights, I'd held Alok close to my chest and made a resolution: I'd ask Denise to marry me. I couldn't ask her to support me financially unless we were actually married. So why not do it? Why not commit to being a family all the way and get married?

It wasn't as if we'd never talked about marriage before. Of course we had. When she was pregnant, I'd brought the subject up—more than once. I'd asked her whether she thought we should be married before Alok was born. And Denise's response was always that we didn't need to rush into anything, that she didn't want us to get married out of some feeling of obligation. She wasn't aching for the title of wife, she'd said, because she'd had it before, and it had blown up in her face (aka hedge fund ex-husband cheats with twentysomething intern).

Nine months ago, I bought an engagement ring. I'd planned to ask Denise on her birthday, two days before Christmas. But then, I didn't. Doubts crept in. We'd dated for such a short time before Alok was born. One minute we were getting to know each other, having late-night sex in the office, falling in love, and then suddenly we were parents, fighting over bath times and feedings and nanny hand offs. Maybe a couple needed more time together before having a baby—to build up a surfeit of goodwill to carry them through the sleepless, sexless, panicked first months of parenthood.

And then, buried deeper under those doubts were other ones, ones I tried harder to avoid thinking about. Like, had Denise's pregnancy really been an accident? Denise was not a person who got sloppy, who made stupid mistakes. But as soon as such thoughts popped into my head, I'd berate myself for thinking them. What the fuck did it matter if it was an accident or not? Alok was here now, and I loved him, and I couldn't imagine life without him. And who did I think I was anyway? An NBA player? What was so great about my sperm that a woman would plot and plan to entrap me? The fucking hubris of it.

As Christmas passed into New Year's, I'd get up in the middle of the night, open the velvet box, and stare at that three-carat Art Deco ring, trying to will all the niggling doubts out of my head. I didn't want to ask her out of a sense of obligation. I wanted to be sure.

I'd been sure once before.

And look how that had turned out. Elena left me. To marry someone else.

Denise's ring was buried at the back of my sock drawer now. And as for my being a stay-and-home dad, I couldn't take the plunge there either. Being the negligible associate to Denise's rock star partner already made me feel small. I hated the smirks and smug looks of some of the men at Tiller. Even though I knew I shouldn't give a shit about what they thought, I wasn't sure my self-esteem could handle being totally financially de-pendent on Denise. To say nothing of my parents' disappoint-ment if their Harvard-educated son became a househusband. Honestly, I wasn't sure what would have upset my parents more.

Finding out that Alok had unmarried parents or that I'd quit my job to parent full-time. Indian men did not do that sort of thing. It would be fine if my sister did that. But not me. Not ever.

I watched the silver-sideburned stay-at-home dad pushing his twin boys, content with his life choices. I envied him.

My pocket began to buzz. I pulled out my phone and a text from Denise popped up. *Did you tell them yet?*

Jesus Christ. Why was she so obsessed with my telling them? She only saw my parents once a year. Twice, tops. She barely knew them. Why was she so fixated on me correcting the record? No—it wasn't just the lying to my parents that could be bothering her this much. I was starting to think she was so worked up about it because I'd never asked her to marry me. That even if she said she didn't need the title of wife, the lie to my parents about us eloping had triggered something in her. Now I was the man who hadn't asked her to marry him and, to add insult to injury, was pretending to his parents that he had.

I sighed, closed my eyes, and tilted my face toward the warmth of the sun.

I couldn't hide at the park forever. I nodded at the silver-sideburned dad. "Well, better head home and get this guy a snack. See you around."

I scooped Alok up by his armpits, lifted him out of the swing, and braced myself for the wails.

14

SURESH

The game room had a new, full-time occupant. And a new Xbox, which had quickly colonized the television.

Mallika's eight-year-old son, Bijesh, whom everyone called Bobby, did not leave home without his Xbox. He seemed to spend inordinate amounts of time playing a game where two muscled men punched each other until one crumpled into a bloody mess.

What a relief that my kids came of age before these times. As far as I could remember, they only played nonviolent video games showcasing two mustachioed Italian immigrants who liked to jump over multicolored mushrooms. Though I had to admit: It was a nice change to hear the sounds of laughter and video game pinging coming from the game room, instead of the usual silence.

"Bobby, you're still playing this? It's lunchtime, and you haven't even brushed your teeth! Please go now," Mallika scolded from the doorway.

"Five more minutes." His eyes didn't leave the screen. He was in the process of kicking a man in the face repeatedly, having brought him to his knees a moment or so before. Blood gushed from the man's neck. *Thud, thud, thud.* His neck kept snapping backward. How was he still alive? This game was at odds with the laws of human physiology.

"No. Right now," Mallika said. Grumbling, Bobby stopped pummeling the bleeding man, put down the game controller, and stomped sullenly out of the room. "Good boy." As he walked by, she ran her fingers through his hair, straightening the wavy locks into something less disorderly.

"Sorry about that." She smiled apologetically at me. "He's usually more cooperative. I think he's just being difficult because . . . well, you know." She looked down at her hands.

Over the past two days, since Mallika and Bobby had arrived on my doorstep (or driveway, rather), I'd learned a great many things about Mallika's life:

(1) She had a son (obviously).
(2) Her husband, Ajay, was not, in fact, named Ajay. His name was Praveen.
(3) Ajay/Praveen was not, in fact, dead.
(4) She and Praveen were not, in fact, divorced. They were, however, separated.
(5) They separated months ago because Praveen, some kind of investment-consultant character, had squandered their life savings in a series of shady investments and dealings, which not only landed them knee-deep in debt, but had also caught the attention of the authorities. Praveen was presently in jail for insider trading.
(6) Over the past few months, creditors had been coming after everything they owned. The only thing keeping Mallika afloat was her job with the octogenarian ophthalmologist, who had recently announced his retirement.

(7) Two weeks ago, she received a notice from the bank that their house (on which Praveen had secretly taken out multiple mortgages) was being foreclosed on.

(8) But everything else she had ever told me was, according to her, one hundred percent true. For instance, Thai food really was her favorite.

She had told me all of this in hushed tones after tucking Bobby into the bed in Nikesh's old room. Given a choice of rooms, Bobby had immediately opted for Nikesh's, with its navy blue bedspread, basketball trophies lining the shelves, and a large yellowing poster of some group called Nirvana (though not a single member looked Buddhist to me). Mallika and I were sitting on the living room sofa. Two cups of tea cooled on the coffee table—though under the circumstances, maybe the Johnnie Walker would have been the better option.

"But why did you come here?"

"We had nowhere else to go. You see, after Praveen went to jail, our friends started avoiding me. I have no family here. I have . . . no one. Except for Bobby. I packed up my car, buckled Bobby in, told him we were going on a trip, and when I sat in the driver's seat, I realized I didn't have any idea where to go. I reached in my purse for my phone, thinking I'd search for a hotel. But do you know what hotels cost in summer travel season? And then I grabbed the paper with the directions to your house, from the last time . . . when I canceled our plans. And before I knew what I was doing, I started to drive here. You were so nice. I'm so sorry I didn't return your calls. I'm so embarrassed." She started to cry, her face in her hands.

I scratched my head. I didn't know what to say. She was here because she had nowhere else to go. She was here because she was desperate and out of money. What could I say to this? I wasn't a charity service. And what about this felon husband? What if they let him out tomorrow, was he going to land on my doorstep too? Who knew if any of this was even true? She had turned out to be a liar, just like all the others. My chest hurt. Could a heart literally sink? I reached beneath the coffee table for a box of Kleenex and handed it to her.

"Thanks." She grabbed one, blew her nose, then apologized. She grabbed another and wiped her eyes; black smudges of eyeliner dotted the crumpled tissue. She leaned against the arm of the sofa. Her hair had fallen out of its clip; it cascaded in loose waves around her. Her cheeks were full of color, her eyes more luminous from the tears.

Well, maybe there was no need to decide anything for the moment. She and Bobby had been tired from the long drive. After an evening of whisky drinking, I hadn't been at my clearest thinking state either. Decisions could be made later, couldn't they?

And now here we were, days later, and decisions still hadn't been made. At some point, I'd have to ask the hard questions: How long do you intend to stay? Do you have any feelings for me, or was your sole purpose for internet dating to find a man with a good credit history, no felony convictions, and a house you could stay in? Is your husband going to be let out of prison soon, and more important, does he possess a violent temper?

But every time I mustered the resolve to ask, one of a few things would happen. Either Bobby would appear with some request for his mother (Can you take me to McDonald's? Can you take me to Best Buy?). Or Mallika would surprise me with some delicious meal, filling the kitchen with the piquant scents I'd been pining for—simmering ghee and turmeric and mustard seed. Or worse, Mallika would express profuse gratitude for my generosity and burst into tears. Any of these scenarios would render me mute—unable to ask those questions that needed to be asked.

Now that Bobby was brushing his teeth, and Mallika and I were alone in the game room, I decided to try again.

"So, what is your plan . . . you know, for the future?" I looked at the television screen, where the bloody images remained frozen in a paused position, waiting for Bobby's return.

"Plan? Of course, we can't burden you for much longer. You've been so generous to us. I don't know . . . how to thank you." Her face started to crumple.

Oh no. The tears. The tears were coming now.

"No . . . please don't," I begged.

"Mom, why are you crying?" Bobby appeared in the doorway, a spot of toothpaste on his chin.

Great—two for one. The crying and the boy. No chance of asking any questions now.

Mallika's choking sobs began to subside. Bobby eyed me suspiciously, which struck me as grossly unfair.

"No, I'm not crying . . . it's nothing," she said, wiping her eyes quickly. "Suresh Uncle was just telling me a sad story . . . about his friend. I'm fine now. Come on—I'll make us all lunch." She smiled weakly at Bobby, and then at me. "But, Bobby, you have to help me, okay?" Bobby nodded, a solemn look on his face.

I watched the two of them leave the room, her arm around Bobby's thin shoulders. I shook my head. What was I to do? My stomach grumbled. Well, I could have lunch, I suppose.

As I turned to leave the room, I remembered the paused Xbox. I placed my finger on the Off switch, glancing one last time at the images on the screen. A man was on his knees, his head thrown back in grim expectation.

I couldn't help but feel a moment of kinship.

"Watch me touch the bottom of the pool!" Bobby's shout came with an emphatic wave.

Shielding her eyes from the sun, Mallika leaned forward in her plastic chair to wave back. "I'm watching!" As soon as Bobby's shiny head disappeared underwater, she leaned back into the umbrellaed shade with a satisfied sigh.

The pool was crowded this afternoon. All around us, perspiring mothers and even some fathers sat at plastic tables reading magazines and sipping sodas, craning their reddening necks every so often to check for the bobbing heads of their children.

"It's so hot today! Should we go for a swim too?" she asked, fanning her face with her hands. She pulled her hair off her neck and twisted it into a tight bun on top of her head.

"I don't know how to swim." I watched a drop of perspiration work its way down her neck to the V-shaped point of a thin blue dress, where it promptly disappeared, swallowed up by velvety flesh. Other droplets had soaked into the blue fabric, creating a slightly darker shade of blue. To distract myself, I began fanning my face with the *Time* magazine in my hand.

Mallika's dress was not much of a dress. It was more like a shapeless blouse, a loose covering for the floral-printed swimsuit beneath it. Mallika seemed perfectly at ease in her swimming costume. Unlike Lata, who never wore such things. Like me, Lata couldn't swim, but she was so afraid of the water that I could never persuade her to dip more than her toes in. I, at least, would put up a brave front for the kids' sake. During family trips to San Diego or Florida or Hawaii, I'd wade knee-deep into the ocean, yelling after the kids if they went too far ahead of me into the waves, trying to pass off my fear as mere frustration that they were leaving their "poor old father behind." In fact, in all our years together, I only saw Lata wade in the water once, and that was purely by accident. Many years ago, we were in Maui and I'd slept late. By the time I'd walked down to the beach, Lata and the kids had already been there for hours. I scanned the sand for Lata in her sensible linen pants and shirt and large hat to prevent her skin from darkening. But I couldn't see her. Then I spotted the three of them in the water: Lata with her pants folded above her knees, Priya and Nikesh holding on to each of her hands, all of them screeching with laughter as they jumped to escape the encircling sea-foam. Unnoticed, I watched them frolic. Nikesh kicked the water and splashed it with his hands. As Lata turned her head to avoid the droplets, I caught sight of her face lit by the midmorning sun. Her expression was pure, unabashed happiness. I couldn't remember the last time I'd seen her face like that. My heart twisted with envy. Because just once, I wanted to put that look on her face. And then my envy turned to dismay when I realized I could never produce such a look on my wife's face—because it required my absence.

"Really? You don't know how to swim?" Mallika said. "Well, next time we come to the pool, I'll teach you."

She took a sip of water from her bottle. Seeing Bobby's head resurface, she waved at him. Satisfied that he was being properly admired, Bobby dived again into the water.

"You know, I was thinking," she said, chewing her bottom lip, "Bobby has had such a difficult week. Maybe we could take a little trip somewhere to cheer him up. How about Galveston? I can teach you how to swim in the ocean. What do you think?" She pushed her sunglasses to the top of her head and looked hopefully at me.

What did I think? I sat silent for a few moments, struggling to keep half a dozen thoughts from spilling out of my mouth. Like, wasn't it premature to be planning weekend trips when she'd yet to utter a word about what her future life plans were? When we'd yet to go on a proper second date? Didn't her son have to go back to school soon? That boy seemed to survive on sodas and video games. As far as I could tell, it wasn't cheer he lacked so much as a clear understanding of multiplication principles. And how did she propose to pay for this trip with no job, a frozen bank account, and a derelict husband who delivered creditors to her door? Was I to be some kind of hairy-fairy godfather to the two of them, meant to shoulder these burdens?

Here was my chance. I cleared my throat. "Mallika, what are you doing? What are we doing?"

Her eyes widened, growing watery. "You want us to leave, don't you?"

"It's not that I want you to leave. But you aren't even divorced yet. Don't you have to look for a job? And what about Bobby—the boy has to go back to school. And what about me? I don't know if I'm ready to take care of a child again. I don't even know what I am to you. A boyfriend, a friend, a motel? Tell me! After that first date with you in Austin, I've hardly spent a day not thinking of you, but who am I to you? Am I just the man who gives you a place to stay? We haven't spent any time alone together. We haven't so much as brushed hands with each other since that first date. It's like we went from a first date to being amiable relatives living in the same house. I wanted to find a soulmate, not a roommate!"

My chair clattered to the ground. I'd gone from sitting to standing, my frustration getting the better of me. Mallika's eyes followed the chair to the ground. Parents on either side of us stopped sunning themselves and stared.

I knelt down and righted the chair. "I'm sorry. I didn't mean to yell. I'm just confused and frustrated. It never seems to work out with people on the internet." I sat down and put my head in my hands, exhausted.

"Oh, Suresh. You must think I'm awful. I show up after one date, dumping all my problems, my son, my suitcases on your doorstep, without a thought to what this is doing to you. I wouldn't blame you for wanting us to leave. We're a burden on you, and you've been more than generous letting us stay for this long."

"No, it's not that. Look, I don't think you're awful. Truthfully,

I don't know what to think about all this. But I know I like being around you. I know you are beautiful. I'd like to go back to where we left off and see if we can try to be a couple. Do you feel the same about me?"

My voice sounded so small, like a scared boy. The truth was: I *was* scared. I was terrified of what she would say. Because if she didn't feel the same, then what would I do? In that moment, I knew I didn't want her and Bobby to go. As strange as the situation was, I couldn't stand the idea of them leaving me in a silent, empty house. Not again.

Bobby's wet head suddenly sprang between us, shedding droplets onto my magazine. "Mom, did you see me? I touched the bottom of the pool five times in a row. Did you see? I'm thirsty. Can I get a Coke?"

Splendid. As if perfectly on cue, the ever-interrupting-caffeine-consumption-machine.

"Another Coke?" Mallika wrapped Bobby's skinny body in a towel. "Okay, but this is the last one. Come on." Mallika looked at me apologetically, grabbed her purse, and followed Bobby to the soda machine.

I groaned and let my head fall on the table. I was never going to get a straight answer.

15

PRIYA

She was acting strange lately.

Little things, mostly. Like looking at herself in the mirror more. Sometimes, I'd catch her in front of her dresser, her face inches from the glass.

"Mom, what are you doing?" I'd ask.

"Oh, nothing. I'm looking for new wrinkles. Priya, do you think I look *very* old?"

I started to giggle. But then I could see she wasn't joking. She looked serious, concerned even. "Um, no. You look fine."

And she did. She hadn't puffed up in the face and around the middle like most of her friends. She dutifully dyed her hair. I stared at her in the mirror, where she started pulling the skin around her eyes, investigating wrinkles. In truth, there weren't many wrinkles to find. Her skin had retained a dewy, youthful glow. I hadn't looked closely at her in a while, but for a late-fifty-something, she kept herself up pretty well. She was beautiful, actually.

"You know, Mom, you are very well-preserved." I thought

she'd appreciate the sentiment. Instead, she slapped a palm to her forehead.

"Well-preserved? You make me sound like a jar of lemon pickle—salted and shriveled."

I laughed. "What, it was a compliment! Why the sudden concern over your looks? Who are you trying to impress anyway, your stupid goth-girl coworker? Because she's irritating. The shredded clothes. All those piercings. That dumb tattoo. Shouldn't she be over her angsty punk phase now—or whatever it is she's trying to communicate? Trust me. You don't need to impress Deanna with your outfit."

Mom pulled back from the mirror and shoved her hands into her pockets. "I'm not trying to impress anyone."

But the more I watched her, I noticed other examples of her newfound vanity. Like wearing heels to work. Since when did she become a daily heels-wearing woman? Growing up, it was something she rarely did—only on special occasions. And even more disconcerting: the lipstick. She wore lipstick every day now. Every day!

And then, the other day, I walked in on her washing dishes and singing—not a strange thing in itself, of course. I knew Mom liked to sing. Throughout my childhood, I'd hear her low, pretty voice float through the kitchen. I'd come to recognize the familiar strains of Hindi film songs and even some mangled pop songs now and then (Madonna's "Papa Don't Breach" was a favorite misquote of Nikesh's and mine). But when I walked in on her the other day, she was singing something altogether different. It sounded familiar, but I couldn't quite put my finger on it.

"Mom, what are you singing?"

"Oh, this? It's called 'What a Little Moonlight Can Do.' That Billie Holiday woman sings it." She said it nonchalantly, and then went back to singing it. Like it was nothing. Like she'd spent our entire life channeling the great ladies of jazz while washing the dishes.

Since when did my mother start singing Billie Holiday? Since when did she know who Billie Holiday was?

This was all because of that man in the library. That old professor who'd asked her about the CD and grinned like an idiot.

This had to be about him.

As soon as the front door closed, I opened my eyes. Mom had finally left for work.

I looked at the clock: eight-thirty. She wouldn't be back until lunchtime at the earliest. I walked into her bedroom and tried to quell the guilty feeling in my chest. It wasn't *really* snooping when it was your mother's room. It was daughterly concern. I opened the jar of Vaseline on the dresser. I ran a sliver of jelly over my lips, and my eyes fell on the CD player near the edge of the dresser. I pulled the CD out and examined it. It had no markings. I put it back. Someone had burned this CD for her. That library man!

Where was the CD cover? I checked behind the player. No cover. I tugged open the top dresser drawer and felt around, careful not to disturb the neatly folded stacks of nightgowns and underwear. No cover. And then I saw something: a thin plastic case peeking out from behind the jewelry box on the other end of the dresser. Like it was hiding. Or hidden.

I pulled it out and opened it. Inside was a folded sheet with a list of song titles:

"Misty" (Sarah Vaughan)

"A-Tisket, A-Tasket" (Ella Fitzgerald)

I scanned the rest quickly, until I got to the bottom. There it was: "What a Little Moonlight Can Do" (Billie Holiday).

I turned the sheet over. Neatly printed at the bottom corner were two names: *For: Lata Raman. From: Leonard Greenberg.*

Strange how one day you just stop thinking of a place as home. How the place you spent so many formative years of your life transforms in your mind from your home to your parents' house. And then, not even that anymore—it was just Dad's house now.

Parked outside, I considered it with the dispassionate eye of a stranger: two-story, orange brick, identical in all but color to every other house on the block, with a sagging basketball hoop in the driveway that got no play unless Nikesh was in town, and an oversized American flag hanging from the roof—an eyesore that Dad had purchased the day after 9/11, for fear that someone would question the patriotism of the only brown family on the block. Yet even I had to admit, the landscaping in front trounced any competition from the neighbors. Bright flowering bushes hugged the corners of the house; vines crept along the wooden fence in an attractive pattern; the lawn was a soft carpet of emerald green. I hadn't pegged Dad for the plant-nurturing type, but damned if he didn't have a knack for it.

I wasn't sure what I was doing here. Fifteen minutes ago, I'd jumped in my car with the intention of driving back to Austin, preferring my own messy life to feigning ignorance about Mom's secret one. Maybe she wanted me gone. Maybe I was cramping her style, preventing her from seeing her new boyfriend. But halfway to the highway on-ramp, I realized I'd left behind my laptop, and I couldn't quite bring myself to turn back around. So I kept driving and let instinct guide me. And instinct led me here.

Back to our old house. Back to our old neighborhood. Well, Dad's still-neighborhood: Majestic Lake. Named after an artificial lake near the entrance of the subdivision. Not even a lake, really—more like a large pond with a few resident ducks. These days, a large sign loomed above the lake, announcing the construction of a new eighteen-hole golf course for the neighborhood.

In the past half hour, I'd become well acquainted with that

sign, having driven by it a half dozen times, changing and re-changing my mind until I finally parked in front of Dad's house. While making that loop over and over, I puzzled (as I often had) over the street names: Columbus, Magellan, Pizarro, and even Dad's street, De Soto. How bizarre that in this provincial town, where people mostly stayed in the same five-mile radius, where the whole neighborhood was oriented around a two-foot-deep, man-made pond (lake, my ass), the streets were named for European explorers who'd crossed oceans to "dis-cover" the New World. Was it possible that the anonymous christener of streets in Majestic Lake had appreciated the irony of those names? Was it some intentional joke, a giant middle finger to the neighborhood that nobody seemed to notice but me?

The rest of the time I thought about what to say to Dad. Al-most two weeks had passed since we'd spoken actual words to each other in my living room. Though other, indirect forms of communication had continued. A week ago, for example, he'd forwarded me a newspaper article about global warming and carbon emission credits for utilities. Totally random, but thank-fully, on a neutral scientific topic, rather than one of those "Women's Eggs Dry Up by Age 30" articles that he was prone to send me. With the global warming article, he left the email mes-sage box blank. Not even his customary, *I thought you would find this interesting. Love, Dad.* Just blank. I suppose he was testing me, to see if I would break the silence first. Or maybe he just wanted to make sure I was alive. So, in response, I'd forwarded him an article about Halley's Comet. Equally random. Equally blank in message box. And since then, nothing. By coming to the house, I was breaking first. But the man was getting old. He lived alone. And at this moment, he was the only honest parent I had.

Besides, I'd resolved to end things with Ashish, so maybe it was time to bury the hatchet with Dad.

I climbed out of the car and walked toward the flowering bushes in the corner. The closer I got to the house, an incredible smell filled my nose—was it jasmine? It was a scent that reminded me of childhood trips to India, my grandmother tucking a cluster of threaded white jasmine buds into my braided hair. I breathed in deeply, and my shoulders relaxed. I brushed my fingers against a row of mustard-colored blooms. I didn't know what they were called, but they were lovely. For a moment, I wished that I too had a green thumb and could make something beautiful come out of the ground. Maybe Dad would cut me a few, and I could take them home.

"Mom, it's so hot. Can I go swimming again? Please?" A small Indian boy sprinted onto the walkway, waving his thin arms.

I crouched in the bushes, hiding myself from view.

"Bobby, I told you, no." Through the leaves, I could see an Indian woman, a pretty one, neither young nor middle-aged, behind the boy, walking toward the mailbox. She opened it and collected the contents. She was dressed in jeans and a *salwar*-styled top, with beaded embroidery across the neck. She ran one hand through her hair, which hung loose around her shoulders.

I'd never seen this woman before. And who was this kid, this "Bobby"? Were these some relatives visiting Dad? I quickly ran through all the aunts we never saw. Dad had a cousin in the States. She lived far away, though—Milwaukee or Cleveland or somewhere Midwestern. And Dad's cousin was way closer to his age. The woman at the mailbox barely looked forty.

"Mom, it's so hot. See—the ground is burning me." The boy was lying down, writhing against the cement like he was having a seizure.

"Why is the front door open? The AC is on." Dad's voice sailed over the walkway.

I pushed deeper into the bushes, and tried to ignore the woody stems poking my back. My eyes darted to my car; it wasn't parked right in front of the house, thank goodness. It was parked across the street. But what if Dad noticed it? The last thing I wanted was to be found hiding in the bushes by Dad and these other people—whoever the hell they were.

"Why is Bobby on the ground?" Dad asked.

"He wants to go swimming but I told him no. And he still needs to practice his multiplication tables. You can't forget how to do math while you're out of school. Bobby, get up before your clothes get dirty," the mailbox woman said.

"But I want to go," the boy wailed.

Dad knelt down next to the boy. "How about this? I'll take you swimming but only if you practice your multiplication tables."

The boy stopped caterwauling to consider the offer. "Can I do them in the car on the way there? Deal? Okay? Deal."

He leapt up from the ground and ran back into the house, before Dad or the mailbox woman could respond. Dad chuckled. "He's a skillful bargainer, that one. Maybe you should put him on the phone with the bank."

Bank? Whatever Dad meant by that, the mailbox woman certainly got the joke. She started to laugh, a belly-driven laugh that shook her shoulders. A second later, Dad joined her, the both of them yukking it up like two lunatics on the walkway. When they finally calmed down, Dad gently took the mail from the woman's hand and motioned for her to go inside. She smiled at him and went into the house. Still chuckling, he followed her and closed the front door.

I stepped out of the bushes and onto the grass. I dusted off dirt from my jeans and stray leaves from my hair. Through the window, I could still hear the boy's excited voice.

I needn't have worried. Dad hadn't noticed my car at all. His mind was clearly on other things.

~ ❧ ~

A few minutes after Dad pulled out of the driveway, I slipped my key into the front door. Once inside, I paused in the foyer and listened. For all I knew, there was another kid stashed away in here, an older kid who had no interest in joining Dad, the mailbox woman, and that odd Bobby kid at the neighborhood swimming pool. For all I knew, that mailbox woman had brought a whole litter of kids with her.

I ventured in a few more steps and listened. Not a peep. The house felt silent, but in a different way from when it was just Dad living here. The air molecules buzzed with the energy of new occupants. The air even smelled different—traces of ginger and cumin (so the woman cooked here!) and a rose scent I didn't recognize. That woman, who was so obviously not Dad's long-lost cousin. Dad never looked that happy around relatives. Never offered to teach their children multiplication. No, that mailbox woman—that undeniably pretty mailbox woman—was clearly his new girlfriend. Maybe even his new wife. Could that be possible? That he would remarry and not tell us? Mom had a secret boyfriend; anything was possible.

"Hello?" I called out. I felt bolder now, quite certain the house was empty.

My sandals slapped against the marble floor. I took them off and carried them. I would be quick, but I had time. A trip to the pool would take at least an hour. For the second time today, I'd play detective. Assessing the living room, I felt my shoulders relax. Everything looked the same as the last time I was here, even the row of family photographs on the mantel. A picture of Nikesh in his second-grade soccer team uniform; a fifth-grade photo of me in a velvet recital dress, hands poised above a piano; Dad, Nikesh, and me posing on an Alaskan glacier.

Satisfied with the living room, I swung left toward the kitchen. A math textbook sat on the breakfast table. I opened the book; at the top right-hand corner was the name *Bobby Reddy* in large, wobbly print. Reddy. I didn't know what kind of

Indian name that was. It didn't sound Tamil, though. As I put the book down, I nearly knocked over a half-finished can of Coke.

Unbelievable. Who let their kid drink Coke? No wonder he was so hyper, flailing around on the pavement like he'd been Tasered. What kind of mother was this woman? But even I had to admit the kitchen was cleaner now. Spotless. No dishes in the sink. Coffee mugs drying neatly on the dish rack. Dad was a slob when left to his own devices. Once, I'd come over to find bowls spilling onto the counter, their edges crusted with three-day-old cornflake bits.

I checked my watch. I'd wasted a good ten minutes already. On to the real stuff: Where was that mailbox woman sleeping?

Quickening my pace, I entered the master bedroom. My eyes went first to the bed. Four-poster, cherry wood, dramatically etched headboard—a bed I'd always considered too grand and opulent for both the size of the room and my parents' personalities. I approached the mattress, slowly. The bed was sloppily made, with crumpled sheets peeking out from beneath the duvet. I exhaled, relieved. This was the hurried, slapdash handiwork of my father. Judging from the spotless kitchen, the mailbox woman had a more meticulous touch.

Nevertheless, I surveyed the rest of the room. No hair clips on the bedside tables. No perfume bottles or jars of cream on the cherry dresser. I pulled out drawers at random: socks, undershirts, extra sheets, but no female items, as far as I could tell.

The master bathroom was next. If I found fancy conditioner in the shower or tampons in the cupboard, then I'd know what was what. I flipped on the lights. The bathroom was muggy, the mirrors caked with soap scum. I scanned the his-and-hers sinks. On Dad's side were familiar sights: Gillette shaving cream, Listerine, a tongue cleaner perched on the toothbrush holder next to his brush. On the "hers" sink side—nothing. Nothing aside from a Dial soap dispenser. I opened the cabinets beneath the sink and above the toilet: no maxi pads, no hair dryer. Relief flooded through me. They weren't sharing the master suite—at least, not yet.

I hoisted myself onto the bathroom counter, leaned back against the mirror, and surveyed the white-tiled room. When I lived here, I rarely entered this bathroom. I suppose by the time we had moved into this house, I'd outgrown my childhood habit of watching my parents' bathroom rituals. The image of Dad scraping the metal tongue cleaner across a flat, grainy expanse of tongue was no longer the hypnotic spectacle it had been when I was five. No, to my prissy, pubescent eyes, it was gross. I picked up the tongue cleaner now. What a weird-looking object. Maybe someday Dad and the mailbox woman would have another daughter, a daughter who'd sit eagerly on this very counter watching Dad scrape detritus off his tongue. I laid the tongue cleaner against the toothbrush holder, just as I'd found it. On my way to the bathroom door, I heard a soft metal ping as it fell to the counter. I shut the light off and closed the door.

I was lying on carpet, gazing at stars. Dim and semi-peeling— they were the same plastic glow-in-the-dark stars I'd stuck to the ceiling of my bedroom closet decades ago, during a short-lived fascination with all things celestial.

I had yet to leave the house. After confirming Dad's solo-occupied room and bathroom, my relief had turned into confusion. If that mailbox woman wasn't sleeping in Dad's room, what the hell was she doing here? Were they just roommates? That seemed implausible. So instead of leaving, I'd trudged upstairs to do more digging. My old room was unoccupied, thank goodness. Judging from the *Star Wars* figurines perched on Nikesh's bed, that Bobby kid was sleeping in there. In the guest room, neatly folded clothes were piled on the bed; an assortment of toiletries were lined on the dresser. And two international-sized suitcases occupied a full corner—suggesting something far longer than a weekend stay.

Well, that was it. I'd reached the end of my investigative capabilities. Columbo, I was not. Who knew where the mailbox woman and her son had come from, what they were doing here, or how long they were staying? It was Dad's secret. Just like the jazz-CD man was Mom's.

I pulled my phone out of my pocket and dialed the number I'd promised myself not to call. If my parents could have a secret life, I could too. After the first ring, Ashish picked up.

"Well, hello there."

"Hi," I said.

"So, did you leave town or something?"

"What makes you say that?"

"I went by your place a few times. Your car is gone. Your lights are off. Your mailbox was dangerously full—I took care of that, by the way. I have your mail. Who's feeding Ann Richards, or did you take her with you?"

"Your wife is feeding her. Didn't she tell you? We're friends now."

"Priya, stop."

"My neighbor is feeding the cat, not that you really care. You hate my cat."

"I don't hate her. I just think cats are pointless creatures."

"I think married men are pointless creatures."

"Wow. Okay then, go ahead and get it all out."

"Your wife is pretty." My voice sounded small. I hated how small it sounded. I cleared my throat and spoke louder. "She's really pretty. Were you serious when you told me she stopped having sex with you? Because at the gym, you seemed like a couple who wouldn't have a problem in that department."

"Priya, I've never lied to you. I'm just in a complicated situation. Our parents are family friends. Our brothers are friends. If I left Chalini, I'd be ruining things for everyone. I feel stuck . . . and confused. It's not a dodge. It's the truth."

"Well, you do not have the monopoly on complicated situations. I'm currently hiding in my old bedroom closet."

"You're at your parents' house? That's where you've been the past week?"

"I've been at my mom's apartment. But she's apparently got a new boyfriend now, and three's a crowd, you know? So at this moment, I'm in my parents' old house—my dad's house now."

"Why are you hiding? Your dad doesn't know you're there?"

"No, he doesn't. He's not home right now. He's with his new live-in girlfriend and her son. He's taken them to the swimming pool." I laughed. "Do you know what's sad? My mom and dad are going to lap me. I mean . . . they're going to marry these new people, and I'll be invited to their weddings, and they'll have new kids—well, at least my dad will. And what will I be doing? My life will be exactly the same. Inertial. I'll still be in love with a married man who will never leave his wife for me."

There was silence on the other end of the phone. "Love? You did say 'love,' right . . . or did I mishear that?"

I sighed. It was love. Wasn't it? Somehow, I'd gone and fallen in love with a married man. Had I become too depleted by loneliness, exhausted into love? Whatever the reason, I was an idiot.

"Does it change anything?" I asked.

"Well, it means something."

"I didn't ask if it meant something. I asked if it changes anything."

"Well, look . . . I don't know if it changes anything in practical terms right this second. But it's still an important thing to acknowledge and consider. Now we can think about our options with the full information, right?"

My chest felt heavy. Lead-filled. I thought I had closed that door. I thought I'd wanted it to be over. He loved his wife. I saw them together. Wasn't that why I'd fled to Clayborn to hide out in my mom's apartment? But now he was talking about "options." What did that mean? Was he going to leave her for me? He wasn't making me any kind of promise. It changed nothing. Did it?

"Priya," he said. "Where'd you go?"

"I'm here. I'm still here."

16

NIKESH

"**D**id you get my note?" Denise eyed me in the mirror. She held a pearl earring shaped like a raindrop against her ear. She wrinkled her nose, apparently unsatisfied with the look, and replaced the pearl with a diamond stud.

We were in the bedroom. I'd finally gotten Alok to sleep, and now I was sprawled on the bed, elbows folded beneath my head, watching Denise get ready for a banquet.

Or was it a gala? I could never tell the difference. Was there even a difference? Anyway, it was a dressy event celebrating some laudable civil rights organization. The firm, in an effort to demonstrate their public interest street cred (aka "we're not just soulless moneymaking assholes whoring ourselves to the financial services industry"), had purchased an entire table at the event. Our original plan had been for me to go too, and for Yvette to stay on through the evening. But having forgotten all about that plan, I'd sent her home early and whisked Alok to the park.

Denise had returned from work at seven, practically sprinting through the door. "I'm so late. We'll never make it on time." Spotting me in cargo shorts stacking Legos with Alok on the floor, she did a double-take: "Wait, why aren't you dressed?" She scanned the room. "Where's Yvette?"

I'd been so eager to spin my early afternoon home as an example of exemplary fatherhood, that I'd cluelessly boasted, "I sent her home early so Alok and I could have an afternoon of father-son bonding. We went to the park. We ate mac 'n' cheese. And now it's Lego time. Right, little man? High-five." I stuck my hand out and Alok swiped back, barely missing it. I tickled Alok's chest, unleashing a torrent of baby giggles. I looked up at Denise and grinned, inviting her to bask in my glorious display of fatherhood.

Instead, she dropped her office tote on the ground with a thud, disappeared into the bedroom, and reappeared holding a hanger with a beaded black gown. "Gala. Tonight. Yvette was supposed to babysit. Any of this ring a bell?"

At that moment, Alok slammed his hand through the Lego stack, sending the colored blocks clanking to the ground. He laughed and said, "uh-oh," an expression he'd picked up recently and seemed to use with uncanny timing.

"Uh-oh," I repeated. "Well, just go without me. No one will even notice I'm not there. I'm just a lowly associate. You're a partner. And you like these events more than I do anyway. I'll put Alok to sleep while you finish getting ready." I should have felt bad about forgetting, but I was relieved not to go.

Denise had shrugged then, either too tired or too indifferent to protest.

The afternoon of park and sun had sent Alok to sleep faster than usual, and so now I watched as Denise made her last touches—dabbing perfume on her wrists, buckling the straps of silver, stiletto sandals around her slim ankles.

"Well?" She stood in front of me, hands on hips.

"You look fantastic, babe."

She theatrically rolled her eyes. "Thanks, Nik. But that wasn't the question. Did you get my note today?"

"Yes. And was interoffice mail really necessary? And making Sheila hand me the envelope instead of delivering it yourself? Couldn't you have just called me? Or texted me? Or I don't know, told me at home like a normal wi—person." In my growing agitation, I'd nearly said "wife." Uh-oh. Was it possible that she'd take pity on me and let that little slipup slide?

Her eyes widened. "Wife-person! See, that's exactly my point!"

Of course she would never have let that go. She was a lawyer, an exceptionally good one, whose specialty was pouncing on weakness, never letting any detail go unnoticed. I closed my eyes and fell back against the pillows.

"You don't even know what to call me because you're too confused with all the lying you have to do! I'm not your wife, Nikesh. You never asked me to be your wife. I playact your wife when we're around your parents because you told them we're married, and that makes me feel like shit. So yes, I used interoffice mail. I've tried every other mode of communication with you and it hasn't worked."

A sound from the baby monitor made us both freeze. We locked eyes and raised fingers to our lips, simultaneously shushing each other. A momentary cease-fire. A few seconds later, the monitor was silent again.

Denise turned back to the mirror, her eyes suddenly tired-looking, despite the carefully drawn eyeliner and smoke-colored shadow on her lids. "Do you want this?"

"What do you mean?"

"This. Us. Our life together. I don't want you to feel like you've been trapped in something that you don't want." Her voice became small, almost a whisper. The question sent a wave of shame through me. Hadn't I suspected her of trapping me? Hadn't I wondered that myself, at weaker, darker moments? I thought of Alok's sleeping body down the hall, his knees curled to his chest, a thumb halfway out of his mouth. She'd given me the best part of my life. I didn't want a life without Alok—without him sleeping across the hall from me every day for the next seventeen years. Denise and I had something real—we did. We loved each other. We were just in some kind of new-parent slump. We could get past it. I had to stop letting doubts—and memories of Elena—get the best of me.

I stood up, walked toward her, and laid my hands on her shoulders. "Don't be ridiculous. We're a family. This is what I want. The three of us together. Okay? I'll call my parents tonight and tell them everything. I'm sorry that I've let it go on this way for so long—that it's hurt you. Forgive me?" I wrapped my arms around her small waist and kissed the back of her neck.

"You really do look fantastic." She did too. Her silky hair was pulled back in a loose, low bun. The beaded dress was cut low in the back, showing off her alabaster skin, a creamy ripple of spine. I ran my hands lightly over the tops of her breasts, jutting out like two graceful hills over the beaded bodice.

She watched me in the mirror—watched us. She leaned back into me, as my hands continued to wander. Her eyes were softer now, but still doubtful. She glanced at the clock and peeled my arms away.

I opened the fridge and cool, still air tickled my nose.

I pushed aside cartons of leftover Chinese food and mason jars of mashed carrots and peas until I found what I was looking for. A six-pack of IPAs hiding in the back of the fridge. Relieved, I grabbed one, flipped the tab open, and let the cold, frothy beer cover my tongue. I sat on a dining chair and rolled my shoulders back.

Alok was sound asleep. And I had a good two hours until Denise was back.

I needed to call my parents. But before I did that, I needed to do something else. I needed to stop letting the past fuck with me.

I reached for my phone and dialed before I could talk myself out of it. Three years had gone by, but the number was still burned in my memory.

I took a long swig of beer while the phone rang. One ring. Two rings. Three.

Finally, she picked up.

"Nikesh, is that really you?"

Her voice. Elena's voice. It sounded exactly the same as I remembered. Not girlish. No-nonsense and with a slight hoarseness to it. A voice that I once told her reminded me of Scarlett Johansson's voice. To which she'd responded: *Well then, if you ever feel like a threesome, you can just close your eyes and pretend. 'Cause that's the closest you're gonna get, man.* Remembering that now made me think of being naked in bed with Scarlett Johansson and Elena. Jesus, it had been so long since I'd had sex.

"Uh, Nikesh?"

I blinked my eyes rapidly, trying to push the image out of my head. "Yeah. It's me. Hey. Sorry—is it too late to call you?"

"No. I'm just really surprised to hear from you. It's been . . . years."

"Three years."

"Right." Silence. I could imagine her long fingers coiling and uncoiling her curls. She always did that when she was on the phone. Coiling and uncoiling. "So, how have you been, Nikesh? I've thought about you, you know, wondered how you were doing."

Oh really? If you'd really been thinking about me, then why didn't you ever call me and tell me you were getting engaged, or why didn't you ever call me after to check if I was okay, or why didn't you ever call me to tell me you were sorry, or why didn't you ever call me to tell me why you married him and not me?

"I'm good. Really good. I have a son, Alok. He's almost one."

"Wow! You have a kid. Good for you." Beneath the excitement in her voice, I could hear the surprise. It annoyed me. Was she so surprised that I'd met someone and had a kid? Did she think I'd been pining for her all these years, my life frozen in place like some pathetic loser?

"What about you? Do you have any kids?"

"Oh no, not yet. Too busy at work right now. But one day . . ." Her voice trailed off. In the background, I could hear a man's voice ask if she wanted aioli on the side. That had to be him— her husband, Adam. He worked with her as a staff attorney at the ACLU Immigrants' Rights Project. I'd learned that from Elena's Facebook page. Apparently, he not only defended the rights of the downtrodden but he also cooked things that required aioli on the side. I was a corporate sellout who did not cook things. But I had a kid. I'd beaten her to that. Maybe aioli-making Adam was infertile. I cheered myself with the thought.

"Sorry, we're about to sit down to dinner. But I can talk for a few more minutes. Nikesh Raman. Man, I still can't believe it's you! I was starting to think I'd never hear from you again. Three years. And you have a kid now. So crazy. I didn't even know you'd gotten married."

I considered my options here. On the one hand, I was happy letting her think I was married. Why not let her picture a beautiful wife making me something aioli-worthy, as a charming baby dozed in my lap? On the other hand, I would gain some satisfaction in letting her know that Denise and I had chosen to have Alok without getting married—offending her Catholic sensibilities that way. After all, I blamed Catholicism for her leaving me.

Elena was the first religious girl I'd ever seriously dated. She attended Mass with regularity—even dragged me along a few times. At first, I found it all sort of interesting—the priest in the fancy robes, the singing, the standing, the bread, the wine. It felt like attending a play or a performance piece at a museum, where the audience had to participate. Aside from my initial nervousness about doing something wrong—like sitting when I should be

standing, doing the hand cross thing in the opposite direction—
I'd enjoyed the spectacle.

Reflexively, I made a cross sign at the dining table. Was it
right to left first? Or up and down first? I could never quite remember.

Her fealty to God always threw me, though. It was hard to
square with her otherwise practical approach to life. Whenever I pointed out this contradiction to her, she balked: "It's
not contradictory. Look, I'm not asking you to throw evolution
out the door and embrace creationism, or to toss any post-
Enlightenment belief in science and rationality into the garbage.
I'm not some dupe who hasn't thought this out for herself, so
don't be patronizing. I like believing in something, even if I can't
see it or prove it or quantify it, okay? Don't come to Mass if you
don't like it. No one's making you."

I knew she wasn't making me. And I tried to be a good sport
about it. Maybe I was even a little envious of her belief. Watching her, I kind of wished I'd been raised in a religious home. My
family was officially Hindu. But aside from my parents buying
us a new outfit on Diwali every now and then, or the small idols
that my mom kept on a shelf in her linen closet, religion carried
no discernible consequence in our house. Though, maybe it
would have been nice to grow up with the sense that things were
part of some divine plan. Maybe it would have been nice to have
a place to go each Sunday, to see the same group of people for
church dinners and mixers and volunteer outings. To have something that connected you with a bunch of other people doing
the exact same thing. Like a football game, but you know, more
meaningful or whatever.

Back in the tenth grade, I'd even considered converting—for
Laura Cunningham. Laura had soft pink lips that you wanted to
kiss and resplendent breasts that you longed to suck and a com-
mitment to her church, which she advertised—like some other
students at my high school—by wearing T-shirts featuring a

bloody hand punctured by a nail. We'd become friendly in ge-
ometry class, and despite my best efforts, I couldn't break past
the platonic boundary she'd raised between us. I feared that
without Jesus on my side, I'd never see the pink nipples beneath
that nail-impaled-hand T-shirt graphic. So one day in class,
when she wore a rather tight-fitting *He Died So We May Live*
shirt, I inquired about the conversion opportunities at her
church. She was ecstatic. My parents were not. One Sunday, I'd
hurried past the breakfast table wearing my best suit and tie, trying to ignore my mother's frantic entreaties: "*Aiyo*, don't let those
people convert you."

Even Dad, usually the more hands-off of the two when it
came to my teenage comings and goings, chimed in, "Always
wanting to convert, these people. They can't leave us alone. All
over the world, these missionaries knocking on doors, bothering
people. Not like our Hinduism. Our Hinduism is a deeply philosophical religion."

Dad tended to defend Hinduism in abstract terms. Aside
from pronouncing it a "deeply philosophical religion," he was
short on particulars. That's because he was, aside from these
strange spurts of defensiveness, an atheist. A man who, when
watching graphic depictions of Middle East chaos on CNN,
would quote Marx with adoration: "Religion is the opiate of the
masses."

In any case, my parents needn't have worried. My tenth-grade
interest in conversion was extremely short-lived. It ended basically a millisecond after Laura introduced me to her college-
aged boyfriend, Peter, who'd just returned home after a one-year
missionary stint in Latvia.

I'd never put it all together before, but maybe I had some kind
of fetish when it came to religious girls. Hadn't Janine become a
born-again too? And Denise, hadn't she spent her youth singing
in Methodist church choirs? Even now, she'd disappear every
other Sunday to commune with God. We'd never explicitly dis-

cussed the role of religion in Alok's upbringing. There hadn't been a need to have that discussion yet. For now, Alok was too unruly to take to a church or any place that required sustained quiet. But in a few years, would Denise insist? Would I be glad if she did—glad that Alok would get exposed to some kind of faith in a visceral way, long before he could become cynical about it?

"So when did you and—sorry, I don't even know your wife's name. When did you guys get married?" Elena asked.

Okay, truth. I'd go with the truth. "Her name is Denise. And, we're not married. Not yet, anyway."

"Ah. Got it," she said.

"What's that supposed to mean?"

"Nothing. I didn't say anything."

"Yes you did. You think it's wrong that we have a kid and we're still not married. I know you, Elena. After all, you left me because I wasn't Catholic."

"What are you talking about? You think that . . ." Her voice got louder and then she stopped talking. Softer now, I heard her say, "I'm going to go outside for a second, babe. I'll be done by the time the table is set."

I waited, listening to the sounds of her breathing, the faint scrape of a sliding door.

"Okay, so this is why you called, isn't it? You want to have this conversation. Fine. Let's have it. I did not break up with you because you weren't Catholic. Adam is not Catholic, for your information."

"Then why?" For three years, I'd been waiting for an explanation. A real explanation.

"Because I . . . fell in love with someone else."

"But we were so happy."

"Were we? I don't think I was by the end. Look, I didn't care that you weren't religious. I could live with that. But it was more than that. You were just so . . . I don't know . . . conviction-less.

Honestly, you didn't seem to care all that much about anything, other than me. You were unhappy with law school, your job . . . everything. I felt like you were just drifting along, taking the path of least resistance, and then feeling constantly dissatisfied and penned in by your life. It was starting to get exhausting, being responsible for your happiness. I didn't know how to convince you to . . . to care about something . . . to choose."

I could feel the blood drain from my legs. Conviction-less? A drifter? That's what she thought about me?

"Nikesh, I didn't mean to fall in love with someone else. It's not like I was searching for someone new when we were together. I can't even explain how it happened. It just did—so gradually that I was deep in it before I even realized how far gone I was. I didn't want to hurt you. I felt so horribly guilty about it. It's why I couldn't tell you at first. And then you never responded to my email about my engagement, so I assumed you were pissed at me and never wanted to hear from me again. I'm sorry. I really am."

She fell in love with someone else. Someone she loved more than me. It happened every day. People in relationships fell in love with someone new. They found someone they liked better. They ditched their husband, boyfriend, wife, girlfriend, and their lives went on with someone new. Utterly unremarkable. Except when it happened to you.

"Look, Nikesh, I really have to go. You can call me again, if you want to. I hope you're . . . happy in your life. I really, really do."

I cleared my throat and forced myself to speak. "Yeah. Enjoy the aioli." I hung up before she could say another word.

I drank my remaining beer in one long gulp and pounded the can on the table. I got up and walked down the hallway to Alok's room. The white noise machine was humming. I tiptoed toward the crib and peeked in. He was sucking his thumb softly. His chest rose and fell in a fast baby rhythm. I adjusted the thin sheet, pulling it over his belly.

Elena was wrong. I did have conviction about some things. I had picked something. I had chosen. Alok.

And Denise. They were my future. I just had to not screw it up.

Speaking of which, I'd made Denise a promise to tell my parents tonight, and I wouldn't put it off any longer. I glanced at the digital clock on the dresser. It was ten-thirty now (nine-thirty in Texas), which gave me anywhere from ten to thirty minutes before Denise walked in the door, champagne-buzzed and inquisitive.

I tiptoed out of Alok's room into the hallway and padded back toward the dining room table in search of my phone.

I had just dialed Dad's number when I heard keys jangling in the front door, followed by the uneven trod of tipsy feet.

Fuck. I'd blown my window.

Denise glided into the dining room, her heels in her hand, her bun artfully disheveled, her red lipstick faded. All the markings of a good night.

I hung up on Dad before he could answer and plastered a fake smile on my face. "So how was it?"

"Oh, you know, the usual. Martinis, champagne, feel-good speeches about the importance of lawyers to humanity. Blah blah blah."

She walked toward me and dropped her strappy shoes on the floor with a thud. She unclipped her hair, shaking out her bun. "So, how did it go? What did your parents say?"

I hesitated. I took a deep breath, and then lied through my teeth. "They took it pretty well."

"Really? They weren't upset or mad or anything?" She furrowed her brows and pursed her lips until they made a pickled "o" shape—her gestures became more exaggerated in her drunken state.

I shook my head, hoping she wouldn't press further. "Nope. Who knows? Maybe the divorce has made them more understanding. Less judgmental. I should have told them from the start."

As I said the words, it struck me that maybe they were truer than I'd let myself believe. All this time, I thought that I was protecting my parents from the truth because it would hurt them. But maybe I'd just been protecting myself from having to answer their questions—questions I hadn't been ready to answer. *Why didn't you ask her to marry you? Why don't you do it now?* I hadn't wanted my parents' questions because I didn't know the answers myself. So I lied to them about eloping. And I made Denise be a part of the lie.

"You most definitely should have." She nodded in agreement. She paused, as if ready to say something more. But then she leaned in and planted a soft kiss on my lips. "I'm proud of you."

I leaned into her and wrapped my arms around her waist, trying hard to ignore the guilty feeling in my chest. "So you and Alok will come to Texas, right?"

"Of course." She started removing bobby pins from her hair, making a small pile of them on the counter.

"We'll stay with my dad, okay? More room there."

She wrinkled her nose. "Can we just stay at a hotel?"

I shook my head. "My dad's all alone in that big house. He'd be devastated if we didn't stay with him. It would be like spitting in his face. It's an Indian thing." I reached for my phone. "Why don't you get changed, and I'll call my dad to let him know."

Denise plucked the phone from my hands and set it back down on the table. Her hair hung loose around her face and her expression was unusually mischievous. "I have a better idea. You come with me now. And you can call him tomorrow."

Tomorrow. I'd tell them tomorrow.

17

LATA

He did not come into the library today.

All day, I waited. I stayed close to the reference desk, in case he came in, never straying too far to reshelve books. And now the library was closing for the day.

It was already Thursday. I needed to tell him today. This way, he could still find someone else to use his extra concert ticket. I owed him that courtesy, at the very least. And I needed to return his CD—the jazz quartet one that was still unopened in my purse. The singing ladies one—well, that was in my bedroom. I had listened to it too many times to return it now.

I looked at my phone. I didn't have Len's number. He had mine, though. He'd asked for it at the yoga studio that day. But I hadn't asked for his. I had been so flustered that I hadn't thought to ask him.

What about his office phone number? It had to be listed on the campus website. I could search for it and call. I was alone at the reference desk. Deanna wasn't scheduled to work this afternoon. Jared had left early for an appointment, leaving me to close the library. No one was standing in line to return books or check them out or ask any questions. There were only a handful of students left at the carrels, and even they were beginning to pack their things, zip up their oversized backpacks. No one needed my attention. No one was paying the slightest attention to me.

I clicked open the internet browser. It was automatically set to the university home page. I clicked on *Faculty* and typed in Len's name. His picture popped up on the screen. He was dressed professionally, in a gray suit jacket and blue button-down shirt. His curly hair was neatly combed. He was smiling in the picture. He was often smiling. He seemed like a happy man. I liked that about him. I hoped that my cancellation would not upset him. Maybe it was a good thing that he had not come into the library today. Doing this over the phone would be easier. I wouldn't have to see the expression on his face, the hurt look in his walnut eyes. I scanned the web page until I found his office number. I took a deep breath and dialed.

It was ringing. I cleared my throat. I reached for the open water bottle on the counter and took a sip.

One ring, two rings. I took another sip.

Three, four, five rings. A recorded message—not Len's voice, but a female computerized voice, telling me to please record a message after the beep. *Beep.*

I hung up.

Of course he wasn't there. It was almost five o'clock. He was probably at home or maybe at Olive's yoga class. It was not as if professors kept regular hours, nine to five, five days a week. Take Priya, for example. Sometimes she'd stay home on Monday and go into the office on Sunday. She left town when she wanted to, for days at a time—like she was doing now—and nobody seemed to care. I didn't understand it. I liked the fixed schedule of my job. Mondays, Wednesdays, and Fridays, I worked until two. On Tuesdays and Thursdays, I worked until five. My weekends were free. If someone wanted to find me here, they knew which days and hours to come by. If someone wanted to avoid me here, they knew which days and hours not to come by. Which was a good thing for Len, because after I canceled, he would know exactly how to avoid me.

Not Len. Professor Greenberg. After I canceled, he would probably go back to being Professor Greenberg.

Maybe I could leave him a note. *Dear Professor Greenberg, Something has come up and I cannot attend the concert with you. Thank you so much for inviting me. I'm so sorry. Lata.* I could attach it to the jazz quartet CD and slip it under his office door.

The music department was in the building next door. I looked at the web page. *Camden Hall, Suite 4010.* I could go by there on my way to the staff parking lot. After all, he would have to come back to his office sometime. Maybe he'd find it tomorrow morning, and that would still leave him time to find another person to take to the concert.

I plucked a sheet of blank paper from the printer. I wrote my note, signed it, and attached it to the CD with a ribbon of Scotch tape.

Okay, I had a plan.

It might not work. But it was better than nothing.

The first floor of Camden Hall was full of practice rooms.

As I walked down the long hallway toward the elevator, sounds floated in the air. Piano trills. Violin strings. A male singing voice, deep and rich and beautiful. A low, brassy sound—perhaps a tuba, though I wasn't quite sure what a tuba sounded like. None of those sounds were intended to go together, and yet, they didn't sound unpleasant all mashed up like this. Under different circumstances, I would have lingered in this hallway. I would have savored the bizarre blend of sounds, relishing the fact that behind every closed door was a student diligently practicing an instrument. But right now, I was anxious and in a hurry. I wanted to finish this errand as fast as possible.

This was only my second time in this building. The first time was over five months ago, the day of my job interview at the library. I was anxious and in a hurry then too.

I had gotten lost that day. My job interview had been at 9:00 A.M., and everything had gone wrong that morning. I couldn't find my favorite pearl earrings—the ones that went perfectly with my soft gray suit. Then I had decided that a suit was too formal to wear for a library position (as I had never seen a librarian wearing a suit), so I changed into my navy pants and a pink silk blouse. Then once I was in my car and on my way—twenty minutes later than I had planned—I realized that I had left my copy of the campus map on the kitchen counter. I knew how to get as far as campus parking. Beyond that, I would have to ask for directions. What I discovered about college students that day was that most of them had no idea what buildings were on their campus. One student directed me to the science building, another to the humanities building, another to the business school.

It had started to feel like a sign from God. That I was a fool for applying for the library job. That I had no business trying to start over now, after never having worked before. At that low moment, when I was ready to turn back and walk to my car, I'd spotted a miracle. A student carrying a guitar case on his back. A music student! At the sight of him, my nerve returned. I could get this job. I met all the listed qualifications. I had a bachelor's degree—many years old, and from India, but it would do. I had a computer-skills certification from the local community college, attesting to my proficiency with computers, internet resources, and a wide range of commercially available software. Two of my professors there had written me recommendation letters, explaining that I had received the highest test scores in the class. Okay, so maybe I did not know much about music, but that had not been listed as a job requirement for the music library. Anyway, I was a fast learner. I was patient with people. I could do the job. I just needed someone to give me a chance.

I followed that guitar-carrying student all the way to this building, Camden Hall. And once I got here, I found a hallway full of people who actually knew where the music library was: right next door. I'd entered my interview just in time and out of breath—and more determined than before. Jared was the one who interviewed me. It all went smoothly until he asked about my prior job experience. I had prepared an answer for that: I was going to allude vaguely to how I used to tutor students in English when I was a college student in India (this was true), and then re-emphasize my enthusiasm for the library position, my recent computer skills, my quick ability to learn, and my capacity for hard work. In other words, I had planned to evade the question.

Jared had looked at me then, his eyebrows raised, dubious. At that moment, I could imagine what he thought: *Why take a chance on this older woman who has never held a real job in her entire life?*

I was losing him, I could tell. So I stopped boasting about my aptitude, my enthusiasm, my computer skills. I told him the truth. I told him how I had deferred my own dreams for marriage and children, how I had felt an emptiness when my children left for college, how I had recently gotten divorced and left the house I'd lived in for so many years, how I needed this. *I needed this.*

"Jared, I know there are other people who have more experience than me. But you won't interview anyone who wants this job more than me. I just need a chance. I need you to give me a chance. You will not regret it."

It was embarrassing, to open myself like that to a stranger. But I had been desperate. And it worked. His expression had softened. "I like you, Lata. I have a soft spot for underdogs. And late bloomers. You've told me a lot of things about yourself, so let me tell you something about me. I didn't come out as a gay man until I was forty. I know something about second acts in life. And I want to help you find yours. The job is yours, if you want it."

A second act. I liked the sound of that. Jared understood. And he had given me a chance when I had most needed it. That was why I didn't join Deanna in mocking him when he did his funny theatrical voices or left early for his mysterious appointments. He had given me my first real chance for a second act.

"Lata? Is that you?" A man's voice rang out behind me just as I reached for the elevator button.

I froze. My pulse quickened. Oh God, was it Len? Would I actually have to do this face-to-face? Would I hand him the note, the CD, watch him read it, all in front of the elevator? This was the worst of all possibilities.

I turned to see Jared's familiar, balding head. My body relaxed. "Jared, you scared me. What are you doing here?"

"I'm practicing." He gestured toward a practice room. "I got the lead in a local production of *Man of La Mancha*. You're looking at Don Quixote, baby!"

I had no idea what Jared was talking about. But he looked so ecstatic, I congratulated him. "That's terrific news."

"It's finally happening, Lata. All those years of trying out for parts. Getting rejected over and over again. But it's finally happened. I can't believe it." A tear had formed in the corner of his eye.

A tear formed in the corner of mine too. I was proud of Jared. He hadn't listened to the cynics or the naysayers, the audible critics like Deanna and the silent critics like me. He had kept trying and failing, trying and failing, until he succeeded. He was living the second act that he wanted. He hadn't been afraid to try.

I hugged my purse close to my body. What about me? Did I

really want to cancel on Len? Was this really about Priya being at my apartment? Or was I just too afraid to try?

"Come listen to me."

"Of course, I'll come to your performance. Just tell me the date and I'll be there."

"No, I mean now. Come listen to me now. In a practice room. Tell me what you think."

"Jared, I don't know much about music. You knew that when you hired me."

"You have ears, don't you?"

I laughed. "It's just that . . . I have an errand to run." I looked at the light above the elevator, blinking above the second floor. It was almost here.

"Lata, didn't you hear me say I have the lead? My very first lead ever! Your errand can wait. Come on, milady." He held out his arm, as if I were a queen and he was walking me to my throne.

The elevator dinged. Two students stepped off, a boy and a girl. She wore a backpack. He wore a large, pear-shaped instrument. A cello, I guessed. The boy had his hand in the back pocket of the girl's jeans. They were laughing.

I let go of my purse strap. Then I hooked my arm through Jared's. "Okay, sir, serenade me."

I placed the Dannon yogurt carton in my cart and hummed.

Jared had been good. Really good. So much better than I could have imagined.

To dream the impossible dream . . .

His voice was strong and resonant and full of feeling. If only Deanna had been there to hear it. You really couldn't judge a book by its cover. It was so true. Not just about books. But every-thing.

I threw two bags of frozen peas into the cart and rubbed the goose pimples on my upper arms. How was I out of groceries already—in the middle of the week? For a girl who was de-pressed, my daughter could certainly eat. Usually, I shopped only once a week: on Sunday mornings, when church was in session, to avoid the crowds. I would buy what I needed for the week, cook a batch of food on Sunday afternoon and eat leftovers all week long. But with Priya here, it didn't feel right feeding her leftovers every day. I had been making her a new dish each day, going down the list of her favorites. Yesterday, it was pepper rasam. The day before that, it was tomato rice. Maybe today, I'd make sambar with okra.

I pushed my cart toward the produce section and picked up an okra. I pinched and sniffed it. Satisfied, I grabbed two hand-fuls and threw them in a plastic bag.

Too bad I wasn't in the mood to make a fresh dinner. What I really wanted to do was grab a frozen pizza and forget the cook-ing today. I felt guilty to think it, but this wasn't a good time for my daughter to visit. She required so much attention and care. So much of my life, my attention had gone to my children. I wanted to pay some attention to myself. Hadn't I earned it?

Obviously, I could never ask her to leave. Which meant that I'd have to find a way to tell her about my date with Len. Be-cause I didn't want to cancel. I didn't want to give him the CD back. I wanted to go to this concert. I wanted to . . . try it. A date.

I pushed the cart toward the bread section and noticed a woman my age eyeing a bag of sesame seed buns. I observed the woman's fingers as she reached for the buns. She had no wed-ding ring. Did this woman go on dates too? She looked slim and neat in her linen dress and chin-length hair. As I bent down for a loaf of wheat bread from one of the lower shelves, I noticed the woman's polished toes peeking out from gold sandals. They were a light pink, like the color of Easter candies. They gave her feet a youthful quality; those toes could easily have belonged to a woman two decades her junior. Did the men this woman went on dates with notice the youthfulness of her toes?

"Are you okay?"

I looked up to find the owner of those pink toes staring at me. "Oh yes, I'm fine. I just noticed that you have very pink toes."

The woman wrinkled her eyebrows, confused.

I blushed. "No, I mean, your polish—it's very nicely applied. Did you do that yourself?"

The woman's face relaxed into a smile. "Goodness no! When I do my own toes, the polish goes all over my cuticles. I get them done at Alice's, down the street. They're the best, very clean and reasonably priced. And they do a great job smoothing out the soles of your feet too—they don't hold back. Just pumice and pumice until they're smooth as a baby's bottom." She laughed, and wiggled her toes for emphasis. Then she gave a friendly wave goodbye and pushed her cart down the aisle.

Slowly, I pushed my own cart toward the checkout line. With each step, I could feel the cracked undersides of my feet pressing against my shoes. They felt nothing like a baby's soft bottom.

Pedicures. It had always amazed me, the amount of money some women spent on such things—like facials and massages and maintaining the bottoms of the feet. It seemed like a waste. Not that I considered myself to be a cheap person. No, I very much believed in spending money on certain things, things that would last for years—gold jewelry, home construction, soft leather purses, silk blouses. But polished toes? They would hardly last a day. They might look nice when you came back from the salon, but the next morning, when you squeezed them into pointy work shoes, wouldn't the polish chip?

Waiting at the checkout line, I looked down at the black pumps covering my unpolished toes. I winced, imagining the hardened cracks and crevices of my feet, white-flecked with dry-ness, deadened skin flaking off.

I looked up at the glossy magazines on display. One an-nounced: "Gel Polish—The Sure Way to Chip-Free Nails." Gel polish—what was gel polish?

I eyed the magazines suspiciously. An entire row of them, glit-tering beneath the fluorescent Kroger lights, showcasing long-haired girls with nonexistent waists and pearly white smiles. Most of them seemed to chronicle the exploits of celebrities or offer advice about dieting and hairstyles, though a few seemed to venture into more disreputable territory, boasting articles on "How to Please Your Man" and "Ten Sexual Positions to Drive Him Wild." Phrases that one did not expect to see while hold-ing a carton of yogurt at the Kroger checkout line. Once, many years ago, I'd found one of these more dubious magazines in Priya's bathroom. I had flipped through it, discovering page after page offering tips for blow jobs and hand jobs. Nothing but jobs, jobs, jobs. As if the human body was a big construction site.

"Do you have a Kroger's club card?" The girl at the counter paused before scanning the carton of yogurt. "If you have a card, it's half price. Ma'am?"

"Pardon? Oh yes." I fumbled in my purse for my card. I handed it to the girl, who, I couldn't help but notice, had per-fectly painted red fingernails. Did everyone pay such close at-tention to their nails? I looked at my own hands, with the nails uneven and the skin around them (what was it called? cuticles?) peeling and dry.

Well maybe this once, a pedicure and manicure would be all right. After all, I was working now. It was my money and mine alone to spend and waste as I saw fit. And anyway, didn't that pink-toed woman say the place she went to—Alice's—was rea-sonably priced? Maybe I'd surprise Priya by suggesting that we get our nails done together tomorrow at lunchtime.

And maybe when we were there, getting gel polish on our

nails, I would tell her about Len and the concert. She would be surprised, but she would understand.

Wouldn't she?

Three hours past dinnertime and Priya was nowhere to be found.

I stirred the pot of sambar half-heartedly and turned off the burner. The clock on the oven read nine-thirty.

I dialed Priya's number for the third time. As it had twice before, the voicemail greeting intercepted before the first ring. "Where are you? I'm getting worried. Please call me back."

Was it possible she had decided to go back to Austin? Surely, she would have waited to say goodbye. I felt guilty for my earlier thoughts. I had resented her being here, and now she was gone and I was worried. It served me right.

I spotted her laptop on the dining table, and relief filled me. She would never leave without that. She wouldn't leave without telling me.

I tried to distract myself from one worrisome thought after another: that Priya had been rear-ended by a bus; that she'd gone for a jog around the neighborhood and been bitten by a rabid dog; that she'd gone for a swim in the apartment pool and drowned in the deep end. The last thought sent me scurrying to the balcony. I leaned over the railing and looked down. The lights lining the pool made everything visible. But I couldn't see anything in the glowing water, aside from a hairy man in yellow shorts doing laps. What if that hairy, yellow-shorts man strangled Priya, put her in his car trunk, and then started doing laps in the pool, to dispel any suspicions that he was a psychotic strangler?

Aiyo. I needed to calm down. And I needed to stop thinking about those horrible prison shows Priya watched. They were putting crazy ideas in my head.

Of course Priya was fine. I should be relieved that she was out

of bed, ready to go back into the world. She was probably working from a coffee shop somewhere, had lost track of time, and
her cellphone battery had probably died because she never remembered to charge it. On the balcony, a cool breeze fluttered
the sleeves of my blouse. I shivered and walked inside.

Now, the sight of Priya's laptop on the dining table was not so
comforting. It introduced a new seed of doubt. Because if she
was working at a coffee shop, wouldn't she have taken it with
her? Were coffee shops even open this late?

I needed to calm down. I could listen to Ella or Billie. I
walked into my bedroom, turned the CD player on and listened
for a few seconds, my hip leaning against the dresser. The music
was not working its usual magic. I couldn't relax. I opened the
CD player, took out the CD, and moved toward the other end of
the dresser to return it to the cover. I slipped my hand behind
the velvet jewelry box, expecting the sharp corner of plastic to
prick my fingertip. But there was nothing. I lifted the jewelry
box off the dresser. The CD case was gone!

Oh God, what if Priya had found it? What if she had been
looking through my jewelry box and it slipped out? She had already met Len at the library. She was probably imagining all
kinds of things about the two of us. Had she called Nikesh and
told him too?

I reached again for my phone and dialed.

"Mom, good timing. I was just going to call you."

"Nikesh, thank goodness you answered. Your sister hasn't
come home yet. I don't know if you know this, but she's been
staying with me for a while. I think she's been depressed. Did
she call you today?" I took a deep breath, preparing myself for
questions about Len and the CD.

"No. She didn't call me. But I'm sure she's fine. Maybe she
went to a movie. Maybe she went to Dad's. So, look, um . . .
while I've got you on the phone, I want to tell you something. . . ."

"Your dad's? You think she went there?" I struggled to keep the panic out of my voice. Was it possible that Priya was so upset she went to talk to Suresh about it? That she told him about the CD from Len? Surely she wouldn't have done that. Would she? I felt nauseous. And then angry. I had not done anything wrong. I had yet to even go on a date with this man, and Priya was meddling in my life and gossiping about something that hadn't even happened. It was terribly unfair.

"You know, Nikesh, maybe you could call your dad and see if she's there? And then you can call me and tell me if she is."

"Mom, are you serious? Are you and Dad really on such bad terms that you can't even call him? Is that what this family has come to?" He groaned.

A wave of shame swept over me. First, I'd lied to my daughter, and now I was trying to make my son do my dirty work for me. "No, it's not like that. I'll . . . call him myself. You know what, I'll do even better than that. I'll drive over and see if she's there. Okay? Bye *kanna.*"

"Actually, Mom, while I've got you on the phone, I want to talk to you about . . ."

In my haste, I couldn't hear the rest of his sentence. I threw my phone in my purse and raced to the door.

18

PRIYA

Dive bars weren't really my thing. Stale with the smell of old sweat and uncleaned bathrooms, the sounds of Carrie Underwood and Shania Twain (or maybe if you were very lucky, Patsy Cline and Willie Nelson) blaring in the background—they weren't places I tended to linger.

But they had one redeeming feature—no, make that two. You could drink all you wanted without fear of judgment. And you could sit at the bar and smoke cigarettes (in small-town Texas, anyway), and no one would bother you about it. Those were not small things in this world. They were, on occasion, estimable things, to be given their proper due.

"What can I get you?" A large woman wearing a Houston Texans shirt, with a smattering of facial hair across her chin, leaned across the bar.

"Can I have a Manhattan, please?" If I had to be unfussy about the urine-tinged smell in the air, the torn vinyl barstool under my butt, and the crushed peanut shells digging into my wrist, then I was going to be fussy about my drink request. It was fair, under the circumstances.

"You got it," she said without missing a beat. She shoved a relatively clean red ashtray toward me.

I felt some pride at having spotted this nondescript place—Elmo's—not too far from Mom's apartment. I scanned the bar: mostly unkempt men in baseball caps squinting at an analog television tuned to ESPN, and a pair of young, skinny-jeaned, hipster types, trying to look nonchalant, as if they weren't changing the chemistry of the bar by their very presence.

After leaving Dad's house, I'd headed back in the direction of Mom's condo, intending to grab my laptop and blow this town. But in a daze, I'd taken one wrong turn and then another (directions were never my strong suit), until I found myself at a stop sign in front of a bar with green doors and a neon sign in front. The parking lot was bordered by a large, graffitied wall.

Instinctively, I read the first graffitied phrase my eyes landed on. It was written in loopy black spray paint: I FEEL IN LOVE WITH HALF A HEART. My breath caught in my chest.

Was graffiti the new fortune cookie, there to sporadically creep a person out with its unexpected omniscience? Well, at the very least, it seemed like a sign. A sign that I should stop and get a drink.

My eyes went to the graffitied phrase beside it, also in loopy black spray paint: DEREK IS A DILDO. Okay, so much for signs. But I'd figured one drink before returning to Mom's couldn't hurt. In fact, a drink seemed necessary. So here I was, with one palm curled around a sweating glass and two fingers gripping a cigarette.

Two cigarettes in an ashtray . . . Patsy Cline's voice began filling the stale air. Well, okay. Maybe things were looking up now.

"Priya, right?" A young woman's voice interrupted Patsy.

I turned to the sight of gray leggings and a shredded black tank top. It was Mom's library coworker—that Deanna girl. For fuck's sake. How was this possible? Was there no other bar in this stupid town for her to go to?

"Yeah." I nodded. "Hi, Deanna. What are you doing here?"

She slid onto the barstool next to mine. "This place is a block away from me. I'm here for the burger—it's the best. I come here all the time. Hey, Brenda, can I get a burger and fries?"

The bartender nodded from the opposite end, where she was handing an old man a bottle of Shiner Bock.

"I thought you were vegetarian. You didn't eat meat at the Chinese place," I said.

"I just ordered veggie that day for your mom. I'm a carnivore."

I took a sip of my drink and considered her annoyingly skinny figure. "I also thought you were anorexic. You barely touched your noodles that day."

"Wow, dude. You're bitchier than I remembered." She shook her head.

"Sorry." And I was. That was incredibly rude, even for me, even on a bad day like today. "It's been a really hard day, and I'm not working on all cylinders here."

"What's so hard about it? You only got to sleep until ten instead of noon? Did you run out of those spongy white idli-things to eat? Life is so hard for you."

"Wow, dude. You're bitchier than I remembered," I repeated, laughing. I tried to get the bartender's attention. "Brenda, can I get another Manhattan?"

Deanna laughed too. "Okay, so we're even. All right, tell me. What's so bad about today?"

I considered her for a moment. Her eyes were wide and curious, with just a glint of mockery. What made her think I was going to bare my soul to her anyway? For all I knew, she was going to turn around and tell my mother. But then again, what did I care if she did? I was leaving town soon enough. And it felt good to be talking to someone. Anyone. Even this girl.

"Hmm, let's see. Where to begin? Well, I'm sure you know all about this, since you and my mom are like BFFs now, but I found a CD in my mother's room from that weird jazz-professor guy, who I can only assume is going to be my new stepdad."

Deanna nodded. "Naturally. 'Cause that's the way it works. First comes a CD. Then comes marriage. And if your mom wasn't postmenopausal, I'd assume she was preggers too."

"Very funny. Anyway, I went to my dad's house, and apparently, he has a new family now. Some lady who's barely older than me and her son have moved in with him. And there's no point trying to tell my brother about any of this, because he's got his perfect kid and his perfect wife and his perfect Brooklyn condo and his life's all figured out or whatever, so he doesn't seem to give a shit about what the rest of us do. If I called him, he'd just tell me to get a life."

Deanna shrugged. "Sounds about right."

"What sounds about right?" The Manhattan was starting to make my brain fuzzy. I was starting to slur my words a little. It would have been a good idea to eat dinner today. Or lunch.

"The you-needing-to-get-a-life part." She bit into her burger. A drop of grease rolled down her wrist.

"What do you know? I mean, wouldn't you be the least bit weirded out if your parents suddenly transformed into lying teenagers, sneaking around behind your back? Parents aren't supposed to change on you like this." I sucked the last few drops of Manhattan out of the glass. It was probably time to stop. "Brenda, can I have another one? These are really something."

And they were too. Who knew that in this tiny nothing of a dive bar in Clayborn, a bearded bartender lady wearing a Houston Texans shirt made the best Manhattans in the world? At any other moment, I'd really revel in that discovery. I'd think something like: *Take that all you asshole mixologists in swanky downtown bars charging twenty bucks a drink! Bearded Brenda totally kicks your ass!* But at the moment, I was too miserable to celebrate Brenda's coup.

Deanna dipped her fry in ketchup and munched. I stuck my hand in her basket and pulled out two fries for myself.

"You want to talk about parents changing," she said. "My dad is my mom's third husband. Three years ago, they quit their jobs and moved to some ashram in northern Oregon, and I've barely seen them since. They're irresponsible jerk-offs, and maybe once a year, they drag their heads out of their asses and remember they've got a daughter." She took an angry bite out of her burger and chewed vigorously.

"Your mom's cool," Deanna continued, a thin trickle of grease on her chin. "At least she gives a shit about you and makes you those white spongy things to eat. Mine just meditates in some corner like a useless blob. At least when you have a breakdown like the one you seem to be having now, you've got someplace to go and hide from the world. My parents don't even have a spare room for me. Forget the spare room, they don't have a job. They don't have health insurance. They don't have a 401K. Who do you think will be paying for their sorry asses when they're old and sick?"

Deanna was funny. I had to give her that. I laughed and reached for another fry. She slapped my hand.

"Oh, you think that's funny, huh? Well, let me tell you something that will wipe that smile off your face. Leonard Greenberg, jazz-professor man, has a huge-ass crush on your mother. And you know what? I think your mom kind of likes him too, if she'd let herself consider the possibility of being happy."

"Wait—so she's not dating him already?" I asked. My face brightened. "She won't go out with him?"

"Listen to yourself. Don't you want your mom to have some happiness? Don't you ever want her to get laid again?"

"Shut up." I groaned and covered my ears.

"You know what I think?" she continued, her mouth full.

"No. And I don't want to."

"I think you're jealous."

"Of you?" I looked disdainfully at her. Who did this girl think she was? The sheer vanity of twenty-year-olds—always thinking that people were jealous of them.

"No, dummy. Your parents." Deanna rolled her eyes and took another bite.

"That's ridiculous." I snorted some Manhattan out of my nose and slid a little off the stool. This was my third and, possibly, I was losing some of my customary elegance. Possibly, I was well on my way toward losing it completely.

She shrugged. "No it's not. You're jealous because they're out there trying to live their lives and be happy."

"I'm trying to be happy! I'm trying! I have a boyfriend—well, sort of. And we've been together for almost two years. And he's smart, and he makes me laugh, and he has great teeth, and I told him that I loved him today." I gulped the rest of my drink down. "And okay, so yes, he's married, but he loves me . . . he told me so. He told his therapist too. And you know, I think he'll leave his wife. Probably. I don't know. She's really pretty. I just don't fucking know. How did this happen to me?" I waved my empty glass.

"Brenda, can I have another one of these?" I couldn't be sure, because things were starting to get a bit blurry, but Brenda seemed to exchange some kind of conspiratorial look with Deanna. Deanna rolled her eyes and shrugged in response, at which point Brenda started to mix another Manhattan. Annoyed, I tapped Deanna's shoulder. "What's your problem with me anyway?"

"I barely know you. But from the little I've seen, I think you're whiny and you blame other people for your problems. Why are you hiding out at your mom's apartment? Aren't you like forty or something?"

"I'm thirty-five! Not forty!"

"Well look, I'm not the best with relationship advice, but if you want to be with this married guy, tell him to leave his wife or go fuck himself. If he doesn't, look for someone new. Simple."

"You think it's all so easy. Look at you, of course you do. You're twenty years old, and life seems like one big . . . plate of fries." I chose the nearest metaphor my eyes landed on. I grabbed her basket of food and waved it around, and a few fries fell onto the counter.

"You try one fry, and if you don't like it, no problem, you can throw it on the counter, because you've got a whole basket more. But just wait a decade or so. Your world—your basket—starts shrinking. All those possibilities, they start disappearing. Until one day, all you've got is one, maybe two fries, tops, left in your basket, and you can't just throw one away, because if you do, then there'll be no more fries left, and it'll just be you all alone with an empty basket. And meanwhile, everyone else you know is filling their basket with husband fries and baby fries, while your basket stays empty, and . . . you never imagine it when you're young that you might end up with an empty basket . . . but time passes so fast and . . . it happens, and you think back that you shouldn't have wasted those fries when you had them in your basket, that you should have paid more attention to the fries that you had, but . . . it all feels too late. Do you see what I'm saying here?"

I pounded the counter for effect. The effort winded me.

"I want fries. Husband fry. Baby fry. Why does everyone else get to have that? Why not me? What's wrong with me? Well, actually, Chalini can't have baby fries, you know? She's infertile." I wagged my finger in Deanna's face.

"Who the hell is Chalini?" Deanna said.

"Exactly. Who the hell is she? What's so great about her?"

The room was blurry. I was tired now. I needed to rest. I lay my head on the counter and tried to ignore the peanut shell pressing into my forehead.

19

LATA

Even in the dark, I could tell the landscaping had been tended. What I had expected, of course, was a mess: untamed grass, overgrown hedges, crepe myrtles bent toward the ground like torture victims begging for mercy.

But no: In the dark at least, everything looked as good as I had left it. Maybe even better. Was it possible that Suresh had actually hired someone to take care of all this? That the home-improvement miser had actually *paid* a gardener? Priya had mentioned something about him gardening now—had he really done this himself? Perhaps the neighbors had shamed him into it.

I hadn't been back here in months. Over twenty years of my life I had spent within the walls of this house. Thousands of hours spent cleaning, polishing, vacuuming, and dusting its endless corners. Hundreds of hours spent planning its creation, choosing every little detail, from doorknobs to grout color, ignoring Suresh's grumblings about the expense of marble tiles, plush carpeting, and real wood floors. It was to be my "dream house," as they liked to say on *Oprah*. A dream house that would make me scream and clap and dance with joy—if not on the outside, like those people on *Oprah*, then at least on the inside. But I'd come to learn that dream houses were a dangerous concept. They gave you license to dream not just of gleaming fixtures and marble tiles, but of a better life within. A dream house fit for a dream life.

But strangely, once I decided to leave the house to Suresh, I found it easy not to miss all those things I had plotted and planned and fought Suresh so adamantly for. It embarrassed me now, my persistence in pushing for those expensive extras. And yet, I had felt such a need for them back then, as if those elegant fixtures were something I could hold on to, to keep from floating away. These days, I felt steadier—my feet firmly on the ground.

I shut the car door and scanned the street for Priya's silver Civic. Had she parked in the garage? Maybe she and her father were both in the kitchen now, sitting side by side on barstools, sharing a pizza and commiserating about my loose morals.

Well, I wouldn't apologize. Forget it. Not in front of Suresh. I hadn't done anything wrong, so what exactly could they accuse me of? I hadn't even been on a date yet. So what if I had accepted a gift—two gifts—from a new friend? I lifted my head high and rang the doorbell. I was prepared to weather any attack. I had nothing to apologize for.

The front door was thrown open by a child. A very good-looking child, who seemed about eight. I was flipping through my mental photo album of our friends' and relatives' children, when two adult voices called out in the background. One was unmistakably Suresh's, yelling, "Bobby, who is it?" The other, a worried female voice, sounded nothing like Priya: "Bobby, you can't just open the front door like that."

The woman reached the door first and placed a protective hand on the boy's shoulder. "Hello, may I help you with something?"

The boy and the woman—a very pretty woman, who looked maybe a handful of years older than Priya—stared curiously at me. Suresh's heavy footsteps were fast approaching. I gripped the door's edge. I did not feel so steady now.

"What are you doing here?" Suresh gasped.

"I . . ." What was I doing here? I was having trouble remembering. I was having trouble focusing on anything but the pretty woman's hair—thick, long, wavy hair, hanging loose around her shoulders. The kind of hair you'd see in a Pantene advertisement.

"Priya. I'm looking for Priya." I tore my eyes away from the pretty woman's curtain of hair and fixed them on Suresh. Drops of sweat had accumulated on his upper lip.

"Priya? Why would she be here?"

"Do you want to come inside?" The Pantene-hair woman opened the door wider, beckoning me inside.

As if it were her door. The mahogany door I'd spent two days touring warehouses to find. The Pantene-hair woman stretched her arm toward the foyer, directing everyone toward it. As if it were her foyer. The foyer in which I'd spent three weeks testing samples of pale yellow paint, gauging hues in various stages of daylight, before choosing one the color of whipped butter. The Pantene-hair woman laughed. "It seems silly, after all, to talk on the doorstep." As if it were her doorstep.

"Yes, of course. Come inside." Suresh now too was gesturing toward the foyer. As if they were hosting a party together and ushering a guest inside.

What could I do—run away? Teeth gritted, I followed them. Once inside the foyer, no one spoke. We all stared, waiting for someone to speak.

"This is . . ." Suresh began, just as the boy said, "Who are you?"

"Bobby, that's not nice," the Pantene-hair woman scolded. She smiled apologetically at me.

"Okay, well, this loud young man is Bobby. And this is . . . ah, his mother, Mallika." Suresh spoke hurriedly, his eyes never leaving my face. "Meet Lata, my . . . ah."

"His ex-wife. Obviously," I said, my cheeks burning.

"What's an X-wife?" Bobby said, looking curiously at me. "Is that like X-Men?"

"Bobby, please be quiet," Mallika scolded.

The boy shrugged and continued to stare at me. I stared back at the three of them huddled close together like a family posing for a portrait, the buttery walls like a canvas behind them. I shook my head clear and marched past them into the living room.

"I'm looking for Priya. She's been staying at my house, but she didn't come home. I need to find her."

Despite my growing panic, I was suddenly struck by the absurdity of it all—that I had rushed over here, concerned that Priya's finding Len's CD would sink her further into the depression she kept denying she was in. And instead, what did I find? Suresh had taken up with a new, younger woman. With a child. Was it possible that Priya knew? That Nikesh knew? That the two of them had purposely kept me in the dark for fear of hurting my feelings, and by not telling me, allowed me to walk into this house like a complete fool?

"Priya has been staying with you? How could she not tell me?" Suresh asked.

I gasped at the gall of his question. "Well, there's been a lot of not telling things, hasn't there?"

For a moment, he looked sheepish. Then, he burst: "I've tried to tell you things, Lata! I called you. I wanted to tell you about our daughter and how she's throwing her life away by smoking and having an affair with a married man. That's right! She told me her boyfriend has a wife. But did you have the common decency to call me back? No! Did you have the common decency to call and let me know that she's staying with you? No! And now look—she's gone missing."

Mallika drew her hand to her mouth and pulled Bobby closer to her, as if trying to shield him from the corrupting stain of our bad parenting.

Priya was seeing a married man? And smoking? I wouldn't believe it until I'd spoken to her myself. I ran up the stairs, shouting: "Priya! Are you here? Priya!"

I opened the door to Priya's old bedroom. Everything was the same: the silvery green bedspread, the large stuffed elephant in the corner, the assortment of trophies on the shelves. But the closet door was open. I stepped inside and heard an unpleasant cracking sound. I bent down and removed an object from beneath my foot: a cellphone.

Priya's cellphone. I'd been telling her for months to get a cover for it, but Priya had, as usual, ignored me. The screen was ruined.

Relief flooded through me. So she'd been here recently. Maybe she was back at my apartment now, safe and sound, and I had just missed her.

Just as the relief came, a new feeling replaced it: rage. How dare he? How dare he blame me? For *anything*. What kind of example was he, anyway? Living with a woman practically his daughter's age, by the looks of her? Who was he to be giving lectures to anyone? There he was: aimless, ill-tempered, overweight . . . and this man, *this man* had found a new girlfriend? One with Pantene hair, no less. Presto, he'd magically started a new life. And meanwhile, I'd been feeling guilty because a perfectly respectable, nice, age-appropriate, educated man had asked me to go to a jazz concert, had offered me a chance to see something new on a Saturday evening instead of staying home alone, shrouded in a blanket, watching television.

This was typical, really. Indian men could get divorced, and before the ink dried on the divorce papers, they'd marry a new woman half their age, have a new kid, start a new life, and nobody cared. They were applauded for it. By their mothers, their siblings, their friends. But a divorced Indian woman my age?

She had one of three options: (1) to live out the rest of her days alone, humbled as if she were a widow; (2) to move in with her adult children, provide permanent babysitting for grandchildren, and act thankful about it; or (3) to move back to India and take care of her aged parents. Those were her socially sanctioned, statistically likely options. But trying to find companionship . . . and with a non-Indian, no less? That was considered ridiculous and implausible.

Waving Priya's cracked phone in my hand like a sword, I ran down the stairs, prepared to do battle. "She was here! Her phone was in the closet. And do you know why she left, why you had no idea she was here? I bet she took one look at you with this new girlfriend half your age and ran out of the house! It's your fault that she's gone! You ruined everything! You ruined our marriage, you ruined our family, you ruined my youth; and if your daughter's life is not what you wanted, if she's ruining her life, just as you ruined yours, then you have no one but yourself to blame!"

And before Suresh could say one word, I threw Priya's cracked phone into his shocked face and ran out the front door and into the safe, warm quiet of my car.

I turned the key in the ignition and paused to catch my breath. My heart was racing so fast, I feared it would stop. I rested my head on the steering wheel, causing the horn to beep.

I bolted upright and looked worriedly in the direction of the house. The last thing I needed was for the horn to cause Suresh to come outside. Thank God, the front door of the house was still shut.

But the horn did cause someone to jump. Out of the corner of my eye, I could see a man at the far edge of the lawn, where the house bordered the neighbor's house. I squinted to get a better look at him. He was holding something in his hand. I couldn't tell for sure in the dark, but it looked like one of those bulky, fancy cameras. Was he taking photographs of the house?

Before I could consider the matter further, my phone started buzzing. I didn't recognize the number, but what if it was Priya calling from a borrowed phone?

"Priya, is that you?" I gasped.

"No. It's Deanna. Your daughter's at my apartment. She's totally fine, but you should probably come pick her up. She's in no condition to drive. Or if it's too late for you to come get her, she can crash on my couch."

"Why can't she . . . ? Never mind. Tell me your address. I'll come right there."

As she spoke, I glanced once more at the man lurking in the yard. Well, if he was a burglar, that wasn't my problem. And Suresh had an excellent security system. I'd insisted on it when we built the house. The cameraman was probably just one of those birder people, who liked to walk and take pictures of birds. Maybe he was taking pictures of night birds. Owls. Or stars. Whatever it was, Suresh would be fine.

Right now, I had a more pressing task: to collect my daughter.

20

SURESH

When I entered the kitchen, Bobby and Mallika were already there. I had slept late—it was after nine. I was still tired, though. And my body ached. I had tossed and turned until three in the morning.

Bobby was sitting on a stool at the counter, eating cereal. Mallika was at the stove, cracking eggs into a pan. The smell of onions sizzling in butter filled the air. Usually, those smells would make my stomach grumble in anticipation. Today, though, my stomach felt like lead. I couldn't get Lata's words from last night out of my head. *You ruined everything.*

"Suresh Uncle, do you want some Cap'n Crunch?" Bobby held out his bowl.

I sat down next to him at the counter and folded my hands in my lap. "No thanks. I don't feel like eating anything."

"Suresh, you have to eat something," Mallika said. "How about some omelet. I'm making it your favorite way—with onions and cheese and chopped jalapeños."

"How come you aren't hungry? You always eat breakfast,"

Bobby said, his mouth half full of cereal. "Is it because of your ex-wife?"

"Bobby!" Mallika exclaimed.

It was such an adult question posed so innocently by a child. I smiled in spite of myself. "Yes. It's because of my ex-wife."

"She should not have thrown a phone at you," Bobby said, wagging his finger. "Mom says you aren't supposed to throw things at people, no matter how mad you get. It's not appropriate behavior."

"Bobby, can you please leave Suresh Uncle alone?" She cast an apologetic look in my direction.

"It's okay, Mallika. The boy is entitled to his questions. After all, he witnessed everything." I turned to Bobby and put my hand on his thin, knobby shoulder. "You are right, Bobby. She probably shouldn't have thrown a phone at me. But on very rare occasions, a person might do something to deserve a phone being thrown at them."

"Like what?" Bobby paused in his cereal munching and watched me with unusual interest.

"Like . . . you say something you shouldn't have said, something hurtful, and you do it on purpose, just to punish someone and make them feel bad."

Bobby considered this. "So when Ryan tells me I throw like a girl or tells his friends I'm an A-rab, I can throw a phone at him."

Alarmed, I looked at Mallika. Bobby's remark had surprised her as well. She dropped the spatula she was holding and it clattered into the pan.

"No, no, don't do that!" I said. The last thing I needed was to be the cause of some disciplinary problem at Bobby's school (when, and if, he ever returned). "Look, Bobby, this phone-throwing exception is only for adults who have a long history with each other. But children are different, okay? Children have no histories with one another. Children can always start fresh and iron out their differences. Children should never throw cell-phones at one another. So promise me that you won't."

"Okay, I promise."

"I know you won't. You're a good boy." I ruffled his mop of hair. I realized at that moment how much I liked him. I hoped that my fight with Lata had not upset him. The poor child had suffered enough—first losing his dad to prison and then being uprooted from his home to a stranger's house.

"Okay." He shrugged. "I'm gonna go play Xbox now!" Bobby jumped from his chair and sprinted out of the kitchen.

"Don't forget to brush your teeth," Mallika shouted after him. She shook her head. "That boy. It was good of you to indulge his questions," she said, nodding at me.

"If I were him, and I'd seen a grown woman shouting and throwing a cellphone at someone's head, I'd be asking questions too." I closed my eyes and sighed. How could Lata have done that to me? She had never been a violent woman during our marriage. She'd never thrown anything at my head before. She might have thrown a plate or two on the floor. But not at my head. What had come over her?

My stomach emitted a low growl. Those oniony-cheesy-eggy smells were starting to have an effect on me. Even before I could tell Mallika I'd changed my mind about the eggs, she approached the counter, heaping plate in hand. She placed it in front of me. "Butter toast is on the way," she said.

I leaned forward and inhaled the spicy, buttery smell. "Thank you. It smells delicious." I lifted a forkful into my mouth.

"Suresh, I think you should talk to them," Mallika said.

"Who?" I responded, between forkfuls of egg.

"Your ex-wife and daughter."

"I appreciate your concern, but they don't want to talk to me. They've made that perfectly clear."

"No, they are upset with you because of us. We should go. We're making it hard for you to put your family back together."

She grabbed a wet dish towel and rubbed circles on the counter-top.

I put my fork down with a clang. The idea of them leaving me alone in his house again was too much to bear. "That wouldn't solve anything. They were upset with me before you came. They're upset with me because . . . I'm not a very good man."

She sat down next to me, her eyes wide and kind. "You are a good man. Let your family see that. Go explain yourself to them."

From the pocket of her robe, she pulled out Priya's cracked phone and placed it in front of me. "She came here to see you. That's why her phone was here. And then, who knows, maybe she saw us and changed her mind. Which brings me to the point I started with—it's time for us to go."

I covered her hand with my own. Hers was still damp from the dish towel. "Please don't go—not yet. I'll talk to Priya, I promise. But stay through the weekend—at least."

Mallika looked thoughtful. She squeezed my hand. "Okay."

Then she tapped the cracked glass screen of the phone. "Here's an idea. Why don't you get your daughter a new phone and then take it to her. Like a peace offering. That might be a good place to start."

I picked up the phone. The cracks etched in the screen made a delicate, weblike pattern. I pressed a button to turn it on, but nothing happened. It was dead.

I didn't share Mallika's optimism. Somehow, I didn't think a new phone would make Priya or Lata change their attitudes toward me. But then again, what did I have to lose at this point? Neither of them was talking to me anyway. And maybe getting Priya a new phone would somehow convince Mallika to stay a little longer.

"Okay. I'll get Priya a new phone. Tomorrow. And I'll take it to her mother's condo."

21

NIKESH

"So when we land, we'll go straight to my mom's condo, spend some time there. And then we'll head to my dad's in the evening and spend the night there."

I stuffed the diaper bag as far as it would go under the seat in front of me and tried to quell my feelings of guilt. Here we were on a flight to Texas, and I still hadn't told my parents the truth.

"Your parents do know, right?" Denise asked.

I froze. Did she suspect something? Had I given something away, like a poker tell?

Denise placed Alok in my lap and started digging into the cushions for her seatbelt straps. "Nikesh, your parents do know that we're coming today, right?"

Relief poured through me. She still believed me.

"Of course my parents know we're coming," I said, shifting Alok so he could stare out the window. "In fact, I emailed both of them our flight itinerary yesterday."

What I didn't tell her is that I had called them both too—twice. But neither of them had answered nor returned my voicemails. It was weird actually. Usually, they called me back pretty quickly—within twenty-hour hours. Maybe it was all for the best this way. I could tell them everything in person when I got to Clayborn. I'd just have to find a way to get time with each of my parents alone, with Denise far out of the way.

"You know how your parents are," Denise said. "Planning and attention to detail is not their strong suit. Remember the last time we visited? We were waiting outside of baggage claim for over an hour because your dad went to the wrong airport in Houston." She rolled her eyes.

"Dad thought we were flying into Intercontinental instead of Hobby. In his defense, most flights do go to Intercontinental because it's fifty times bigger than Hobby. It's an easy mistake to make. Anyway, this time, we're renting a car in Houston and driving to Clayborn ourselves, so you don't have to worry about that."

Irritated with her needling, I shoved the window shade farther up, so Alok's view was unobstructed. I pointed out the baggage handlers loading luggage onto the plane. "Look, buddy, they're putting suitcases on the plane."

Alok probably had no idea what I was talking about, but I'd recently heard some parenting segment on NPR about adults narrating their actions to babies to aid verbal development, or something like that. Plus, it was a convenient way to ignore Denise.

Okay, so maybe her criticisms were not entirely unfounded. I knew my family was not the best when it came to travel details. Or punctuality. But in their defense, it was a cultural failing. Indian people were constitutionally incapable of being on time or attentive to details when travel was concerned. For evidence of this, you could just go to any train station in India. Or bus station. Or airport. Maybe it was one reason why the British were a poor fit, as far as colonizers went. That is, if one was ranking the fit of potential colonizers like one would party guests or vacation companions. Which was an insane way of looking at it, as there was no such thing as a "good-fitting" colonizer. They were assholes, the lot of them.

"Well, are they ready for this birthday party? It's still happening, right? Because that's the whole reason we're here."

"Obviously, it's happening. Alok's birthday is like the highlight of my parents' existence right now. He's basically all they have to look forward to these days."

But even as I spoke, doubts sprouted in me. Not only had neither of my parents returned my calls yesterday, but they hadn't uttered a single word about Alok's birthday in weeks. Dad—well, he wasn't the type to chatter excitedly about a child's birthday party. Or any kind of party, really. But Mom?

A few weeks ago, she'd called me up, asking if she could invite the Chandrasekhars to the party, since they'd been "dying to meet Alok." And I said, yes, of course, she could invite whomever she wanted. Then she pressed me for a party theme, and I suggested *The Very Hungry Caterpillar,* but Mom said she didn't know what that was, so I said: "Okay do *Sesame Street* then. The kid loves Elmo." And then she prattled on about going to Target to look for Elmo-themed paper plates and napkins and decorations. But since that conversation, not a word about the party.

And during the last phone conversation I had with her, she'd been so bizarrely freaked about Priya being out late that she'd basically hung up on me before I could talk about anything. Was that why they weren't retuning my phone calls? Because Priya was having some kind of early midlife crisis?

"I think my sister has been staying with my mom for a while," I said.

"Oh, then I'm definitely glad we're staying at your dad's. Your sister is basically an asshole to me. Your mom becomes mute around me. And your dad is mostly indifferent, which makes him my favorite of the lot."

"Hey," I said, covering Alok's ears.

"What? You know it's true."

Denise was right to be frustrated with my family. They had never gone out of their way to welcome her. But it wasn't as if she'd really tried to get to know them either. The few times she'd been around them, she found any excuse to disappear into a "work call" or a "work email" or a "work emergency."

"You're right. My family could try harder with you. I'll talk to them about it. But don't you think that maybe you could try a little harder too? Just a tiny bit? I really want you all to know one another better." I had high hopes for this weekend. That call with Elena had been shitty but clarifying. I wanted to make things right with Denise. I wanted my parents to see a different side of her than they'd seen so far—and vice versa.

Denise rolled her eyes.

"Please? For Alok's sake, if not mine." I turned Alok around in my lap and rested my chin on his head.

"Ma-ma," Alok said, clapping. Perfectly on cue. The kid was a fucking genius.

Denise laughed. "Okay fine, I'll try. At least with your dad. And maybe with your mom if she actually deigns to talk to me. With your sister, all bets are off. If she comes for me, I'm going to let her have it." She closed her eyes and sighed. "Well, at least this trip, I don't have to pretend we're married. The truth is out. That's something."

"Right." Jesus. I had to figure out how to corner each of my parents as soon as we got to Clayborn, so I could tell them both before Denise said something that gave it away.

Our seats began vibrating in preparation for takeoff. I rubbed my temples.

Maybe this trip was a really bad idea after all. We should have just had a birthday for Alok in Brooklyn and called it a day.

Well, it was too late for second thoughts now.

I turned Alok back to face the window. He pounded his little palms on the glass and said "bah-bah," a trail of drool on his lower lip.

I wiped it away. "That's right, buddy. Say bye-bye to New York. We're going to see your *paati* and your *tatta* and your crazy *attai* Priya."

22

PRIYA

"Don't you have any clothes that show off your boobs more? You've got them. Why hide them behind three layers of clothing?" Deanna said. She scowled at my mother's outfit—crisp black pants, cream silk blouse, and thin red cardigan.

I sat on the bed, watching Mom twist left, then right, assessing her outfit choice in the dresser mirror. Deanna stood to her left, shaking her head derisively.

"What do you want her to dress like—a Vegas showgirl?" I said. "You're trying to torture me."

"I'm not trying to torture you. It's just one of the perks of truthful commentary here. Look, Lata, you look pretty damn good for fifty-whatever. So why not dress more youthfully? I mean, can't you wear a skirt or something? It's a date, not a driver's license test."

Mom did what she'd been doing for the past hour: She ignored us. She reached for a tube of lipstick and ran it over her lips.

"So, Mom, what time do you plan to be home? Take your phone, just in case."

Deanna snorted. "You're such a pill."

"Deanna, I don't know who officially inducted you into this family, but I'm about two seconds from throwing you out."

"Girls, stop! I'm nervous enough as it is." She shot stern looks at both of us. "I thought you were both here to help, but all you've done for the past hour is argue." She put her palm against her forehead and sighed. "Deanna, would you make me some tea? The kettle is on the stove and the teabags are in the top left cupboard. If I drink a cup now, I can be sure that I won't fall asleep if this concert goes past eleven." She looked meaningfully at Deanna.

"Eleven? You're staying out until eleven?" I said.

Deanna left the room, sending another snort of disgust my way.

Mom sat next to me on the bed. "I thought we talked about this."

"What do you mean?" I asked, assuming an expression of innocence.

A mixture of disappointment and exhaustion settled on her face. It made her look the tiniest bit older, which made me happy.

I had very little memory of my mother collecting my drunk, lifeless body from Deanna's, but it couldn't have been pretty. After waking up with a splitting headache yesterday morning, I'd stumbled into the kitchen, where Mom was unloading the dishwasher. "Mom, I'm sorry," I said. "I don't usually get drunk and pass out on barstools. I don't even know how Deanna got me into her car and into her apartment. She weighs about as much as a ten-year-old." I was trying for some levity. All I got in response was a tautening of mouth.

"Um . . . no, seriously. It was nice of her to take care of me. She told me more about Leonard, the guy who made you that CD. He's your new friend?"

"Yes. He's my new friend. He asked me to go to a jazz concert with him tomorrow. And I've decided to go. I don't have to ask permission. I'm free to do what I like. Why do you give your father that luxury, but not me?" She put a mug in the cupboard with such force, it probably chipped. "I went to the house. I know what you all have been keeping from me."

I sat on the countertop and drew my knees up to my chin. "I didn't know either."

"Really? You didn't know he was living with someone? A woman barely older than you, with a child?"

"Well, I knew he'd been, you know, going on dates or whatever, but I didn't know he was dating anyone seriously; and I definitely didn't know this woman and her kid moved in with him. It was a shock to me too." I paused for a moment. "Your CD was kind of a shock too. It was a shocking sort of day. That's what led me to, you know, get drunk or whatever."

Mom wiped the moisture off a plate with a dishcloth. "Is that what you do when you're distressed? You get drunk enough to pass out in public? Your father says you smoke: Do you?"

"Not usually." She looked suspiciously at my mouth, as if scouting for tiny lines that would reveal the truth. "Well, not that much. And I'm quitting. I haven't been doing it here, see?"

She shook her head. "Who knows what any of you do."

"If you're upset about Dad's new girlfriend, does that mean . . . you have feelings for him?" I asked.

"No, Priya. I was upset that you disappeared from this house without a word. I was upset to walk into that house and look like a fool in front of your father. But I have no intention of going back to him, or to that house."

I nodded. "He's done a pretty good job with the landscaping, though. Come on, you have to admit that."

She smiled at last. "Yes, I'll admit that. It looks better than when I was doing it, even."

Seeing an opening, I pressed further. "So what about this jazz-professor guy? Is he just a friend, or are you, like, really dating him?"

"Right now, he's my friend." She shoved the dishwasher door shut—her way, I suppose, of saying the subject was closed.

After that, we had a daylong truce. No incendiary subjects— Dad, Len, smoking, et cetera. And then came this evening, bringing with it an ill-timed visit from Deanna, who was dropping off my wallet, which had somehow fallen out of my purse and into her car during my drunken state. And so here we were now, my mother and I, returning to those subjects we could no longer avoid.

Meeting my mother's disappointed gaze, I shot her one of my own. "Don't you think it's weird that I'm getting you ready for your first date, when . . . you never did this for me?" My voice quavered.

Mom blinked once, twice, a pained look on her face. "I'm sorry, but I just . . . wasn't prepared back then. We didn't have a relationship like that, and now that I'm older, I wish it had been otherwise. I wish I could have helped you with that part of your life, given you good advice. But I don't know if I could have. What did I know about dating? What advice could I have given you? Maybe I could have just listened. Maybe I should have asked more. But what good is regretting all that now? I did the best I could. You can't keep thinking about the past, wishing you'd done things differently. You have to move on. Or life becomes very hard." She wiped a tear from her freshly kohl-rimmed eye. "And lonely."

"I understand loneliness too."

To my surprise, I started to cry.

"What's all this your father says about a married man? Is it true?"

"I'm ashamed of the way it happened. But I'm not sorry. I think I love him." I wiped my eyes and reached for the box of Kleenex on the bedside table. I was too sad to be afraid anymore of what my mother thought.

"Does this man feel the same way about you?"

"I think so. He says he does. But I don't know if he'll leave his wife." Something about saying these words out loud to my mom made the situation feel more hopeless than I'd allowed myself to admit. My eyes welled up again. "Oh, Mom. It's a big mess."

Mom nodded. "It sounds like a big mess."

She put her arm around my shoulder and pulled me close. I sank against her, inhaling the familiar citrus scent of her perfume, waiting for her to tell me that everything would be all right.

She did not tell me that everything would be all right.

23

SURESH

So this was the complex where Lata lived?

I stared at the beige stucco building in front of me, flanked on either side by identical beige stucco buildings. The complex was called The Tuscany, though I was sure none of its inhabitants were fooled into thinking they lived in an Italian villa. I stood in the pillared entrance, next to a wall of mailboxes and a metal contraption that dispensed plastic bags for picking up dog shit. Its sign read: *Be a good neighbor. Clean up after your pets.*

Those ridiculous Chandrasekhars. They already had a six-thousand-square-foot house—why hold on to a condo on top of that? Hopefully, Lata had the good sense to push for a reduced rent. For all she knew, Mala was overcharging her. That Mala was crafty. I had no doubt she'd cheat her best friend if it allowed her to purchase a dozen new saris or a glittery jewelry set during her next trip to India.

Well, whatever Lata paid to live here, I had a hard time imagining her satisfied with condo life. As I remembered it, Lata liked wandering through rooms. When we lived together in our house, I'd enter the kitchen, and soon enough, she'd wander into the bedroom to look for something. Or I'd go to the bedroom, and she'd wander into the guest room to collect an extra blanket. A compulsive room-wanderer she was, going from room to room, fussing about, organizing trinkets, straightening pictures.

Our house had thirteen distinct rooms, if you counted the living room, dining room, study, game room, kitchen, bedrooms, and bathrooms. How did she manage her compulsive wandering here? Did she wander to the pool? The gym? The communal mailbox? Did she sit on these wooden benches and watch her neighbors collect their dogs' turds from the grass?

I studied the post office Change of Address Confirmation form in my right hand: *Apartment #2413*. The form was addressed to Lata, obviously, as she was the one who had requested the U.S. Postal Service forward her mail from our house to this odious place. I had hidden the confirmation form in my desk ever since it arrived a few days after she moved out. Even before that, Lata had offered to give me her forwarding address. But I'd refused to take it: "If you don't want our home to be your home, I have no interest in knowing where you live."

As far as Lata knew, that was the end of it. But then this confirmation form came, and I couldn't quite bring myself to throw it away. I wondered if a time would come when I'd need to know her address. I'd imagined a dozen scenarios where my pocketing of this change of address form would be heroic. Say, for example, Lata called me in a panic because a bookcase had fallen on her foot. Or she called me in a panic because she slipped in the bathtub and broke her nose. Or she called me in a panic because her apartment was on fire. But I never imagined using it under the present circumstances. So far from heroic.

I crumpled the form into my right pocket. In my left hand, I held a Best Buy bag with Priya's new phone in it. I pulled out the box and studied it.

It was a brand-new, top-of-the-line iPhone. Even the box looked like it belonged in a museum—slim, sleek, and white. The salesman had assured me it had every feature a person could want: maps, GPS, email, music library, everything. For a second, I had considered buying something cheaper. But I decided against it. This was, after all, a peace offering. Wasn't that how Mallika had put it? What Mallika had not given me, however, was a script to follow. I had no idea what to say—to Priya or Lata.

Well, that was if I ever actually found Lata's apartment. The numbering system at The Tuscany was extremely confusing. The numbered placard on the building wall said *Apartments 6001–6336*. Was it possible that there were 6336 apartments in this complex? And, if so, where in God's name was 2413?

A ponytailed young woman walked by me with a small, bushy white dog. "Excuse me, miss. Do you know where 2413 is?"

She chewed her gum, considering my question. "Oh, it's on the other side. Take a right at the pool and keep walking until you're at the second-to-last building in the complex."

"That makes no sense. Why not use a numbering system that starts with one? And proceeds in some kind of logical order?"

She raised her eyebrows and shrugged. "Got me."

Got me? Got her what? Was I to consider this the current vernacular for *I don't know and I don't care and I've never bothered to find out*? Before I could ask, she bounced away, her dog yapping in tow. This was clearly a generation that communicated in monosyllables and shrugs.

After walking the length of what felt like a full city block, I came upon the pool. Despite the warm temperature, the pool was empty. I kneeled by the edge of the water and dipped my right hand in. The water was cool without being cold. I made small clockwise circles in the water, and a funny thought came into my head: What if I took off my clothes and jumped into this pool? Put aside the fact that I couldn't swim or that I would never do such a thing. But just imagine the look on that mono-syllabic woman's face if she came back from walking her dog only to find me so. Would a nude brown man floating in the water merit a response more emphatic, more erudite than "got me"?

Or, for that matter, what if Lata came down tomorrow, only to see my naked, drowned corpse being fished out of this water? Would she feel remorse, a scintilla of regret for having accused me of ruining everything? *Everything?* Was one man even capable of wreaking that much havoc? Well, there was Hitler, I suppose. And Stalin. But they were sociopathic autocrats.

Besides, Nikesh had turned out fine. He was married, had a beautiful son, an impressive career. He was thriving. Didn't I have something to do with that?

I changed the motion of my right hand to counterclockwise and watched the ripples shift direction. The water was refreshing. A soothing tonic for my burdened psyche. I really should have learned to swim a long time ago. When I first came to this country, before the kids were born—I should have learned then.

Maybe I could convince Mallika to stay a little longer by promising to take them on that trip to Galveston. I would let her teach me how to swim. In the Gulf of Mexico. Maybe a man could start re-creating himself, one new learned skill at a time. Maybe it was never too late.

"Hey, are you okay over there?" A voice rang out from across the pool, startling me.

I dropped the Best Buy bag into the pool.

Oh no. No, no. Not the iPhone.

Who was that yelling idiot? The bag was starting to float away from the edge of the pool. I crouched over the edge and reached for it.

"Hey, are you okay?" the man yelled again. For God's sake,

why couldn't he just shut the bloody hell up and mind his own business?

I reached farther . . . almost had it. That damn phone. It was too expensive to drown. Just a little bit farther . . . there . . . got it.

An instant later, all I could feel was cold water entering my nose, and the sensation of sinking.

24

NIKESH

"Your mom's condo is here?" Denise gazed doubtfully at The Tuscany.

Her eyes scanned the stucco façades, the pillared entrances, the manicured hedges, the enormous parking lots with rows of cars baking in the sun (including our own rented Prius). She wrinkled her nose in barely veiled disgust.

I hoisted the stroller out of the trunk and sprang it open. While Denise unfastened Alok from the car seat, I grabbed the diaper bag and strapped it across my body. "It's a bit grim, I know. But she's just here temporarily. It's her friend's condo, and she's getting some discounted rate."

"Still, isn't it weird that your dad kept the house and your mom lives in this monstrosity? No offense."

"Come on, it's not that bad. Well, maybe it's pretty bad. But Mom didn't want the house. I still don't know why she didn't."

"Well, I can't say I understand her decision to live here. But whatever floats her boat, I guess. Let's get this show on the road. What's the apartment number again?" Denise said.

I uncrumpled the piece of paper in my pocket with Mom's address on it. "Apartment 2413."

"Is there a doorman for this building who can point us in the right direction?"

"No doorman. It's the South, ma'am, not New York." I pushed Alok's stroller, and the swishing sound of its wheels echoed through the concrete hallways. The first apartment we passed said *6316*. The second one said *6460*.

"What imbecile came up with this apartment numbering system?" Denise asked.

We strolled Alok down one long concrete hallway and then another and another until we spotted a large atrium with a pool, where two men bobbed violently in the water.

"Are those guys fighting in the water?" I wondered aloud.

Denise squinted. "No. I think one of them is drowning, and the other is trying to help."

"Wait here." I handed the stroller to Denise and began running to the pool. As I drew closer, I saw that it was Dad's head in the water, his arms struggling against the other man. "Dad!" I ran faster, my heart skittering in my chest.

By the time I reached them, the two drenched men were safely on the concrete, gasping for air.

"Dad! What happened?"

"Nik—" He started coughing uncontrollably.

"Easy there," the other guy said. "You're his son?"

"Yes. What happened here?"

"Nik . . . what are you . . ." Once again, Dad started coughing.

"Dad, don't try to talk." I patted his back, hoping to ease the coughing. I only made it worse, so I stopped patting, and turned to the other guy.

"I'm not entirely sure what happened. This man—your father—nosedived into the deep end of the pool fully clothed.

The next thing I know, he's flailing his arms, yelling for help because he doesn't know how to swim. So I jumped in and pulled him out."

"What? Oh man, thank you so much for doing that," I said.

I watched the man squeeze water out of his slacks and the sleeves of his button-down shirt. He was clearly dressed to go somewhere.

"I'm so sorry. Your clothes are ruined," I said. "I'll pay for the dry cleaning. I insist. Denise, do you have any cash on you?"

Denise pushed Alok toward us. Alok was waving his arms, saying "spla." "Spla" was his way of saying "splash," a word he liked to babble in the bath.

Dad was still struggling to catch his breath. Seeing Alok, he waved, unleashing a coughing fit.

"Dad, why did you go in the pool when you don't even know how to swim?" I got down on my knees. What was he even doing at my mother's condo? I thought they weren't really talking to each other. Was it possible that they were planning Alok's party together? A flicker of hope lit up in me. But the sight of Dad's nearly drowned body quickly put it out.

"You haven't been drinking again, have you?" I inspected his face for signs of drunkenness. But it was too hard to untangle the signs of drowning from signs of drunkenness.

"No, of course not!" Dad cleared his throat. "I dropped the phone into the water and . . . Oh no, where did the phone go? Is it still in the pool?"

"You dropped your phone into the water?" I said.

"No! Priya's phone. It's in a Best Buy bag!" Dad started coughing again.

"You mean, this?" Denise leaned over and grabbed a soggy blue plastic bag floating near the edge of the pool.

Dad reddened at the sight of Denise, as if embarrassed to be caught in such a compromised state. "Denise, hello. Yes—that's the bag I was trying to get!" *Cough, cough.*

"Dad, forget the bag. We need to **get you inside**," I said. "What's Mom's apartment number again?"

"Apartment 2413," Dad gasped.

The wet man stopped squeezing water out of his sleeves and looked curiously at us. "Did you say 2413?"

25

LATA

The tea was doing nothing to soothe me. I gazed hopelessly at the oven clock. Len was thirty minutes late.

"He's probably stuck in traffic," Deanna said, following my eyes. "It doesn't mean anything." Deanna refilled the kettle with water and set it on the burner.

I didn't say anything. It was a Saturday, so there was no work traffic. And the fall term had not yet started, so Clayborn's student population was largely gone. Besides, Len seemed like the kind of man who would call from the car if traffic was delaying him. I cupped my hands around the mug of tea and brought it to my face, letting the steam waft into my nose.

Priya watched me across the dining room table. "You know, this complex is not so easy to navigate. When I came here the first time, I wandered around for twenty minutes before I found your apartment."

I nodded. Yes, perhaps that was it. I too had gotten lost the first few times after moving here. In fact, I'd mistakenly put my key in the lock of an identical-looking apartment on the other side, 6414, the first week after I moved in. It was so embarrassing when a large man wearing a Gold's Gym T-shirt opened the door and peered suspiciously at me. Maybe Len was ringing that same man's doorbell at this precise moment. But then, what would stop him from calling and asking for directions? Had he forgotten his phone at home?

"Or maybe he got into a car accident," Priya said.

Startled by the suggestion, I nearly spilled my tea.

Priya raised her hands in the air, palms turned outward. "I wasn't suggesting it was likely, just a possibility."

Deanna rolled her eyes. "You're impossible."

"Look, I don't want my mom to think she's being stood up on her first-ever date."

For a moment, I pictured Len in his Montreal Jazz Festival hat, next to a policeman, surveying the damage from a three-car collision. And though I knew it was wrong, the image made me feel better.

"I knew this was a ridiculous idea. I should have said no." I went to the sink and rinsed my cup. I stood on my tiptoes, pushing my shoes off my feet. They were brand-new high-heeled pumps (not sandals, since I'd never gotten that pedicure) that dug painfully into the backs of my ankles. What was the point of keeping them on now, anyway? The doorbell rang: an answer to my unspoken question.

"See, it was traffic. I knew it," Deanna said triumphantly.

I stepped back into my shoes and stood frozen next to the sink. The bell rang again.

"Lata, aren't you going to answer it?" Deanna asked.

I wiped my hands on a dish towel, and then smoothed my hair. I walked to the door slowly and took a deep breath. The bell rang again. And then again.

"Well, he's in a goddamn hurry, isn't he? Kept you waiting for thirty minutes, and now he can't give you thirty seconds to answer the door," Priya said.

I tried to ignore the anger in Priya's voice and to prevent my own anger from creeping into my face. I opened the door with what I hoped was a pleasant and forgiving expression. Like Mother Teresa's. It was an expression that faded instantly. Standing in the doorway was a sopping-wet Suresh, propped up on one side by Nikesh and on the other by a wet Len. My eyes darted from one to the next in shocked confusion.

"Mom, I'll explain everything in a bit," Nikesh said. "But we need to get Dad inside." The next few seconds were lost in the commotion of wet bodies and water-soaked footsteps in the apartment.

Priya leapt from her chair and came running forward. "Nikesh? What are you doing here? And why is Dad wet? Dad, are you okay?" Suresh was coughing loudly. "Do you need to go to the hospital?" Priya asked, as Len relinquished Suresh's left side to her.

"I'm okay," Suresh said, gasping. "I don't need a hospital."

"Priya, can you stop talking for one second?" Nikesh said. "Let's get Dad situated first. Denise is walking Alok around the complex, and I'd really like to get the hysterics out of the way before the baby comes back."

Priya helped her father onto the couch and scowled at her brother. "Okay. He's situated. Now explain: What the fuck happened here?"

"Priya, don't use bad language," I scolded. I didn't know why, in the midst of the strange scene in front of me, I'd chosen to fixate on Priya's vocabulary. But it seemed the only constructive, black-and-white comment I could form at the moment. That I disliked my daughter's language was clear. Nothing else was.

Len cleared his throat. "Perhaps I should excuse myself and let you all discuss this privately." Everyone turned to look at the sopping man standing awkwardly near the front door.

Len's gray curls were wet and plastered against his forehead. His slacks and dress shirt stuck to his tall, narrow frame. Even his glasses seemed to have taken a beating; they were bent at a strange angle on his nose. But the expression on his face was concerned, and it was directed at me.

"No, don't go!" I said it with such force that everyone in the room stopped staring at Len and began staring at me.

"I mean . . . have some tea, or something before you go? You must be cold," I said, trying to sound as calm as I could.

"I guess that's my cue." Deanna turned toward the kitchen.

"Yeah, man, stay and have a cup of tea," Nikesh said.

God, I loved my son. Though I still wasn't sure why he was here. Why were any of them here right now? There weren't even enough chairs in my apartment for everyone to sit in. I didn't have enough teacups for this many people. I didn't understand: Why were they all here? The jazz concert would have started by now.

"Everyone should know what you did. This man saved Dad's life. He jumped into the pool and rescued him because Dad can't swim."

Now I understood why Len was so late. He was saving my idiot ex-husband from drowning. Suresh always managed to ruin everything for me. I glared at him.

Suresh was glaring at me too. Somewhere between the pool and my apartment, Len must have told them why he was headed over here—to see me.

"Well, that was good of him and all, but why was Dad in the pool fully clothed in the first place?" Priya asked.

Suresh cleared his throat and chest with one long, unappealing, phlegm-generating grunt. I had not missed that sound.

"I was just dipping my arms in the water, and then that man"—he pointed accusingly at Len—"yelled at me, causing me to drop the phone in the water, and then when I reached for it, I fell in! It's all his fault that I fell. And he hurt my arm too!" Suresh held his arm up and pointed to a faint blue bruise on his forearm. My children's questioning eyes swung toward Len.

"Now wait just a minute," Len said. "For the record, I shouted

'Are you okay' at him because he looked like he was ready to fall in fully clothed. And the next thing I know, he did. He's flailing his arms, yelling for help. So I jumped in to get him out. As for his arm, I told him to keep still, but he wouldn't. He kept fighting the water and me, and the only way I could get him to stop was to hold his arms down." Len shook his head in disbelief and turned to Suresh. "I apologize for hurting you, but I couldn't think of another way to get you out of the pool safely."

"Dad, the man rescued you from drowning. And he ruined his clothes in the process. You can't deny that. What's a little bruise compared to not drowning?" Nikesh said. "Len, we owe you a big one."

Nikesh looked my way, a slight smile playing on his lips. "So, Mom, what's this I hear about you going to a concert tonight?"

Len let out a small, hollow laugh. "Well, I think maybe there's been enough performance and excitement for one night." He turned toward me. "Lata, maybe a rain check on the concert? It looks like you have quite an evening in store."

I felt a lump form in my throat, and for a moment, I didn't trust myself to speak. "Yes, that's probably best," I whispered. I opened the door for him. "I really don't know what to say. Thank you, and I'm sorry for all of this . . . for your clothes."

He shook his head. "Don't worry about the clothes. They'll be fine. I'm just sorry we didn't get to do this properly. Maybe another time?" He took my hand and squeezed it gently.

I watched him walk down the corridor. His wet shoes squeaked against the concrete. I kept waiting for him to turn back and wave. But he didn't.

I couldn't blame him for wanting to escape me as quickly as possible.

PART THREE

26

PRIYA

If one were to look up the definition of "awkward" in Webster's, one might come upon the following set of images:

(1) A man, wearing his ex-wife's bathrobe while waiting for his pool-soaked clothes to dry, shifts positions on the couch, but his inexperience with the mechanics of bathrobe-wearing renders him totally unaware that his genitals are partially exposed with each shift;

(2) Said man's ex-wife, sitting at the dining table, her eyes distracted and forlorn, makes painstaking conversation with the unwelcome wife of her oblivious son, who has, true to form, arrived without a word of warning; both women gamely pretend not to notice the aforementioned genital-baring bathrobe situation of said man;

(3) Said oblivious son feeds his almost-one-year-old cubed cheese while making ill-conceived jokes about his mother's ruined date, unaware that each comment causes his mother to wince and his father to shift unnecessarily in his bathrobe.

Deanna, the lucky bitch, had availed herself of the luxury of not being related to any of us by bolting the scene a few seconds after Len had left.

And where was I in this charming scene? I was now hiding in the laundry room, pretending to busy myself with the task of drying my father's clothes so that, in this literal den of awkwardness, at least one problem—the genital-baring bathrobe situation—could be rectified.

"What are you doing?" Nikesh's voice startled me, causing me to jump. He grabbed the shirt from my hands. "Are you going to hide in the laundry room forever? Come out already."

Glaring at Nikesh, I chucked the shirt back into the dryer. I jabbed the Start button so hard, my pointer stung. "I'm trying to finish Dad's clothes, so he can get the hell out of here."

"So Mom was going out on a date tonight? That's crazy. I didn't expect it from her. But you know, Len seems like a nice enough guy. And he saved Dad's life. Maybe he's a little hard on the eyes, but"—he shrugged—"I suppose Mom could do worse. There probably aren't many choice offerings in the sixty and above bracket."

Why was he talking so loudly? "Shhh, keep your voice down. Do you have any idea what's been going on here? How stressful it's been? Between Dad having a new family and Mom finding out about Dad's new family, and Mom's new girl-about-town antics, and now you? You decide to drop on her doorstep without any warning?"

"For your information, we didn't drop on anyone's doorstep. You know perfectly well that we're here for Alok's first birthday. I told you about it weeks ago. I talked to Mom about it weeks ago. I even emailed Mom and Dad yesterday to remind them. So it shouldn't be a surprise to anyone that we're here. I'm actually pretty hurt that none of you seems to remember or care that we're here. And what do you mean, 'Dad's new family'?"

"Dad didn't tell you? There's some Indian lady and her kid

living with him. You might be interested to know that she looks about the same age as your wife. Maybe younger."

Nikesh was speechless—finally. I savored the look of astonishment on his face as we walked back into the living room.

Dad was still on the couch playing the genital-baring bathrobe game. Mom had escaped awkward small talk with Denise, and was now on the ground, stacking plastic rings with Alok. The room was silent, except for the sounds of Alok's baby babble and plastic rings thumping.

Denise cleared her throat and said: "Perhaps this isn't the ideal moment to ask, but is this birthday party for Alok tomorrow still happening? Not to put you guys on the spot, but my son is turning one for the first and only time, and that was kind of the whole point of coming all the way down here. So if that's not happening, then it would be good to know, so we can start making some alternate birthday plans." Denise cradled her phone in her palm, pointer poised like she had some party planner extraordinaire on speed dial.

The nerve of that woman. Who was she to make demands of my parents? Did she think we all had nothing better to do for the past few weeks than make birthday party preparations?

"Thanks for doing us such a big favor, Denise. God knows how hard it must have been for you to sit on a plane and come *all the way down here*," I said.

"Excuse me?" Denise said, just as Nikesh jumped in: "That's so out of line, Priya."

A second later my mother chimed in. "That's enough, Priya. Denise, please ignore her."

Why was Mom taking their side? Why did she always take Nikesh's side?

"Well, it's not like our lives stop just because they deign to visit us," I said.

Before Nikesh could respond, Mom put her hand out to silence us—a red plastic stacking ring in her hand. She stood, turned to my father, and said in a tight voice. "Suresh, why did you come here?"

It was the first time she'd spoken to him since his wet form had stumbled into the room, ruining her first (and maybe last) date with Len. I tried not to enjoy the fact that Mom's date was canceled. The rational part of me knew it was wrong and childish to feel that way. But I couldn't help it. I didn't want her life—our lives—to change this fast. I didn't want her to date someone new, marry someone new, have a new family. Where would that leave me? I still needed her.

My father shifted in his bathrobe nervously, causing Denise to cover a chuckle. I couldn't take it anymore. I ran to the laundry, grabbed the clothes from the dryer, and threw them at his waist. "They're dry, mostly."

"You still haven't answered, Suresh. What are you doing here? Why did you come here?" Mom's eyes simmered with frustration. She threw the plastic ring on the ground. Alok, thinking it was part of a game, clapped.

Dad sighed. "I came to give Priya a new cellphone. Since the one she left in the closet was broken, I bought her a new one." He looked at me. "I bought you a brand-new iPhone. Top of the line, with GPS, music, email, internet, all of it. But it fell in the pool. It's ruined now."

He looked down at the semidamp clothes piled on his waist. "What a wasted effort it all turned out to be. Hopeless, wasted effort." There was such defeat and resignation in his voice, I couldn't bear it.

My father had almost drowned. All so he could bring me a new iPhone. Despite the fact that I was a homewrecker who hadn't talked to him in weeks.

I leaned down, put my hand on his unshaven cheek, and kissed the top of his head. I felt tears well up. "Never wasted, is kindly effort."

Dad grabbed my hand, his eyes shiny.

"You sound like Yoda," Nikesh said. "Never wasted, kindly effort is," he croaked.

"Stop it, you idiot." I laughed, grateful suddenly for his stupid joking.

Nikesh laughed. Dad laughed. Even Denise laughed. All of us, probably laughing harder than the occasion merited out of sheer relief. Only Mom didn't laugh. For a few seconds, she watched us laughing. Then she got up from her chair, walked to her bedroom, and slammed the door.

27

SURESH

We drove home together in my SUV, as it seemed ridiculous and environmentally suspect to take three separate cars.

Denise complained about having to remove the car seat from the rental and reinstall it in my car. But for once, my son refused to give in to the bossy woman. "No, we're going together in one car," he said firmly.

The "we" excluded Lata, of course. Not that I expected her to come anywhere near my house—not after her cellphone-throwing antics the other day. But even putting that incident aside, her behavior over the last few hours had been inexcusable.

After storming into her bedroom, she hadn't come out—not even to say goodbye. More than once, Priya tried to enter the bedroom, only to find it locked. When Priya asked if Lata intended to eat dinner, Lata said, "I'm not hungry. I want to be alone. Why don't you all go to your father's house and spend the night there."

And so, like their father, my children were Lata's castoffs—at least for the night. For a few hours, they too could taste the bitterness of being banished from their mother's kingdom, from her good graces. Was it so wrong of a father to take a bit of solace in this newfound solidarity with his children? Not that I'd wish for a permanent rift between my children and their mother, of course. But after an evening of untold humiliations: the pool, *that man* causing me to fall, and then getting a hero's welcome from my flesh and blood, the utter indecency of my ex-wife whispering sweet nothings into the wet ears of *that man*! Was it wrong that the only thought buoying me was that my children had, for once, at long last, witnessed a chink in Lata's saintly maternal armor?

She was flawed. She was petty. She was craven. She was a cellphone-throwing hypocrite, laid bare for all the world (okay, at least her children) to see.

As if reading my thoughts, Priya exclaimed, "Can you believe she threw me out? Me? What did I do? It's not like I ruined her date by nearly drowning in the pool."

"Stop saying I nearly drowned in the pool." I clicked the signal to change lanes.

There was no traffic. I didn't know whether to be relieved or disappointed about that fact. On the one hand, I wasn't in a hurry to get back to the house. I didn't know what Mallika's reaction to this crowd would be—or worse, theirs to her. No doubt she was wondering what was taking me so long to return. Stupidly, I'd forgotten my own phone at home, so I couldn't even call ahead and warn her.

Where would everyone sleep tonight? With Mallika in the guest room and Bobby in Nikesh's old room, there wouldn't be enough rooms for everyone. I did some quick rearranging in my head. Priya would insist on her old room. Maybe Mallika and Bobby could share the guest room. And that would leave Nikesh's family with Nikesh's old room. Would the three of them fit in there? They could figure it out. There was even an air mattress in Nikesh's closet if need be.

So spoiled, these children, with all their needs for beds and space and separate bathrooms. In India, twenty-five people could live comfortably in a house as big as mine.

Suddenly, a different worry entered my brain: What if in my absence, Mallika had gone back on her word and left with Bobby, without a forwarding address, without a way to find them? With all these contradictory worries, I didn't know whether to rush home or take an extra-long detour.

"So, Dad, this Mallika woman is staying with you now?" Nikesh's head poked between the front seats.

I could feel Priya staring at me too, from the front passenger seat.

I chewed my lip. "She has been staying with me for a little while, yes."

"And her son too," Priya said.

"Yes, his name is Bobby. He is eight. He's a sweet boy—a little hyper at times, but sweet."

"Wow, Dad," Nikesh said. "I thought you told me you only had one date with her and then she stopped answering your calls. And now she and her son live with you? Isn't that moving fast? What's her . . . um . . . financial situation?"

"What do you mean?" I was surprised and hurt by Nikesh's questions. I'd expected this kind of inquisition from Priya, but not Nikesh. He was supposed to be on my side.

"He means, is this lady some kind of penniless gold digger who's using you for your money?" Priya said.

"Jesus, Priya," Nikesh said. "Can't you ever be diplomatic about anything? But, you know, Dad, it's kind of a fair question, isn't it?"

Was it possible to change the subject back to Lata? To direct the hot glare of my children's judgment back toward their loose-moraled mother?

I knew if I told them the truth about Mallika's situation, it wouldn't sound good. They would be convinced her motives were bad, that she was using me for free room and board. And maybe to some extent, she was. But here's what they didn't know: I wasn't ready to let Mallika and Bobby leave yet. I had been happier with them at my house than I had been alone. Eating meals together, taking trips to the swimming pool, helping Bobby with his math. They had let me pretend that I was part of a family again. That I was needed. That I wasn't alone. Did that mean I was using them too?

Luckily, I didn't have to say anything at all. At that moment, Alok saved me. From the back came the sounds of gagging and coughing.

"Nikesh, he's throwing up!" Denise said. "I told you not to give him that much cheese at your mom's."

"Oh shit," Nikesh said. In the rearview mirror, I could see my son hunched over the back seat, searching for the diaper bag.

"Nikesh, where are the wipes? We need wipes fast! Orange vomit is all over his clothes."

I did not like the way Denise was talking to my son. He did so much for the baby as it was—feeding him, putting him to sleep, bathing him. Far more than I ever did when my kids were babies. He acted more like a second mother than a father. His wife should be more appreciative of him.

"Just relax. I'm getting it. I'm getting it." Nikesh's voice was muffled, buried in the diaper bag.

Perhaps picking up on his parents' frustration, the baby, who had thus far seemed unconcerned by spit up, began to wail.

I pushed my foot against the gas pedal. The answer to my dilemma had come in the form of orange vomit: I'd get us home quickly.

Despite all the ruckus, I could feel Priya's eyes on me.

She was still waiting for my answer.

28

LATA

The library was deserted at this time of night. Moonlight filtered through the large windows, bathing the empty carrels and silent stacks in a soft yellow glow. There were no sounds but the gentle hum of computers set to energy-saving mode.

I had never been at the library so late before. I let myself in with my key. I dropped my body into the one chair at the counter—Jared's usual chair—and swiveled slowly. In the darkness, the room looked smaller somehow, more drawn in, like a swaddled version of its daytime self.

It was just a silly concert. A small thing, really. What did missing one silly concert matter when untold horrors were taking place all over the world? Children were starving, villages were being bombed and plundered and sacked. A few weeks ago, I'd barely thought of jazz as anything other than background music for car commercials and elevator rides. So what did it matter now, if I missed this one silly concert?

I thought of Len's CDs; they would be my first, last, and only gifts from him.

Oh God, what must he think of me now? I lay my head on

the countertop and closed my eyes. How was it that even after divorce, Suresh could cause me such embarrassment? Wasn't thirty-six years of it enough?

Quietly, I let my tears fall. Under different circumstances, I might have worried about my tears mixing with the kohl around my eyes, worried about black-speckled drops staining the countertop. But it was dark, and no one was here, so I just let them fall.

As a parent, I'd spent so much of my life coaxing my children not to cry, describing the virtues of dealing with disappointment dry-eyed and clear-minded: "Nikesh, I know you wanted to win that soccer game, but crying doesn't help anything. . . . Priya, I know you wanted that blue dress with the pink polka dots, but it's too expensive and crying won't change that. . . ." But here I was, unable to convince myself: "Lata, I know you put on your best pearl earrings and gold bracelets and new black heels; I know you spent the day contemplating clever things to say during the car ride, stories to lean forward and share when the band took a break; I know you imagined sitting at a table covered with a crisp white tablecloth and goblets of wine; imagined closing your eyes and letting the music swirl around you like a heroine in a movie; imagined your head swaying and a smile on your lips and the light dancing on your skin; imagined Len casting appreciative glances in your direction and placing a warm, firm hand on yours, both of you tapping your feet and enjoying the moment together. But crying doesn't help anything, and an old woman like you should know better."

I lifted my head from the counter and wiped my eyes. I reached in my purse for a packet of Kleenex, plucked one out, and wiped the smudged kohl from beneath my eyes. Then I turned on the desk lamp, plucked another tissue, and wiped the countertop, making sure to erase all traces of my kohl-flecked tears.

Well, that was that. It had been a pleasant set of imaginings, and it would be nothing more. I gathered my purse and stood. I surveyed the silent library. At least tomorrow, I'd still have this: my private kingdom.

I leaned over to switch the lamp off. A soft rapping at the door made me jump. Was it the campus police? I used my key to get in, of course, but perhaps I'd unknowingly triggered some kind of alarm. I looked at the glass door, expecting to see a security guard holding a flashlight. Instead, I saw Len's face, his familiar gray curls pressing against the glass.

"Lata, it's me—Len." He waved, his voice muffled by the glass.

I rushed to the door and let him in. "What are you doing here?" I said. "It's so late."

"I might ask you the same thing," he said.

"I wanted to get out of my house. And this is the first place that came to mind. It's the one place that usually makes me happy. Why are you here?"

He shuffled his feet awkwardly. "After I left your apartment, I went home and got cleaned up. And then I thought about going to the concert alone, but I couldn't quite bring myself to do it." He shrugged his shoulders, his expression glum. "And then, I started to feel angry, but I didn't quite know who to be angry at. Your husband seemed like an obvious first choice."

"Ex-husband," I corrected.

"Right, ex-husband. He's a bit of an odd bird, I take it?"

I tried to laugh, but the sound came out more like a snort. I covered my mouth, embarrassed. "That's a tremendous understatement. Especially coming from someone who saw him fall fully clothed into a pool."

Len chuckled. "Right. Well, anyway, I tried being angry with your ex-husband for a while. I called him some names in my head and then some other ones out loud. And then, I started getting a little angry at you. I started wondering if maybe you just agreed to go to the concert with me out of politeness or something, and who knows, maybe you were trying to work things out with your ex-husband. And then I thought I couldn't face you at the library tomorrow, and that I'd just drop off what I needed to return tonight in the drop box, when nobody would be here. Great plan, huh?"

"No," I said. "I suppose if you were trying to avoid me, your plan backfired. But then, nobody asked you to knock on the door. If you had simply dropped your library items off without knocking and then left, I would never have seen you." I struggled to keep a composed face, to mask the tightening of my chest.

"Well, that's the thing: I got here, and I saw the light in the window, and I saw you standing at the counter by yourself, look-ing . . . well, beautiful. But a little tragic too—like a wronged heroine in an opera who's about to belt out a tearjerker of an aria. And then I felt foolish about being angry with you. And it oc-curred to me that you've probably got a lot going on in your life right now, and maybe you could use someone to talk to. A friend, at least. And that maybe I could be that person, regardless of how else you felt about me. So there you have it. A very long answer to your question." He leaned against the counter, as if winded by his many confessions.

I wasn't sure what to say. There were a thousand things I wanted to say, confessions and questions and clarifications of my own, ranging from: *You can rest assured that I'm not trying to work things out with my ex-husband* to *You thought I looked beautiful?* to *What's a "tearjerker of an aria"?* to *I didn't agree to go out of polite-ness, but because you are the first man I've ever met who made me something because he thought it would give me happiness. And it did.*

But sometimes, wanting to say too many things at once makes it harder to say any of the things you want to say in the right kind of way. And then, with each passing moment, the words mash and collide in your mind until it's one messy jumble of feeling. I saw the glimmering concern in his walnut eyes, and I reached for his hand. It was large and dry and warm.

"Do you think that maybe you could make me another CD of the singing ladies?"

He laughed. "I already did. It's in my car. I'd planned to give it to you after the concert."

29

PRIYA

"Bobby, forget it little man, you don't want to buy New York Avenue. Save your money. Trust me," Nikesh said, trying to coax the dice out of Bobby's small hands.

"But it's orange, and it's on a corner. And Priya said corners are good. You want to buy the corners, right?" Bobby looked at me questioningly.

"Come on, Big Sister, tell him I'm right," Nikesh said, winking at me.

Nikesh was not giving Bobby good advice. He was as unscrupulous as our mother when it came to playing Monopoly with people under the age of ten. And under ordinary circumstances, I'd have warned Bobby to trust no one in this family in Monopoly matters. But tonight, I wanted this game to end early. I wanted Bobby to be vanquished soon, so he would leave us alone to gossip about his mother.

Where was his mother anyway, that Mallika? Why didn't she insist her son go to sleep? It had to be ten, at least.

"Yeah, you don't want that one. It's not a good property." I shook my head at Bobby.

Just as he was about to hand the dice over to Nikesh, a soft voice asked, "Why are you giving him bad advice?"

It was Mallika. She'd tiptoed in without us seeing. She smoothed the front of her pink tunic and kneeled down beside Bobby.

"No, it's not like that," I said, just as Nikesh said, "It's Raman-rules-of-the-jungle-guerilla-style-Monopoly. Every man, woman, and child for themselves. Don't trust anyone but your own instincts. Sorry, Mallika, but Priya and I can't help it. We both learned this game from a Gordon Gekko–style teacher of Monopoly: our mom. When I was eight, she convinced me to sell her Boardwalk for a hundred dollars. She was pretty ruthless when it came to this game."

He grinned at Mallika and Bobby. "No hard feelings, okay?" Mother and son quickly relaxed and smiled back at him, apparently charmed by the big idiot. I rolled my eyes; it was so typical.

"Did you hear that, Bobby? You and I need to watch out for these two." Mallika wagged an index finger at the two of us. She put her arm around Bobby and surveyed the properties he'd acquired—a rather meager assortment, mostly railroads.

"If you're up here, what are Dad and Denise doing?" Nikesh asked Mallika.

"The last I saw, they were in the kitchen," Mallika said.

"Together?" For a second, Nikesh appeared alarmed. But he recovered quickly. "Well, if Dad and Denise are together, then I'd better go rescue her. Or him. Not really sure who I'm rescuing here. Both, probably. I need to talk to Dad about something anyway."

Well that sounded mysterious. What did he need to talk to Dad about? Was he going to ask more questions about why our father was letting strangers live in his house? Because I'd be curious to hear those answers too.

Nikesh handed his properties to Bobby. "All right man, I'm giving you all my holdings. Give her hell." He pointed in my direction. Then he remembered that Mallika was in the room and corrected himself, "Heck, I mean. Give her heck." He winked at Bobby and fled the room.

Inwardly, I groaned. Of course he'd leave me here alone with Mallika.

Not surprisingly, she'd looked puzzled when Dad pulled into the garage with a car full of hungry people. After a round of awkward introductions, her hands had fluttered toward the dining table, where a single plate of food had been carefully Saranwrapped. "Oh gosh, I had no idea we were having guests . . . or I would have made . . ." Her voice had drifted off, nervously.

"Well, it's getting quite late and Alok must eat something before he goes to bed," Denise declared, frustration evident in her voice. "Could we order a pizza?"

I had glanced from one woman to the other, trying to decide whose declarations annoyed me more: Mallika, for insinuating that Nikesh and I were guests that ought to have provided advance notice before entering the house we'd spent the bulk of our lives in, or Denise, for suggesting that this woman or anyone else ought to have procured a dinner for her sooner. It was a toss-up, really.

"Pizza? I want pizza!" Bobby chimed in. He was wearing cotton Spider-Man pajamas, and his hair was freshly wet, emanating the fruity smell of shampoo.

"Bobby, no. You already ate," Mallika scolded.

From his perch on Nikesh's hip, Alok had eyed Bobby's every move with fascination. Alok sucked his thumb contentedly, perfectly oblivious to the adults' tension and the bright orange cheese-vomit stain across the front of his onesie.

"Mom, it's not fair. If he gets to eat pizza, why can't I?" Bobby whined, pointing accusingly at Alok. Bobby's lip quivered and his face began to crumple.

Denise knelt down in front of Bobby and stuck out her hand. "Hi, Bobby, I'm Denise. I plan to order a pizza with no cheese and a lot of extra vegetables. A super-healthy pizza. What do you think? Still want some?" Her voice was measured and her eyes focused, as if she was negotiating a corporate deal with an adult. Like she was just laying out the cold, hard facts for him to do with as he wished.

Bobby had stopped whining and considered both her outstretched hand and her offer. Apparently, the proposal sounded as unappetizing to him as it did to the rest of us. He scrunched his nose in disapproval and left the kitchen to resume control of the remote in the living room.

In spite of myself, I'd been impressed. Maybe there was more to Denise than met the eye; she apparently had some clever tantrum-evading strategies for eight-year-old boys up her sleeve. Mallika should have taken notes, because the two times I'd seen her try to reason with her son, she'd failed miserably. I tried to catch Nikesh's eye, with a look intended to say *Hmmm, this wife of yours, maybe she doesn't suck at this mothering thing*. It was a peace offering of sorts, to make up for my earlier hostility at Mom's apartment.

But Nikesh hadn't met my look; his eyes were otherwise occupied. He'd been staring at Mallika. Not in a leering gross way, thank God, but in a curious way, the surprise evident on his face that Dad had managed to attract a roommate of such doe-eyed, full-lipped, blouse-straining, old-fashioned-Bollywood-ish prettiness. Keenly aware of this myself now, as Mallika leaned over to collect a Community Chest card, I tried not to stare or visibly shudder.

"So, I hear you're a history professor," she said.

"Yeah, I am." I took the dice from Bobby and rolled. Six. I began moving the shoe, which was always my Monopoly piece—had been from the very first game we ever played. Nikesh was the top hat. There was a symbolism in that, I think. Maybe our fates would have been different if we'd each started our Monopoly-playing lives with different pieces.

"That must be very interesting. Are you on vacation now?" she asked. She couldn't have been more than a few years older than me, but she asked questions in a very Indian-aunty kind of way, replete with emphatic nodding and singsong intonation. Maybe these conversational tics were endemic to Indian-born women, regardless of their generation. Mallika had an accent, so I assumed she was raised in India.

"Fall classes haven't started yet," I said. "So in that sense, I suppose, I'm on vacation. Though, for me, it feels more like a temporary medical leave than a vacation, really."

I had no idea why I was sharing so much unnecessary information with her. I didn't know a thing about her, besides the fact that she'd dragged her son to move in with a stranger she'd met online. All evidence suggested that she was a nutcase or a gold digger or both, and that my father was too dumb or blinded by her looks to notice.

"Oh, are you physically unwell?" she asked.

"No, mentally." I held up $220, the cost of purchasing Kentucky Avenue, for Mallika and Bobby to see, before placing it in the "bank" (i.e., the board game box). "Honestly, I'm just trying to escape my life for a little while."

She nodded again, a faraway look in her eyes. "You're lucky that you can escape to your parents' house. For some people, that's not possible."

"Where are your parents? Are they . . . um . . . dead?" I asked.

She shook her head. "No, they're alive. They live in Bangalore now. But for all practical purposes, they may as well be in another world." She covered her face with her hands, and her upper body began to quake.

Oh for pity's sake. What was I supposed to do? "Hey, um, are you okay?" I patted her shoulder awkwardly and looked to Bobby for help. He crawled onto his mom's lap and buried his face in her heaving chest. Well, great, some help he turned out to be.

"I'm sorry," she apologized, wiping her face. "It's just . . . what you said. About needing to escape from your life. It triggered something in me, that's all." As she spoke, a strange look crossed her face—some mix of sadness and fear—though I didn't know her well enough to say for sure.

"Enough of this boring, gloomy talk." She clapped her hands, causing Bobby to lift his head from her chest. "Okay, Bobby, that's enough Monopoly for tonight. Time for bed."

"We're not done playing yet. I want to finish," Bobby whined.

"You can play tomorrow." Her voice had lost its singsong intonation now and become something harder and sterner. She pried the cards from his hands, threw them in my direction, and dragged him from the room.

Whew. Alone at last. I leaned toward the half-colonized Monopoly and spotted a weird brown stain near the board. Maybe it was coffee that had spilled onto the carpet and dried into the shape of South America. Well, apparently Mallika's meticulous kitchen cleaning didn't extend to the game room.

Dad really ought to do something about this disgusting stain. Seriously, the man didn't need a loony tunes girlfriend. What he needed was a good, solid housekeeper.

30

SURESH

Well at least she wasn't an unnecessary talker—I could say that much about her.

I considered Denise's silent form next to me at the kitchen sink. Every few seconds, she'd pluck a sopping dish from my hand, dry it with a few swift strokes of her towel, and place it in the cupboard. She hadn't said a word in the few long minutes since Mallika left us to check on Bobby. Did she come from a long line of silent Nordic types?

I tried not to stare at the pale, almost bluish hue of her skin, the sparse blond hairs sprouting from her forearm. Her coloring reminded me of that other girl that Nikesh had brought home several years ago, what was her name? Janet? Jenna? Janine! The one who wouldn't stop talking inanely and caressed Nikesh at the dinner table in a way that turned Lata's face gray.

No, I much preferred the quiet stiffness of Denise. Her silence was a blessing, really. For what was more irritating than a woman who needed to jibber-jabber to fill the silence? Silence was good. Silence was gold.

I gazed longingly at the doorway. It was empty. Shouldn't

Priya and Nikesh be helping with these pizza-crusted dishes? Why had they left this woman—this unspeaking, unsmiling woman—all alone to shoulder the burden? Why had they left me?

As if reading my mind, Denise finally spoke. "Just a few dishes left to go."

I nodded. "It's a shame the dishwasher is broken. It's been that way for a few weeks. I guess I should call somebody to fix it. But I don't know who to call. This sort of thing was usually Lata's department. And now I'm a helpless bachelor." I lifted my palms up and smiled, trying to lighten the mood with a self-deprecating joke.

"Can't you just look up 'dishwasher repair' on Google?" Denise asked, grabbing a wet fork out of my hand. Her drying had outpaced me to an uncomfortable degree. Her hand kept reaching out for the next dish before I'd finish rinsing it.

"Here, why don't I take care of these last few," she said, nudging me out of the way. She finished the dishes in roughly half the time it would have taken us together.

Watching her brisk, efficient movements, I sensed that Denise would not be impressed by my musings on the concept of learned helplessness—my conclusion that Lata, by taking care of everything associated with the house and leaving me in the dark about her methods, had, in fact, done me a grave disservice. No, I could only presume that any concept of helplessness, learned or otherwise, would be lost on this girl. So instead I said, "Yes, I suppose you are right. I should just google it."

She dried her hands on the dish towel. "We could do it now."

"Do what now?"

"Google 'dishwasher repair.'"

"Oh, no . . . you're a guest, you don't have to. . . ."

"Well, it's not like we're doing anything else right now. And you need to get this thing fixed. So, where's your computer?" She stood with her arms crossed, her eyebrows raised.

Something about her stance reminded me of my sixth-standard math teacher: Sister Mary Alice. Every day she'd write an unfinished formula on the board in her perfectly symmetrical handwriting, and then turn toward us, brows raised and black eyes sparkling, challenge written all over her young face. We had all nursed uncomfortable crushes on her, even though her hair was hidden by a habit and her thin figure lacked the soft ripeness of the actresses' photos we ogled in secret. But she had a bossy confidence, an assuredness to her movements that was fetching. Such women were hard to argue with and harder to refuse; one tended to oblige them.

Wordlessly, I led Denise down the hallway to my study. I turned on the lights and motioned for her to sit in front of the computer. Before sitting down, she ran her hands lightly over the silver spines of several *Funk & Wagnalls* encyclopedias. They sat on a bookshelf above the desk. The set was incomplete, missing volumes "P," "Q," and "Y," among others. She pulled out a volume, "M," and flipped through the pages, an amused expression on her face.

"Encyclopedias," I said. "One of the many things that the internet has rendered obsolete. Now their only purpose is to prevent my bookshelves from looking too bare."

She smiled. "I loved encyclopedias when I was a girl. I'd sneak into the school library during lunch and pull out a different volume of *Encyclopaedia Britannica* each day. I'd close my eyes, let the book fall open, and spend lunch reading about something random, like Mount Kilimanjaro or pasteurization or the monarch butterfly. I begged my parents so many times to buy me a set. But they could never afford them." With a look of regret she closed the book and returned it to the shelf.

I'd never heard Denise talk this much before. I tried to imagine her as a young girl, in pigtails and a dress, burrowing her head in encyclopedias during lunch and avoiding the prying eyes of school librarians. It was a charming thought.

"What do—did—your parents do for a living?" I corrected

myself quickly. Her parents had died. Of course, I knew that. Whatever my divorce-addled state of mind had been when Nikesh first brought Denise home, I remembered that. One did not forget a fact like that, the fact of being the only living grandfather to your grandson.

"My dad owned a hardware store and my mom was a real estate agent. Mostly, my mom's income kept my dad out of debt. He was devoted to his store, even though it stopped being profitable for the last few years of his life. His prices couldn't compete with the chain stores."

"I'm very sorry to hear that." I didn't know whether I was apologizing for the futility of her father's professional ambitions or the fact of her parents' death or both. It was an all-encompassing apology.

She sat down in the chair. "Well, I suppose that's life. You have to face facts. You can't bury your head in the sand and pretend everything is okay when it's not. My dad was a kind man. Everybody liked him. But he left all the practical questions to my mother. I wish I'd been closer to both of them before they died." She brushed a piece of hair away from her face and tucked it behind her ear. A slight quiver in her upper lip betrayed her distress. "It's really nice that you and Nikesh are so close."

"He's a good son. I'm lucky." A feeling of warmth ran through me. Had I misjudged this girl, unfairly dismissed her as a cold-and-unfeeling type? Maybe we had just never had the chance to talk before. There were always other people around, Alok needing attention, other distractions.

"Okay, do you want to type in your password so that we can look up dishwasher repairmen?"

I bent over and typed: *06221972*. My password for everything was still the date Lata and I got married. It was blind habit. I didn't even think about it, really. Whenever I was asked for a password, I always typed in that date. But it struck me now, as Denise watched me type, that I should have changed the password for one particular purpose at least—that keeping my anniversary date as my password for dating websites was, as my kids would say, "messed up."

Denise clicked and my dating profile page popped onto the screen, four unanswered messages blinking in the mailbox. I had set it as my home page some time back and forgotten all about it. In fact, I had barely used my computer since Mallika and Bobby arrived. Denise raised her eyebrows and looked questioningly at me. "Should I . . . close out of this?"

Embarrassed, I grabbed the mouse from Denise and clicked the page closed. She patted my hand in a comforting manner. "It's nothing to be embarrassed about, Suresh. Divorce is hard, grueling, and lonely. After my divorce, I holed myself up at work and didn't go on a date with anyone for a year. Then, I did some online dating too. It didn't really work out for me, but at least it was a distraction."

Divorced? This woman was divorced? It wasn't enough that she was old enough to be Nikesh's mother. Okay, that was an exaggeration. I assumed she was in her early forties. Though I could never quite tell with some of these very pale women; they often looked prematurely aged. But divorced as well? Why had my handsome, brilliant son tied himself to this elderly divorcée?

"Here, I found one. They call themselves Dishwasher Repairers. What a clever name," she quipped.

I cleared my throat. "You're divorced?"

"Yes."

"Does Nikesh know?" I asked feebly.

"Of course," she said. "Does it bother you that I'm divorced? I mean, you're divorced. And Nikesh said you were fine about us not being married and all." Her voice trailed off just as Nikesh entered the room.

What was she saying? She and Nikesh weren't married? It

made no sense. They had eloped and gotten married at city hall many, many months ago—before Alok was born. That was what Nikesh had told me. Was that not true? My head was spinning.

"So this is where you two are hiding," Nikesh said, walking toward us.

"Nikesh, you never told your dad that I was divorced?" Denise said, her face darkening.

Nikesh blanched, staring at her and then at me. "I just didn't see the point in sharing everyone's sordid life history."

"Sordid?" She stood up from the desk, emitting almost visible fumes of fury. "Let's get something straight. I'm not embarrassed by my life history, okay? But you know what I am embarrassed by? You. Your lying. Your spinelessness. Did you really tell them that we're not married the other day, or were you just lying about that too? Because from the look on your dad's face, I'm guessing you didn't do it."

"Denise, can we talk about this later, in private?" Nikesh said, his voice low.

She snorted in disgust and then turned to me. "Suresh, you seem like a decent-enough man who deserves to know the truth, so I'm going to level with you here, okay? I'm going to lay it all out on the table. I'm not your son's wife. I got pregnant four months into dating him. We have no plans to get married—not that I know of, anyway." She gave Nikesh a furious look and then turned back to me. "I'm divorced because I had the poor sense to marry a jerk when I was twenty-four, and the even poorer sense to stay with him through all the years he cheated on me. I'm a decade older than your son. I'm his boss too— marginally, but nevertheless it poses some distinct challenges. I'm a Methodist, and when the time comes, I want to raise Alok as one too. Now, I'm sorry if any of that displeases you, or if you pictured a different woman to be with your son and to mother your grandson. But we can't always choose what happens to the people we love, can we? That's just life. We have to deal with it."

A tear collected in the corner of her eye. I felt bad for her. I hated seeing women cry. Unlike Mallika, though, Denise seemed uncomfortable shedding tears in front of an audience. As soon as they appeared, Denise wiped them with the backs of her hands and stormed out of the room.

I turned to Nikesh, full of questions. But the look on his face stopped me midsentence.

He shook his head. "Not now, Dad. Please, not now. I have to talk to her." And then he too fled the room.

31

LATA

We were in Len's car, listening to the first song of the new CD he had made me. As soon as it ended, I pressed the button to play it again.

Heaven, I'm in heaven.
And my heart beats so that I can hardly speak.

"Lata, that's the third time you've played this song. At this rate, it'll take you a month to get through the CD." Len laughed, and signaled right to pull into the parking lot of a Denny's restaurant.

"I can't help it. Ella Fitzgerald's voice is magical." I fell back into my seat.

I didn't want to confess the other reason I kept replaying it: that by focusing on the giddy exuberance of Ella's voice, I could keep my own exterior calm. I could just let Ella be the mouthpiece for my own swirling, nervous excitement at being in Len's car at ten-thirty at night, headed toward any open restaurant that would serve us coffee and dessert.

"Here we are. Not quite the restaurant I'd planned on, but I guess you can't be too picky at this hour."

In the time it took me to remove my seatbelt, Len had already walked around to the passenger side of the car and opened the door for me. It really did make me feel like the heroine of a movie.

We walked to the front door of the restaurant. The bright neon glow of the Denny's sign reflected off his glasses. It had been years since I'd eaten at a Denny's. The last time was during a family car trip to New Orleans. Priya might have been four-teen or fifteen—an irritable and unhappy time for any girl, but her especially. A picky eater, she'd made quite a show of disgust at a Denny's somewhere off Highway 10. She spat out the first bite of her club sandwich, declaring it "insipid." I remembered her using that oddly adult word in particular: "insipid."

"Is this all right?" Len asked. He held the door open, looking confused as to why I hadn't walked through it.

"Oh, sorry." I stepped forward. "I was just recalling the last time I was at a Denny's."

"When was that?" he asked, guiding me to a booth in the back of the restaurant.

Given the late hour, the Denny's was surprisingly full. We passed booths of sullen teenagers awkwardly clutching cups of coffee that their taste buds had not yet fully accepted, and a few couples here and there, scraping the last bits of a meal off their plates.

"About twenty years ago. We stopped for lunch on the way to New Orleans."

"You and your ex-husband?" he asked.

"And my son and daughter. It was a family trip, though not a very good one. No, I shouldn't say that. There were parts of the trip that were wonderful: drinking chicory-flavored coffee and eating those delicious donut-things—"

"Beignets?"

"Yes, those, and walking by the river, and seeing all those stalls of handicrafts, and hearing the sounds of music."

"The music!" Len said, clapping his hands together with delight. "I love New Orleans. There's amazing music everywhere; not just in concert halls or music venues, but incredible musicians play on street corners. And that spicy Cajun food! I can't get enough of it." He frowned at the plastic Denny's menu in his hands.

"Have you been there many times, then?" I asked, turning to the dessert page.

"My ex-wife and I got married there. We used to go to New Orleans almost every year on our anniversary—well, except after Hurricane Katrina. Such a tragedy. So I guess that makes, let's see"—he tilted his head, calculating—"about twenty-two trips."

"Goodness, so many. I've never visited any place that many times, not even India."

He laughed. "Well, lucky for me, New Orleans is a lot closer than India."

I smiled and looked down at the pictures of various dessert offerings: a banana split with caramel and fudge, a cheesecake with strawberry topping, a large waffle with a mound of whipped cream. The colors were garish.

"That's nice, that you and your wife shared a connection to a place," I said. "Suresh was never a big fan of traveling. He hated it. He didn't like going to India. We never went to Europe. We traveled more when our kids were young—to places like Disneyland and San Diego and other beachfront places that the kids enjoyed. We all went to Maui together once. That was a lovely place."

"We did share a love of New Orleans. At least, I think we did. Sometimes I wonder, though, if she was just humoring me. Maybe she would have preferred to go somewhere else once in a while, you know? When you've been married that long, a person can lose track of the things they liked before marriage."

I nodded in agreement. "Yes, that is definitely true. How did you meet, if you don't mind my asking?"

"On a blind date, when I was in graduate school. We were set up by my then-roommate's girlfriend. Susie—that's my ex-wife's name—and my roommate's girlfriend were teaching at the same elementary school at the time. What about you? How did you meet your ex-husband, the swimming champion?"

I shook a finger at him, in mock disapproval. "That's not very nice."

"Just kidding. I think I'm still blaming him for the fact that instead of taking you to a concert, I have to eat one of these scary-looking desserts." He pointed to the picture of the strawberry-topped cheesecake. "This pink color is fluorescent; it's blinding."

I laughed. "Yes, these pictures are not very appetizing. I'm thinking of ordering the carrot cake, if for no other reason than that there's no picture of it."

"Not a bad idea. Maybe I'll order the apple pie for the same reason." Len waved to an unhappy-seeming waitress, a young woman whose uniform looked two sizes too small for her robust figure. She took our order, snatched the laminated menus from our hands and disappeared.

"So, how did you meet him?" Len said. "From our brief encounter, I'd say the two of you seem different."

"I guess you can say that we too met on a blind date of sorts. One worked out by our families," Lata said.

"Ah." He nodded. "Does it make the ending of your marriage any easier, knowing that you didn't really choose him? I mean, you can't blame yourself for having failed to spot the red flags before you got married, to see all the personality differences."

I considered his question. It was one I'd never asked myself—mostly because it seemed so beside the point. "No, that doesn't make it any easier," I said, more forcefully than I intended. "I might not have known Suresh before we married, as you and your wife did, but we made a life together for over three decades. We raised two kids together, built a house together, lived through our parents' deaths together. When you go through so much with someone, it doesn't matter . . . how it began. The origins of your union become irrelevant." I struggled to find the right words, words that would give fair due to the marriage I had without suggesting lingering regret in having left it.

"I'm sorry. I didn't mean to minimize your loss or hardship in any way."

"I know you didn't. . . ." My voice trailed off. There was, of course, one way that the origins of my union did matter—and mattered a great deal. I was completely unprepared for my present situation.

Suddenly, I felt very exposed—I shivered. I looked around at the occupied tables and thought of how ridiculous I must seem to all those young couples, those teenagers. An old Indian woman on a date. What would Mala say if she saw me like this? What would my dead parents say if they'd been alive to see me?

"I'm just not . . . sure how to do this," I said weakly.

"What do you mean? How to cope with divorce?"

"No. This," I said, waving at him, the table, the restaurant. "I've never been on a date before. Maybe it was ridiculous to think I could. At this age, after all these years. I think maybe I should go home. It's very late, and it's been such a long, strange day." I looked down at the table, unable to meet Len's eyes.

But I could feel him staring at me, willing me to change my mind, to try. "Lata, no . . ."

The waitress appeared and plopped down our desserts. "Can I get you folks anything else?" she asked.

"Just the check. And can you wrap these to go please?" I said.

⸰⸵

We drove in silence to the library parking lot. Not even the CD player was on. Len made a sharp right turn, causing the Styrofoam cartons of uneaten dessert to shift in my lap.

I glanced at his hands, gripping the steering wheel. In the dim dashboard light, his skin appeared taut and ghostly white around his knuckles. I couldn't bring myself to look at his face, to see if the tense distress of those hands was mirrored there too.

It was all my fault. I should never have said yes. It wasn't fair to him. I should never have pretended to be one of those women who could bravely face the humiliations of this dating business. I imagined that lady from the supermarket with the beautiful toenails sitting across from Len at the Denny's booth, freely dipping her spoon into his pie, not giving a second thought to how it might seem to others. Not her children, or her ex-husband, or the surly waitress, and certainly not the other diners that she'd never see again. She would have let herself be happy—would have allowed this man to try and make her happy.

Len turned into the library parking lot. Soon, he'd be pulling up next to my Camry. And then we would say our goodbyes. And that would be it. I would never see his face light up at the sight of me in the library. I would never look down at my buzzing cellphone with a mix of excitement and panic, wondering if it might be him. And if I happened to catch myself humming jazz songs as I loaded the dishwasher, I'd wear the pink flush of humiliation instead of a smile.

Even at this time of night, there were several cars scattered about the parking lot. "I wonder who these cars belong to," I said, eager for any topic to break the unhappy silence. "The library has been closed for hours."

"The chemistry building is nearby. Those cars probably belong to graduate students, burning the midnight oil in a lab."

I considered the cars surrounding Len's and mine: they were all small, inexpensive, and battered-looking.

"My father was a chemistry teacher," I said. "He passed away years ago, but he taught chemistry at a secondary school. Sometimes I think, if he'd been born in a different generation, maybe he would be in one of those labs, burning the midnight oil as you say."

"When did he pass away?"

"Twenty-two years ago. Pancreatic cancer. Though there are still times when I forget he's gone."

Len tugged the parking brake. We were silent again. I knew I had no reason to stay in his car anymore, but I couldn't quite bring myself to get out either. So I kept talking. "He was a very kind man, my father. He never had a harsh word for anyone, especially me. Though I imagine he would be able to come up with a few if he could see me now."

Len leaned back in his seat, his expression thoughtful. "My father was an Orthodox Jew. He wouldn't be so thrilled about this either. Or who knows? Maybe he'd think that his son is sixty and should forget about what anyone thinks of him and just be happy. I'm not sure kids ever know what their parents really think or want for them. I'm pretty sure my kids don't."

A few more seconds passed. Without pausing to think, I jabbed the Play button on the CD player. A song came on. A slow song: a song that I'd heard somewhere before, on a commercial perhaps, but this was the first time I had paid any attention to the lyrics.

> *Birds do it. Bees do it.*
> *Even educated fleas do it.*
> *Let's do it. Let's fall in love.*

Len cleared his throat. "Cole Porter was really a lyrical genius. But we can, uh, fast-forward to the next one. Or shut it off. You can take it with you." With hurried motions, he pressed the Eject button on the CD player, stuffed the disk into the plastic case, and held it out to me.

I watched his hands. His fingers were long. A few gray hairs sprouted from his knuckles. In the moonlight, they looked like threads of silver. I imagined his hands on both sides of my face, caressing my cheeks. My mind started wandering to those grocery store magazines, to the ones I'd found in Priya's bathroom so many years ago, with those pictures of cleavage-baring women advertising all those bodily jobs, describing the mechanics of delivering pleasure in a way that sounded about as romantic as car repair. I shook my head, banishing the images.

This generation talked too much. Some things were better left unsaid. Silently, I compared Len's hands to Suresh's—hands that were smaller than Len's, thick-palmed and dry, with black hairs sprouting from knotty knuckles. Hands that had explored my twenty-year-old skin, supple and firm, bursting with life; and then, my thirty-year-old skin, soft and dewy even after two pregnancies had thickened my midsection and slackened my breasts. Hands that had touched me into my forties, rarely, but every once in a while, caressing the skin that was no longer as soft or supple, but still there—alive, breathing, warm.

I turned toward Len and pulled the CD from his hand.

He leaned in, and kissed me.

32

NIKESH

I pushed a glass tumbler against the filtered water nozzle in the fridge. Nothing came out.

The filter light blinked; it needed replacing. First the dishwasher. Now the water filter. Nothing worked around here. Why didn't Dad know how to fix anything?

Whatever. I didn't want water anyway. I wanted something stronger. Whisky. Vodka. Even beer would do. I put the glass on the counter and leaned my head against the fridge door.

My conversation with Denise had not gone well. "Conversation" was not even the right word to describe it. Pleading was more like it. I'd pleaded with her to forgive me for lying. I'd pleaded with her not to book a flight for herself and Alok and leave tomorrow. I'd pleaded with her not to bolt from my dad's house and stay at a hotel for the night. On counts two and three, I'd succeeded. She said she'd stay the night and that she and Alok would stay for the birthday. But on the first count, forgiveness, I was shit out of luck.

Who could blame her? I was a liar. I'd brought her to Clayborn under false pretenses. I'd made a fucking mess of it.

Though, in my defense, I had planned on telling Mom and Dad as soon as I got to town. How was I supposed to know that everything would be so crazy around here? Between Dad nearly drowning in Mom's pool and Mom's hissy fit about missing a date with some random dude she'd met at the library and Dad's new houseguests—how was I supposed to confide in either of them?

I opened cabinet doors at random, hoping to find the alcohol that had made Dad so drunk that one day. Anything? Nope. Just a mismatched assortment of plates and cups and Tupperware.

I opened the fridge door again and fished around for beer. Once again, nothing. Maybe he'd drunk all of his liquor, whatever and wherever it was. Or maybe Mallika didn't approve of drinking, so Dad had gotten rid of it.

I really shouldn't have been surprised. Dad didn't usually keep alcohol around. And since he and everyone else in this family had apparently forgotten about Alok's birthday party tomorrow, Dad hadn't even bothered to buy beer or any other party beverages. No juice. No cans of sparkling water. No Cokes. Nothing.

What a family I had. Everyone was too fixated on their own lives to stop and consider that my son was turning one tomorrow. Nobody seemed to give a shit about it. Hadn't Denise predicted this on the plane? She was right to be doubtful of my family's ability to plan a birthday party. They couldn't even be counted on to do that.

"Who died in here?" Priya's voice startled me.

"Hey. I'm just looking for beer."

"Dad doesn't drink." Priya made her way to the fridge, glass in hand.

I rolled my eyes. *Yes, Miss Know-It-All, Dad doesn't drink. Except that time I called him and he was drunk.* "The fridge filter needs to be replaced."

"Okay, tap water it is then." She walked to the sink, filled her glass, and turned toward me. "So is that why you look so pissed? Because you can't have filtered water?"

"No. How bougie do you think I am?"

"Pretty bougie. Fancy lawyer with the Brooklyn condo. I picture you brushing your teeth with bottles of Fiji water." She took a sip, raised her eyebrows, and smacked her lips.

I laughed in spite of myself. "I bathe in it too. That is what we of the upper crust do."

"Speaking of upper crust, where is Denise? Is she already asleep? I haven't heard a peep from her since dinner."

"Since when do you go out of your way to hear Denise talk? All you do is go out of your way to be hostile to her," I said, the joking tone out of my voice.

"What's up your ass? It's not like Denise goes out of her way to be nice to me. When was the last time she asked me about my job or my life in Austin? Half the time she's staring at her phone or she's off in a room doing work. It's obvious she wants nothing to do with any of us. A bad relationship is a two-way street. I won't take all the blame."

I hung my head, defeated. Why couldn't any woman in my life make things easier? Usually, I could count on Mom. But even she'd let me down this time.

Priya blew a stream of air out of her mouth. I guessed that she was itching for a cigarette. How many times had she—we— snuck out of this house during trips home from college to the backyard to share a smoke? I'd quit during law school. Elena hated the smell of cigarette smoke. And I'd never picked it back up. It was always more of a social thing for me anyway. Something to do at a party or during a friendly chat with a stranger on a balcony or with your sister while commiserating about your parents' weirdness. Thinking about those backyard cigarettes with Priya made me sad now. For so long, we used to be this team—united against our parents. But ever since the divorce, we'd turned into these sniping siblings.

I walked to the sink and stood next to her. I pointed out the window toward the unmanicured, woodsier edge of the backyard. "Remember how we used to sneak out late at night and smoke together?" I said.

Priya turned and followed my finger. "Of course I remember." She chewed her lip. "We could go back there now and have one if you want." She patted her pocket.

I shook my head. "No, it's been too long. I don't think my lungs could handle it now. You should really quit, you know. Nobody smokes anymore."

"Bastard. That was entrapment. You set me up so you could lecture me about not smoking."

I laughed and put my arm around her. She was really funny sometimes. I missed her. I missed how we used to be.

"You're right. That was a dick move. Sorry." I was sorry about a lot of things.

We stared out the window together. A half-moon peeked out between the trees, making the branches look silver. It was the perfect yard for a party—spacious and green and well shaded.

Tomorrow, my son was turning one. It was a big fucking deal. And he was going to have a party. So what if everyone forgot to plan one. All you really needed for a party were a few decorations, food, drinks, and a handful of people. I could make that happen.

"Okay, Big Sister, we're going to Target."

"Right now? Why?"

"We're going to get birthday party stuff for your nephew."

33

SURESH

I'd been parked outside Lata's apartment complex for over half an hour.

After Denise and Nikesh's fight in the study, I'd left my house to get some fresh air. I needed to clear my head. I walked out of my house into the moonlit night, intending to head toward Majestic Lake. But instead, I'd gotten into my car and driven here—to Lata's complex. Once in the parking lot, I stayed put in my car, contemplating what to do. After all, I couldn't very well go knocking on Lata's door at midnight without some kind of explanation. And the truth was, I didn't have an explanation. I didn't know what I was doing here. Before this afternoon, I'd never even been to this stupid condo complex. But for some reason, I'd come here. I guess I wanted to be near Lata. I wanted to tell her about Nikesh not being married, about Denise's anger at him for lying. Lata knew how to say the right things to the kids—how to console them and cajole them. I never knew the right things to say.

An old green Jetta had pulled up and parked a few cars away. It was a Saturday night in a college town, so I expected some beer-flushed college students to stumble out. I rested my gaze lazily on the Jetta, my thoughts still occupied by the question of whether to knock on Lata's door, when out she stepped. From the passenger side of the Jetta—Lata.

I squinted, disbelieving. It was definitely her. In the moonlight, I could make out the waves of her black hair, still thick and youthful after all these years, the slope of her shoulders, the gold bangles twinkling at her wrists.

But it was midnight. Where had she gone? Where was she returning from at this late hour? And then the Jetta's driver stepped out.

That man! Len, was it? Leonard. Whatever stupid name he had. I shrank back in my seat and watched *that man* take Lata's arm and disappear with her into the pillars of the complex entrance.

And that was fifteen minutes ago! I squinted at the dashboard clock. *12:15.* The numbers glared at me, green and menacing.

How long did it take to walk a woman to her door? I knew from this afternoon's grim experience that Lata's complex was a hellish labyrinth of hallways. But still! The contents of my stomach swished. I felt as if I were on a capsizing ship. Was this the reason she'd kicked her children and her only grandchild out of her apartment? So she could meet up with this white man and take him to her apartment afterward to . . . to . . . No, it was unthinkable.

Out of sheer desperation, I turned on the radio. It was set to NPR, and classical piano music plinked and trilled in a frenzied, ominous manner. Music to match the dread filling my heart. I increased the volume, wishing the music would drown out my thoughts.

I checked the dashboard clock. *12:17.*

I glared at the Jetta, willing it to disappear. A decade-old Jetta, by the looks of it. It probably didn't even have airbags. All evening, *that man* drove my wife around in a piece of junk that didn't have proper safety features. What if some drunk college students had careened into their car? Lata could have died. *12:18*.

I jumped out of my car and slammed the door shut. I advanced toward the Jetta slowly, like a hunter toward prey. Not that I'd ever been hunting before. But for a moment, I wished I had. I wished I was the kind of man who knew how to shoot a gun. A man who carried around a hunting rifle in the back of his car, like Clint Eastwood, or one of those men in Westerns, with their menacing stares and scarred chins and pointer fingers resting comfortably on gun triggers. But I was not that kind of man. It would never occur to me to buy a gun or keep one in my house, much less my car.

Several years ago, Lata and I had returned home from Nikesh's law school graduation, only to find that our back door locks had been meddled with. In our absence, someone had tried to break into the house, and nearly succeeded too, as the door hinges were barely hanging on. But something had apparently stopped them, convinced them the risk wasn't worth the effort—maybe the house alarm or the neighbor's barking dog. Lata had immediately called a locksmith to repair the hinges, because how could we sleep at night knowing that the burglars might return to finish the job? The locksmith had been one of those Clint Eastwood–type fellows: unkempt hair, blue jeans, heavy boots, the smell of cigarette smoke emanating from his denim shirt. He looked like a man who carried a rifle in the trunk of his car. He told us we needed to replace our entire door, which would take a few days.

"But what are we supposed to do in the meantime?" Lata had asked. "What if the burglars come back?"

"Well, ma'am," the Clint Eastwood locksmith had said, calmly collecting his tools from the floor. "My advice would be to take your gun out of the closet, sleep with it under your pillow, and if they come back, blow their goddamn brains out."

What kind of advice was that? Of course, Lata and I hadn't seriously considered his proposal. That Clint Eastwood locksmith could not have found two people more unreceptive to his advice. In fact, the only thing more frightening than the thought of burglars returning to our house was the prospect of a human-killing instrument lying beneath our pillows, inches from our brains. I'd been a Texan for the past thirty years, but I'd go to my deathbed never having purchased—or even having held—a gun.

Now, suppose that Clint Eastwood locksmith found himself in my current predicament: standing before the car of his ex-wife's boyfriend. He would probably find a creative use for a gun. I could easily picture him shooting out the Jetta's tires. Or the windshield. Or, who knows, maybe the Clint Eastwood lock-smith would shoot *that man* himself.

But I was not the locksmith. Not even close. And while usually that thought would have given me some comfort, at this particular moment it did not.

I backed away from the Jetta. I checked my watch. *12:20.*

In the distance, I could hear the faint sounds of footsteps on concrete—growing less faint with each second. I ran to my car, slammed the door, and slumped low in the seat. Peeking through the window, I watched as *that man* emerged from the pillared entrance of the apartment complex, opened his car door, and drove away.

I held my breath, waiting for the Jetta to grow smaller and smaller in the side-view mirror. He was gone. He hadn't stayed. I felt so relieved I could have cried.

I sat back up in the seat. This was my chance. Lata would still be awake. In a few minutes, she'd change into her nightgown and brush her teeth and comb out her hair in long, careful strokes. Hair that still reminded me of the first time I ever saw her in the living room of her parents' house. Hair that, even after all these years, I ached to stroke in the dark.

I'd knock on her door, and she'd answer it and . . .

And then what? Who was I kidding? She wouldn't listen to me. Even if I could somehow conjure up the right words to say, she wouldn't listen to me. She wouldn't give me a chance.

Not now. Not tomorrow. Probably not ever.

34

PRIYA

"So how do you feel about these?" Nikesh held up a package of plates shaped like trains.

I shrugged and rubbed my arms, wishing I'd brought a cardigan to the always over-air-conditioned Target. "I don't know; is Alok into trains?"

Nikesh chucked the plates into the shopping cart. "He's not old enough to be into Thomas the Tank Engine yet. But I don't see any of the *Sesame Street* stuff around here, which he *is* pretty wild about, so I guess Thomas is the next best thing. The only other stuff they've got is Disney princesses."

"How do you know Alok's not into the Little Mermaid?" I studied a placemat in the shape of a mermaid's face. Her cheeks and eyelids were covered in glittery color. Like a showgirl or a stripper.

Nikesh threw two stacks of matching train cups into the cart. "If his early interest in cars and balls is any guide, I'm guessing princesses are not going to be his thing. But who knows? We'll cross that bridge when we come to it. If he likes princesses, so be it. Is there any chance you're going to be the least bit helpful during this shopping trip? Your nephew turns one only once, you know."

"I said I'd come with you to Target. I didn't say I'd be helpful." As far as I could tell, empty plastic bags would be just as interesting to Alok from a decorative standpoint than any of this crap in the party decoration aisle.

I pushed the cart behind Nikesh as he headed toward a shelf of colored streamers.

"What do you think?" He held a package of streamers in each hand. "Should I get blue and red or orange and green? Or blue and orange? Or green and blue?" He scratched his head. Then he grabbed a half dozen streamer packages, threw them into the cart, and slammed the handlebar. "What the hell am I doing?" he shouted.

A young woman in a red Target shirt sorting toothbrushes in the Oral Health aisle across from us looked warily at him. If Nikesh didn't cool it soon, I feared she'd call security on us.

"Hey, calm down," I said. "How about you just step away from the cart and take a breath here. You know, Alok's not going to care. I'm no expert, but I imagine birthdays are too abstract a concept for a twelve-month-old. Why are you getting so worked up about this decoration stuff? I mean, is anyone even coming to this party except us? We'll just order pizza—with extra cheese this time, I don't care what your wife says—and we'll call it a party, and that will be that. Easy. I think they even sell cupcakes here."

Nikesh groaned and rubbed his eyes. "It's not the party."

"I sort of figured it had to be more than that, but you never know. I thought maybe you'd turned into one of those psycho parents who needs to have perfect kids with perfect birthday parties or else they'll never get into Harvard or some shit like that."

Nikesh snorted. "I'm so screwed."

"If it's not the party, what is it? Denise? You guys are fighting, right?"

"I don't think Denise is going to be talking to me for the rest of the trip." He shook his head ruefully.

"What did you do?"

"Well, it's more what I didn't do. We're not married. I told you all that we eloped, got married at city hall. But we didn't. We never got married. I promised Denise I'd set it all straight before coming down here, but I didn't. Not only that, I never told any of you that she was divorced either. She told Dad everything I hadn't told him. And now she's furious. She feels betrayed. As she should. What's the matter with me?" He shoved the cart and sank to the floor.

I sat down next to him. Through my jeans, I felt the cold lino-leum. For a moment we were both silent, listening to the faint hum of fluorescent lighting, the occasional squeak of carts in the distance. "So why didn't you guys get married?"

"I don't know. Neither of us pushed the idea when she got pregnant. I got her a ring, you know. Months ago. I was going to ask her at Christmas, but then I didn't. I guess I was still think-ing about Elena. Fucked up, right? To have a kid with someone and still be thinking about your ex."

"No, it's not. You loved Elena. What happened with her?"

"She fell in love with someone else. While we were together."

"Oh. I'm sorry."

"But here's the thing. I'm finally over it—over her. I am ready to commit to Denise, but now she's pissed at me. She doesn't trust me. I've blown it."

"No, you haven't. You just have to find a way to convince her." I put my arm around him and leaned my head against his shoul-der.

And then, out of nowhere, I giggled. I slapped a hand over my mouth, trying to shove the laughter back in.

"You're the worst." Nikesh shook his head, disgusted, and pulled away from me.

"No, no," I said, gasping. "It's not like that. I don't want you to be . . . unhappy." I caught my breath and continued. "But for so long, I've thought your life was so perfect. Living in this amazing Brooklyn condo with your high-paying job and your crazy-successful, fashionable wife, and your adorable baby—well, except for that car-cheese-vomit business, which was pretty gross. But anyway, I was convinced you'd figured your life out despite being five years younger than me, while my life is a mess."

"Your life is a mess?" Nikesh said. "You have a tenure-track job doing what you love to do. You're living life on your own terms. That sounds pretty good to me."

"Are you kidding? Who knows if I'll actually get tenure. And I'm not married and probably never will be. I don't have a baby. And all the time, I think maybe I should have married Darren when he wanted to marry me, and we should have just had that baby instead of . . . and maybe that was my only chance, and I blew it. And I've made all the wrong choices and now I'm alone, and I've completely wasted the past two years dating a married man who won't leave his wife for me, and it's all so messed up and I've done it all wrong and I can't undo it, and . . ." I doubled over, my forehead nearly touching the cold floor.

When I came back up for air, I felt sick to my stomach. I'd never told anyone about the baby before. Nikesh was staring at me, his eyes wide and concerned.

I leaned back against the shelf of streamers, shoulder to shoulder again with my brother.

"Priya . . . a baby?"

I shook my head. "I really don't want to talk about it."

He nodded. "Is that why you're weird with Alok?"

"It's hard for me sometimes. I don't regret what I did . . . it was the right call for me at the time. It's just that I remember it when I see Alok. I really do love him though. He's a great baby."

I mussed Nikesh's floppy black hair. "And you're a really good dad. You're so patient with him. Like you're a natural."

Nikesh sighed. "I don't know about that. I've had my bad parenting moments, for sure. Getting frustrated when he has a tantrum, which he's doing a lot more of these days. I know this is the age when babies start to get fussier. But sometimes, I wonder if he's reacting to us—like he's somehow intuited that he was born to parents who never fully committed to being with each other. It's not right to subject him to this kind of uncertainty."

"Nikesh, Alok is a baby—all that's important is that he feels loved by his parents. I mean, look at us. How sure did Mom feel about Dad for all those years? Why are you romanticizing what it's supposed to be like for a kid growing up when you didn't have that yourself? It wasn't ideal, but there were plenty of good moments. And you turned out okay. You felt loved, right? We all loved you—love you."

He put his arm around me. "Why can't you be nice like this all the time?"

"Shut up, you stupid idiot."

"So what about the married guy? What's the story there?"

I blew out a stream of air. This talk would have been better somewhere they let you smoke.

"I love him. But he won't leave his wife."

"He sounds like a prize."

"I know. It sounds bad. It is bad. But for some reason, I can't . . . let him go. I feel like it's my last chance or something. Like if it's not him, I'll end up alone."

"Don't be stupid. You're only thirty-five." He gently tugged my ponytail. "Look at Mom. She's almost sixty and she found a new dude."

I groaned. "Yeah, but you can't have a baby at sixty."

"So have one on your own if you want one so badly. But don't just stick with this guy because you're afraid you don't have other options. You do." He tugged my ponytail again. It was getting annoying. "And for what it's worth, I never liked Darren. He was pompous. He wore those stupid blazers with the patches."

"All right you can shut up now. Believe me, I have plenty of things to say about the people you've dated too. So don't tempt me."

He lifted his hands in mock surrender. "Okay, truce."

We watched as a harried-looking woman in her early thirties barreled her cart into our aisle, clutching a piece of paper. Spotting the Little Mermaid plates, she exclaimed with relief: "Oh, thank the Lord. Thank you, thank you, thank you. They have them."

Afraid someone might have overheard, she peeked over her shoulder and spotted the two of us. She clutched the Little Mermaid plates to her chest. "You don't understand. My daughter's fourth birthday is tomorrow and I totally procrastinated. If Target didn't have these, I'd never hear the end of it."

We nodded at her, sympathetically. She grabbed an armful of packages, threw them in her cart, and sped away.

Suddenly inspired, I hopped up off the floor, smoothed out my jeans, adjusted my ponytail, and held my hand out to my brother.

"Okay, so we're a pair of screwups questioning our life choices. But you know what we're not going to mess up? This birthday party. We're going to throw Alok the perfect birthday party. Yes, we might be the only two people there who are actually talking to each other. But so what? Let's buy these streamers in every color. We'll buy some over-the-top banners and more of those train plates and cups, party hats, balloons, cupcakes, the works. We'll do this one thing right."

35

LATA

Could lips vibrate? I peered into the mirror, running my fingertips over my lips.

They looked the same now as they did a few hours before. But they felt so different. Vibrating with excitement, as if ready to fly off my face.

How strange this dating business was. One minute, you were in a Denny's, so embarrassed you wanted the vinyl booth to swallow you up. And the next minute, a kind man was kissing you in a moonlit car.

I shook my head in disbelief and picked up my toothbrush.

Just like that, Len had leaned toward my face and kissed me, his lips soft and dry on mine. And then, an even more amazing thing had happened: I kissed him in return. And I didn't feel embarrassed or worried that I was doing it all wrong. I just closed my eyes and let myself feel like the heroine in a movie—still young and lovely and alive. The next few minutes were a beautiful blur. Lips and fingertips on my face. A hand in my hair. Laughter—mine and his and mine again.

I ran the toothbrush across my teeth, back and forth, back

and forth. Even my gums seemed to be humming. Was that possible?

When we pulled apart, Len had said, "Why don't you let me drive you home? It's so late."

I had nodded. "Yes. I'd like that."

The entire drive to my apartment, we talked. I asked him about his children. He had two sons, the younger one a chef in Seattle who worked far too much, and the older one a dentist in Dallas. We parked outside The Tuscany, and he insisted on walking me into the complex and all the way to my door. And during the walk, we continued talking. We paused at a small courtyard, not far from the pool, and sat together on a wooden bench. I confessed to him my worries: about Priya being unmarried (though I couldn't bring myself to tell him about that affair business); that Nikesh had married a woman whom I still found hard to accept, not so much because she was older or non-Indian but because she lacked a bubbling warmth—a merry, talkative, easygoing quality—that I'd always expected in the woman my son would marry. Len told me about his older son's wife, apparently a delightful hygienist who assisted with his son's dental practice, and then he told me about his younger son's having come out as a gay man a few years before and how that had surprised and worried Len at first, but then he'd gotten used to it.

And then we fell silent, staring at the pool. I couldn't read his thoughts at that moment, but I assumed they were similar to mine: that a date, which had started so disastrously with a nearly drowned ex-husband and soaked clothes and tears and doubts and fears, had somehow turned into something lovely and easy and fun.

Len took my hand and squeezed it. "I'm glad I met you." And I leaned my head against his shoulder.

I shook the water drops off my toothbrush and placed it in the toothbrush holder, next to Priya's. The sight of Priya's toothbrush caused me the slightest flicker of guilt. I hadn't thought about any of them—Priya, Nikesh, even the baby—for hours. What were they all doing at the house now? Probably they were all sleeping, given the late hour. For a second, I felt bad for having sent them away so abruptly. Nikesh and his family had, after all, traveled all the way from New York. And despite their long trip, I'd made it clear I didn't really want them around me today.

Well, it wasn't as if they had nowhere to go. They were spending time with their father at the very house they'd grown up in. They would have gone there eventually. I just sent them a bit sooner than they planned. And anyway, wasn't that how it would have to be from now on? When Nikesh or Priya visited, they would spend time at the old house with their father and then separate time with me, here. The kids could hardly expect that we'd all spend time together at the old house as one big happy family. Especially not if that Pantene-hair woman was living there.

My mood momentarily darkened, imagining her scurrying around my old kitchen, turning knobs on the stove, cooking food for my children, for my grandchild. Though that woman was so young, she probably didn't know how to cook anything. Girls her age—Priya's age, practically—didn't know how to do anything in the kitchen. They could barely boil water.

I dotted my cheeks, nose, and forehead with cream, rubbed the dots in circular strokes, and tried to refocus my thoughts in a happier direction: on Len. Who cared if that Pantene-hair woman was there? Suresh was free to do what he wanted with whomever he wanted. It wasn't even my kitchen anymore. I'd chosen to leave it and everything else in that house. And at this moment, I felt very sure I'd made the right decision.

I climbed into bed, pulled the sheet tight around my body, and let thoughts of lips and a moonlit car guide me to sleep.

36

SURESH

I stood near the lake's edge: close but not too close. I'd learned my lesson about that.

The moon shone against the water, giving the man-made pond a glimmering grandeur that almost seemed worthy of its name: Majestic Lake. I held a small pebble in my hand, then threw it into the water and listened for its gentle ping. All the while, the image of *that man* holding Lata's arm and guiding her into the apartment complex burned in my brain.

Lata was never coming back home. She had moved on. She had forgotten me.

For a second, I considered calling Pinky, to ask if she'd like to meet me at the lake. We could stand in silence and ponder the disappointments of life together. But that was a ridiculous idea, of course. It was well after midnight now, and to call at this hour would only send her the wrong message about my intentions. No, no, I couldn't go stirring that can of worms. The poor woman had been through enough in her life already.

I would just stand here and contemplate this lake and life's disappointments all alone. At least I didn't have to worry about disturbing any neighbors. No houses surrounded Majestic Lake. Just a parking lot and a playground, and beyond that a patchwork of trails leading through a dense wooded area. And then, on the other side of the lake, a partially constructed golf course.

When we first moved to this neighborhood, I often brought Nikesh to this lake to feed the ducks. He loved them. Priya was harder to please in that regard; she was nearly a teenager by the time we moved and had already begun considering such outings beneath her. One time, when Nikesh and I were feeding the ducks at dusk, he'd turned to me with a look of concern, his small hands clutching pieces of stale bread. "Where do the ducks sleep at night? Do they have nests in the water?"

I hadn't known the answer. Those were the days before Google and these new iPhones, when accurate answers to such questions were not literally at a parent's fingertips. So I did what any parent would do in those technologically backward times: I made up an answer.

"Well, they sleep in the trees, of course, safe and dry."

The answer had satisfied Nikesh, allaying his concerns about the well-being of his beloved ducks. He contentedly tossed bread into the water and never asked the question again. A few years ago, I'd learned the actual answer—on Google, of course. Ducks slept on the water, their heads turned backward into their feathers, the most natural of pillows. They slept in a line, where the ducks on the ends would sleep with one eye open, watching for predators. It would have been a truthful and consoling answer to Nikesh's question, had I been able to find it then. Looking at the lake now, I scanned the dark for a silhouetted row of sleeping ducks, two slivers of open eyes on each end. But I couldn't see anything except dark water, tiny ripples reflected in the moonlight.

It was all so much easier when your kids were little children.

When they asked you questions and listened carefully to your answers—even if those answers were made up and wrong. Then they grew up and didn't care what you thought about anything—had zero interest in hearing your answers to the questions they didn't ask, even if your answers were right.

I had a daughter who was having relations with a married man. For all I knew, she was still seeing him. And my son had a child outside of marriage with a divorced, forty-year-old woman—a woman he still hadn't married, even after all this time. I simply could not understand the choices they had made. They were making bad decisions, one after the other, and I couldn't do anything about it. They were fully grown adults. If I offered advice or reproach, they'd ignore me. Or stop calling me altogether.

Parenting adults was so much harder than parenting children. Why didn't anyone ever tell you that? Yes, a small child was completely dependent on you, but at least you had control. If a child didn't see things your way or refused to do what you wanted them to do, you had powerful tools of persuasion at your disposal. You could put them in time-out or send them to their rooms or prevent them from watching their favorite show. Even as they grew into middle-schoolers and teenagers, you could still ground them or take away their Nintendo or refuse to lend them your car or provide them money. With a grown child, you had none of the control. Just the worry.

And the guilt. Because if they were making the wrong choices as adults, if they were proceeding down dubious paths, then all you could do about it was stay up at night staring helplessly at a lake and wondering if it was somehow your fault. If you'd set a bad example for them. If you'd been too busy or distracted or depressed about your own life to teach them important lessons when they were still young enough to listen to you. All you could do now was ask yourself if you'd failed to keep a watchful eye open. Like those damn ducks.

Sometime after one, I stepped into the house. The front light was on. Mallika had probably turned it on for me, so I wouldn't trip on the steps or struggle to find the keyhole in the darkness. I doubted anyone else would have remembered. The thought of Mallika flicking on the front light in anticipation of my return touched me. I didn't know how much longer she would stay. And I knew her feelings toward me weren't romantic, as mine had been for her. But she cared what happened to me—cared for my happiness, my safety. That was more than Lata seemed to feel for me.

The house was dark and still. Hopefully, everyone was asleep. In a few short hours, Alok's morning cries would puncture the silence. I walked through the kitchen, where two glass tumblers sat on the counter—one empty and one half full of water.

I walked into the living room. Through the French doors, I caught sight of two figures in the backyard. The patio lights were on, and I could see Priya and Nikesh, throwing rolls of colored paper between them. They were hanging glittery banners from the branches of trees. I walked closer to the windows and watched them. Every few seconds, one of them would hold some shimmery decoration against a tree or a pillar or a chair and ask the other one for an opinion. I could see a near-empty bottle of Johnnie Walker Black Label atop the patio table— probably the same one from Chandrasekhar that nearly killed me some days ago.

I watched them for a long time, smiling. Neither of them saw me by the window. They were transforming the backyard into a fiery mess of color. It was for Alok's party, I assumed.

I hadn't seen them together this way in so many years. I was transported to a time when they were small children sitting at the dining room table, a jumble of paints and crayons and glitter and glue spread between them.

Well, whatever I'd done wrong—whatever, *we*, Lata and I, had done wrong—they were still ours. These children. Our children.

I opened the French doors and walked outside to join them—to offer my help, whether they wanted it or not.

37

LATA

"Mom, are you on your way?" Nikesh sounded excited, his voice higher pitched than usual.

I squinted at the clock on the nightstand. It was just after ten. I never slept this late.

An array of images and sounds from last night flew into my head: a vinyl booth at Denny's, Ella's voice on the car stereo, two lips, foggy car windows, a silver moon, a courtyard bench. I rubbed my eyes and swung my feet onto the floor.

"On my way where?" I struggled to remember any discussion from the previous day about plans to meet. Honestly, I had hardly paid attention to anything my family had said after Suresh's pool debacle and Len's walking away. In my distracted state, had I mindlessly agreed to some Sunday family plan?

"To the house. Alok's birthday party, remember? We decided to have it here. We stayed up half the night decorating the back-yard. Priya's at the grocery store getting helium balloons and a cake as we speak, and Alok's going nuts in the backyard, grab-bing colored streamers and flinging them in different direc-tions."

"Oh, the birthday party. Is that still going on today? I just assumed that after yesterday's . . . events . . . it would be, you know, postponed."

I couldn't believe it. They were having a birthday party at Suresh's, today? Had that Pantene-hair woman stayed up half the night too, tying colored streamers to the trees, laughing and planning party games with my children? All of them working together to make a party for my own grandson that I was being instructed to attend like some last-minute, afterthought guest.

Phone against my cheek, I stomped into the kitchen, my feet smacking the tiles. I filled a cup with water, took a sip, and calmed myself down. I had to admit, even if they had called me yesterday evening to help, I probably wouldn't have answered my phone.

"Mom, come on. Don't be like that. You can't still be upset with Dad. In fact, why don't you invite Len? That will even out the situation, right? It's only fair. Mallika's here and that's, like, weird for you. So in exchange, you should bring Len if you want. In fact, I insist. Let's all start being adults about this. No more weirding out. And anyway, this is a birthday party—the more bodies we have the better. Come on. Please don't be difficult. It's your grandson's first birthday, and you can't miss that. You're his *paati*. You have to be a part of it."

I took in a deep, long breath. And then exhaled. If this event was for any other reason and for anyone other than my grandson, I'd refuse. But this—how could I say no? My only grandchild was turning one. And it was my own fault that I'd forgotten about Alok's birthday party, that I hadn't taken control of the plans and hosted it somewhere else, far away from Suresh's house. I'd been too distracted by Len, and now it was far too late to make alternate party plans. So whatever humiliations lay in store for me, I'd just have to bear it. It was only one day of my life. Not even an entire day, really, just one afternoon.

I sighed, resigned to my fate. "Of course I'll be there, *kanna*."

"And Len?"

Was Nikesh right? Would it make me feel better to have Len by my side, as a kind of shield against Suresh and his Pantene-hair woman? Or would it make the party even more awkward?

Well, it was all presumption anyway. Because who knew if Len would even want to come. After all, the last time he had been subjected to Suresh's company, he'd ended up fully clothed in a pool and then berated by the very man he'd saved from drowning.

"Okay, I'll invite him. But I'm not sure he'll be free to attend so last minute. Or that he'd even want to come."

"Oh, Mom, I'm sure he'll change his plans for you. After all, you're like twenty times better-looking than him."

Despite myself, I laughed. How easy it was for Nikesh. Nothing seemed to get the better of him, to unsettle him. Even as a baby, he was easy—a happy boy, always quick to laugh. With Priya, there'd been so many tears, so many hurt feelings to soothe over the years. But sometimes I wondered whether Nikesh's life was more complicated than he let on. He had spent so many years making it easy on us, never complaining, never sharing his doubts, that it had become his habit around us.

In fact, if I was being really honest with myself, I knew that even his elopement, by some measure, had made things easy on us. Of course I'd been hurt when my only son left me out of the biggest event in his life. But then later, after the shock and disappointment began to wear off, I realized that maybe the alternative was even more unthinkable. What if Suresh and I had been tasked with planning a full-blown wedding for our son? I struggled to imagine it: inviting the four hundred guests, flying in family from India, ordering the food, the cake, the flowers, the *mandap*, the priest—and all of that right in the midst of our separation? It would have been impossible. Yes, even Nikesh's elopement had made it easier on us, in a way. But what a terrible thought for a mother to think! Was it possible that Nikesh had eloped, had denied himself a genuine wedding celebration to spare me—us—from discomfort? I leaned against the sink, my body suddenly heavy with guilt.

Oh, my easy, easy boy. But no one's life could be easy. Especially with a busy job and a small child. Nikesh too had to worry and fret and succumb to dark thoughts at times. But who did he confess those to? Who soothed him? Was it Denise? I hoped so, I really did. Whatever my reservations about her, I hoped she was a source of comfort to my easygoing baby. I hoped, but didn't quite believe, that was true.

"*Chi.* Silly boy. I told you I was coming to the party. You don't have to flatter me."

He laughed. "Okay, Mom. No more flattery, then. We don't have time anyway. Alok's got about one good hour in him, maybe two if we're lucky. Then he'll start getting antsy for his nap. So hurry."

Len wanted to come. It surprised me how relieved I was to hear him say yes. Within twenty minutes of my call, he picked me up and we were on our way.

I tried to quiet my nerves by concentrating on the music from the speakers, on the passing cars, on the traffic lights. Beneath those sounds, I began to hear a buzzing sound, which I assumed was part of the music until Len said, "Lata, I think your phone is buzzing."

I grabbed it from my purse. "Hi, Lata! So look, we're on our way to your apartment for Alok's birthday party." It was Mala.

"What? How do you know about the party?" I asked.

"You told me a few weeks ago, remember? You said it would be at the condo's clubroom. It's such a great clubroom, isn't it? There's that Ping-Pong table, and after the party is over, you don't even have to worry about cleaning because they have a cleaning service. You know, before we bought our house, Raj and

I threw some great parties there. Sometimes, I think we should have moved into the condo ourselves. It would make life so much easier." Mala laughed, both to assure me she had no serious designs on the condo and to convey the absurdity of the suggestion. Of course, Mala would never move out of her house just so she could use some silly old clubroom.

I didn't laugh. Instead, I struggled to remember this supposed conversation with her. What was happening to my mind? Was my forgetfulness a sign of early onset Alzheimer's? I'd seen a pamphlet about that too at my doctor's office the last time I was there.

But now it was coming back to me—a dim memory of telling Mala about the party for Alok. And how, in an effort to convince my friend that I wasn't lonely or deserving of her pity, I'd perhaps overstated my plans, describing a big bash with catering and a clown and decorations in the condo's clubroom.

Oh God, why did I ever open my big fat mouth? I should have convinced Nikesh to throw the birthday party in Brooklyn and have us fly out there instead. Well, it was too late now. Now I had to figure out some way of disinviting my friend.

"You know, Mala, I'm so sorry, I forgot to tell you that . . ."

And just as I was about to tell her that we'd canceled the birthday party for Alok because Nikesh had too much work in New York and couldn't travel to Clayborn, I realized that Len would overhear my lie. And then I'd have a new and potentially bigger problem. I'd have to explain to Len that I lied to my best friend in large part because I was too embarrassed to have her know anything about him. Which was the lesser of two evils here? To have Mala at the party, and by extension the entire Clayborn Indian community who'd hear everything about everything because Mala wouldn't be able to resist relating such good gossip? Or to lie to Mala and risk offending Len?

"Lata! Are you still there? Did the phone disconnect?"

Ah, okay now: Here was a potential third option. Maybe I

could just pretend my phone had stopped working, and then I wouldn't have to lie to Mala or explain anything to Len. But then, Mala and Raj would drive all the way to my condo complex, knock on my door, and wait for me to answer in their dressy silk clothes with birthday presents in hand; and that would be such mean treatment for friends who'd helped me so much over the years.

Aiyo. All my options were terrible. I'd just tell Mala the truth and hope for the best.

"Mala, I forgot to tell you the party is at the house . . . I mean, Suresh's house." I cleared my throat and glanced at Len from the corner of my eye. His eyes stayed on the road.

"Oh. Really?"

"Yes, so sorry for the change in plans. It's just . . . you know, the backyard is so big, and Alok will have lots of room to run around and play, and the clubroom is better for an older kid's party because Alok can't play Ping-Pong or do anything like that. I'm sorry you had to drive out of your way."

"No, Lata. It's no problem at all. Actually"—she laughed— "you know, we're still in our driveway. Raj forgot this bottle of wine he wanted to bring, so we drove back for it. We were going to be late anyway, and now this is perfect because we're closer to your house . . . I mean, Suresh's house . . . and so this all worked out great." Mala's voice became louder and higher with each word. If she tried any harder to convince me this party situation was ideal, she'd puncture my eardrum.

"Okay. We're . . . I'm on my way too. See you there." I hung up the phone quickly, cutting off Mala's ear-splitting commentary.

Len's eyes were still focused on the road. He stopped at a signal, and I explained. "I forgot I invited my friend Mala to this birthday party. It completely slipped my mind. So much has happened in the past few weeks."

Len nodded. "Lata, would you prefer if I just drop you off? I don't have to come in, you know." His eyes stayed fixed on the road ahead.

I wondered how it was that he always seemed to know the right thing to say. Even if he struggled to mean it at times, like now, at least he knew what he should say. That was something, really, in and of itself. Something I'd learned never to expect from Suresh.

"No, I want you to come. You can meet my friend Mala and her husband, Raj—Dr. Chandrasekhar. He's a nephrologist." I didn't know why I highlighted this particular detail. It wasn't as if a jazz history professor and a kidney specialist would have immediate discussion topics in common.

"And besides, Suresh will have his new . . . lady friend there too. So with or without you there, I'm pretty sure Mala will have plenty of good gossip to make her head explode." I shook my head and laughed. It all seemed so ridiculous now. I felt less like the heroine of a movie and more like her empty-headed best friend—the one who always got herself into ludicrous situations for the amusement of the audience. Well, movie heroine or bumbling sidekick, one thing was becoming clear to me: I felt calmer when Len was around.

We were getting close to the house now. Through the car window, I could see the murky water of Majestic Lake—a stupidly grand name, I'd always thought. A few kids and parents were at its edge, pointing at the ducks. Maybe if the party became unbearably awkward, I could say I was taking Alok to see the ducks and escape for a while.

"Okay, then, if you're sure." Len squeezed my shoulder with his free hand. Then he clicked the signal and turned his car onto De Soto Drive.

38

PRIYA

The decorations had turned out pretty good in the end—if your aesthetic was color-blind clown. Streamers in bold shades of green, blue, red, and yellow zigzagged through tree branches. A blue tablecloth with smiling, anthropomorphized trains lay draped across a long, foldable card table that Nikesh had fished out of the garage. He'd also found a half dozen folding chairs to go with it.

A huge cluster of weighted helium balloons formed a boisterous table centerpiece. The birthday boy was transfixed by them. Standing in his mother's lap, Alok kept pulling the balloon strings toward him and clapping as they sprang back up. He was awfully cute, with his hair neatly combed and dressed in a navy sailor outfit. Denise wore navy too, a cheerful sundress with piping—though her expression was glum. Apparently, she and Nikesh hadn't made up yet.

I held a cold bottle of Corona against my cheek, hoping it would wake me up. Nikesh and I had stayed up until three, decorating the backyard. Even Dad helped for a while, though we sent him to bed soon after he started snoozing on a chair. I wasn't sure if it was the old age or the (surprising) finger of whisky he drank with us that sent him to sleep so fast. But together, we pulled it off. Somehow we made a party happen.

Food lined the table: sprinkled cupcakes, bowls of chips, pretzels, and popcorn, a veggie platter with dip, freshly delivered boxes of pizza. Not a gourmet feast by any stretch, but it would do. An assortment of beverages chilled in the cooler. Even the weather was cooperating. It was half past eleven, and the temperature was hovering just above eighty degrees—the sun obscured by gray clouds. Rain was forecast for the evening, long after the birthday festivities would end.

We even managed to get a few extra people here. Nikesh invited a friend of his from high school—Eugene, who'd moved back to Clayborn to become the town's orthodontist. (The old one—Dr. Benson, who'd fixed our teeth back in the day—had apparently died.) Eugene had a three-year-old daughter he brought with him. She was trying to shove a whole cupcake into her mouth. Expensive dental work was probably in her future; good thing she had an inside track.

The other extra body was Deanna. I could see her now, pulling slices of cheese pizza onto her plate. She was dressed (surprisingly) normally, in a sleeveless black T-shirt dress. Though, apparently, she couldn't be bothered to put on a bra. I had texted her at seven this morning to invite her to the party. Since we needed some bodies here, I figured Deanna was one person who might actually say yes—out of some sense of obligation to my mom. Her text response was noncommittal: *Why the fuck are you texting me so early?*

But here she was. At a party for a one-year-old she didn't even know. It struck me that Deanna might be lonely—a loner. She was alone at that bar—Elmo's—when I ran into her a few days ago. And at work, she'd glommed onto my mom, a woman nearly three times her age. Didn't she have any friends her own age? A boyfriend? A girlfriend? I'd never asked her. I should have asked her.

Well, I guess I was kind of a loner these days too. Unlike Nikesh, I'd lost touch with everyone I'd been friendly with in high school. And the few friends I'd kept from college and graduate school had disappeared into a haze of husbands and toddlers and mortgages; I barely saw any of them anymore. I barely saw anyone other than Ashish. He had somehow become my best friend. Which made it even harder to cut him off and stick to it.

I held up my beer to Deanna in a gesture of greeting. She held up her pizza slice in response. Two loners at a one-year-old's birthday.

"Priya, here you are!" Mala Aunty grabbed my arm and gave me a heavily perfumed hug. Her chunky gold necklace pricked my collarbone.

No, please no. Did Nikesh invite them? Was he so desperate for bodies at his son's birthday that he'd actually called Mala Aunty? Deanna was one thing. The Chandrasekhars were quite another.

"Why do we see so little of you? You really should visit your mom more often. Divorced life must be very hard for her . . . so lonely, you know. Don't you agree, Raj?" Mala Aunty tsk-tsked and shook her head from side to side, and her husband mm-hmm'd in agreement.

Clearly, these two had no idea what my mother was doing with her free time. Part of me wanted to tell them about Len, just to see their reaction. At that moment, I even felt a pinprick of pride that my mother had created a life for herself after the divorce—that she wasn't just some pathetic sad sack living in Mala Aunty's cast-off apartment.

"Oh my, that Alok is such a cutie pie!" She waved at Alok, who was too busy trying to suck on a balloon to notice. "And I see your brother coming out of the house now. My goodness, he looks so handsome in his checkered dress shirt and slacks. Why didn't you dress up for this party, Priya? This is an occasion!" Mala Aunty's eyes went up and down my outfit, scrutinizing.

I was wearing denim cutoffs and a white V-neck. I looked at Mala Aunty's outfit: a red silk salwar kameez, black strappy heels, and that garish (and painful) gold necklace. In my opinion, she was the one who was dressed ridiculously for a one-year-old's outdoor birthday party.

"I can't believe Nikesh's son is already turning one. When is it going to be your turn, Priya? We're all waiting for your wedding. Right, Raj?"

"Oh yes, I will definitely bring my dancing shoes to that!" Raj Uncle swayed his hips back and forth in a goofy way.

I rolled my eyes. I didn't make it a habit to be rude to my mother's friends, but seriously: If you were an unmarried thirty-five-year-old woman, then Indian people my parents' age were simply the worst kind of people to be around. One thing I knew for sure: I was not going to give them the satisfaction of telling me all about their perfect daughter and her perfect son and her perfect impending-baby-number-two. No way. My eyes scanned the backyard for an escape. But Mala Aunty's hand was still on my arm—in some kind of vise grip. As if she knew full well I was planning to ditch her.

Desperate, I tried to wave Deanna over. I could pawn the Chandrasekhars off on her. Midway through a pizza bite she caught sight of my frantic waving. She squinted, appraised the situation I was beckoning her into, and turned back toward the food table.

Damn it. Well, nobody said that girl was a fool.

"So, Priya, tell me, are we going to hear wedding bells for you sometime soon?"

I sighed. The woman was relentless.

At that moment, I spotted Mom stepping into the backyard

through the fenced side entrance. She wore a gauzy yellow blouse and fitted black pants. She looked slim and elegant, not overdone and tacky like her nosy friend. And right behind Mom was Len. He was looking sort of dapper too—well, compared to the last time I saw him. At least he was dry, in pressed tan slacks and a white button-down. His hair, however, was another story. Gray curls all over the place. He really needed to get a handle on that situation.

So Dad's pool antics hadn't scared him away after all. Fine. I was too sleep-deprived to spend energy resenting his presence. In fact, I was kind of glad Mom brought him along. If anything would distract Mala Aunty from haranguing me about my spinsterhood, it would be the sight of Mom with a boyfriend.

"Mala Aunty, look, it's Mom. And she brought the man she's been dating, Leonard. He's a jazz history professor at the university. A really interesting guy . . . very good at . . . burning CDs. You guys should go say hello. I'm sure she's dying to introduce you."

"Oh." Mala Aunty abruptly let go of my arm and brought her overjeweled hand to her chin. "Isn't that . . . nice."

I savored the look of shock on her face. And boy, was that look going to get even better. Because Dad and Mallika were coming out of the house now with a tray of samosas.

"Oh and look, Aunty, there's Dad coming out of the house with the woman he's living with: Mallika. And that's her son, Bobby, right behind them."

At that, Mala Aunty's mouth dropped open. Even Raj Uncle, who'd been uncharacteristically quiet for a while now, let out an audible gasp. "Oh gosh. Wow. Okay, then."

And just like that, I was free.

39

LATA

I dried my hands on the towel in the powder room—the bathroom for guests—just off the kitchen. The hand towel was neatly hung and freshly washed. Clearly not the handiwork of Suresh.

I steadied myself against the sink. In the mirror, my lips looked pale and dry. I dug my fingers into my purse and pulled out a tube of lipstick. Carefully, I outlined my lips in mauve, blotted with a square of tissue, and flushed it down the toilet. Then I stood there, watching the pink-flecked tissue churn down the drain. I racked my mind for anything else I could possibly do to avoid going back out there. I pulled the hand towel off the bar, shook it loose, and refolded it. Then I hung it on the bar, taking my time, making sure the edges were perfectly even.

Well, that was it. There was nothing else to keep me in here.

Honestly, I didn't know what was more unbearable. Having to witness Mala pepper Len with question after question, as if she were hosting a Barbara Walters interview special. Or having

Suresh glare at me and Len from across the yard with such fury that I could almost feel the heat burn a hole in my forehead. Or having to watch that Pantene-hair woman flitting around the party with a tray of samosas in her hand, laughingly asking guests if they'd had enough to eat, urging them to try the mint chutney, playing the grand hostess at my grandson's birthday like she'd already signed the title to this house. My God, the nerve of that woman. The nerve of Suresh. The nerve of Mala. I wanted to wash my hands of all of them.

So here was my new plan. I would march out of this powder room, find Nikesh and ask him to bring the cake out for cutting. I would tell him I had a terrible headache and needed to go home. Or better yet, I would tell him my stomach was upset because the Pantene-hair woman's samosas had given me food poisoning. (Not that I'd eaten a single oily-looking one, but Nikesh didn't need to know that.)

Feeling bold now, I swung the door open with such force, it slammed against the door stopper with a loud, rubbery thud.

"Oh my gosh! Who's there?"

I heard a racket of metal from the kitchen. As I stepped out of the powder room and into the kitchen, I saw a mess of samosas on the floor. A few had slid so far across the room that I almost stepped on one.

Oh God. It was her. The Pantene-hair woman. She had oven mitts on her hands and a shocked expression on her face. The oven door hung fully open, little waves of heat spilling out between us.

"They're all ruined." She looked at me accusingly. "The bathroom door—it startled me. You startled me. And I dropped them."

The nerve of this woman! Interloper in the house I designed, using the KitchenAid oven that I'd carefully chosen, criticizing me for opening the bathroom door! All these years, I could count on one hand the number of times I'd used this tiny powder room off the kitchen. It was a *guest* bathroom, after all. For guests. When I lived here, I hardly ever used it. Did this woman have any idea how strange it felt to be invited to this house as a guest? For my grandson's first birthday, no less? Did this woman have any idea how being here, in the same house as her and Suresh, made my organs churn like I was getting tossed on a roller coaster? I was about to tell her exactly how I felt about her oily samosas—how all the guests were better off with them spread out on the kitchen floor—when she ripped off the oven mitts and dropped her forehead into her bare hands.

"I'm sorry, Lata. Of course it's not your fault. I'm on edge today." She looked up and smiled weakly at me. "I know it must be strange for you too, seeing me in here, using your old kitchen like this. I just wanted you to know that Suresh and I—"

Before she could finish, I cut her off. "No, no, you don't need to tell me. It's none of my business what you and Suresh are doing."

"Yes, but that's just it. I want you to know that we're not—"

"Mom! What's taking you so long?" Her son—Bobby, was it?—came bounding into the kitchen, his voice echoing off the marble countertops. "Are you ever bringing out the samosas? You came in here forever ago, and I'm starving!"

"Oh, Bobby, they're no good. I dropped them." She bent down and began piling samosas on the baking sheet that had clanged to the floor.

"But I really wanted one! I'm sick of pizza! Pizza, pizza, pizza, that's all they eat around here. Can we go to McDonald's?"

"Bobby, we cannot go to McDonald's."

"It's not fair! How come we never do what I want to do? This birthday party is stupid. All the kids here are babies. There's no one for me to play with." The boy's face wilted, and tears began filling his eyes.

This poor boy. It could not be easy, having to tag along with his mother to a complete stranger's house. As odd as I felt being back here, how must it feel for this boy? I bent down, so I was eye level with him. "Bobby, do you like Indian food?"

"No, it's gross," he said between sniffles. "But I like samosas. With lots of ketchup."

I smiled. "My son used to eat them that way too." Samosas, vadas, dosas—the only way I could get Nikesh to eat any of it was by squeezing a dollop of ketchup on his plate. And now, maybe this boy was going to grow up in the same house, make the same complaints about eating Indian food in the same kitchen, make the same pleas for hamburgers and hot dogs, squeeze the same large dollops of ketchup on his plate, play video games in the same game room, throw basketballs into the same goal in the same driveway. This boy—with the large, tear-filled, beautiful brown eyes, and the same long, floppy black hair that Nikesh used to have.

I ran my hand through his hair, pushing it away from his eyes. "You know what. The samosas aren't ruined. We can just put them in the oven for five more minutes. It will zap all the germs off." I made exploding motions with my fingers. "Zap, zap, zap."

His eyes widened. "Really?"

"Yes, really." I looked up at the Pantene-hair woman . . . at Mallika. I bobbled my head from side to side, a conciliatory gesture. "Look, why don't you take Bobby outside. I'll bring these out when they're done."

"Come on, Mom, let's go!" Bobby yanked Mallika's arm, pulling her out of the kitchen. She mouthed a "thank you" to me and let her son drag her away.

I bent closer to the ground and began picking up the rest of the samosas. I laid them in neat rows on the baking sheet. They actually looked quite good. Not so oily as the last batch, the edges crisp and golden brown. I did not know how to make samosas from scratch. If I had made snacks for this party, they would have been pakoras.

"Mom, there you are!" Nikesh appeared before me in the kitchen, just as I laid the last samosa on the pan.

"Why are you on the floor? Len just asked me if I knew where you were."

Oh God. Poor Len. I'd left him alone for so long. By now, Mala had probably uncovered his bank account balance, his social security number, and his ex-wife's contact information.

I stood up, baking sheet in hand, and slid it into the still-open oven. "I have to finish these. Just a few more minutes. Why don't you keep me company until they're done?"

I had barely seen my son since he arrived. Some of that was my fault. I had been so distracted and angry yesterday, when they were at my apartment. But even otherwise, getting time alone with Nikesh was a rarity. That's what happened when a son got married. Seeing Bobby with his mother, the way he needed her, pulled on her arms and legs for her undivided attention—was it possible both to miss something and to feel relief at its being gone at the same time?

"Oh, okay, sure." He seemed distracted, feeling around his pants pocket for something—a baby pacifier perhaps? "So what do you think of the party?"

"It's . . . unusual."

"Why do you say that? Do you mean because you and Dad brought dates, and because Denise isn't speaking to me?" He laughed—a hollow, unhappy bark of a sound.

"What do you mean she isn't speaking to you? Did your dad do something?"

"No. Believe it or not, Mom, not everything that's wrong in this family is Dad's fault. This one's all on me, I'm afraid."

I wasn't sure what to say. It was not like Nikesh to confide in me about his marital problems. My easy boy. "I'm sorry to hear that. Do you want to tell me what happened?"

The oven beeped, startling us both. The samosas were done.

Nikesh shrugged. "Don't worry, Mom. I'm fine. We're fine."

He jammed his hand into his pocket again, clasping something. Lines creased his forehead.

Despite the confidence in his voice, my son did not look fine.

"Don't worry," he repeated. "I know how to fix this."

40

NIKESH

I was losing the thread somehow.

My knee dug into the ground. A twig poked my ankle. An airplane buzzed in the sky, leaving a hazy white tail in its wake. I wanted to be on that plane, going somewhere else, anywhere else. I wanted to stand back up.

What was the appropriate length of time to kneel before you could stand back up? Was there some kind of proposal etiquette to conform to?

Everyone was staring at me. At me and Denise. A jagged half-ringed audience around us: there was Mom, holding Alok in her arms, standing next to Len; then Dad with Priya on one side and Mallika and Bobby on the other; there was my old high school friend Eugene holding his little girl with blue cupcake frosting on her lips; there were my parents' friends, the Chandrasekhars; and even that strange girl who worked with Mom at the library (Deanna, was it?), who I'd met at Mom's apartment yesterday. I avoided eye contact with everyone—other than Denise. But I could feel all their eyes on me. So many eyes.

And still, Denise had yet to utter a word.

I cleared my throat. "Um, I'm gonna stand back up now." I brushed the grass from my knee and stepped backward.

In my right hand, I held a blue velvet box, still propped open to that Art Deco ring I'd bought Denise all those months ago.

Denise cleared her throat. Since I'd begun my (admittedly) rambling proposal, she'd been staring mostly at the ground. Possibly she was shocked, and her silence was a reaction to shock. Or perhaps she found that pilled anthill mound on the lawn a fascinating, near-hypnotic sight. Or perhaps I'd grossly miscalculated this proposal, and she was contemplating how to turn me down in a way that would minimize the spectacle I'd made of both of us.

"I'm . . ." She looked up at me with what seemed a mixture of surprise and confusion and frustration on her face. It was not unlike the look she'd given me when I'd once surprised her with a bouquet of yellow lilies that caused her to erupt in a fit of allergic sneezing—a look that told me that my grand gestures, no matter how right they seemed in theory, would somehow always fall short in practice. But then her eyes softened, turning to concern. She reached out for the box. "It's a lovely ring." Gently, she took the box from my hands and closed it shut: a thud heard round the neighborhood.

I heard someone cough. Dad, maybe? No—it was a woman's cough, less guttural than Dad's. Maybe Priya? Jesus, this was mortifying.

"Maybe we could go inside and talk for a bit. Excuse us, everyone."

She clasped my hand and pulled me away with her—away from all their staring eyes, toward the empty house.

41

SURESH

They left us to watch their disappearing backs. And now, we all had to pretend like nothing had happened.

We had to stand stupidly by the food table, like a herd of confused cattle, picking at the congealing Domino's pizza and carrot sticks and onion dip on our plates, lifting bottles of beer and sparkling water to our lips, and making forced conversation, like this was a normal birthday party.

For God's sake, what had my son been thinking? All right, so I was not the best when it came to picking up on social cues. How many times had Lata told me over the years that I lacked tact and timing and powers of observation when it came to other people's feelings and comfort? And yet, even I knew better than to propose to a woman when I wasn't one hundred percent certain she would answer yes. And in public, no less—in the middle of a child's birthday party!

Why had Nikesh done this here? Today, of all days? The woman was furious with him yesterday. I had a front-row seat to her anger. Why not give her some time to calm down—a month, a week, at least another day? And to think that during all these months when I'd sought Nikesh's advice about dating and women and relationships, it had never occurred to me that my son might also have no idea what he was doing.

And why were all of these people still here? Nikesh was inside with Denise, and any mood for celebrating was done for. As the titleholder of this house, did the responsibility for ending this debacle of a birthday party now fall to me?

Maybe Priya could tell everyone to go home. After all, she'd done so much of the decorating. Wasn't this party as much hers as Nikesh's?

I glanced meaningfully in her direction, informing her with my lifted brows and rapid eye blinks that it was her responsibility to ease the awkward quiet that had settled over the group like a fog. In response, Priya announced she was going to grab a bottle of wine from the fridge and dashed for the kitchen. Oh, that clever coward!

Well, Lata then. She could do it. Half the guests were her invitees anyway. Like those Chandrasekhars, who seemed to follow Lata everywhere, and that skinny teenage girl with an assortment of metal piercings in her ears and eyebrows who was piling pizza and carrot sticks onto her plate. I had no idea who that girl was, but I did recall her being at Lata's apartment the day *that man* caused me to almost drown. And speaking of the devil: the audacity of *that man* to show up here—at my house!

Did it even occur to Lata to ask me if I wanted these people at my house before she invited them? Of course not. Lata did whatever she wanted, whenever she wanted, and with whomever she wanted. If she felt license to invite every Tom, Dick, and Chandrasekhar to my house, then she could damn well find a way to entertain them all. Mallika and Bobby were my responsibility. Everyone else—Lata's problem.

I shook my head and walked quickly to the fenced entrance near the side of the house. I opened the wooden door, slammed it shut, and kept walking until I reached the front yard. I looked up at the windows to Nikesh's room. The blinds were closed. Were they making up? Were they breaking up? Were they packing bags and leaving early?

I spotted a few weeds peeking through the manicured bushes. I yanked them out and began looking for more. Hoping for more. Weeds would distract me. I knew how to fix the problem of weeds.

The strange thing was: I was starting to like Denise. She was strong and clear-headed and methodical and decisive; traits my son did not always have. Maybe she could forgive him for lying to her. They were still young; they could work out their differences and stay together. My heart ached at the thought of Alok having to shuttle back and forth between his parents, moving between apartments and bedrooms, like a rootless boy.

A weed. I needed to find more weeds. I hunched closer to the ground.

"Suresh, what are you doing out here?" I felt Mallika's hand on my shoulder.

"Pulling weeds."

"You can't just leave the party. Suresh, look at me." She tugged my arm, and I turned toward her. Her face glowed from the humidity.

"Some party this turned out to be," I said.

Mallika chuckled. "I thought they were already married. I didn't even understand that he was proposing to her at first."

"He's been lying to me—to all of us—about being married."

Mallika patted my shoulder sympathetically. "Well, it's hard sometimes to tell one's parents embarrassing truths. I still haven't told mine about Praveen being in jail."

I shook my head. "What will happen to Alok?"

Mallika shrugged. "He'll adjust. Kids adjust to all kinds of situations. Look at Bobby."

Bobby had followed Mallika to the front yard, where he was pretending to karate chop the crepe myrtles. We watched him for a while, vibrant in an orange shirt, joyously kicking and punching and shouting "hi-yah" around the yard, oblivious to the world of adult problems. It was a comforting sight.

As we watched, a silver Lexus approached the house and parked next to the mailbox. For God's sake, had Lata invited more people to this birthday party? Some other pair of our old Indian friends who hadn't bothered to call me after the divorce? Some other strange colleague of hers from the library?

A tall Indian man stepped out of the car. I didn't recognize him. He seemed no older than fifty and was dressed like an accountant—in black slacks, blue dress shirt, and shiny black loafers. A pair of thin wire-framed glasses sat on his nose.

Other than that tattooed girl, were all of Lata's new friends men? Heat coursed through my arms and hands. I dropped the weeds I was holding and shouted, "Look, the party is over, okay? You can go back home."

"What party?" the man asked just as Bobby began running toward him and yelling with glee: "Rahul Uncle!"

The man's face erupted into a huge smile at the sight of Bobby. He picked him up and spun him around. "Hey, big man. You've grown so tall!"

I looked at Mallika for an explanation. Her eyes had grown big and round, almost fearful. "What are you doing here, Rahul?" she said.

He let go of Bobby and walked toward us. He held out his hand to me. "I'm Mallika's brother-in-law." He said those words so pointedly that I pulled my hand back.

"How did you find me?" Mallika whispered.

"Well, you see, a friend of mine happens to be a private investigator. He told me that you and Bobby were staying here—at the house of some old man." He paused, letting the insult sink in. "I wanted to see for myself how my dear nephew and his mother were doing. And I was curious to meet the old man too." Again, he paused. "And now I have. So tell me, how do you know Mallika?" He glared at me, his eyes no longer pretending civility.

"Rahul, stop this. You had no right to hire a private investigator to follow me." Mallika shook a finger at him.

"No, you're wrong, Mallika. I had every right to know what had become of my brother's wife and son. In fact, I saw Praveen last week, and he was worried sick about you both. He said he hadn't heard from you in many weeks. He was missing Bobby terribly and desperate for a visit. I promised him I'd find you both and bring you back to live with us." He shook his head. "You didn't make it easy. But luckily, my private investigator friend is very good at what he does. All your visits to the pool helped things too. Once he'd zeroed in on Clayborn as your hiding ground, he figured that with an eight-year-old in the summertime, a municipal pool would be a good bet on finding you. And he was right."

Between clenched teeth, Mallika said, "I won't take Bobby to that awful place. That prison. I won't let him see his father that way. And I won't take him back to live with you. It's your fault that Praveen got in trouble in the first place. He never should have gone to work for you. You've ruined your brother's life. And mine. And Bobby's. And you want us to come live with you? I'd sooner die." Mallika was near screaming now. "It should be you in that jail and not Praveen!"

I didn't know what to do. Whether to call the police, or to ask Mallika to lower her voice so she didn't scare the neighbors, or to ask Mallika to shout even louder so that some neighbors would show up and help me scare off this shady brother-in-law character.

Rahul moved to grasp Mallika's arm, and at that moment, my equivocation stopped. He wouldn't be laying a finger on her—that much I knew. I stepped forward, inserting my body between them.

"You should go home. Any further conversation, you can continue over the phone." I tried to keep the fear out of my voice. The man might be dressed like somebody's accountant, but he was four inches taller than me, a decade younger, and if Mallika was right, he was a crook to boot. If he had this private investigator on speed dial, who knew what other questionable characters were in his pocket?

"Who do you think you are?" He poked his finger into my chest. "You're just a sick old man preying on a confused woman who is still married. She has a husband. That's my brother's wife and my brother's kid. I'm here on his behalf. Who do you think you are, telling me what I can and can't do with my own family? You're nobody in this. Got it? You're nobody to any of us." His face was so close to mine, I could smell the garlic on his breath and see a piece of spinach lodged between two bottom teeth.

"Hey, get away from my father! Or I will call the police!" Priya shouted. I turned my head in the direction of her voice. She was standing on the front stoop of the house, a wine opener still in her hand. She must have seen us arguing through the window and come running to investigate.

Rahul jabbed his finger into my chest again. "Sick old man," he spit out.

I didn't care what this particular scoundrel thought of me. But it suddenly occurred to me how my actions might look to an outsider. Would it look as he said? That I was some sick old man preying on the misfortunes of a disturbed young woman? Was it possible? The thought was so discomfiting that, for a moment, I nearly forgot about Rahul's finger in my chest and his garlic breath on my face.

"Rahul, stop." Mallika slapped at his arms. "It's not his fault. He didn't know I was married when I met him. He didn't know about my husband being in jail. He didn't know any of it. I was desperate to get away . . . from you . . . from everything; and he's been nothing but kind and decent to us. He's been a real friend."

"You're married?" Priya yelled. "And your husband is in jail?

Why did you drag my dad into your bullshit? Dad, I warned you that these internet women were crazy!" Priya was right next to us now, pointing the wine opener at Rahul, then Mallika, and back at Rahul again.

Rahul stepped back, away from me, away from all of us. "You can put down your corkscrew, okay?" he said to Priya. "I'm going home now. Mallika, I'll give you until tomorrow to come back. Or else I'll return here for you both. Please end this nonsense and come back to your family, where Bobby can see his father, play with his cousins, go to a good school. What you're doing is so stupid and selfish—you have to see that. You can't just hide forever."

Rahul's face and voice softened, no longer menacing but pleading. "You know I didn't make Praveen do anything. He's a very adamant person. No one can tell him what to do. In your heart, you know that. You want to blame me because you want to blame someone. But you know."

Mallika's lip quivered, and tears began to fall from her eyes. Rahul's eyes began to tear too, both of them no doubt thinking of the same man. Perhaps this Rahul was not such a scoundrel after all.

Rahul rubbed his eyes with his sleeve and turned around. "Bobby! I'm leaving. Come give me a hug." He scanned the front yard. "Where did he go?" he asked us.

In all the commotion, I had forgotten about Bobby. He was right here a few minutes ago, and now he wasn't. "Did he go inside?" I asked Priya.

"I didn't see him," Priya said.

"Maybe he ran to the backyard?" Mallika said, worry filling her voice. "Bobby! Bobby!" she began yelling. She looked at us, panic in her face. "Where did he go?"

"Don't freak out," Priya said. "All the shouting adults probably scared him. I'll go check inside, and you guys check the back. He's here somewhere. I'm sure of it."

42

LATA

"Bobby? Bobby?" I cupped my hands around my mouth as I called the boy's name.

He hadn't been in the house or the backyard. According to the panicked telling of Priya and Suresh and Mallika and that other Indian man that nobody bothered to introduce, the boy had simply vanished from the front yard.

So I was leading half the attendees of this disastrous birthday party—Len, Mala, and Raj—along one tree-covered trail near the lake to search for Bobby. In the meantime, Suresh, Mallika, and the mystery Indian man were going to search the playground and then another trail close to the lake. Priya and Deanna (not sure what she was doing here, as I didn't remember inviting her) were planning to drive around the neighborhood calling Bobby's name out of the car windows, in case the boy was wandering the streets. Even Nikesh and Denise—whose (suddenly) unmarried state I'd barely had any time to process—had volunteered to push Alok in his stroller around the block and knock on neighbors' doors, in case Bobby had slipped into one of their backyards. That just left Nikesh's friend Eugene and his little girl at the party—in case Bobby found his way back to the house before the rest of us.

How could a boy just disappear? Wasn't Mallika watching him? Wasn't Suresh?

Though, to be fair, children had a knack for disappearing when you least expected it. How many times had I taken a school-aged Nikesh to a department store, turned my back for a split second to inspect shoes or a duvet cover, only to discover he'd run off somewhere? Panicked, I'd always run to customer service, ask them to make an announcement over the PA system: *Nikesh, your mother is looking for you. Please go to the nearest cash register and tell the cashier that your mother is waiting for you at customer service.* We had that routine perfectly practiced by the time Nikesh left grade school.

And Priya, oh God, she'd been far worse, choosing to pull her childhood disappearing acts at cavernous theme parks, like AstroWorld, Sea World, Disneyland. Disneyland had been the breaking point, though. At Disneyland, Priya had disappeared for nearly an hour. At Disneyland, I'd become hysterical before a security guard found her spinning happily in a teacup ride called the Mad Tea Party. I would never forget the name of that repellent ride. In fact, for years after that episode, I refused to watch any Disney movie. Even seeing the logo on the screen would trigger the same bile-flavored fear. The taste that was starting to fill my mouth now.

No mother deserved this—the feeling that her child may be lost. Or taken. The waking nightmare that haunted every parent.

I quickened my steps, racing ahead of the others. "Bobby! Bobby!"

"There seems to be a bike path over here. I'm going to follow it to see where it goes," Len said. "You guys keep following the main path and I'll catch up with you." Raj nodded in agreement, "I'll come with you." Both men disappeared into the trees, while Mala and I continued on the main path.

"Has Suresh known this woman Mallika and her son for long?" Mala asked.

I looked sharply at my friend, shocked and disappointed that she would choose such a moment to fish for gossip.

Mala flinched. "Don't misunderstand me, Lata. I only mean, has the boy been here long enough to have made friends in the neighborhood? Some other little kid that he may have run off to play with?" Mala asked.

I shook my head. "I really don't know. I didn't even know they were staying with Suresh until a few days ago."

Mala nodded thoughtfully. "Len seems like a very nice man."

I slapped my palm to my forehead. "Mala, I don't know what I'm doing. Who do I think I am trying to date someone new at this age? What do I think is going to happen? That someone is going to marry me again?" I laughed a hollow, brittle-sounding laugh.

This time, Mala looked sharply at me. "And why not? Why wouldn't someone want to marry you? Don't think so meanly of yourself, Lata."

"Mala, don't take this the wrong way, but I thought you would be more disapproving. That you'd tell me to be careful with this white man I barely know. That you'd tell me I don't know the first thing about dating, and I'll just end up getting hurt and looking foolish."

She sighed. "Listen, I was going to wait to tell you this. But there's no time like the present, I guess. I was diagnosed with breast cancer."

"Oh God, Mala, no." I stopped walking and gripped my friend's arm. "I just saw you a few weeks ago for tea, and you didn't say anything."

"I was hopeful then that the lump would be benign. I only found out this week that it isn't. Strange, isn't it? One minute, you're celebrating your daughter's pregnancy and the next a doctor tells you that you have cancer."

"Mala, I'm so sorry." I squeezed her arm. I couldn't believe it. This day was getting worse and worse.

"I'll be okay. It's early stage. But the reason I'm telling you now is this: Our lives are short. The blink of an eyelid. And you never know what will happen, when someone will suddenly tell you that you're sick, or dying. We have to squeeze every moment of joy that we can. If Len makes you happy, don't pay attention to what anyone says or thinks. Not your kids. Not your friends. Nobody. If he makes you happy, that's what matters."

I put my arm around Mala's shoulders and drew her close to me. My dear friend for so many years. A friend I had envied for her seemingly endless good luck. A friend I should not have underestimated—not today, and not before.

"Oh, Mala, what if we don't find this boy?"

"That poor woman. We'll find him. One of us will find him."

43

NIKESH

"Bobby!" I called out. We hadn't made it very far. Just a few blocks. At each house, I'd ring the doorbell, and if someone answered, I'd explain the situation and ask if I could peek in their backyard for a missing eight-year-old Indian boy. So far, nothing.

"Did someone call the police?" Denise said. Her forearms rested on the stroller handlebar. Beads of sweat dotted her upper lip. Inside the stroller, Alok sucked on a pacifier attached to a small stuffed elephant, sound asleep.

"My dad already did. They said they're sending someone over. But it's been less than half an hour since Bobby's been gone, so I'm guessing we're not the highest priority right now. Between the eleven of us searching, one of us will find him. He's eight. How far could he have gone? He's probably just wandering around the neighborhood."

"What an insane day. I still can't believe it. Nikesh, what came over you? Why on earth did you choose to propose today, in front of all those people, half of whom you barely even know?"

I ran a hand through my sweaty hair, embarrassed. It seemed like such a stupid decision now. "I don't know. Seeing Alok at the party, sitting in your lap, looking so happy in the same yard I'd played in as a boy, it all just stirred something in me. You were so upset last night—and for good reason. I wanted to show you how important you are to me. I want us to be a family. So, I went with the feeling. I tried not to overthink it—for once."

"Nikesh, we'll always be a family because we have Alok. Whether we're married or not, we are a family. Always. But we're not doing Alok any favors if we just stay together for his sake."

"But that's the thing, Denise. It's not just for his sake. I want to marry you."

"The past few months haven't been good, Nikesh. They really haven't." She shook her head.

"I know they haven't. But we're still adjusting to having a baby. And let's be honest—we haven't really tried to make time for each other." I waited for her to say something.

"I don't know. Is it just new baby stuff that we'll move beyond, or is it something bigger?" She looked down at Alok and adjusted his head pillow. "I think I've fixated on you lying to your parents about us being married because it's been the easier thing to fixate on. It's easier than wondering if we would still be together if I hadn't become pregnant."

I didn't say anything. I knew what I should say: *Of course we would still be together.* But how could I say that when I didn't know—when I had wondered the same thing myself? Anyway, it was beside the point. What did it matter what we would have done in an alternate universe without Alok? He was here. We were a family. We had to try.

Almost as if she could read my mind, she said, "Look, for Alok's sake, we'll try. We'll try making more time for each other. We'll try counseling. And if all that doesn't work, then maybe we can try living separately for a while."

"Separately? What about Alok? Who would he live with? He needs both of us. He needs me."

"He'll still have you. He'll have both of us. And if it comes to that, we'll buy the condo next door—for you. If that's what we need to do to make it easier for Alok, we'll do it." She reached out and grabbed my hand. "If we do go that route, though, you'll probably have to return the ring—to help with a down payment."

"Um, did you just make a joke?"

"Maybe," she said, a small smile on her lips.

"I was starting to think you'd forgotten how."

For the next half block, we walked silently together, one of her hands in mine, the other pushing the stroller.

"Do you think we'll make it?" I said.

She squeezed my hand. "We'll try as hard as we can."

A drop of water landed on my nose. It was starting to drizzle. "The rain's early. It wasn't supposed to happen until evening." I bent over the stroller and pulled down the hood so it covered Alok's body.

"Poor Mallika. She must be out of her mind with worry," Denise said. "Do you think we'll find Bobby before it starts pouring?"

I squeezed her hand. "We'll try as hard as we can."

We walked together, hand in hand, calling out Bobby's name.

44

PRIYA

"What are you doing here?" At the end of my parents' driveway was the completely improbable sight of Ashish. He stood next to his black Audi, hands stuffed in his pockets, surveying the front of my parents' house.

"Nice to see you too. I'm glad you're not still hiding in the closet." He grinned. The stupid asshole grinned.

"Seriously, what are you doing here? How did you find me?"

"I need to talk to you. When you didn't come back, I snooped around your apartment and found an address book with your parents' address in it. So old-fashioned of you to keep an address book." He moved forward, as if to embrace me.

I backed away, my arms raised protectively in front of my chest. "No. I don't have time for this"—I waved my arms up and down—"whatever this thing is that you think you're doing. Bobby is missing."

He looked past my shoulder at Deanna. "Who's Bobby?" It wasn't clear if he was directing the question at Deanna or me.

"Bobby is the kid of the woman that Priya's dad is shacking up with."

"Deanna, please shut up. They're not shacking up."

"She lives here, right? They met online. So yeah, shacking up. I'm Deanna, by the way."

She stepped forward and stuck her hand out to Ashish, her tone suddenly formal and respectable, like she was interviewing for a job.

He shook her hand. "Nice to meet you." He ran his eyes over her piercings and bralessness, with an amused glint in his eye. "And how do you know Priya?"

"I work with Priya's mom at the library. And Priya here texted me this morning to invite me to her nephew's birthday party. I wasn't sure about coming because Priya can be a pill and I planned to sit on my couch and watch the first season of *The Sopranos* on DVD. But then, I thought there'd probably be some of those spongy white idli thingies here, which are like, addictive. And then it turns out, this party is even better than television. Rejected marriage proposal. Missing kid. Lots of excitement. Though, no spongy idli things to eat. That part was pretty disappointing." Deanna looked accusingly at me, as if the lack of idlis was my doing.

"Deanna, I only invited you because we were desperate for bodies. No offense."

"Oh, Priya, you know you love having me around, even if you pretend to hate it." She blew me a hostile kiss and turned toward Ashish. "Okay now, who are you? Oh wait, let me guess. You're the married dude Priya's sleeping with."

Ashish coughed, disconcerted at last. "That's one way to put it, I guess. Priya, do you think we could go somewhere and talk privately for a second?"

I shook my head. "No, we can't actually. Bobby's missing. We have to find him. I don't know why you thought showing up at my dad's house was a good idea, but you picked a hell of a time."

"I left my wife," he said. "I left Chalini. I want to be with you."

"Nice. Very classy," Deanna said.

"Deanna, shut up." I stared at Ashish's face, stunned. His eyes were wide and pleading. My phone buzzed in my hand: a text from Dad, asking if we'd found Bobby.

I shook my head. "I can't get into this right now. We have to find Bobby." I looked up at the sky. The gray clouds had multiplied. What if the rain came early? My heart started to beat faster.

"Since you're standing there with your keys, and your car is blocking us in anyway, why don't you drive us around to look for him?" Deanna said, pointing at Ashish's car. It was parked at the end of the driveway, blocking Deanna's car and my father's SUV, which I'd planned to use for our search.

"Sure, I can drive you wherever you want. Priya?"

"Yes, fine, drive us."

We climbed into Ashish's car, me sitting in the front seat next to him, and Deanna sitting in the back, like we were on some family trip and she was our sullen, rebellious teenage daughter. Except she seemed only too eager to be with us. "Feel free to discuss this whole wife-leaving thing. Pretend I'm not even here," she chirped from the back seat. "Look, I've even got my earbuds in. I'm going to listen to music and totally ignore you both."

I rolled my eyes and tried to ignore the frantic beating of my heart. It was beating so ridiculously fast. Was this what a heart attack felt like? What was going on here? I mean, wasn't this what I had been waiting for him to say for two years—that he was leaving his wife for me? So why wasn't warm, tingly relief coursing through my veins? Maybe it was just my worry over Bobby. Maybe it was clouding all my emotions, spraying a fine mist of panic over everything, even Ashish's big news. I rolled down the window and stuck my head out.

"The AC is on," Ashish said.

"I don't care," I said, gulping in the warm, sticky air. I ducked back inside and rolled up the window.

"I get that my timing isn't ideal here," Ashish said. "But I want you to know that I'm serious about this—about us. I really left Chalini. And I'm not going back. I want to be with you." He reached out and rested his hand on my bare knee. His skin felt hot on mine—too hot.

"A few days ago, you weren't ready to leave your wife. And now you are? What changed exactly?"

"I don't know. Maybe it was you being gone. It clarified things for me—how much I missed you. How much happier I am when you're in my life."

I could hear faint whistling from the back seat—a familiar tune, though I couldn't quite place it. If Deanna was trying to blend into the background, she was doing a shitty job of it. I blew a stream of air out of my mouth. I needed a cigarette.

"Look, for two years, you've made me feel happy and also really, really shitty. The thing is, I don't know how to trust you, Ashish. I've only ever known you as a cheater. How am I supposed to magically forget that?"

"That's not fair. It's not like you weren't a willing participant in this. I love you, Priya. I left my wife for you. I want to have children with you. Doesn't that mean anything to you?"

Deanna's whistling was growing louder now. Just as I was about to spin around and scold her, I finally recognized the tune. "Your Cheatin' Heart."

Hank Williams.

Was she sending me a message? If my own heart wasn't such a bloody mess right now, I might have burst out laughing. In her own devious way, she was egging me on, urging me to stick up for myself. I remembered Nikesh's words from last night, on the floor of Target: that I should stop being stupid; that if I really wanted a family—a baby—I could do it on my own; that Ashish wasn't my only option. I had time. I had choices.

"Yes, it means something to me. It just doesn't mean everything to me anymore." I moved his hot hand off my knee. "I don't think this is going to work."

"Maybe this isn't the right time to talk about this." He sounded exasperated. "You're preoccupied with the missing boy, so let's focus on that. Can you tell me where we're going? Or am I supposed to just drive in circles?" he asked.

"Turn left here. We'll start by circling around the lake, and then if we don't find him, we'll . . ." I closed my eyes and leaned against the window.

What if we didn't find him? Bobby didn't know this neighborhood. What if he'd fallen into the lake or something? I imagined his drowned lifeless body, a T-shirt clinging to his small torso, the messy mop of black hair that reminded me of Nikesh's when he was a boy plastered to his lifeless face. Or what if some sicko had tricked him into a car, luring him with candy or ice cream or Coca-Cola? Surely, Bobby's mother had warned him against strangers—had taught him to run screaming from men in white vans promising sweets and soda? I shut my eyes and a sob escaped my lips.

"Hey." Ashish put his hand on my shoulder and squeezed. "Don't worry. We'll find him."

I nodded, pushing out all thoughts of drownings and strange men in white vans. Majestic Lake was a man-made pond that was two feet deep. And Bobby most likely knew how to swim. Hadn't he begged to go to the swimming pool just the other day? And this was quite possibly the safest neighborhood in all of Clayborn, and therefore, the world. I was being ridiculous. Bobby probably just ran off to play somewhere. Maybe he spotted a cute puppy and followed it, and the puppy's nice, law-abiding owner, a young mom in yoga pants with three kids in tow, was currently calling Mallika's phone to inform her that her son was safe and sound, eating a healthy snack of celery sticks in her living room.

Deanna rolled down her window, stuck her head out and began yelling: "Bobby! Bobby!"

I rolled mine down and did the same.

Ashish drove. He made a loop around the lake. And then another.

"I don't think he's here," Deanna said.

"One more time. Make another loop. Go the long way, around the golf course too this time," I said. I wasn't ready to give up.

As Ashish drove by the far end of the golf course, a section messy with cut trees and construction equipment, I could make out a speck of orange. Hadn't Bobby been wearing an orange shirt with some superhero on it? "Stop—stop the car!" I shouted at Ashish.

Ashish had barely stopped the car before I bolted out of it. I sprinted toward the orange, barreling over pieces of metal and construction debris, ignoring the twigs and branches cutting into my ankles.

"Bobby! What are you doing?" I panted.

He was sitting on the dirt, next to a quivering duck. A pathetic little creature that had veered far from the lake, far from the other ducks. Bobby's face was streaked with tears, his shirt a mess of leaves and branches and dirt.

"They were . . . yelling." He was crying so hard it was difficult to make sense of his words. "Rahul Uncle was yelling at my mom. And Mom was screaming." Tears rolled down his face.

I crouched down next to him and held his little hand until his sobs started to lessen.

"So I ran and ran." Still whimpering, he said, "And then I saw Wolverine."

"Wolverine?"

"The duck. I named him Wolverine. And I followed him. Through the trees. He was lost. And I wanted to make sure he was okay."

"Of course you did." I dug into my pocket, hoping to find a

Kleenex stuffed somewhere in there. I found one and held it out to Bobby. He blew his nose loudly.

"Why don't we get you back to your mom? And I'll get my friends over there"—I pointed to Deanna and Ashish, both of whom were walking toward us—"to make sure Wolverine gets back to the pond safely."

"I want my daddy." His face crumpled, and he began bawling again.

"Oh, honey, I don't know where your dad is."

"She said Daddy was away at work. But today, she yelled at Rahul Uncle and said he was in jail. I want to go home. I want to see my daddy. I miss my daddy." He was near hysterical with tears.

I didn't know what to do. I didn't know why his dad was in jail. All I wanted to do was lie to him: to tell him that his dad would come back soon, that his family would return to normal, and that his helplessness at not being able to control the events around him or the people he loved was just a momentary set-back, just a function of being eight rather than an intractable condition of being human.

I drew him into my arms and rocked him. "I know you do, sweetie. I know you do. I miss my daddy too."

45

LATA

The boy was safe.

I transferred the uneaten samosas—no longer crisp or warm to the touch—into a large Tupperware container. Without thinking, I bit into one, letting the cold, spicy mush of potato and peas coat my tongue.

What a relief that Bobby had been found. It was Priya who'd found him, alone on the golf course. Our search party had returned home after everyone else. I had yet to even see the boy, or his (no doubt, very relieved) mother, or even Suresh (thank God).

Bobby was upstairs now, being given a long bath. And quite honestly, after walking through those trails and then twice around the lake, I could have used a long bath too. I smoothed my hair, and a small twig came out in my hands. I gazed at the cuffs of my pants, coated in mud.

Oh well, I would be back home—my own home—soon enough. Len and I couldn't leave this house quite yet, because the party wasn't over—not officially. Alok was still napping. According to Eugene, who'd left with his daughter a few moments after we returned from the lake, Nikesh and Denise had carried the entire stroller contraption up the stairs, so as not to wake the baby.

But any minute now, he would wake, and we could finally—finally!—do this cake cutting. And then, Len and I could finally—finally!—leave this place.

I looked out the window into the backyard. Len was shaking out a wet tablecloth. The rain had come and gone quickly, drenching all the backyard decorations, the plates, the cups, the cardboard boxes of pizza. A few feet away from Len, Raj was holding open a Hefty garbage bag as Mala tossed in the pieces of wreckage.

I took another bite of samosa. All the walking had made me ravenous. The only reason these samosas were edible and not rain-soaked like the rest of the party food was because I'd had the good sense to serve them outside in a covered CorningWare casserole dish. And the only reason I'd done that was to keep the flies and mosquitoes away from them. It turned out I'd been worried about the wrong things ruining the samosas.

In fact, when it came to this entire party, I had been worried about all the wrong things.

On the way here, my big fear was that Mala would find out about Len and judge me for it, that she'd gossip to our friends. My big fear was that I would have to face Mallika, would have to watch her move about my old kitchen as if it had always been hers, erasing me from the place I had worked so hard to create. My big fear was that Suresh would corner me with accusations and complaints, that we'd get into a humiliating fight in front of everyone and ruin our only grandson's first birthday.

What I should have been worrying about was the children. An unhappy eight-year-old boy running off and getting hopelessly lost. My unmarried son proposing (unsuccessfully) to the mother of his child, his expression so hurt and embarrassed in that moment that I could feel my own heart split in two. My daughter's married boyfriend showing up and causing lines of worry so deep in her forehead, she was practically looking middle-aged. Right now, both my son and daughter were off having hushed arguments with these people in their old childhood bedrooms; the same rooms where they once dreamt about their happily-ever-afters were now the site of difficult conversations and adult decisions.

I opened the fridge and stuffed the samosas next to a gallon of milk. Well, I did not know how to solve any of these children's problems. Bobby wasn't mine. And my own children were fully grown adults who had to make their own decisions, for better or for worse. But in this moment, I could do one thing. I could make everyone some soothing masala tea.

I tugged the jug of milk and set it on the counter. I opened the same cupboard doors I'd opened so many times in my life, hunting the shelves for cardamom and cloves, letting the familiar scents tickle my nose.

"Oh. It's you. What are you doing?"

Oh God. That familiar voice cutting through my silent, peaceful kitchen. Somehow I had managed to avoid him the entire party. My luck had to run out sometime. I took a deep breath and turned toward Suresh with two jars in my hands. "I'm making tea. I'm surprised you still have these." I set the spices on the counter beside the milk, the glass clinking against the marble.

"I haven't touched any of those things since you left. How the devil do I know what to do with them? I'm surprised you didn't take them all with you. Along with all the good plates and bowls that you took."

"*Aiyo*, please don't start an argument. It's your grandson's birthday, after all."

He eased onto a barstool, a thoughtful look on his face. "Okay, okay. Speaking of our grandson, he is finally awake. Nikesh says they'll be down in a few minutes for cake cutting."

I nodded. "Good." We were both quiet for a few moments. I

busied myself pouring milk in a large saucepan and setting it to boil on the stove. "Did Nikesh say anything else to you? Is he okay? Did you know he was not married?"

"I only found out yesterday. She's divorced too. Did you know that?"

I winced. "I'm realizing I don't know very much about our kids' lives. Nikesh is not married. Priya's boyfriend is married. Denise used to be married. I guess they will decide to do whatever they decide to do. They are not children anymore." I added spices to the milk and reduced the heat. "You know, when Bobby ran away today, it reminded me of those times our kids would wander away and get lost when they were that age—like that time at Disneyland, when we lost Priya. Remember how terrifying that was?"

Suresh nodded. "Yes, I remember. I was so scared."

"Even if we can't understand their lives now, at least we can be relieved that those days are over."

"Oh, I don't know. I wouldn't mind doing those days over again. Doing them differently—better." Suresh stared at me, his eyes large and sad.

I looked away from him, a sudden ache in my chest, a glimpse of how things might have been. Well, what good came from wishing you could do things differently now? Those years were gone. You could not rewrite them, magically erasing all the bad parts.

I shrugged and turned back to the stove. "It looks like you'll have a chance to do things differently with Bobby . . . and Mallika. Are you going to marry her?"

"What? No! Why would you say that?"

"She lives here. What else am I supposed to think?" I reached back into the cupboard for the tea.

"No, I am just her . . . friend. The truth is, she's still married. Her husband is in jail for insider trading."

I was so shocked, I dropped the tin of tea on my foot. "Ouch!"

"Are you okay?"

"Yes, I'm fine. Jail? Suresh, what are you doing? You have to be careful!"

"I know, I know. But what can I do, Lata? These women on the internet, you would not believe it . . . they don't tell you the truth!"

The internet? Suresh was meeting women on the internet? Oh God. I could not help it, I started to laugh.

"It's not funny, Lata. It's my life. All because you abandoned me!" He slammed his hand on the counter.

My shoulders were shaking so hard, I struggled to strain the tea bags in the milk. I cleared my throat. "Okay, I am done laughing now."

"So what about you? Are you going to marry that ugly white man who nearly drowned me?"

I stirred the bags in the milk and lowered the heat to a simmer. "He saved you from drowning. And I like how he looks." I turned and glared at Suresh. "And more important, he is unselfish. He is kind to me. Look at him now." I pointed out the window, where Len was peeling wet streamers from tree branches. "This isn't even his family's party, but see how he's helping. You don't even have to ask him to do it. And you—look at you. Sitting here uselessly. Just calling him names."

Suresh's face twisted into a look of hurt. I felt something soften in me, a little pricking of guilt even. Here he was, harboring the wife of a criminal, his life one big mess, and what was I doing? Rubbing his nose in it. Kicking the dog when he was down. "*Aiyo,* I will not be marrying any man anytime soon, okay? Maybe not ever. I am enjoying my freedom. I am enjoying my single life."

At that, Suresh's expression seemed to brighten, before turning glum again. He rubbed his forehead and groaned. "Well, at least one of us is enjoying it."

I started to laugh again. God help me. Sometimes the man

was funny. A big pain in the buttocks—always. But sometimes, he was funny. Suresh grimaced, as if he was about to scold me for laughing again. Which only made me laugh harder, my chest heaving and little tears forming at the edges of my eyes.

He watched me like that for a few seconds, his expression stern. And then, a small smile cracked his stony face. "You might be laughing now, Lata. But just you wait. This dating business— it's no joke. You'll see."

46

SURESH

It was time to cut the cake—at last.

Alok stood on a chair in the dining room, his chubby knees wobbling. His parents were positioned on either side, keeping his body steady, their palms against his diapered waist. On the table sat a large square cake with train-shaped blue icing and one candle lit in the middle. Alok eyed the flickering flame suspiciously and sucked his thumb. His hair was still mussed from naptime, curls sticking out in all directions. Apparently, neither Nikesh nor Denise had thought to comb it. They probably had bigger issues on their minds.

I suppose we all did—the lot of us, singing "Happy Birthday" in a semicircle around Alok with cheer so forced, it felt, quite frankly, insane. Shouting the song's inane words as if to drown out our own heartbreaks and worries.

Happy birthday to you.

Nikesh's shoulders slumped. Denise's fingers were still ringless.

"Don't worry, Dad," he'd said to me, before bringing out the cake. "We're going to figure out a way to make this work."

I watched my son and his not-yet-wife, their eyes distracted as Alok teetered back and forth between them.

Happy birthday to you.

And then there was Mallika, a few feet away from Denise. She was standing behind Bobby, her hands squeezing his shoulders as if terrified to let him go for even a second. Mallika had started wailing like a captured animal when we couldn't find Bobby. Wailing until Priya called to tell us that she'd found him. When Priya had returned home, she was carrying Bobby in her arms. He'd been clinging to her, like a monkey to a tree—his arms around her neck, his legs encircling her waist. I watched them walk up the front lawn in the rain, suddenly overcome by pride that Priya had been the one to find him, that she looked like a mother. I had never seen her that way before. Priya had whispered something in Bobby's ear, and he reluctantly let go of her and let himself fall into the waiting arms of a weepy Mallika. My heart ached in that moment—not for Mallika or Bobby, but for the sight of Priya's empty arms.

Priya stood a few feet from Nikesh, next to me. She too was singing, her voice high and clear. But she seemed distracted. Every few seconds she'd tug the string of a blue balloon tied to Alok's chair. Then she'd glance toward the back of the room, her eyes landing on a youngish Indian man in dark jeans, sneakers, and a white button-down shirt. Ashish, his name was? Priya had introduced him to the party as "her colleague, who'd come by to drop off some papers." A ludicrous introduction that had sent the skinny, tattooed girl into peals of laughter. Obviously, he was Priya's married man.

My instinct was to hate him, of course. But as I watched him watching Priya fiddle with the blue balloon, I began to hate him less. He was clearly besotted with her. He followed her every move hungrily, like she was a fresh dosa and he hadn't eaten in a year. All right, so it was true that he had turned her into a mistress (that loathsome word). But maybe (and I hated to admit this), Priya had been a willing accomplice. And maybe this man's intentions had started out poorly but then turned into something true. And maybe she would find happiness with him. Or maybe she would kick him to the curb. Who could know? Certainly not me. I was not qualified to dispense advice in romantic matters.

Which brought me again to Mallika. She and Bobby were planning to leave the next morning. I wasn't surprised by this news. Bobby had spent the last hour crying for his daddy; and even before Mallika assured him they'd go back to Austin the next day, I could read the writing on the wall. It was the right decision. And while Bobby took a bath, Mallika explained how for now, they'd stay with Rahul. And then she would think about her next steps—she would likely call her parents, tell them about her situation, and maybe even take Bobby to India for a time.

So, that was that. Another failed internet romance. Another woman who had lured me into her life with lies.

I would miss her, though.

And anyway, I guess we were all guilty of telling untruths—if not to one another, then to ourselves. Certainly, everyone in this house was guilty of that. But probably everyone in the whole world was. Most of the time, what we thought of as truth was threaded with self-serving distortions.

I have two children. *Fact.* I love my children. *Fact.*

I was a decent husband to Lata. *Truth.*

As a husband and father, I haven't done as well as some, but I did the best I could do, given what I knew and the cards I was dealt. *Truth.*

See, there were facts. And then there were truths—as we each saw it.

Happy birthday dear Al-o-ok.

Even the Chandershakers had their problems, it seemed. I watched Mala, singing half-heartedly next to the windows. She seemed smaller somehow. Her skin more sunken in than the last time I'd seen her. New wrinkles lining her brow. Even the irritatingly boisterous Raj was subdued. A few minutes before the cake cutting, he'd presented me with a bottle of wine in the kitchen.

"Here's a bottle of Cabernet I think you'll enjoy. I know you're not a fan of whisky, so I thought I'd try a wine on you this time."

"Thank you." I took the bottle from him and rubbed my hand over the elegant cream-colored label. His efforts searching for Bobby had moved me—a little. He could have left the party hours ago, but he'd stayed and loyally scouted for the missing boy.

"You know, Raj, I never properly thanked you for the Johnnie Walker that you gave me all those years ago. I drank a good deal of it in one sitting."

Raj looked surprised. "Well, I'm glad you liked it. But as a doctor, I would advise you to restrict yourself to one small portion per sitting."

I laughed. "Raj, do you ever wonder what you would have done if you hadn't become a doctor?"

"Sometimes," he said. "When I was a child, I wanted to be a cricket player. Or a journalist. But there's a time for childish dreams, and then there is the world of adults, with mortgage payments and children's college tuition. Anyway, I'm glad I am one now. Being a doctor means I can ask the right questions when there are medical issues . . . in my own family. I'm no less helpless in the face of illness, of course. But I don't feel quite so ignorant." His eyes grew cloudy.

I didn't know what he was thinking about, but it was clear his mind was heavy. "Look, I want to apologize to you, Raj. I know I haven't always been kind to you. And sometimes I think it's because you always seemed so pleased with yourself . . . with your life. I've lived so long in this town of professors and doctors, and it used to make me ashamed that I had never finished my PhD, that I'd given it up. Maybe I was envious of you—your career, your unwavering happiness."

Raj nodded, considering my words. "Nobody's happiness is unwavering. But you have to appreciate what you have and take care of the people in your life. Unselfishness—that's the key to happiness, I think. Anyway, I hope you find happiness in your life, Suresh." He shook my hand and patted me on the back.

It was quite possibly the soberest conversation I'd ever had with Raj. Was it possible that he and Mala were getting a divorce too? Hope leapt up in my chest. I wasn't proud of it, but what could I say? It would be nice to have company in this particular tent of failure—the divorced-man tent—even if that company was Raj Chandrasekhar.

Though from where I was standing now, I could see Raj's hand intertwined with Mala's. They were leaning against the windows, their shoulders touching and their heads bent toward each other, in the comfortable way of a long-married couple that would probably die in their sleep together. It was painful to look at them.

I shifted my eyes away—and onto Lata. She was singing too. She was standing on Mala's other side, holding tightly on to Mala's other hand for some inexplicable reason. And then next to Lata, with his shoulder practically touching hers, was *that man*. That Len character. Him, I still hated. So what if he helped look for Bobby too, trotting back to the house with twigs in his hair as evidence of his efforts. So what if he helped clean up the backyard. I would still count the minutes until he left my house. Until he left our lives. He wasn't going to last, I was sure of that much. Lata would come to her senses soon enough. She wasn't cut out for the dating life. This was her first experience of it. She was a total novice. She had no idea what she was getting herself into.

Happy birthday to you!

The song was over, and everyone began clapping and cheering. Someone—that skinny, tattooed girl, probably—got her hands on a noisemaker and began honking it.

Yay Alok! Hooray!

And what of me, then?

Well—I would wait. For Lata, maybe, if she came to her senses soon enough. Or else, who knows—the internet was a vast, daily-expanding cornucopia of women. Surely, one of them would work out for me. Surely, one day, in the not-so-distant future, one of them would enter into my life with honesty and openness, ready to accept the love and affection and humor and care I was willing to offer.

And in the meantime, I still had them: these children, this beautiful grandson. I wasn't alone. And there was time left. Time to be a better father, a better grandfather, a better man. This was America, after all. It was never too late. You could always re-create yourself—Suresh 2.0.

I moved in closer, inserting myself between Priya and Nikesh. I wrapped my arms around their waists, hugging them to me.

"Okay, Alok, blow out your candle!" I said.

"Dad, I don't think he knows what that means," Priya said. "Do you, buddy?"

Alok popped his thumb out of his mouth and looked curiously at us.

Priya laughed. "Well, maybe he does."

"Alok, come on," I said. "We'll do it together. Ready? One. Two. Three. Make a wish!"

I was nearly sixty years old. It was too late in life for me to believe in God or fate or fairies granting wishes. But I could still believe in luck. And second chances. And love. And my family. I closed my eyes, made my wishes, and blew.

ACKNOWLEDGMENTS

Thank you to my amazing agents, Kim Witherspoon and Jessica Mileo. Your thoughtful guidance made this book so much better. Thank you to Andrea Walker, for your insightful comments, kindness, and enthusiasm for this novel. From our very first conversation, I knew my book was in the right hands. Thanks also to Emma Caruso, Noa Shapiro, Andy Lefkowitz, and everyone at Random House who worked on this book. Thank you to Nicole Dewey for your astute advice.

Thanks to my first creative writing teachers—Whitney Otto, Julia Fierro, Cynthia Weiner, and Lucinda Holt—and workshop peers at Tin House, Sackett Street, and The Writers Studio, for making a young lawyer believe she could write fiction. To Marcy Dermansky and Zahie El Kouri, for invaluable feedback on early drafts. To my creative writing colleagues at Georgia State University, for giving me a writing community in Atlanta, and to Sheri Joseph, for helpful writing counsel.

Enormous thanks to my friends and family. Thank you to Vidhya Sriram for being my tireless cheerleader. No one makes me laugh like you. To my College Station crew, for the decades of love and support. To Jean Shin (who read more drafts of this novel than anyone should have to), there is no one I'd rather talk books with than you. To Reshma Saujani, for never letting me give up on this dream. Thank you for always believing in me and shooing my (many) doubts away.

Thank you to my in-laws, Kuldip and Sudarshan, for making me feel like a daughter from the moment we met and for being such devoted grandparents. To my brother, Anand, for your humor, compassion, and love. Watching you become a husband and father has been a delight. To my parents, Rajan and Prabha, your nearly five-decade marriage inspires me, and your unconditional love and support sustain me. I am so ridiculously lucky to have you as my parents.

To my husband, Nirej, a true partner in parenting and life. I could not have finished this book—and kept my sanity—without you. Thank you for taking care of us. To my children, Nishan and Sania, my favorite people in the world. Being with you is the greatest joy of my life. Thank you for showing me how endless my love can be.

ABOUT THE AUTHOR

Deepa Varadarajan lives in Atlanta with her husband and two children. She is a legal academic and a graduate of Yale Law School. She grew up in Texas and received her BA from the University of Texas at Austin. Her short fiction has appeared in *The Georgia Review,* and her legal scholarship has appeared in *The Yale Law Journal* and many other publications. *Late Bloomers* is her first novel.

ABOUT THE TYPE

This book was set in Caslon, a typeface first designed in 1722 by William Caslon (1692–1766). Its widespread use by most English printers in the early eighteenth century soon supplanted the Dutch typefaces that had formerly prevailed. The roman is considered a "workhorse" typeface due to its pleasant, open appearance, while the italic is exceedingly decorative.